W9-DBP-441

'Twas the night

SANDRA HILL

"Trademark Sandra Hill [is] filled with lots of humor, some of it laugh-out-loud fun. She has that magical touch."

—*Romantic Times*

"Ms. Hill knows how to mix laughter and sensuality just right."

—*The Belles and Beaux of Romance*

KATE HOLMES

"Those who enjoy a light-hearted romp need look no further."

—*The Romance Reader* on *The Wild Swans*

"Ms. Holmes has written a humorous love story, filled with fantasy and enjoyable characters."

—*Romantic Times* on *The Wild Swans*

TRISH JENSEN

"Trish Jensen has got a great comedic touch and an ear for dialogue."

—*The Romance Reader*

"Charming and delightfully humorous, *Against His Will* is nonstop fun."

—*Romantic Times*

'Twas the Night

by

Sandra Hill
Kate Holmes
Trish Jensen

Bell Bridge Books

Bell Bridge Books
PO BOX 300921
Memphis, TN 38130
ISBN: 978-1-61194-002-2

Bell Bridge Books is an Imprint of BelleBooks, Inc.

Originally published in a mass market paperback edition titled *Here Comes Santa Claus* by Leisure books, and imprint of Dorchester Publishing Co., Inc.

Printed and bound in the United States of America.

We at BelleBooks enjoy hearing from readers. You can contact us at the address above or at BelleBooks@BelleBooks.com

Visit our websites – www.BelleBooks.com and www.BellBridgeBooks.com.

10 9 8 7 6 5 4 3 2
Cover design: Debra Dixon
Interior design: Hank Smith
Photo credits:
For *'Twas the Night*:
Various holiday graphics © Dianka | Dreamstime.com

:Ls:01:

DEDICATIONS

Sandra Hill:
To my Internet soul sisters:
Anne Holmberg, Trana Mae Simmons, Karen Fox,
Sharry Michels, Pam McCutcheon, and Janice Tarantino.
They have shared their writing expertise with me over the
years, but more than that, they have become good, good
friends, even though some of us have never met in person.
Someday, ladies, we are going to get that pink limo with
The Elvis wobble doll. I promise.

Kate Holmes:
To Sandra and Trish,
With heartfelt thanks for inviting me to play in your world.
Stan and I had a GREAT time on that bus!

Trish Jensen:
To the ladies and gents of the READ list,
An eclectic and fabulous online conglomeration
Of readers, author, reviewers and booksellers.
I adore you, one and all.

Dear Reader,

Welcome to our most unusual anthology. In fact, it is so unusual that we refer to it as a non-anthology.

When the three of us decided to write this book about three former orphans (a Blue Angels pilot, a bounty hunter and an ex-NFL football player) forced to return to their hometown for a Christmas Eve wedding, the only thing we knew for sure was that they would be riding on a bright red Santa Brigade bus filled with senior citizen Santas. Almost immediately we discovered that we would have a chronology problem if the stories were written in the usual manner . . . three separate novellas.

Instead we decided to write this anthology round-robin style. Sandra wrote all the chapters from Sam's point of view; Trish wrote Kevin's; and Kate wrote Stan's. In other words, every chapter was written by a different author, each of us picking up where the last chapter left off.

We were very pleased with the final result, an anthology that reads like a single novel. Please let us know how you like this unique method for telling our funny, poignant love story.

Best,
Sandra Hill www.sandrahill.net
Kate Holmes anneavery1@earthlink.net
Trish Jensen www.trishjensen.com

Prologue

You are cordially invited to join

GEORGE GARRISON
AND
MOLLY OLIVER

In the joyous celebration of their wedding

At 7 p.m. on Friday, December 24, 2010

At Our Lady of the Snows Chapel

Snowdon, Maine

Reception to follow at

The Holiday Inn.

RSVP Requested by December 18th.

CHAPTER ONE

SAM

Monday afternoon, four days 'til Christmas Eve.

"Jingle Bells, Jingle Bells, Jingle all the way . . ."

"American Airlines, Flight One-oh-one to Boston is cancelled. Passengers are directed to the information desk for further instructions.

"Jingle Bells, Jingle Bells, Jingle all the way . . ."

"U.S. Air, Flight Six-seven-three to Syracuse is cancelled. Passengers are directed to the information desk for further instructions.

"Jingle Bells, Jingle Bells, Jingle all the way . . . "

"United Airlines, Flight Nine-eight-five to Bangor, Maine is cancelled. Passengers are directed to the information desk for further instructions."

"Jingle Bells, Jingle Bells, Jingle all the way . . ."

On and on the staticky public address system went with cancellations of what appeared to be all northbound flights in the face of a coming blizzard. The only planes taking off today from Philadelphia International Airport were those headed south, or to the western U.S. Since the southbound storm was headed this way and would probably hit full-force tomorrow, chances were there wouldn't be any northbound flights tomorrow, either.

As a backdrop to the distressing announcements, speakers in the airport terminal piped out, over and over and over, like a stuck record, a bouncy version of Jingle Bells. Meanwhile, holiday travelers—those not stunned over being land-locked at this all-important time of the year—laughed and called out to strangers with jolly "Merry Christmas" greetings as they hurried along toward their designated gates.

One person in particular was feeling less than jolly. "I hate snow. I hate that sorry song. In fact, I'm beginning to hate Christmas." Navy Commander Samuel Merrick slunk lower in his Naugahyde booth and glared out the window of the airport coffee shop. He watched grimly as fat snowflakes were beginning to come down like celestial post-it notes . . . reminders that mere mortals and their technological advances, such as aircraft, could be frozen in place on a whim of the gods.

In the midst of Sam's grumbling to himself, Lt. Andrew O'Dell slid into the opposite booth and handed him one of the two cups of coffee in his hands, the whole time smiling. "Now, now, Slick. Since when did you become the Bluebird of Christmas Happiness? Or rather, the Blue *angel* of Christmas *un*-Happiness?" he corrected, staring pointedly at the distinctive blue and yellow Blue Angel badge with the F/A Hornet Jets in a diamond formation that was positioned proudly on Sam's uniform . . . just as it was on his.

He and Andy were current members of the renowned six-man Blue Angels Flight Demonstration Squadron. Considered the best of the best, these jet pilots performed high-precision, aerobatic maneuvers in breath-taking, razzle dazzle air shows across the world. Although their flying talents were famous, the Blue Angels' main role was to serve as role models and goodwill ambassadors for the U.S. Navy and Marine Corps.

"Easy for you to say, Andy. You're not gonna be stuck in the City of Brotherly Love for the next day or two. You're almost home . . . just a short puddle jump to Harrisburg."

Andy didn't look a bit sympathetic . . . probably because his thoughts were consumed with his fiancée—a dairy farmer, of all things—whom he hadn't seen in three months. He and Andy had come up from Pensacola, homebase to the Blue Angels, less than an hour ago. It should have been a short layover for them. Then, after Christmas, they'd travel to NAF, the Naval Air Facility, in El Centro, California, where the squadron wintered.

"Knowing you, Slick, you'll find something to occupy your time," Andy said in an awestruck voice.

Oh, swell! Another Navy nugget suffering from a bit of misplaced hero worship.

As if on cue, an American Airlines flight attendant walked by, gave Sam a quick once-over, then flashed him a not-so-subtle smile that said clearly, "Hey, sailor, I'd like to know you better," before sitting down with companions at a nearby table.

"See, see!" Andy hooted in an undertone.

"It's just the uniform. Women have this thing about men in a killer uniform."

"Hah! You don't see them going ga-ga over me, do you?"

"Ga-ga?" Sam questioned with a raised eyebrow, even as he instinctively returned the woman's once-over. His slow, lazy perusal registered her trim figure and attractive facial features and the fact that she could pass for a red-headed version of Cameron Diaz. Even better, her legs were a shade longer than a Hornet jet stream. Still, he turned back to his coffee with an "Oh, well." shrug. Reciprocating her smile would amount to an invitation . . . one he was not interested in. In fact, he'd become bored with the whole dating game for a long time now.

Sam wasn't a vain person . . . well, not too vain . . . but he'd had no trouble attracting females since he was thirteen years old and discovered that his dark hair, blue eyes and tall frame were assets to be milked for all their worth. But it wasn't just his looks. Hell, he'd gotten charm down to an art form before he'd turned ten, and earned his nickname of Slick which had stuck all these years, right down to being his call name in the Blues. Yep, charm had been a necessary survival skill when dodging the law and criminal elements in the inner city neighborhood where, during his early years, he'd been raised—or, rather, ignored—by a druggie mother, who'd been practically a kid herself.

But now Sam was feeling all charmed out. He didn't give a flying fig about meeting another woman—gorgeous or not. He was tired. Perhaps it was this forced trip back to Snowdon, Maine . . . a place he had studiously avoided for fourteen years, ever since his high school graduation. He had no choice now, though. His old mentor, George Garrison, was getting married, and he couldn't let him down. He'd promised he would be there by Christmas Eve, and he would be, by damn . . . blizzard or not.

"Man, oh, man! I can't imagine what it must be like to have women . . . and men, too . . . do double takes when you pass by . . . just because you're so good looking. God, I envy you." Though he was in perfect physical condition, as required by the Blue Angels regimen, Andy would never be described as handsome . . . not with all those freckles and his gap-toothed, David Letterman smile and a cowlick sticking up on his crown, in spite of his short haircut.

Sam was only thirty-two, but he felt old compared to the exuberant, impressionable and over-talkative Andy, who was a mere twenty-six. Andy had just joined the Blues this past year, while Sam was in his third year with the Blues . . . including ten years with the Navy, after college.

Taking a deep breath, he said, "Andy, I envy *you*."

"Me?" Andy was clearly taken aback.

"I've seen the pictures of you and Cindy . . . and the farm she inherited when her parents died. You can tell, just by looking at the glow on her face, how much she loves you. And that farmhouse will be perfect when you start to raise a family. Hell, you've already got a readymade family with those younger sisters she's helping to raise." He shrugged, at a loss to explain himself further. "You've got it all."

Andy's Adam's Apple bobbed up and down a few times before he choked out, "Yeah, I guess I do."

"Tell me what your Christmas will be like," Sam encouraged, wanting to take the attention away from himself.

Andy smiled and his face lit up like a Christmas tree. "Cindy and I both come from big families. I have three brothers and two sisters. She's got three younger sisters. Then, there are lots of aunts and uncles and grandparents. Loud, that's the best way to describe our Christmases. And crowded. Plenty of good, homegrown food. Always a stuffed turkey *and* a baked ham. My mother makes the pies . . . eight of them . . . two each of pumpkin, apple, mince meat and lemon meringue. Aunt Nellie makes the cakes; my favorite is Devil's Food with boiled icing. Yummm. We probably never got as many big ticket items as other kids did, but I can't recall feeling deprived."

He thought for a moment, still smiling.

"It's a happy time."

That's exactly how Sam had always imagined a family Christmas should be. The Waltons . . . only better.

"How about you, Slick? What do you do on Christmas?"

"Get drunk."

Andy tilted his head quizzically, not sure if he was kidding or not.

"How's this for a dose of reality? My earliest Christmas memory is of me grabbing the bell from the Salvation Army lady, whacking her over the head with it, and stealing all the money in the kettle."

Andy narrowed his eyes at him. "Exactly how old were you?"

Sam blinked several times in rapid progression. What had come over him to reveal a memory he'd thought long-buried? Finally, when Andy refused to accept his silence as a reply, he told him, "Eight."

"Ah, Slick!"

"It was a long time ago. No big deal!" he said gruffly.

Andy seemed about to say more, then cut himself off. "Hey, I have an idea. Why don't you come home with me for Christmas? Good grief! My cousin Valerie would go *ga-ga* over you. She's a massage therapist." Andy jiggled his eyebrows meaningfully.

Sam laughed. "I wish I could. Especially with a *ga-ga massage therapist*. But I have to be in Maine by Friday."

Andy put his hand on Sam's forearm. "You seem really down in the dumps. It's not just the weather delay, is it?"

Thank goodness, Sam's cell phone rang then. He was spared from answering Andy's question . . . a procedure which would involve even more painful revelations.

"Merrick here," Sam said, flicking up the lid of his cell phone with a thumb and holding the mini console to his ear.

"Samuel! It's so good to hear your voice," a jovial voice spoke out.

It had to be George. He was the only one who could get away with calling him by his given name.

In the background could be heard the loud barking of dogs . . . lots of dogs. George was a veterinarian, and the man who had practically saved his life as a wayward teenager, along with the lives of his best buddies, Kevin "JD" Wilder and Stan Kijewski, fellow inmates . . . uh, residents . . . of the White Mountain Home for Boys in Snowdon, Maine. Kevin, a former cop and currently a D.C. private eye, and Stan, until recently a pro football player with the San Diego Typhoons, were supposed to meet up with him in Maine.

Sam could pretty well guess why George was calling now. He had asked the three of them to come back to Snowdon this week to be best men at his wedding. Now, George was checking up on him . . . like he always had. "When can Molly and I expect you? Chowder's on the stove, just the way you always liked it. The weather's getting a mite rough up this way, and I wanted to make sure we get to the airport in time to pick you up."

George's deep Maine burr was a welcome melody to Sam's ears. Furthermore, "a mite rough" to a Maine old-timer meant ten-below temperatures, wind chill equal to a North Pole gale, and snow to the rooftops . . . what the rest of the world considered emergency crisis conditions.

"Uh, George, have you turned on the TV today?"

"No. Mable Gentry's poodle was constipated again. I keep telling Mable not to give her dog cheese doodles."

"Mrs. Gentry still has that poodle? Bella was her name, right?" Sam had worked enough in George's kennels as a teenager that he knew his regular customers, even after all these years.

"Yep! Bella. Mus' be more'n fifteen years old. But what was that you said about the television?"

"Huh? Oh. I asked if you've turned on the TV today."

There was a long sigh on George's end." Don't tell me, you're on TV again. Goldurnit, boy, you've got more moxie than good sense. I couldn't believe that somersault you did in your aeroplane over the White House last summer. I hope you're not gettin' yourself in trouble again with my weddin' so close."

Sam smiled, loving the way George's conversations tended to ramble. He even loved the sounds of all the yips and woofs and bow-wow's and meows that always seemed to surround him. Most of all, he loved the way George was concerned about him, as if he were still "Slick Merrick, Teenager-In-Trouble" . . . *again.*

"George, you are in the midst of a major storm, and it's headed this way. I'm stuck at the airport in Philly, with all flights northbound being cancelled for the time being, possibly the next two days."

There was a long pause of silence. "Does that mean you're not coming?" George's voice was soft when he spoke, and full of disappointment. Just like it was the time Sam had shoplifted those condoms from a convenience store when he was fourteen . . . or when he'd gotten picked up by the police for speeding when he was fifteen . . . or when he'd broken both legs skiing down Suicide Run after an ice storm when he was sixteen.

"No . . . no, I'll be there. I mean, I'm almost certain I'll be there. It's just a delay for now."

"Hold on a minute." George could be heard talking to a female in the room with him. Probably his fiancée. Finally, he came back and informed Sam excitedly, "Molly came up with a perfect solution for you." He paused in a ta-da manner before suggesting, "You can hitch a ride on the Santa Brigade bus."

"What the hell is a Santa Brigade?" Almost immediately, he added, "I beg your pardon, sir." Old habits died hard. George never tolerated bad language.

"The Santa Brigade is a troupe of volunteers from Winter Haven. And they're headed back up this way any day now. They better be. They're all invited to the porchbreaker of a weddin' celebration we're planning."

"Winter Haven? The retirement community?" Good Lord! What did a retirement community have to do with him?

"Yep. For years, a bunch of the residents have been dressing up as Santas, entertainin' kids hereabouts with magic and stuff. Then, three years ago, they rigged up this special bus so they could travel down the eastern seaboard visiting homeless shelters and such for a couple weeks before Christmas. They're famous, boy. Haven't you ever heard of 'em?"

He paused to listen to the female in the room again. Before finishing. "Molly just reminded me. They were on *Good Morning America* a few years back. Dint'ja see 'em? Diane Sawyer sat on Morey Goldstein's lap. That old fart's gonna have a head so big when he gets back here his hat won't fit. You remember Diane Sawyer. She passed out in a Blue Angels plane 'bout the same time. I saw it myself on the TV."

Sam braced an elbow on the table and put his forehead in his palm. Between George's rambling and the approaching snow storm, Sam felt the mother of all headaches beginning to throb behind his eyes. "George, what do all these geriatric Santas have to do with me and my cancelled flight?"

"Be careful how you use that word geriatric, boy. I'm in that category now, too."

"Sorry."

"Those geriatric Santas, as you call them, are the answer to your prayer, Samuel."

What prayer? Call me crazy, but I don't recall praying for a long time . . . probably since the time my mother told me she was abandoning me when I was ten. Sam shook his head, hard, to clear it. He was becoming way too maudlin today.

"At this moment, they're at the Good Shepherd Shelter in Allentown, Pennsylvania. That's right down the road from you."

"I hate to tell you this, but Allentown isn't down the road from Philadelphia." Andy whispered some specifics to him. Then Sam informed George, "It's a two-hour drive under good conditions."

George was talking right over him. "Molly's ringing up their bus driver right now. You remember Betty Morgan."

"Betty Morgan is the bus driver? *The* Betty Morgan? I thought she was a Marine." Betty, nicknamed Betty Bad-Ass by him and his buddies, had caught him necking one time behind her father's garage with Sally Sue Simpson. She'd given him a lecture that day, complete with blue language that still turned his face red in memory, on the need for always carrying proper rubbers. And she hadn't been referring to boots, either.

"Retired. Now she's a NASCAR mechanic . . . famous, actually . . . and a bus driver for the brigade on her off-time. Orders everyone around like a drill sergeant. What's that you say, Molly? Oh, Betty wants to know if you can be in Allentown by fifteen hundred hours?"

"I can't be there in one hour," he replied testily, glancing at his wrist watch and making some quick mental calculations. "It's already two o'clock. I have no means of transportation handy. There's not enough time. And the weather's getting bad." *Besides, I have no desire to ride for a day or more in a crowded bus with a bunch of senior citizen Santas through a blizzard. Not to mention Betty freakin' Bad-Ass Morgan. She'd probably give me a more up-to-date lecture on condoms.*

George ignored all his protests, and was giving him the number of Betty's cell phone, which Sam jotted down on a napkin.

"Don't let me down," George said then. The wily old fox was manipulating him to his will, just like he always had.

"I'll try to find a way to get there in a day or two, George, but I'm not coming on a Santa bus," he pronounced firmly.

"Now, don't rule it out. There are no guarantees that the storm won't get worse, and you'll be stuck in Philadelphia through Christmas. Talk to Betty. See what you can arrange."

"I'm not coming on a Santa bus."

"Maybe you could hire a taxi to Allentown."

A taxi? Is he nuts? "I'm not coming on a Santa bus."

"Oh. Molly just reminded me about somethin'. The director of Winter Haven is on that bus, too."

So? "I'm not coming on a Santa bus."

"You know who that is, dontcha?"

I don't care if it's Julia Roberts. "I'm not coming on a Santa bus."

"Reba Anderson."

The wind was knocked out his stomach, and his heart raced wildly. Jet pilots and astronauts, and especially Blue Angels who performed tight maneuvers fighting gravitational pull, were taught to lift weights regularly and learn how to tense their abdominal muscles as if to prepare for a stomach punch. It was called "hooking." Without it, they might lose consciousness. In essence, the news about Reba hit Sam like a lethal G-force, and he'd had no chance to "hook."

Through discipline and occasionally alcohol, Sam had kept

thoughts of Reba banked in the recesses of his memory. Now, they all came rushing forward, like a burst dam.

Reba . . . Reba . . . Reba . . .

"That was a low blow, George," he said when he could finally speak with a modicum of calmness.

"Huh? All I said was that Reba was on the bus. I know you had a crush on her when you were kids."

Yep, George is manipulating me, bigtime. "A crush? I was crazy about her."

"Well, ya mighta told her that . . . before you skipped town like a cat with its tail on fire."

"That was fourteen years ago. I was headed for the Naval Academy," he pointed out, then took several deep breaths to control his temper, before adding, "She's married, George. Why rake up dead ashes?"

George gasped. "Samuel H. Merrick! You are ten kinds of a fool. Reba Anderson got divorced more'n ten years ago. I don't think she was married for six months before she discovered that Whitby boy was light in the loafers."

Reba isn't married? he marveled. *Thank you, God!* Apparently, he hadn't forgotten how to pray, after all.

The most incredible feeling swept over Sam then. It took him several moments to realize that it was happiness, the kind of happiness a little kid experiences, awakening on Christmas morning, when he believes that everything is possible.

He caught himself smiling like an idiot before he spoke into the phone again, "It appears I'll be riding on the Santa bus, after all, George."

A burst of static erupted in the phone, and just before the line went dead, Sam thought he heard George murmur, "I thought you would, son. I thought you would."

Reba? After all these years, I'm going to see Reba again?

I wonder if she's changed. I wonder if she'll think I've changed. Will she be happy to see me?

Does she still care?

Do I still care?

Apparently, he did. Why else would he be feeling so goofy? His heart swelled and almost burst from his chest. His brain raced at shutter-speed with images of him and Reba over an eight-year period, from the time he first arrived, mid-year, to be a reluctant student in the

Snowdon, Maine, public schools, while residing at the White Mountain Home for Boys. Reba had befriended the cocky ten-year-old he'd been then, somehow sensing that he'd been shaking on the inside.

Whereas he'd been self-confident, at least on the outside, and popular, Reba had been self-conscious and shy. Always on a diet, she'd claimed to be perpetually twenty pounds overweight. She was tall . . . at least five-foot-nine; so, it never showed as far as Sam could tell. He'd always thought she was just right . . . rounded in the right places. And soft.

"Hey, Slick, come here!"

Sam was jarred out of his reverie by Andy who was in the corridor outside the coffee shop, talking to two men carrying camera equipment emblazoned with the WBZ-TV logo. After placing a few dollars on the table, Sam walked outside.

Andy introduced everyone all around. It turned out one of the fellows, Larry Bassinger, had been a frat brother of Andy's when they were in Lafayette College together a few years back.

"I heard you talking on the phone about needing to connect with The Santa Brigade in Allentown," Andy explained.

"Yeah," Sam said hesitantly.

"Well, guess what? Larry just told me, they did a feature story on those cuckoo-birds last night when they were in Philly."

Larry nodded. "Our phones have been ringing off the hook all day. People want to know more about them."

"Soooo?" Sam addressed his question to both Andy and Larry, the whole time watching out of his side vision as the other guy, Frank Butler, was setting up his microphone equipment, as if to begin an interview.

"So, they have a helicopter, ready to take off. They're supposed to be doing some weather shots, but what the hey!" Andy threw his hands up in the air as if he'd just produced a miracle.

Why is everyone rambling around me today? Can't anyone just get to the point? He folded his arms across his chest, a clear sign of impatience.

Andy continued to beam at him. "They're willing to help you, and in return you help them."

"That's about as clear as pea soup in a ship's galley."

"You give them a feature story, and they get you to the Santa Brigade in Allentown."

"Huh?"

"I'm thinking we should title the piece, 'Blue Angel Drops Out of the Sky'," Frank told Larry.

"That would be good, that would be good," Larry said. "Or how about 'Santa Gets a New Helper.'"

As understanding began to dawn, the only thing Sam could say was, "Oh . . . my . . . God!"

"Geez, Sam, now that I think about it, this is *not* a good idea. Really, you could get in serious trouble with the Navy, not to mention the FAA, and any number of local agencies." Andy was frowning with concern.

"Yeah," Sam agreed, but all he could do was grin. Man, oh, man, did he love a challenge!

But this was a helluva dilemma. Was he really going to parachute out of a news helicopter to join a wacky Santa group wheeling up the highways to Maine in the middle of a snow storm?

Hmmmm.

It would be really dangerous.

I've done crazier things in my lifetime . . . lots crazier.

I could be risking my career, just like Andy said.

Been there, done that, what's new?

I might be making a fool of myself.

Damn straight.

Reba Anderson is there.

He smiled to himself then.

Santa Brigade, here I come!

Reba Anderson was one happy camper . . . well, Santa Claus.

Even with snowflakes the size of cotton balls drifting around her, Reba couldn't feel anything but happy. She and her nine fellow Santas had just provided some much-needed holiday cheer to thirty-one homeless adults and children at the Good Shepherd Homeless Shelter in Allentown, Pennsylvania—their twenty-eighth entertainment program of the holiday season. They had only six more to go before returning to their homes in Maine on Christmas Eve, four days from now.

Dressed to the gills in St. Nick attire, she stood near the fold-down steps of the souped-up Santa Brigade bus, hitching up her Santa belly. Smiling to herself, she recalled a time when she was so self-conscious she never would have donned a fattie outfit, too worried over what others might think. Although she had never been fat, she was proud of her now svelte figure—one which she'd maintained for ten long, jogging-filled years. It was a sign of her growing self-confidence and contentment, she supposed, that she no longer cringed over her appearance . . . or that of the bus which sported a bright, fire engine red paint job and a hokey Rudolph hood ornament.

She was checking off on her clipboard each member of the outrageous, endearing, senior citizen Santa troupe as they emerged from the shelter—actually, a church annex—and made their way carefully through the cascading snow and over slick sidewalks to their mobile home-away-from-home, which was parked in the empty church parking lot.

Reba's heart swelled with pride as she watched the members of her group chat and laugh together about the act they'd just completed. Truly, they'd become like a family. A family of Santas.

Maudeen Livingstone, who was known affectionately as Cyber Granny because of her fascination with computers, stuck her head out of the bus window and informed Reba, "I just got an email from a dollar store in Scranton. If we can stop there on the way to Poughkeepsie, they have a load of gifts for us, including," she chuckled gleefully, ". . . a couple dozen more Chia pets." The seventy-five-year-old Maudeen was a wiry, irascible grandmother who had operated Snowdon's one and only hair salon/barbershop for many years, Clip 'n' Curl. She had a penchant for ever-changing hair-do's. Today her hair was fiery red and curly.

Reba joined Maudeen in chuckling. Their beloved Cyber Granny used her computer like an industrial clearing house for donations and requests for help, matching supply with demand. At any one moment, she could tell you exactly how many fruitcakes they had on hand, or Lincoln Logs, or doll babies or whatever. The Santa Brigade relied almost totally on donations from private and business concerns. And they weren't picky, either. Nosirree. The first time someone had donated Chia Pets, they had all groaned, figuring only idiots would want those cornball items. But it turned out they were very popular in the mostly colorless homeless shelters, which were bereft of any greenery.

Sometimes business concerns were devious in their donations, just looking for tax write-offs for bad merchandise, like The Budget Bazaar which gave them twenty-five wreaths with hidden motion detectors that were supposed to play "Jingle Bells" when someone passed by, but instead played, "Here Comes Peter Cottontail." The only time

Reba had refused a donation was when Good Times Haberdashery in Newark tried to pawn off three dozen samples of "The Real Man's Christmas Belt." Mistletoe hung from the belt buckles.

"Scranton wouldn't be too far out of our way," Maudeen said, interrupting her preoccupation.

"Talk to Betty about any stops you want to make. You know the approaching storm is a concern." Betty, a retired Marine officer and current NASCAR mechanic, was their bus driver.

"Yep," Maudeen agreed. "We've gotta get back to Snowdon by Christmas Eve, guaranteed. Don't want to miss George's wedding. Plus, my grandkids are coming in from Boston that night."

Even as they talked, Betty completed a second check of the air pressure in the huge tires and was now flipping up the hood of the bus . . . not an easy feat for most women of her diminutive size. But Betty was not like most women. The feisty, no-nonsense woman, with the CB handle, "Tough Cookie," had trucker and police connections all over the eastern seaboard to make sure their Santa troupe would get where they needed to go.

"Should we be worried about the weather conditions? Maybe we should stay overnight here in Allentown."

Betty slammed the hood of the bus shut, after having checked the oil and antifreeze, then addressed Reba. "We'll be fine . . . for now. I want us to make as good a time as possible today, though, hopefully to Poughkeepsie, do the show there, and move on northward. I don't think the blizzard will affect us, seriously, 'til we cross the Vermont line. I'm not saying we won't have to take it easy, but I can handle a little snow."

Reba nodded, more than willing to leave all the transportation worries in Betty's capable hands. She turned to check off the last of her passengers. That's when she noticed that Betty was staring with amazement toward the sky. It took a lot to amaze Betty.

"Look! Look!" Several of the Santa Brigade members had rolled down the windows of the bus and were pointing to the sky.

Reba joined them in gazing skyward where the thwapping sound of a helicopter was clearly audible overhead, and visible, even through the thickening shower of snowflakes. It was one of those news helicopters . . . the type that did traffic and weather reporting . . . in this case, WBZ-TV. But that wasn't what had excited her senior Santas, or the people streaming out of the homeless shelter to gawk at the heavens. There was a man parachuting out of the helicopter . . . no, two men. The first was wearing some kind of military uniform. The other was obviously a TV cameraman who had his lens pointed at the other person and at the gathering crowd below.

"Maudeen!" Reba yelled.

Maudeen jumped in her window seat near the front where she'd been continuing to work with her laptop.

"Did you arrange another publicity stunt?"

Maudeen craned her head out the window and looked up to the sky. Even in those few seconds, snowflakes were covering her curly red head. "Nope, but I woulda, if I'd thought of it. There's no such thing as bad publicity," she pronounced and ducked back inside with a decided shiver.

Reba wasn't so sure about that. It wouldn't be good PR for their Santa Brigade if one of these yahoos broke a neck skydiving. And, really, they didn't have time now for another interview, although God bless the media, big and small, who had covered their trips the past few years. The exposure they gave them brought in the gifts and monetary donations that made this charitable endeavor possible.

"Oh, for Pete's Sake! I think I recognize that fellow in the uniform," Betty declared with a sniff. She was staring up at the sky with a pair of binoculars . . . one of many that had been donated by a bankrupt sporting goods chain. "Isn't it just like *him* to pull such a stunt?"

"Huh?" Reba said. "Let me use those." With the aid of the binoculars, she squinted upward at the figures who were rapidly approaching the parking lot. Suddenly, a prickling sensation tickled the back of her neck. *No! It isn't possible. He wouldn't show up here, of all places. Not now. Not after all these years.*

Reba handed the binoculars back to Betty, who seemed equally stunned with disbelief as the men landed safely and disengaged themselves from their harnesses and parachutes. They both removed helmets and dropped them to the ground. People from the homeless shelter rushed forward, along with a few cops who had pulled up, sirens screaming. Everyone was talking at once.

The man in uniform, who must be frozen to the bone since he hadn't worn a jumpsuit like the other fellow had, pushed doggedly toward the bus, ignoring the crowd and shouted questions. His gaze swept the bus area, as if searching for someone . . . then locked on her. He started resolutely to close the short distance between them.

Reba's heart skipped a beat as she backed away slowly.

"Sam Merrick?" she asked in a voice hardly more than a whisper. Or was it a whimper?

He must have heard because he nodded.

Oh, he looks so good. His dark hair was much shorter than the last time she'd seen him, fourteen years ago. Not the buzz cut normally associated with GI's, but short on the sides and neck, nonetheless. There were fine lines crinkling the edges of his eyes and mouth, both of which appeared oddly vulnerable as he stared at her. If anything he looked better than he had before, and he'd always been stop-traffic handsome.

How must I look to him? she wondered, realizing suddenly that she still wore the Santa suit with the big belly, though she had removed the hat and beard, which she clutched in trembling fingers? *Like a fool, that's how.*

As if in answer, Sam's scrutiny swept over her in that slow, sensual way he'd perfected with women since practically toddlerhood. His perusal lingered over her midsection, and a smile twitched at his lips. Then he stared directly into her eyes.

"Reba," he said huskily, "you look just the same as always."

She gasped, clutching at her big belly. Over the years, she'd practiced many scenarios and scripts in her mind, imagining what he would say or do if she ever met him again. And what does he say? That she hasn't changed at all. Well, she had. And not just on the outside. He should have noticed, she decided irrationally. He should have come back sooner. *The louse! The two-bit jerk! Where is his famous charm?*

"What are you doing here?" she blurted out.

He chuckled, and, oh, what a familiar sound that was! Sam had the sexiest chuckle in the world. "I was stuck in the Philadelphia airport, and when George told me that you were here, well, I decided on the spot that I had to come, and . . ." His voice trailed off, and he just shrugged.

"You came here to see me?"

He hesitated with uncertainty. "Uh-huh. And because I need to hitch a ride to Snowdon with your bus . . . you know, for George's wedding. I talked to your bus driver on the phone and she gave me directions to—"

Reba's head swiveled to Betty who leaned against the side of the bus, blatantly eavesdropping on their conversation. "You never mentioned Sam to me," she accused.

"Ooops!" Betty said. "Guess it slipped my mind." She wasn't

fooling Reba. The old fool had deliberately withheld that news from her.

Tossing her hat and beard to the ground with disgust, she turned her attention back to the Show-off Jerk before her. She put a fist on each of her padded hips and demanded, "You heard I was here and just had to come *all of the sudden* . . . by parachute?"

"That's the short story. Can we go somewhere private? I'll fill in all the details later."

Reba had finally come to her senses. Who the hell did he think he was? Who the hell did he think she was . . . some clueless teenager who would be impressed by his romantic gesture?

"You haven't changed at all, Sam Merrick. What a juvenile prank! Guess you figured I'd just swoon all over the place, like all your other women."

"Other women?" he sputtered. "What other women?"

She gave him a look that told him exactly what women she was referring to, as if she didn't read the tabloids, or get reports back from George on occasion. Did he think she was a clueless twit, stuck in the Maine boonies?

Sam put both of his fists on his hips, mirroring her actions, and glared back at her. "What's got your Santa belly all a-jiggle, Reba?" he asked, a teasing tone to his voice. "I thought you'd be pleased that I . . ."

Reba was not in the mood for being teased. "Ooooh, you are a real piece of work, *Slick.*"

Sam had always hated it when she'd called him by that nickname, even though he'd accepted it from everyone else. Apparently, he still didn't like the appellation coming from her lips because his jaw tensed and his fists got tighter.

But then he softened, and the look Sam gave her spoke volumes, caressing her soul. He told her, without speaking, that he wanted her . . . only her.

For that moment, anyway.

The man is smooth . . . I'll give him that. Good thing I caught myself in time. I'll be damned if I allow him to turn that famous charm on me. "Do you expect me to be jumping with joy when you *finally* show up after fourteen years?"

"I heard . . . I heard that you got married. In fact, until today, I thought . . . well, I thought . . . you still were . . . and, after all, how was I to know that . . . " The usually cool Sam stammered as he spoke.

"Give me a break! I was married ten years ago. Where were you thirteen years ago? Or twelve? Or eleven? You know, those first three loooong years after you left?"

"I can explain," he said and tried to reach for her.

She stepped aside . . . not an easy task for a hefty Santa . . . and put up a halting hand. With tears welling in her eyes, Reba realized that her long-buried dream had come true . . . Sam had finally come back. But it wasn't like her dreams at all. In fact, this was her worst nightmare.

"I've never forgotten about you. Never."

Reba could have wept at the sweetness of those words. If only they were true! But it was undoubtedly a phoney sentiment meant to achieve some ulterior motive . . . as always. A Slick-ism. "Cut the crap, Slick. That doesn't even pass the giggle test."

"Reeebbbaaa," he cajoled huskily.

Really, it was untenable. The jerk still thought he could charm the pants off her. Well, darn it, he probably could, if she wasn't careful. Inhaling deeply to calm herself, Reba looked at Sam. Then she looked at the snow bank behind him where city crews must have plowed the parking lot during a previous storm. Then she looked back at Sam again. Finally, she did the only thing a once-jilted female could do . . . she shoved a world-famous Blue Angel in the chest, knocking him flat on his back.

"Charm *that*, Slick," she said and stomped off toward the bus.

Nine Santas clapped in appreciation of her long-overdue spunk. And a television camera filmed what would be heralded in the evening news programs as, "Blue Angel Gets Wings Clipped."

Reba should have felt silly, or regretful, but she felt damn good.

Sam was feeling good . . . damn good.

It didn't matter that he was lying flat on his back in a pile of snow. It didn't matter that Reba was so pissed at him that smoke practically steamed from her ears. It didn't matter that a whole bunch of people were gaping at him. It didn't matter that the TV camera was rolling, and geriatric Santas were voicing their opinions right and left. It didn't even matter that a blinking police light nearby indicated some serious questioning on his horizon. He was exactly where he wanted to be . . . within radar range of Reba. Now, the real work began. If there was one thing Samuel H. Merrick, Commander, U.S. Navy, knew how to handle, it was a challenge.

In one fluid motion, he rose to his feet, dusted off his butt, and took off after Reba, whose fat Santa ass had the cutest wobble to it. Later he might inform her of that anatomical fact, but not right now . . . unless he wanted to land in the snow again.

She was about to board the bus when he grabbed her by the upper arm. Before she could say, "Buzz off, bozo!" or something equally appropriate, he pulled her—feet dragging, free arm flailing, mouth sputtering—toward the church annex. Once inside what appeared to be the vestibule of a chapel, attached to a church homeless shelter, he drew her into an alcove.

Privacy, at last.

Reba, at last.

"Let . . . me . . . go," Reba said through gritted teeth, struggling vehemently, but to no avail. He had her backed up against the wall, his flat stomach pressed against her pillowed stomach, her two hands held above her head, locked in place by his fingers entwined with hers.

Sweet mother! She is the sexiest Santa in the world.

"Let . . . me . . . go," she repeated.

"Never! Never again!" He basked in his first close-up examination of the girl he had loved . . . who was now the woman he . . . loved? He wasn't sure about that, but, before this Christmas was over, he was going to find out, for damn sure.

The adrenaline rush he got when making a rifle-shot pass down a runway before streaking toward a clear blue sky was nothing compared to this. The beauty of a four-plane diamond formation, wing tip to wing tip, at five hundred miles per hour was nothing compared to this.

Pilots had an expression called "flying too close to the flame." Well, he'd thought he'd done just that on a hundred different maneuvers, but it was nothing compared to this. With sudden insightfulness, he realized that Reba was his flame, and always had been. And that's why he'd stayed away.

In many ways, she looked the same, just as he'd told her, though more mature, of course. He was so very glad she hadn't changed much. In his convoluted logic, he figured she'd stayed in place for him.

Long, honey blonde hair fell to her shoulders and beyond in a thick swath that he'd always loved and she'd always hated. He wanted to take a strand between his fingers and rub sensuously, but he wasn't taking a chance on releasing her . . . yet.

Her eyes were the same caramel brown, but different; they'd seen pain. That saddened him a bit. He'd always told Reba she had smiling eyes; a person could tell she was smiling without ever seeing her mouth. He would make her eyes smile again. Yes, he would.

And speaking of her mouth . . . Blessed Lord, what a mouth! That hadn't changed, thanks be to God and genetics. Her upper lip was fuller and puffier than the lower. A supremely kissable mouth.

What would she do if I grazed the pad of my thumb across her bottom lip?

Bite it off, no doubt, he answered himself with an inner chuckle. "Reba," he said in a husky whisper, his head lowering. "I'm going to kiss you, honey."

"No."

"Shhhh, don't resist. I know we have lots to discuss. Please, just give me a chance."

"No."

"I've made mistakes. I owe you a million apologies."

"No."

"You married another man, for chrissake! All these years I thought . . . I was picturing you with . . . " His voice choked up so he couldn't continue. "Later. We'll talk about this later. But, first, God help me, I want . . . *I need* . . . to kiss you. Just one kiss, babe. Just one."

In that flutter of a second before his lips met hers, she moaned. That's all. A moan. But he recognized the moan for what it was. Despite her "No, no, no's," she wanted this kiss as much as he did. Where he and Reba were concerned, there was magic when they touched . . . always had been.

He closed his eyes and inhaled deeply. The scent of holiday evergreens, beeswax candles and incense permeated the air. In a closed room upstairs, he could hear children's voices raised in a screechy version of "Silent Night," probably preparing for a Christmas recital. Were they homeless children, or students from a religious school affiliated with the church? Or angels that God had sent to serenade his reunion with Reba?

Above all the Christmas ambience was peppermint. He smelled it on Reba's breath before he tasted it on her lips. She must have candy canes in her Santa sack, he surmised with an irrelevance that surely bordered on madness.

"Sam," she breathed.

"Reba," he breathed back.

At first, he just settled his lips against hers, and, miracle of miracles, they still fit together perfectly.

Then he set about the serious business of kissing. And, yes, he took his kissing seriously . . . especially with Reba.

Slanting and molding, parting her lips with his. Deeper. Harder. Then softer again. Pleading and demanding. Once, when he came up for breath, he whispered, "I love kissing you."

Smiling against his mouth, she said, "You always say that." She was right. He *had* always said that before . . . during and after their hours and hours of kissing . . . the kind of hormone-heavy torture only teenagers could inflict on each other, and enjoy the process.

"You're trembling," he informed her with male satisfaction.

She laughed. "You're gloating." And she didn't even seem annoyed over that. He must be making progress.

"I love kissing you," he said again, because it felt so right. Time spiraled backwards then. It could have been now, or fourteen years ago. Some things never changed.

He kissed her and kissed her, with all the expertise he could gather and with all the yearnings he could not bank. One long, never-ending, forever kiss. If he stopped the kiss, the dream might end. The magic might disappear. He kissed her soft and coaxing 'til her lips went pliant. Then, blood thickening and senses inflaming, he kissed her deep and wet 'til her knees buckled, and he had to release their interlaced fingers so that he could put his hands on her pillowed behind to hold her up.

"I'm a fool," she whimpered on a sigh. "Like always, I'm a fool where you're concerned."

"My fool!" he agreed. "Be a fool for me, baby. Only me. That's right. That's the way."

To his surprise and delight, Reba put her arms around his neck and drew him closer.

He was the one who whimpered then, especially when she opened her mouth wider and touched his tongue with hers.

"You taste like peppermint," she said against his mouth, not breaking contact.

"I taste like you," he answered with a growl. "And you taste like . . . home."

That seemed to snag Reba's attention because her body went still. Taking his face in both her hands, she broke their kiss and held his head away. "Home?" she asked, her voice grainy with arousal, and something else . . . something much more dangerous . . . *hope*. "Are you really coming home, Sam? For good?" The expectant expression on her face about broke his heart.

No, no, no! Now is not the time for somber questions. "Later, honey," he murmured, and tried to resume the kiss.

She would have none of that and averted her face. "Sam, are you coming home?"

He could feel his face flush. "Of course. I'm coming home for George's wedding. JD and Stan will be there, too. It'll be great." Even he recognized how lame that sounded.

She shook her head at his evasiveness. "Are you coming home for good?"

How the hell do I know? Man, my blood turns cold just thinking about living in that town again. But Reba would be there. And I'm a grown-up now. A Blue Angels pilot, to be precise. Well, golly, Merrick, there's a big call for pilots in Podunk, Maine. Oh, shit! Oh, damn! Oh, God, let me say the right thing.

He hesitated a moment too long, and Reba pushed her hands against his chest and ducked out of his embrace. She put several feet between them before he had a chance to gather his testosterone-foggy senses. "Reba, this is all happening too fast. I need time."

"Time!" she spat out. "You've had fourteen years to make up your mind, Sam. If you don't know now, you never will."

"You don't understand."

"Yes, I do, Sam. I understand more than you can imagine. Perhaps it's best that we met like this again. I needed the closure." She regarded him with soul-wrenching disappointment.

"Closure?" A tight vise was squeezing his chest walls, and he could barely breathe.

"It's over. Finally, and forever." There were tears in her eyes, but Sam could tell that she meant every word.

"But the kiss. You can't deny the kiss, Reba. The magic is still there between us, no matter what you say."

She stared at him for what seemed like an eternity through misty brown eyes. Then she declared flatly, "That, my friend, was a goodbye kiss."

With that, she was gone.

CHAPTER TWO

KEVIN

Tuesday, three days 'til Christmas Eve

"You're *where?*" Kevin Wilder asked into his cell phone.

"You heard me," his childhood friend, Sam Merrick, growled. "I hitched a ride with this Santa Brigade bus thing."

"Santa Brigade?" Kevin turned and captured a glimpse of himself in a mirror hanging on the wall, right below the train schedule. Man, he needed a haircut. Bad. Between his shaggy head, two day beard-growth, his bomber jacket and beat-up jeans, he had the feeling he looked one step above a thug. Or possibly one step below. He turned from his image, recognizing why the girl at the information desk had appeared petrified when he'd stalked over to her earlier. "*The* Santa Brigade? The traveling seniors from Winter Haven?"

"You've heard of them?" Sam asked in an undertone.

"Everyone in the Western Hemisphere has heard of them."

"Not me. Until yesterday, that is."

"Doesn't surprise me, Slick. Your head's been up in the clouds, literally, for years." Kevin stifled a grin at the mental picture of his buddy stuck on a bus with a truckload of Snowdon's finest. "Exactly how in hell did this happen?"

"Long story," Sam breathed. "Suffice it to say the alternatives were none and none. Think Philadelphia airport, cancelled flights, the works."

Kevin pulled his cell phone from his ear and stared at it for a moment. Finally he asked, "Why are you whispering?"

"Naptime," Sam whispered.

"Excuse me?"

"Forget it. So, where are you? Already make it to George's?"

"Hardly." Kevin scowled at the sign above the arched

entranceway of the train station. "I'm in Schenectady."

"Schenectady? What in hell are you doing there?"

"I took a little detour. I wanted to stop and scope out the area a bit for a case I'm working after George's wedding."

"Yeah, spy guy? What kind of job?"

"Nothing earth-shattering, trust me. Some dress maker jumped on a subpoena and disappeared. She's originally from this area and still has family here, so I thought I'd stop and look around, see if anyone's caught sight of her."

"Well, haul your ass out of there and get yourself to Maine."

"The thing is, Slick, sometime between when I landed here and now, the trains north have stopped running altogether. Something about an obstruction up ahead."

"Hmm, that sucks. So when will you hit Snowdon?"

"At this rate, next April."

Sam swore softly. In the background, Kevin heard a hauntingly familiar voice. "*Samuel* Merrick, you watch your language."

"Oh, Lord," Kevin muttered, shuddering. "That's not Mrs. Smith, is it?"

"I'm sorry, Mrs. Smith," Sam said, in the same repentant tone Kevin remembered from eighth grade English class.

"You're stuck on a bus with Pinch-face Smith?"

"She's one of the traveling Santas," Sam replied in a low growl. Despite his frustration over the transportation problem he was facing, Kevin laughed. "Lucky you, Slick."

"She's mellowed. She's only corrected my grammar twice in the last few hours."

"I heard that, young man," Pinch-face admonished. "You're not too old to get the ruler, you know."

"She hasn't mellowed much," Kevin noted.

"Hasn't aged much either. None of these folks have. There's got to be something in the water at Winter Haven."

"Well, with old man Anderson running the place, it's probably bootleg whiskey."

"Actually, he passed away."

Kevin's heart gave a lurch at the news. Although Reba Anderson's dad pretty much disapproved of her friendship with the three of them, he hadn't forbidden it, either, unlike most other folks in town. "I'm sorry for Reba," he said quietly. "I wish I'd known. She was a fun kid." *And* at one point Slick had been crazy about the girl. But Kevin didn't mention that part. As cool and smooth-tongued as Slick had been back then, somehow he'd always been kind of goofy around Reba.

"Yeah, well . . . you ought to see her as an adult."

Kevin frowned. "Say again?"

"She's the tour director for this Santa thing."

"Reba's on the bus?" Kevin burst out laughing. "Well, that explains why you're there, loverboy."

Seeing Reba again was probably driving Sam crazy. So changing the subject seemed like a real good idea. "So, fly boy, got any suggestions for getting me to Maine?"

"Give me your exact location, JD."

Kevin winced a little at the old nickname. He didn't mind so much that his best buddies called him JD, but at the origins of the letters. They stood for "Juvenile Delinquent," the assignation he'd been given by the disapproving adults in Snowdon within weeks of his arrival at White Mountain Home for Boys. He headed over to a porter. "Where am I?" he asked bluntly.

The guy looked at him like he was a few slices shy of a loaf, but finally gave him a precise enough directional location to relate to Slick, which he did. Slick said, "I'll call you back," and hung up before Kevin could respond.

Shaking his head, Kevin flung his backpack over his shoulder and headed back to the information desk. The teenybopper behind the counter swallowed audibly as Kevin approached. He ran a hand through his shaggy hair and plastered as engaging a smile as he could muster on his face. If he were Slick, the girl would have fainted dead away. As it was, she merely returned his smile. "Is there something else I can do for you?" she asked.

The only thing she could do for him was find him a way to get to Maine. He had the feeling that feat wasn't in her repertoire. He opened his mouth, but she quickly interrupted. "Has anyone ever told you that you look exactly like Harrison Ford?"

That stopped him. "Harrison Ford?" The man had to be in his fifties.

"Oh, yes. Just like him. You know, Indiana Jones."

Well, that wasn't too bad, he supposed. Harrison had been a good bit younger in his Indie days. "Nope, never heard that one," he mumbled. "Got any good news for me since last time we talked?"

Her hand fluttered to her neck. "You mean, since ten minutes ago?"

"Right."

"Uh . . . no. The track north of us is still out, and probably will be for the next week."

Damn. "Have any suggestions for alternative forms of transportation?"

"I'm afraid not," she said, her brown eyes sympathetic. "All bus routes northbound have been suspended, and all of the airports within a hundred miles are closing down in anticipation of the storm."

Double damn. He glanced around. "What are all of these stranded people going to do?"

She brightened considerably, and the Christmas ornament earrings she wore jangled as she nodded. "There's a Motel 6 right next door. Why don't you go on over and settle in until the storm passes?"

"I'm afraid I can't do that," Kevin replied, shaking his head. "I *have* to be in Maine in three days. He held up his hands. "I'm best man in a wedding."

"I'm sorry."

With a nod, Kevin moved to turn away, but just then his cell phone started belting out Jingle Bells. He rolled his eyes as he pulled it from the pocket of his bomber jacket. He *really* had to keep his secretary, Mrs. Boswell, away from his toys. He *still* hadn't gotten over what happened the night she'd borrowed his hand cuffs.

"Wilder."

"Hey, JD," Slick growled.

"Tell me you're flying up here to pick me up."

"No can do, but I've got the next best thing."

"What's that?"

"If you can get to the truck stop on Route 8 within the next hour, Betty Morgan says we'll be able to veer off course a little and pick you up."

"We?" he asked suspiciously. "I *hope* you don't mean the Santa Brigade."

"That's what I mean, buddy."

"Let me see if I've got you here, Slick. You're offering to stick me on a bus with Mrs. Smith, and a whole bunch of other Snowdon residents who probably still believe I'm the devil incarnate?"

"They were all real pleased to hear you're not doing twenty to life in Attica."

Kevin scowled. "And you *cannot* mean *the* Betty Morgan."

"The one and only."

"Betty Bad-ass is driving that bus?"

"In between trying to order me to drop and give her twenty, yes."

"Only twenty? Then she's definitely mellowed."

"Uh . . . not really. She just can't supervise more than that in the rearview mirror."

Through the phone Kevin could hear a chorus of folks singing cheery Christmas carols. Everywhere he looked in the train station, people were greeting each other jovially, as if they didn't have a stranded care in the world. He'd landed in the holiday Twilight Zone. "Not a chance I'm boarding that hell on wheels."

"You have a better offer, do you?" Sam asked.

Kevin glanced around wildly, silently praying for Santa and his sleigh to appear. Anything but facing the elder statesmen and women of Snowdon. Although he was secretly proud of the fame his hometown folks had achieved with the yearly Santa Brigade trek, he also knew that many of those self-same philanthropists had written him off as hopeless a long time ago. Only George had had faith. Only George had refused to give up on him.

"I think I'd rather hitchhike and take my chances with a deranged trucker."

"But see, we've got Betty! There's no more deranged than that."

"Merrick, you get KP at the next stop," Kevin heard a voice bark in the background.

Sam swore.

"Samuel!" Pinch-face Smith said.

"Oh, God!" Kevin muttered. There was no way he was getting on that bus. "No way I'm getting on that bus."

"Do you want to see George tie the noose or not, JD?"

"Yes, but—"

"Look, Maudeen went online and checked all options, JD."

"Maudeen? Maudeen of *Color Me Bad* fame?"

"That's the one."

"This is getting scarier by the second."

"You are *not* going to find a better offer," Sam said, ignoring his complaints. "Most roads are closed or nearly impassable. This is about the only boat on the move."

"How is that, anyway? How's Betty getting around all the road blocks?"

"You wouldn't believe the connections this broad has. Not to mention, this bus is so souped up, a blizzard couldn't stop it. Much as

I hate to admit it, JD, this is your best and safest chance at making it to George's wedding."

"Shit," Kevin muttered, as he watched an Amish woman emerge from the station diner and head in his direction. Why she captured his attention, he couldn't say. There were tons of Amish folks in this part of the state, and she was dressed just as drably from head-to-toe as the rest of them. But something in the way she moved was seriously graceful. And although her plain blue dress and white smock exposed not an ounce of flesh, there was something blatantly sexy about her.

He turned away, snorting in self-disgust. He was either deranged or sex-deprived. Or both. "This sucks."

"Actually, I think you'd be wildly in awe here, JD. I know I am."

Considering Slick was a member of the elite Blue Angels, who flew some of the most sophisticated military birds in the air, Kevin was somewhat impressed. "Really?"

"Not to mention, think how much fun we can have regaling these folks with all of our heroic accomplishments. You can lie about yours."

"Kiss ass," Kevin said, but he grinned.

"Come on, JD. This'll give us more time to catch up," Sam said in his best Slick voice. The one no one on the planet seemed able to resist. Including his sucker friends, apparently. "This could be some serious fun," Sam added.

"Oh, yeah. About as much fun as getting ambushed by a FTA."

"A what?"

"Failure to appear. Never mind, just bounty hunter lingo, Slick. Way above your IQ."

"I'll let that one slide, seeing as you're probably real proud of yourself for finally learning what IQ stands for. But what's this bounty hunter crap? Is the PI work not panning out?"

"Nah, I've got more work than I can handle. But this is gravy. And I could use the bucks for law school."

"Law school? Holy shit, JD!"

"Samuel!"

"Sorry, Mrs. Smith." Sam coughed. "Cop, private dick, bounty hunter, and now law school? You're going downhill fast, pal."

"This from a guy who gets his rocks off doing wheelies in mid-air. What can I say? I'm a work in progress."

Sam chuckled. "Come on, JD, what do you say? Let Bad-ass Betty and the Santa gang rescue you?"

Kevin wanted to get on that Santa bus about as much as he

wanted to... miss George's wedding. No, the very last thing he wanted to do was miss George's wedding. Wonder of wonders, George Garrison was getting married. And there wasn't a chance in hell Kevin would miss that event, even if he had to walk to Maine to get there.

A scent invaded his nostrils. Or scents. It seemed like a combination of perfume and cinnamon. Then, as he wrestled with his choices – which seemed to have dwindled to one very unappealing choice – he heard the info babe behind him say, "Hey, Miz Zook. How are you?"

"Ah, good, thank you," a petal soft female voice answered, in a somewhat foreign accent that sounded strangely . . .not quite right. "And a good holiday to you."

"What kind of pies didja deliver to the diner today?" the young girl asked. Out of the corner of his eye, Kevin saw that the girl was addressing the Amish babe. The unfathomably sexy Amish babe.

"Pumpkin, rhubarb and pecan today," the woman said.

That voice traveled straight through Kevin's body, as if caressing his insides with velvet. Kevin ignored it. "Okay, I'll bite," he said. "What do I have to do to meet the bus?" He shuddered at the thought.

"Make it to a place called 'Truck You' within the next two hours. We're going out of our way to rescue you, so be grateful, JD."

He felt as grateful as a five-year-old getting coal in his stocking, but he gritted his teeth. "'Truck You?' You've got to be kidding me."

"Nope. These road folks have a real good sense of humor."

"Where is that again?" he asked, then grimaced when he was bumped from behind.

"Route 8. Betty says it's pretty close to where you are right now."

"Hold on." Kevin swung back to talk to the info babe, and came face-to-face and almost breast-to-chest with the Amish woman. He sucked in a breath.

She sucked in a breath.

He stared into pale green, startled eyes that literally made his heart kick into his ribs.

She stared back unblinkingly, and Kevin knew a fleeting moment of wondering if she liked what she saw.

The moment was fleeting, because he could tell right away she didn't like what she saw at all. In fact, her startled expression gave way to growing horror, as her eyes swept over his face.

Obviously she didn't share info-babe's Harrison Ford observation.

But the alarm in her eyes was pretty damn insulting. He knew he wasn't anything that special, even when he cleaned up, but he also wasn't the hunchback of Notre Dame. Unless he'd just broken out in a horrid disease, he couldn't find a good reason for her reaction.

Even horrified, she was gorgeous. Her heart-shaped face and pink lips begged for a man's touch. Which was utterly ridiculous because her outfit and bonnet said loud and clear, "Back off, bucko."

Amish babe's amazing eyes dropped instantly, and she murmured, "This is for you," to the info chick, giving the girl a small, gaily wrapped package. "And now I must go," she added, before beginning to hustle out of there like a world class sprinter.

"Wait!" info babe said. "I have something for you, too!"

The Amish honey stopped abruptly and reluctantly, then turned back to the desk, her head hanging way low. "You needn't have done such a thing," she protested in that soft, smooth voice and strange accent.

Kevin realized that the delicious smell he'd just encountered actually emanated from her. The bakery scent he could understand. But he could swear there was perfume mixed in there. Chanel No. 5 if he wasn't mistaken. And he was pretty sure Amish people wouldn't be allowed to wear Chanel No. 5, although he didn't know that for sure.

As he stared at her profile, his gaze once again landed on her lips. They were full and lush and he could swear covered in a pastel lip gloss. He was almost positive lipstick would be a no-no in Amish country. Vanity being one of their seven deadliest sins.

His eyes happily drank in her profile and the rest of her features.

If she wasn't wearing blush, then she was a natural blusher. And if she wasn't wearing mascara, she had some awesome eyelashes. Her nose needed no help. It was just plain cute.

A tingling sensation tickled his gut. It was a reaction he'd come to learn over the years that told him something wasn't quite right. He took a closer look at the Amish chick and the tingling intensified. He'd never known any Amish folks personally, but somehow she seemed eerily familiar. Did she resemble some woman he'd dated in the past?

He really mourned that ugly cap on her head. He'd love to know what color and length her hair was. Just out of a PI's natural curiosity, of course.

"JD?" he heard shouted from the speaker of his phone, which had somehow lowered from his ear.

He shook his head and lifted the receiver. "What?"

Slick cussed, and again Kevin vaguely heard Mrs. Smith in the background, chastising.

"If we're picking you up," Slick said, after apologizing once again, "we have to know in about one-point-five minutes. It means a different turn-off."

Kevin dragged his gaze from the Amish babe back to the info kid. "Do you know where a place called 'Truck You' is?" he asked. He thought he heard a low gurgle from Amish beauty, but couldn't be sure, with all the noise around them.

Info babe smiled, apparently happy to have good news this time. "Sure! It's right up the road, just a couple of blocks."

"Can I catch a cab?"

The girl's happy smile faded. "Yes, sure, I think so. As long as they're still running when your number comes up on the waiting list."

"Waiting list? How long is the waiting list?"

She checked a clipboard. "You'll be number thirty-nine if I add you right now."

Kevin started to curse, but remembered the Amish babe just in time. "And what's the ETA of that cab thirty-eight passengers from now?"

"This is just a guess, but about three hours?"

He bit back more cussing. "There's a hundred dollars in it to somehow slip my name up in the top five."

"Oh, I don't know if I'm allowed to do that!" the young girl said, looking distressed and greedy all at once.

Kevin decided to help her enjoy the morality of it by letting her get a peek at the green herself. He reached into his jacket pocket for his wallet, and found the space aggravatingly empty. That couldn't be. He *always* kept his wallet in his left hand pocket. But just in case, he patted himself down, then growled, "Hold on," as he dug through his backpack, tossing the tools of his trade aside, digging through his skivvies and toiletries, and practically chewing off his tongue to keep a string of epithets that would singe the hair off a bear from passing through his lips.

This time he did swear. He just did it silently. "Appears with all the other fun adventures this trip is promising," he told Sam, "I've been robbed."

Out of the corner of his eye he watched the Amish woman try to tug back her freedom from the info girl who seemed hell-bent on holding onto her for dear life.

"Hell, JD! Sorry, Mrs. Smith. For a cop, JD, you sure are a dumb one."

"Ex-cop. But, yeah, looks that way now. You're going to have to lend me money when I get there."

"How the hell you going to make it there now?"

I'm just a couple of blocks away," he said. Glancing out the window, he watched the fat snowflakes falling fast and steadily. "I'm going to have to walk, but I can make it, if I don't die of exposure." He glanced at info kid. "I'll need directions."

"Ms. Zook can show you the way," she chirped, her hands still clutching Amish babe.

She's staying at the farm right past the truck stop."

Kevin suddenly loved info chicks worldwide. He'd jump over the desk and hug the girl, if it weren't for the fact that the blushing Amish lady had just paled to snow white, and shook her bonneted-head frantically before she realized he was watching.

"I'd be so appreciative," he boomed, because the thought of checking this woman out for a while longer appealed. Really appealed. The tingling hadn't stopped, and he was happy for a few more moments to try and figure out its source.

She looked at him then, full-face on, and the tingling exploded. Green eyes. About five feet three inches tall. Slender. Beautiful. Just like the glossy of Cassandra Lee Brandt that was sitting in his backpack. If he could pull the bonnet off of her head, he'd bet the ranch, so to speak, that it was covering wild ebony hair.

When he'd first studied the picture that had accompanied the file on her given to him by defense attorney Willard Plunkin, he'd looked at that hair and decided that no one could hide in a crowd with that hair, it was so distinctive. The woman would surely have to cut it off, which was a real shame. He hadn't counted on her disguising herself in a get-up that effectively kept her mane under wraps, so to speak. Clever. Too bad for her, he was even more clever than that.

Busted, baby.

"Ach, but I'm sorry," she said. "It would not be proper."

He offered up his winning smile. "But wouldn't it be nice — especially at this time of year — to offer a stranger a favor? Just come outside with me and point me in the right direction."

"For a hundred dollars," she blurted, and there wasn't a hint of German in her voice, but a whole pile of desperation.

Greedy little Amish babe, wasn't she? Kevin glanced at the gaping info girl, then back at greedy Amish babe, and while he kept his eyes focused on her general face area, his peripheral vision took in her drab attire. And though he was no fashion expert, he had to concede that as far as plain clothes went, hers were tailored quite nicely. As if sewn by a professional dressmaker type person.

Definitely busted, baby.

He sure wished he could rip off that bonnet and catch her with her hair down, framing that heart-shaped face even cupid couldn't rival.

But he wasn't about to do that in public. He'd probably get arrested for assaulting a poor defenseless religious person.

"Well?" little heart-faced-larcenous-fake-Amish-babe demanded.

"Well, what?" he responded, with all the brains of a snowflake.

"I shall show you," she said, resuming that bad accent and speaking very, very slowly, like he needed to absorb the words in bits and pieces, "the way to the truck stop."

"Deal."

"For one hundred English dollars," she added, holding out her hand, palm up. It didn't help her Amish disguise that she rubbed her thumb over her fingers in the international "show me the money" signal.

"Deal," he said again. "You'll get it the moment my buddy shows up at the truck stop."

"Yeah, 'Truck You,'" the goody-two-shoes-greedy-gorgeous-faux Amish babe whispered under her breath, probably not realizing that Kevin had amazing hearing, too, in addition to amazing skills at recognizing a fake when he smelled the perfumed scent of her.

"Thank you for all your help," he told info babe, then grabbed the elbow of the faux Amish lady and smiled. "Where does our chariot await, milady?"

Callie Brandt was ready to scream. If Kevin Wilder had figured out who she was, he was being really cool and innocent-acting about it. Why didn't he just get it over with and arrest her?

And how badly did the lawyer in New York want her, if he'd sent the most notorious – and, unfortunately for her at the moment, most successful – private investigator in the state?

Anyone who lived in New York and didn't recognize the name or face of Kevin Wilder didn't read newspapers and didn't watch television. In the last five years the man had appeared in more high-profile court cases than F. Lee Bailey. He'd been dubbed in all the newspapers and local news stations as "Mister Justice, PI."

Was it possible that she was wanted badly enough by the New York court to warrant sending their number one guy to track her down? And how *had* he found her?

She supposed she should be happy that he wasn't making a huge scene in front of all the people milling around and looking lost in the train station. But she was pretty sure she should be protesting his big hand on her elbow, making certain she didn't run away.

Callie thought through her options, and came up woefully empty with alternatives. This being on the lam thing sucked. Especially when she was stuck in a floor length bag of clothing that itched and made forging a successful getaway somewhat improbable.

She wished she had more experience in this fugitive business, but unfortunately, she was short on criminal knowledge. But one thing she knew for sure: she had to keep this guy from taking her in until after Christmas.

"Ms. Zook, is it?" this heathen said. This very, very good-looking heathen.

"*Ja,*" she answered, keeping her head low, and trying unsuccessfully to disengage her elbow from his hand.

They approached the side entrance, and when she attempted, once again, to gain her freedom, he stuck to her as if sealed to her with Crazy Glue. Callie blew up. "Would you get your freakin—" She cleared her throat. "Please, sir, release me,"

"Freaking?" Kevin asked. "Is that German?"

"Yes, sir. German for donkey, you see."

"You're calling me an ass?"

"Yes, sir."

He let her go, but dogged her steps. Callie would have loved nothing better than to kick back and shatter a knee cap, but if she remembered correctly, her Amish friends were the non-violent types. Too bad. It might have been better if she'd grown up as neighbors of mobsters, instead of these gentle folks. For sure, the wardrobe and transportation would be much improved.

They passed by the rest rooms, and inspiration struck. "Please, sir," she said, going for demure. How did an Amish person ask to be excused to go to the bathroom? "I must . . . freshen up before I go."

For a mere instant his eyes narrowed, and he hesitated. But then he glanced at the ladie's room door and nodded. "Be my guest."

She didn't rush until she got inside the bathroom. Luck was with her, as it was completely empty. She rushed right to the window, which she'd always thought was strange to have in a bathroom, but right now she blessed it for the escape route it was. The window was high up along the wall, way too high for her to reach the lock standing on the ground.

Glancing around frantically, she found a small step stool, probably there so the cleaning staff could reach the panes to clean them. "Bless you, bless you," she whispered, while speakers piped in cheery Christmas tunes. Feverishly she worked the rusty lock, which wasn't all that interested in cooperating with her. She put her heart and soul into it, desperate to get away from the turkey who was going to ruin her life if she didn't make good her escape.

Well, truth was, her life was probably already ruined, she thought glumly, as she tried to battle stark raving hysteria. But if she could just hide out until after Christmas, at least she'd be making others have some final happy moments. And that meant more than anything.

She finally wrestled the lock free of its crusty nest, "Yes!" she grunted, as she fought to lift the recalcitrant window pane. "Come on, come on," she pleaded, as if that would help. She worked out with weights. She might be small-boned, but she wasn't a weak woman. But this window was bound and determined to fight her all the way.

Finally, finally, it gave an inch, then another. After what seemed an eternity, she'd created enough of an opening to slip through. With a triumphant grunt, she hauled herself up to the sill. Behind her, the speakers belted out a hearty rendition of "Grandma Got Run Over By a Reindeer." She was feeling ebullient enough to sing along as she made her getaway. She just altered the lyrics a little to "Bad Guy Got Outsmarted by a Rookie."

She was so busy feeling smart and wicked and felonious—in the most innocent type of way, of course—that she squawked in alarm when a hand clamped around her ankle. She peered back over her raised butt and almost groaned when said bad guy stood there, calm as you please, eyebrows raised in inquiry. "Trying to get some fresh air?" the idiot asked as he tugged her back from the window, wrapped his arms around her waist and swung her down into his arms. "That's no way to earn a hundred bucks, you know."

She wanted to scream. She wanted to pummel him with her fists. But her ruse was all she had left. So she lowered her lashes and resurrected her accent. "Please, sir, unhand me."

To her surprise, he set her down gently, rather than dump her straight on her rump.

"You should not be in here!"

"I was gettin' real worried about you, darlin'."

"Sir, I must insist you remove yourself."

"How about you removing yourself, doll?" he said, and before she knew it, he untied her bonnet and flung it off her head, and all of her hair came tumbling down.

"Oh, honey, that is some pretty hair," the gorgeous jerk said. "The unforgettable kind, you know? The kind where if a guy sees it on, say, a wanted poster, he never forgets."

She sputtered in pure anger. "Sir! You take horrid liberties, you stinking swine of a lowlife . . . something!" as she tried to grab back her bonnet.

"Awww, Ms. *Zook*, I'm sorry to hear you feel this way. I'm a swine, no doubt about that. But really, I'm usually a great guy."

"You do a real dandy job of hiding it," she said, not even trying to keep the German accent. Truly, the gig was up.

He laughed. "Aw, honey, you wound me deeply," he said, rooting around in his backpack.

Then to Callie's horror, his hand shot out and grabbed hers. She felt cold, cold steel slap around her right wrist. "Cassandra Lee Brandt," he said, "I'm taking you into custody in the name of the State Of New York, on an outstanding warrant for your arrest and recovery." As she glared at him, he had the nerve to smile. Then start singing. "Rookie just got busted by the good guy."

She wanted to slump down and cry, but that never got her anything but puffy eyes and a stuffy nose. So she shot daggers at him instead and said, "You're a real bastard, you know that?"

"Born and bred. Now let's start heading toward that truck stop, sweetheart." He stuffed the bonnet thing back on her head. "Put this back on. I couldn't stand for my prisoner's pretty pink ears to get frostbit."

"How'd you find me?" she asked, still biting back the need to sob.

"You found me, honey. All I was looking for was transportation to Maine."

"Where are you taking me now?"

"The way things are looking, appears you and I have a date with Santa Claus."

"You have got to be kidding me," Callie sputtered. "You are *not* going to frisk me. No way, no how."

"Now be reasonable, Ms. Brandt. You can't really expect me to let you waltz on a bus with a bunch of innocent senior citizens without making sure you're no threat to them."

Callie snorted at the good-looking bully. As many times as she'd seen him on TV, semi-respectable looking when testifying in court, she had to admit that he appeared a boat-load sexier—and more dangerous—in his *Urban Cowboy* attire. "I look like a real thug, don't I?" she asked sweetly.

"And John Hinckley was a choir boy. Look, this will be painless, I promise."

"Oh, yeah, your word means plenty."

"Hey, I promised to make sure your horse and buggy were taken care of, didn't I?"

She couldn't argue that, so she ignored it. "This has *got* to be violating my civil rights somehow."

He winced a little, but kept tugging her toward an alcove in the nearly deserted truck stop. Even the coffee shop had shut down. "I'm not feeling you up, lady. I just want to be sure you're not carrying."

"I'm not."

"Good, then you've got nothing to worry about, Cassandra."

"It's Callie, all right? *Callie.*"

"Yes, ma'am," he said, even as he pushed her coat off her shoulders and began feeling up and down the arms of her dress. "Nothing up your sleeves," he said brightly.

"You jerk," Callie said, horrified to find that even while she felt utter outrage, she also felt something else. Like the warmth of his big hands seeping through the rough cotton.

"And what puny arms you have, I might add."

"Turkey," she said, and wasn't happy the word came out a little breathy.

"Now don't take offense here, but a woman's bodice is a good hiding place."

"You wouldn't—stop that!" she said as he started patting her chest. She tried to slug him with her fist, but unfortunately it was the one shackled to his, and he just held his hand out where she couldn't connect.

To his credit, although she hated giving him any credit at all, he didn't actually touch her breasts. Just all around them. Nonetheless,

"I'm going to press charges."

"I know, darlin', I know. Almost done." His hands whisked over her waist, her hips, then her butt and she squawked again. He ignored her again, and just glided down the outside then up the inside of her legs, from thigh to ankle. She almost wished she were packing heat, so she could blow a hole the size of Manhattan through his heartless chest.

"Nothin' up the pantaloons, either," he said, grinning as he straightened.

"Oh, you're going away for a long, long time, mister."

"Just one more thing," he said, ignoring her some more.

When she saw where his hand was headed, she jerked violently. "No! You can't go looking in—"

But his arm was already buried in the pocket of her coat. "Well, what do we have here?" he drawled, withdrawing his hand. "Damn, damn, damn," Callie muttered.

"Why does this wallet look familiar?" he asked. "Oh, that's right, because it's mine."

Callie tried to widen her eyes innocently. "How'd that get there?"

"Sticky fingers Brandt, add petty theft to your sins."

"Hey, Slick," Kevin said, and was a little embarrassed at the husky emotion in his voice. He stuck out his hand.

Sam stared at his outstretched palm in surprise, then glanced up. "What the hell is that, JD? Come here." Then Sam grabbed him around the shoulders and pulled him closer for a bear hug. Which of course managed to yank Callie closer, too. "Good to see you again, buddy."

"Yeah, you too," Kevin said, returning the hug one-handed. "You're not too much uglier than last time."

The woman shackled to him made a snorting sound. Kevin figured it was her way of commenting on the relative good looks of the two of them, and finding Kevin falling way short. Kevin was fairly used to that kind of reaction. Beside Slick, Brad Pitt would look like a dog. Still, it irritated him. After all, according to the info babe, Kevin resembled Harrison Ford. A *younger* Harrison Ford. And though Kevin wasn't an expert on the matter, women tended to find Mr. Ford sexy.

"And you're still as charming as ever," Sam said, grinning and stepping back. He swiveled toward Cassandra. "Now who's this poor thing?"

"Slick, meet Cassandra Lee Brandt. Ms. Brandt, the overblown fly-boy here is Sam Merrick."

"It's Callie, actually," the shrew said, gracing Slick with a smile that she sure as hell up to now hadn't used on Kevin. Not that he could blame her, but still it irritated him. She'd done nothing but scowl and cuss at him the entire trip.

The woman thrust out her right hand—and his left hand in the process—which he'd covered with the blanket to hide the cuffs binding them. The blanket dropped to the ground.

Sam started to return her handshake when he spied the silver bracelets encircling their wrists. He glanced up sharply. "Holy shit, JD! What kind of sick—"

"He's kidnapping me," Cassandra Lee said, puffing out her lower lip. "I demand to be released into the custody of a sane person."

"Boy, have you landed in the wrong place," Slick commented, then turned his attention back to Kevin. "You're kidnapping an Amish woman? Even for you this seems a little . . . bizarre."

They were standing outside the outlandish-looking, very, very red bus, and Kevin was acutely aware of eyes glued to them, watching with a great deal of interest. Kevin growled. "She's about as Amish as I'm Turkish. She jumped on a subpoena, and there's a bench warrant for her arrest in New York. I'm taking her in."

"Taking her into where? This bus is headed for Maine, buddy."

"We just need Betty to make a quick pit stop at the nearest Sheriff's Department so I can hand her over."

"You're turning in a poor Amish lady? At Christmas?"

"Trust me, she's not Amish and she sure as hell isn't a lady."

"Look, you toad—"

"How are you going to explain to the Santa Brigade that you're shackled to an Amish woman?"

"Listen real carefully, Slick. She's not—"

"Merrick! Wilder!" Betty Morgan barked, loud enough to set off avalanches in hill country. "Get your asses on board ASAP or you're walking to Maine."

"Be right there!" Sam yelled over his shoulder. He turned back to them. "How are you going to explain dragging a criminal on board?" he asked, eyes squinted with humor.

Hmmm. Kevin hadn't thought of that.

"I am *not* a criminal," Cassandra said.

"Last I heard, pick pocketing is still a crime, darlin'," Kevin reminded her.

She had the grace to blush and look away. Still, shame didn't shut her up. "You were a pretty easy mark."

Sam stared, before bursting out laughing. "She swiped *your* wallet?"

Kevin bristled. "I wasn't exactly expecting to get robbed by an Amish woman."

"You're dragging her off to jail for pulling one over on you?" Slick said. "That's kind of harsh."

"Oh, that's only the icing on the cake. Add to that the warrant in the city. Not to mention falsely impersonating a religious woman. Then there's that gawdawful German accent."

"Hey!"

"Merrick!" Betty Morgan bellowed.

Sam sighed. "Come on, JD. We'll work this out on the bus."

"I'm not getting on that bus!"

For a gorgeous young thing, Cassandra Lee Brandt was a pain in the ass. Kevin felt a twinge of guilt, though. It *was* Christmas, and her crime was fairly harmless in the scheme of things. So she'd disappeared so she wouldn't have to testify on behalf of a two bit thug? He couldn't blame her. On the other hand, the defense was desperate for her testimony, and was adamant about filing a bench warrant. And he was being paid good money to track her down and bring her in.

But then his sense of justice somehow got involved, and all he could think of was that she'd broken the law, and she needed to pay for it. At least he thought so.

"Your call, JD," Sam said, although Kevin could swear he was looking at the woman sympathetically. Still, Slick would never, ever question his friend's judgment, no matter how screwed up he might believe it to be.

Kevin sighed. "I'll tell you what," he offered the exasperating woman. "You're getting on this bus. I'm cold and tired and I don't want Betty stranding us. But if you can convince me between here and the closest Sheriff's office that you have a real good reason for what you've done, I'll consider forgetting I ever saw you." He smiled. "In the spirit of Christmas and all."

"I'm touched by your generosity," she said, leaning into him, eyes shooting daggers.

"Ho, ho, ho."

"Jerk, jerk, jerk," she muttered under her breath, but allowed herself to be tugged along to the bus.

As they headed toward Kevin's worst nightmare, Slick pounded him on the back. "This should be interesting," he said.

"You can say that again," Kevin grumbled.

As they approached the bus, Kevin figured out what all that green around the edges of the windows was. Holly and mistletoe. *Good Lord.*

Betty Morgan stood at the door to the bus, tapping her fingers against her crossed arms. "Well, if it isn't the Wild Child," she said, squinting at him.

"Ms. Morgan," Kevin said, "You're looking as beautiful as ever."

"Cut the crap, Wilder." She nodded at Cassandra Brandt. "And who's this? Merrick didn't mention anything about a second passenger."

For some reason, Kevin didn't have the heart to embarrass his prisoner. She might be on the run from the law, but she still had feelings. "This is my girlfriend, Cassandra."

Cassandra made a stifled shrieking noise and narrowed her eyes on him, but to her credit, she pressed her lips together and swallowed any rude comments flitting through that pretty head of hers.

"Your girlfriend," Betty said. "Right. And I'm Mother Teresa."

"Oh, we're madly in love, aren't we, cupcake?" he said, then wiped a fallen snowflake from the tip of her nose.

She pressed her lips even further.

"She's shy," Kevin said.

"Have a tough time hanging onto your women, Wilder? Does that account for having to shackle her to keep her from running away?"

"We're into . . . games, if you get my drift."

"Right. What game are you playing today? The Amish woman and the outlaw?"

Considering *he* was the upstanding citizen in this crowd, he almost protested. But he swallowed the retort just in time. "Yes. It's one of our favorites."

"Uh-huh," Betty grunted. "Well get your cans on the bus. We're wasting time and the storm is just winding up." She looked around them then. "Where's your luggage?"

"We're traveling light."

"Uh-huh."

Kevin tugged on Cassandra's arm, then gave her a gentle shove through the door.

She turned and glared at him a final time before resignedly climbing the steps.

Kevin himself wasn't all that eager to get on the bus, but this was the only option presenting itself. So he hauled himself up, only to be confronted with a busload of elderly Santas.

A chorus of "Hello, Kevins" greeted him, and he conjured up a smile. "Hi, all. It's . . . nice seeing you again."

"Oh, yes, I'm sure," one very tall Santa said. "Hi, JD."

Kevin grinned. "Hey, Reba." He went to hug her, but the clanking of the cuffs and the swift swing of Cassandra's arm sort of ruined the reunion. He smiled an apology. "My girlfriend, Cassandra."

"Right."

"I'm Callie, and he's kidnapping me," Cassandra said.

Her proclamations were becoming irritating. "She's such a kidder," he retorted.

"Find a seat," Reba said. "Or seats. We'll talk," she added to Ms. Cassandra, who was going to get it.

"We will," Kevin said, before nudging his charge forward. He whispered in her ear, "Keep this up, and I'm testifying against you."

"Truck you," she whispered back.

"I've got twenty on him being in custody," one Santa said.

"Fifty that the Amish woman's with the FBI," said another. "He's under house arrest."

"You need a haircut, Kevin," one said, even as she clack-clacked on a keyboard.

Considering the purple hair peeking out from under a Santa hat, he had a pretty good idea who that one was. Maudeen, owner of the Clip 'N' Curl in Snowdon. "Hello, Maudeen," He stopped in front of her and pulled off Cassandra's bonnet. "What would you do with this?"

Maudeen stared at the wild black hair that sprang loose, then went back to her typing. "I'd tell her there's good money in modeling."

"Maudeen Livingstone, this is Cassandra Brandt. Cassandra, Maudeen."

"Actually, it's Callie Brandt," the woman retorted. Jeez, she was even fighting him over her name.

Maudeen glanced up from her laptop. "Callie Brandt? I have a couple of Callie Brandt numbers. Knock-offs, of course. Who could afford the originals? Any relation?"

Callie Brandt numbers? Did that mean she was a numbers runner, too?

Callie actually smiled. "That would be me. I hope you like them."

"Oh . . . my . . . God. Really, that's you? The pants suit is my absolute favorite, and the peignoir is a favorite among my gentlemen friends, if you get my drift."

"I'm glad," Callie said, while Kevin looked back and forth between them in total confusion.

"Hey, everyone!" Maudeen yelled, standing and turning around. "We have *the* Callie Brandt, the famous fashion designer, on our bus!"

A chorus of delighted squeals greeted that announcement as Kevin just stared at his prisoner. She wasn't just a dressmaker, but a *famous* fashion designer? Maybe that's why she'd looked a little familiar when he'd first seen her picture. Although he didn't follow such things, it was impossible to live in New York and not see the television coverage of movie and play premieres. And it seemed like those things were always attended by people like that Calvin Klein guy. Of course, Kevin's knowledge of fashion ended with a guy named Levi Strauss.

For the first time Maudeen spied the handcuffs. "Oh, my! Now there's a fashion accessory that could prove interesting." She studied Callie with a sharp eagle eye. "But honey, that dress has *got* to go."

CHAPTER THREE

STAN

Tuesday afternoon, three days 'til Christmas Eve.

Snow, snow, and more snow.

Stan Kijewski cursed as he fought the rented Mercedes through the frozen, snow-covered ruts. Who knew Vermont had so damn many mountains? And why would anybody in their right mind be living smack dab in the middle of them at the end of a road that hadn't been plowed since the Pilgrims landed?

He should have stayed in San Diego.

No, what he should have done was take that luscious brunette he met last month down to Cancun for the holidays. A few weeks of sand, sun, and hot, no-strings-attached sex would have fixed him right up. He'd been on the point of asking—Bridgette? Brittney?— when the White House had asked if he could do that kid's Christmas fitness program with Schwartzenegger, and then George had called, and that had scotched Cancun and sex and Babs or Boobs or whatever her name was.

He was really sorry about missing the sex.

Not that there hadn't been possibilities since, of course, even though D.C. wasn't as well stocked with luscious, leggy brunettes as San Diego. But while he was all for no-strings fun, he wasn't in favor of one night stands. One month of togetherness was about right. Two was okay. Hell, he'd even gone as long as nine months once, but a week or less—uh huh. A man had his standards, even if they were low.

The steering wheel jerked as the Mercedes' front end fought to dive into the snow-packed ditch. Stan fought back, cursing the road and his shoulder and the throbbing pain in his damaged leg.

If he'd realized that George's forest ranger friend lived this far beyond the back of beyond, he'd have rented a Humvee instead of a

Mercedes. No, he'd have had the good sense to refuse to pick her up, no matter how much wheedling old George inflicted on him.

Just the thought of the unknown woman was depressing. Dana Freeman, forester. What kind of woman became a *forester*, for God's sake?

Visions of plaid flannel shirts and khaki pants on a lumberjack's muscular body flashed through his mind. She probably drove an old Jeep and lived in a log cabin with an outhouse and spent her winter evenings down at the local pool hall, arm-wrestling for fun.

Paul Bunyan in a bra. Swell.

For this he'd traded in a perfect 38-22-38 in a bikini? No two ways about it—the gods really did have it in for him.

The Mercedes bucked its way around a curve and there, up ahead on the right, was a picturesque little Victorian cottage set amidst snow-covered pines and winter-bared maples and oaks. Though it was still early afternoon, someone had turned on the colored lights that trimmed the eaves and outlined every window, offering a bit of unexpected color on this snowy gray day. The lights on the Christmas tree visible through one of the lace-curtained front windows winked in welcome.

Stan stomped on the brakes, bringing the Mercedes to a skidding halt. Victorian cottages and Christmas lights and lace curtains? *Here?*

A pang of something that felt very much like longing, but couldn't be, hit him hard.

Except for the ancient International Scout that was parked to one side, the place looked like something Hallmark had done up for a holiday special. Had he, perhaps, taken the wrong turning?

But, no. He'd double-checked the sign on the mailbox before he'd turned off the paved road. This was the only house he'd come to and the road clearly didn't go any farther. "Can't miss it!" George had assured him. "It's the only house on the road!"

Stan glared at the Christmas-card perfect scene. Why would anyone bother with Christmas trees and decorative lights out here where nobody but the squirrels would see?

And why did he think it was so right that they had?

Shaking off the thought, Stan set the Mercedes at the last little uphill run to the front yard, fighting his way over ice and yet more frozen, snow-covered ruts before coming to a stop beside the battered Scout. A Scout, he couldn't help noting, that had a small snow plow mounted on its front bumper. Just the sort of thing a lumberjack would have. That made him feel a little better about that unexpected pang.

Forget about the house and the decorations, Stan told himself firmly, reaching for his cane. He'd been right about the transport. It only remained to meet Ms Freeman to find out he'd been right about her, too. And he *wasn't* thinking this was the kind of house a fellow should come home to for Christmas. Of course not! No one who'd grown up in an orphanage had any illusions about the season or what lay behind a few electric lights.

And yet . . . No, forget that.

Stretching a little to ease the dull ache in his shoulder, he opened the car door and awkwardly swung his feet to the ground. Snow swallowed his shoes and snuck down his socks.

Wonderful.

More curses as he struggled out of the car. He didn't have half these problems in a properly paved parking lot.

Moving carefully and feeling his way with the tip of his cane, he managed to get ten feet from the car when a woman walked around the corner of the house.

"Mr. Kijewski?"

Unadulterated shock almost landed him on his ass in a snow bank. "Ms Freeman?" It came out more of a croak than a question.

She nodded. "I wasn't sure you'd make it."

Stan cleared his throat and tried to keep his eyes from bugging out. He'd been right about the transportation, wrong about the house, and dead wrong about Ms Freeman.

Dana Freeman was tall, all right. She was also slender as a reed, but with curves in what looked like all the right places. He couldn't be sure about the top because she was wearing a bulky turtleneck sweater under a puffy, waist-length down vest, but below the vest . . .

His eyes slid down the length of her.

Below the vest was Heaven. She had a narrow waist that curved out into slender hips, followed by long, long, *long* legs. Beautiful legs. Perfect, sexy, drive-you-to-wet-dreams long legs. He could tell because they were encased in a pair of those form-hugging pants that revealed every perfect curve and tempting line of her.

God bless the makers of Lycra.

Stan forced himself to start breathing, then dragged his gaze back up—and promptly stopped breathing again.

Dana Freeman was, quite simply, gorgeous. She had the delicate perfection of one of those Renaissance Madonnas some girlfriend had dragged him to the museum to see, years ago. He'd forgotten the girlfriend, but those faces with their wide eyes and smooth skin and perfect mouths had stuck with him, coolly beautiful, distant and untouchable.

Dana had that kind of face, a perfect oval with fine-cut features and a soft, inviting mouth. Her skin was the same pale, petal-soft skin that made you think you could see light shining through if the angle was just right. Unlike those dusky Madonnas in the museum, however, Dana had hair so blonde it was almost white. It hung straight to her waist like a shimmering silk scarf whose colors changed subtly with each movement and shift of light. Her eyes weren't brown, either. They were pale blue ice and they were fixed on him with unnerving directness.

Cold pale blue ice Stan realized, coming back to earth with a thud as her gaze slid down his body as coolly as his had slid down hers. "You can come in while I get my bag," she said, clearly unimpressed. She gestured to the cane. "Do you need any help?"

"No!" He immediately regretted the shout. It made him sound too defensive. Too . . . surly. "Thanks."

"All right." She didn't seem to care, one way or the other. Without another word, she turned and headed toward her front door.

Puzzled, and manfully stifling the urge the cuss, Stan followed after. Since when did he care about surly? And what kind of person left another person with a crippled leg and a cane to flounder through the snow on their own, even if he had said he didn't need her help? And he absolutely, for sure, definitely was *not* pissed that she hadn't been impressed. No way, no how, just didn't happen. He was not, repeat, *not* pissed!

Dana thought her heart was going to pound right out of her chest. Stan "The Man" Kijewski, star quarterback for the San Diego Typhoons until someone ran a red light and ended his career, was even more compelling in person than on the playing field, and that was saying a lot. Dangerously, tantalizingly compelling.

She ought to know. She'd watched him play football for almost twelve years now. On Saturdays when he was in college, then every Sunday afternoon or Monday night after he'd turned pro, she'd made sure she was close enough to a TV set to be able to catch the game.

With her line of work, that hadn't always been easy, but then, what in life ever was?

It was all George's fault, of course. He'd rescued her from the Beerson Home for Girls, which was fifteen miles and one town over from the White Mountain Home for Boys where Stan had grown up. George had taught her to love the wilderness, football, and Stan Kijewski, though not deliberately, and not necessarily in that order.

And now Stan was here and all she could think about was that he was gorgeous and she was still tall, gawky, and tongue-tied. Worse, he clearly didn't want to be here. He'd scowled when he looked at her and half bitten her head off when she'd asked if he needed any help. And since when did a man like Stan Kijewski need anyone's help, anyway?

Although she tried to pretend indifference, she was acutely aware of him behind her. She could hear the muffled thud of his cane hitting the frozen ground and the scraping, shushing sound as he dragged his damaged leg through the snow.

The thought of his injuries, and what he'd lost because of them, broke her heart. It wasn't fair, but then, life wasn't any more fair than it was easy.

Stan Kijewski deserved better than that, though. Despite the hard knocks life had handed him, he'd had the courage and talent to make it to the top in a mercilessly competitive field. She'd retreated into the woods and the often solitary job of a forester because they filled some, at least, of the loneliness in her. Not all, but enough. Unlike him, she'd never had the nerve to try for anything more.

"Shit! Arrrhhhh!"

Dana whirled about to find the Typhoon's star quarterback—*former* star quarterback—spread-eagled on his back in the snow. "Damnit! Stupid ice! Stupid snow!" He flailed at the thick stuff, but succeeded only in burying himself deeper.

Dana blinked down at him, fighting to retain her self-control. He looked so incredibly . . . desirable. Snow dusted his unruly brown hair and clung to his arching brows and outrageously thick eyelashes. A crystal drop of melted snow quivered at the corner of his mouth and dragged her thoughts down dangerous paths where she had no business going.

His elegant black coat—cashmere, she'd bet, though she'd never actually seen anything so expensive up close—had fallen open to reveal the lean, broad-shouldered body that had danced through her dreams more times than she'd care to count. He was dressed in a tweed sport coat over soft green turtleneck sweater—more cashmere from the look of it—that clung intriguingly to a well-muscled chest and washboard abdomen that she'd fantasized finding under those heavy shoulder pads he wore during a game. His pleated slacks looked expensive and, sprawled as he was, revealed more of the tempting male body beneath than he realized.

She forced her gaze from the impressive bulge at the bottom of his zipper, on down the long legs to the out-sized feet at the end of them.

Thank God for the feet.

She let out the breath she'd been holding, relieved. Only an idiot, or a man who'd forgotten what a New England winter was like, would have worn those expensive loafers with their slick leather soles. A good pair of hiking boots with a good tread on the sole would have made more sense, especially for a man with a leg and hip that were still healing after being broken in seven different places.

Still, she couldn't help but picture him with bare feet. And bare legs. And bare chest. Not to mention bare—

All right, she couldn't help picturing him stark naked, but then, she'd been picturing him like that for so long it was almost second nature. Seeing him in the flesh, so to speak, even if he was fully clothed and flat on his back in a snow bank, was like having Christmas and Valentine's Day and the Fourth of July rolled into one neat, very tempting package.

"Are you going to spend the next hour staring, or are you going to help me up?" he growled.

His eyes looked hot enough to burn holes right through the snow . . . or her.

Because what she was feeling, what he *made* her feel, was so wickedly, dangerously tempting, Dana did what she always did— she retreated.

"You said you didn't want any help," she said coolly.

"I changed my mind." Even growling, his voice was that kind of rough baritone that roused shivery prickles on her skin. He held up his hand. "Help me up."

Not *please* help me up, just, help me up! The rudeness made it a little easier to take the hand he offered.

She heaved. He came halfway up, wincing and clearly trying not to. His injured leg obviously wasn't cooperating, so she pulled a little harder. Her feet slipped out from under her as neatly as if she'd been on skates.

"Aaack!" she screeched.

"Damnit!" he swore, toppling back into the snow bank. "Ooof!" he added as she landed on his chest. Hard.

His arm came around her instinctively, pinning her against him.

"Unh," said Dana, and blinked snow out of her eyes.

His face was white as the snow he lay in. His eyes squeezed shut and his mouth curled with pain.

"Shit." He sounded a little breathless when he said it.

Dana hastily shoved off his chest, making him wince.

"I'm sorry. Did I hurt you? I didn't mean to hurt you. It's so slick and you're so big and—"

He waved his hand limply, as if even that much hurt. His eyes were still firmly shut and there was a set look about his mouth that said he was hurting and he really wanted to swear some more but was trying hard not to.

"I'm fine."

"You don't look fine."

He opened his eyes at that and scowled up at her. "No man looks fine when he's on his ass in a snow bank."

You do. She didn't say it.

And you have a great ass.

Of course, she hadn't actually seen his ass so far, clothed or otherwise, but she'd admired it plenty when it was covered in those tight football pants, and there was one poster in her bedroom—

No, better not think about the bedroom. And better not let him anywhere near it, either, she reminded herself, remembering the posters and the clippings from sports magazines that were pinned on the walls.

Dana rocked back onto her knees, this time taking care not to shove against his chest. She looked at him, trying to think of him as a rock, maybe, or a downed tree, or a lame moose, even. She knew how to deal with a lame moose.

"Let's try it again, shall we?" she said, like a woman with places to go and people to see once this annoying little matter was dealt with.

"Let's not," he said, and carefully shoved to a sitting position. Using his right arm, she noticed. The arm that hadn't been damaged in the accident. The arm that wasn't his throwing arm. *That* arm he hugged to his chest. The line of white around his mouth and the hard set of his jaw said all she needed to know about whether the fall had hurt him.

She couldn't tell if the arm or the leg bothered him more, and didn't have the courage to ask. Ever since the accident she'd been suffering from fantasies of her soothing his fevered brow. Good-looking men were always grateful when you soothed their brows and nursed them back to health. *Very* grateful. She'd read it in a book somewhere.

Dana shoved the thought away, irritated. She wasn't usually this confused.

She wasn't usually six inches from the man of her dreams, either. "So, how do you want to do it?" she asked, putting a little bite into her tone just to be sure he didn't get any wrong ideas.

He didn't, drat him.

Instead, he glared at the snow, which was a nice change from glaring at her. "I don't know. I've never landed in a snow bank before. Not like"—his glare switched to his injured leg—"this."

"Well, let me know when you do," Dana said, and stood. The way she figured it, the more distance between them, the better.

He growled. Honest to God growled. "Look, if you'll just stand there and not move, I'll . . . uh . . . climb up you. Use you for a brace. Sort of. Is that all right?"

I'd rather you climbed on *me*, she thought, and blushed. "Sure," she said. "Whatever works. Here's your cane." He didn't bother to thank her.

Using the cane for leverage, he cautiously got to his good knee. His bad leg stretched at an awkward angle and the snow wasn't doing a thing for the creases on his trousers, but at least he was halfway there.

"Come a little closer," he said. "That's it. Brace yourself. Great."

Leaning against her for balance, he slowly, painfully, struggled to his feet. She had to fight against the urge to wrap her arms around him and help him. Or drag him back into the snow bank. That brief time she'd been lying on his chest, his mouth had been only a few inches away. Next time, she'd remember to take better advantage of her opportunities.

No she wouldn't. Who did she think she was kidding? She'd never have the nerve and she knew it.

She almost did, though, when his hand briefly curved over her braced thigh. Only the knowledge that he'd have preferred a sturdy wood handrail restrained her. She'd never had much success with men, but she didn't usually come in second to a handrail, either.

While he grumbled and muttered and tugged his coat into place, she stared at the snow-shrouded forest that backed up to her house and wished that George had never suggested this mad arrangement, or that she'd have had the good sense to decline.

Indulging in unrequited fantasy at a distance was a time-honored female tradition, and she'd always believed in female traditions even if she wasn't very good at them. Seeing your fantasy this close was something else entirely, however, and she had absolutely no idea how to handle it without being rude or making an utter fool of herself.

Neither choice held much appeal, but of the two, she'd take rude any day of the week. Rude was safe. People kept their distance when you were rude, and with Stanley Kijewski, a little distance was a very good thing.

The tingling of her thigh where his hand had pressed, just for an instant, was proof of that. The disconcerting ache a little higher up where her thighs joined her hips was like a buzzing alarm telling her to beware.

She had to fight against the urge to squeeze her legs together, hard.

"You okay?" she said, sounding cold and uninterested and rude. "Fine," he grunted, not looking at her. He brushed the last of the snow off his coat. The last he could reach, anyway. There was a patch at the back of his shoulder and another on his left buttock. She didn't offer to brush them off.

"Be careful right there," she said, pointing but not looking at him. "And watch the steps. They're even worse."

They crawled up the path, her in front, him following, the back of her neck prickling with charged awareness every inch of the way.

Dana kicked the snow off her boots on the steps, then, once inside the door, knelt to take them off.

"You don't have to take your shoes off," she said, deliberately not looking at him as he awkwardly tried to balance on his bad leg so he could scrape the snow off his other foot.

She set her boots on a scrap of rug set at one side to catch the drips. He toed off his loafers and nudged them onto the rug beside her boots. She studied the over-sized, stocking-clad feet, but resisted letting her gaze slide higher.

She didn't dare, because what she really wanted was to stare and stare and stare, to devour him with her eyes. Of course, she wasn't going to do that. She wasn't even going to glance at him.

No more than was polite and normal, anyway.

She glanced at him. She'd swear he was even better looking than he'd been five minutes ago.

He didn't look one whit happier, though.

"Coffee?" she asked. He shook his head. "The john's that way." She waved vaguely. "I'll be right back."

"Sure. Whatever," he muttered behind her.

She barely stopped herself from slamming her bedroom door behind her, but she couldn't stop the unexpected wobble in her knees or the loud pounding of her heart.

She stared at the big poster pinned on the opposite wall. Stan, left arm pulled back for a pass, eyes narrowed and dangerous behind his face guard. Of all the posters and clippings, this was her favorite, but right now, it might as well have been wallpaper.

Stan "The Man" Kijewski was here. In her house. And in a few more minutes they were going to be in the same car together for . . . hours.

She almost collapsed against the door at the thought.

Stan glared at the hallway where she'd disappeared. He'd met stevedores with more manners.

None with as great an ass, though.

Dana Freeman had a truly magnificent ass, the kind that made a guy think of grabbing hold and—

No, he wouldn't think of that. Especially not about Ms Freeman.

She might have a body made for hot dreams and hotter sex— she'd taken off the vest on the porch to reveal generous curves in all the right places, even under the bulky sweater—but the woman had ice water in her veins. Had to have. The way she looked at him made him wonder if he had a social disease he didn't know about.

Not to mention she weighed a lot more than she looked. It had *hurt* when she'd landed on him. His shoulder and leg ached from the fall, but he was getting used to that. What he wasn't used to was a woman who was so damned oblivious to his very existence.

When he was crawling to his feet, he'd deliberately put his hands a couple of places that would have earned him a slap under any other circumstances. She hadn't so much as giggled. She certainly hadn't blushed. And if she knew how to bat those beautiful, ice-blue eyes of hers, she sure as hell hadn't given him a demonstration.

Stan suppressed an urge to charge down that hall, throw open her bedroom door, and sweep her into an impassioned kiss, just to show her what she as missing.

He really should have opted for the brunette and Cancun.

Since he hadn't, he'd have to make the best of things. All he had to do was survive the next few hours locked in a car with her, then he could forget she even existed.

In the meantime, he might as well indulge his curiosity.

While he waited for Dana Freeman to emerge, Stan gritted his teeth against the pain and clumped around the living room, shamelessly poking into the books on the crowded shelves that lined one wall, opening cabinet drawers, and shuffling through baskets.

The house surprised him. *She* surprised him.

He would have expected the books on forest management and the professional and outdoor magazines, but there were a lot of well-read paperback romances mixed in with all those high-brow literary and non-fiction books. He would have expected the comfortable, practical furniture but not the needlepoint pillows—pillows he suspected she'd created herself, if the half-finished piece in the basket by the easy chair was anything to go by. He might have expected the pine cones in the brass bowl by the hearth, but not the carefully tended African violets on the glass shelves by the window.

Dana Freeman wasn't anything like the bruising woman he'd imagined, but he couldn't quite get a feel for what she *was*. Except beautiful. *That* he'd gotten in one swift, satisfactorily lustful glance. Also rude, unhelpful, and cold.

Yet nothing about this house said *cold*.

Not that it mattered, of course.

When she finally emerged a few minutes later, he couldn't help but feel a little disappointed. She'd changed the leggings for loose, practical jeans. She still wore the sweater, but had casually looped that incredible hair at the back of her head, then fastened it with one of those claw thingies that always made him think of a steel trap.

She paused for an instant. Stan had the uncomfortable feeling she was taking in every inch of him and that he was somehow coming up wanting. In spite of himself, he straightened, putting more of his weight on his good leg and less on the cane.

He thought of her offhand acceptance that he hadn't needed any assistance, out there in the yard, and scowled.

"Sure you don't want some coffee?"

Her voice was low, yet clear and carrying with just the right touch of huskiness to make it sexy as hell. The kind of voice that could whisper sweet nothings in the bedroom, or get attention in a crowded room.

"No coffee, thanks." He glanced out the window. Because he wanted to check the weather, he assured himself, not because those calm, ice-blue eyes had any unsettling effects on him. "We'd better get going. This weather doesn't show any sign of getting better any time soon."

"Have you had lunch?"

"No." Right now everything hurt too damn much to think about food. What he really wanted was to stretch out on that long, inviting-looking sofa, to put his leg up and prop some pillows under his shoulder and spend the next hour staring at the lights on the Christmas tree and letting the homey, pine-scented warmth of this place seep into his bones. And if Dana Freeman wanted to spend the time soothing his weary brow and whispering sweet nothings into his ear, that would be fine, too.

He sure as hell didn't want to get back in that car. Just the thought of it was enough to make everything hurt more than it already did. But pain was something he'd learned to live with. Pain and wanting things he couldn't have.

Dana studied him thoughtfully. No matter what he said, the man was hurting. The fall, then her landing on him, had probably jarred every healing bone and joint in his body. Not that he'd admit it, of course, any more than he'd admitted to being in pain when he'd played the entire fourth quarter of that game against Dallas with a severely cracked rib.

"Mind waiting while I fix myself something to eat?" she said. She wasn't above a little subterfuge if that's what it took to get him to rest for a bit. The weather could wait.

She had to fight not to smile at his obvious relief.

The incipient smile died when he limped into the kitchen after her. That same electric awareness she'd felt out in the yard made her body come alive, charging every nerve ending to acute awareness.

Behind her, he crossed to the tiny kitchen table and pulled out a chair. She didn't need to turn and look. If she were suddenly struck blind and deaf, she would know where he was and what he was doing.

A hot flush stained her face. To hide it, she wrenched open the door of the refrigerator and stooped to look inside. The cool air was welcome relief. She took her time fishing out lettuce and meat and cheese.

Behind her she could hear a soft, groaning sigh as Stan settled into the chair and stretched out his leg.

Adding mayonnaise and mustard to her haul, then a half-empty carton of milk, she nudged the refrigerator door closed with her hip and dumped everything on the counter. She didn't once glance his way, but she knew he was watching her. Her nerve endings told her so.

"Nice house."

She jumped, not expecting the sound of his voice, and glanced over her shoulder.

His eyes were the clear green of old glass, and they were fixed unwaveringly on her. Was it her imagination, or did she read approval in his gaze? Approval and, maybe, just a little bit of interest?

"I wasn't expecting to see Christmas decorations out here." His gaze slid down her jeans-clad legs and up again. "Do you bake Christmas cookies, too?"

"Yes, but I give them all away." Dana concentrated on setting the meat and cheese out on a plate. He was probably looking at her skinny rear and thinking she ought to eat a few herself.

When she was sure she wouldn't embarrass herself by more blushes or any hungry, yearning looks, she set the plates and food on the table, including a setting for him. The strained look of silent suffering that had been on his face ten minutes ago was gone, but there was still a tension about his jaw that spoke of pain. She would, she decided, give it a little while longer before she agreed to leave.

He didn't protest about the extra plate. The sandwich he built would have done justice to an army of lumberjacks and he was working his way through his second glass of milk before she was halfway through her first.

Thankfully, he kept the conversation on safe topics like the weather or her work. She didn't think she could have kept up her facade of indifference if he'd ventured into more personal territory.

Just being this close to him was doing strange, unnerving things to her, making her heart pound and her palms sweat, making her think thoughts she'd tried, until now, to keep strictly for her hottest, most secret dreams. If he ever guessed at what she was thinking, she'd die of mortification, right here at her kitchen table. It was all she could do not to fling herself across the table and into his arms, and to hell with the ham, cheese, and mayo.

Stan dug into the simple meal with immense satisfaction. Dana

Freeman wasn't anywhere near as uninterested in him as she tried to pretend. Not *anywhere* near.

What he couldn't explain was why that fact pleased him so.

Granted, she was gorgeous, but he was used to gorgeous. Maybe not quite *that* gorgeous, certainly not in that slightly ethereal, Renaissance Madonna way that was uniquely hers, but still gorgeous. And he'd known a couple of women with similarly deep, soft voices, but none whose simplest utterance could make electricity skitter up and down his spine.

Maybe it was because it was so damned comfortable here, sitting in this warm, bright kitchen, talking while the snow fell soft and heavy outside. The aches and pains and nerve-tightening tensions of these last few weeks were fading away, leaving him feeling more relaxed and contented than he'd been in a long, long time.

Maybe it was the faint scent of pine and cinnamon that hung in the air, or the quiet ticking of the grandfather's clock in the living room. A house—a real *home*—should always smell of pine and cinnamon and have an old clock tick-tocking somewhere in the background. The nine thousand square feet of house in San Diego where he stored his extra shoes and socks had neither. It was a nice house, though it had never been a home. But this little cottage tucked away in the Vermont woods . . .

Stan sighed in sudden contentment and glanced about the kitchen with its white painted cabinets and old china plates on the wall and the Santa tea towel looped through the handle of the refrigerator.

This was a home, a place where you didn't have to be anyone but yourself. A place where you belonged instead of feeling like you were just passing through.

Stan dragged his gaze back to Dana.

Or maybe it was just her. She was so . . . calm. So sure of herself. Even though she was as intensely aware of him as he was of her, there was still a quiet reserve about her, a gentle dignity that he found strangely tantalizing. Every time he looked at her he found himself wondering what she would be like naked in bed with that soft, deep voice grown rough with desire and that reserved dignity blown away by the mind-bending sex they were sharing.

The fantasy shattered when she abruptly pushed away from the table.

"I suppose we'd better think about getting on the road before the weather gets any worse," she said, flushing slightly under his gaze.

Before he could respond, his cell phone rang. With a sigh, he fished it out of the inner pocket of his sport coat and snapped it open. "Kijewski."

"Stanley, you ugly bastard, where the hell are you?"

Stan grinned. "Try calling me that to my face, Slick, just try."

"What? You object to the truth?"

Stan laughed. Slick knew it wasn't the masculine endearment of "ugly bastard" that he objected to. The first time they'd met, they'd both been about ten years old. Slick had called him "Stanley," and Stan had beaten the shit out of him. Of course, Slick always claimed it was he that beat the shit out of Stan. Whichever way it was, they'd emerged from that fight bloody, bruised, and friends for life.

"Actually," Slick continued, "I'm calling to find out where you are."

"Me? I'm sitting in a comfortable kitchen with a beautiful woman for company."

The back of Dana's neck went red as she bent over the sink. Stan had to repress the urge to walk over there and take that crazy clip out of her hair so all that white-gold silk could tumble into his hands and—

He forced his attention back to the phone. "This weather sucks."

"Tell me about it. JD and . . . uh . . . a friend just joined us."

"Us?"

"Me and Reba Anderson—you remember Reba?" There was an odd note in Slick's voice when he mentioned Reba. "And the Santa Brigade."

"The what?"

"I'll explain later. But we've got a bus that's the only thing running right now and Betty Morgan's driving and—"

"You're on a bus with Betty Bad-Ass? What in hell—"

" . . . we thought you might want to join us, too."

"Join you?"

Dana dumped the last of the dishes in the drainer and glided out of the kitchen. Stan craned around in his chair to watch her go. On a scale of one to ten, that woman's ass rated fifteen, even in jeans. And the rest of her—

"Anyway," Slick said in his ear, bringing him back to attention, "Betty says we'll be hitting Vermont in a couple of hours and maybe we can meet you somewhere."

Get on a crowded bus when he could have Dana all to himself?

Slick had to be kidding. But then, he hadn't met Dana.

"Nah. Thanks, anyway. I think we can manage just fine, Slick. I've—" He stopped as Dana abruptly appeared in the kitchen doorway, gesturing for him to wait. "Hang on a minute, will you?"

"The roads are closed," Dana said, that beautiful Madonna face suddenly looking grim. "All of them. I just called and checked."

"All of them?" Stan had a sudden vision of holing up with her for the next few days, just the two of them here in the kitchen, or cuddled in front of the fireplace, or in her bed—

"*All* of them. If your friend has a bus that's still getting through, it may be our only way to get to Maine by Friday."

Friday. George. The wedding.

Hell.

"Uh, Slick? We may have to take you up on that offer after all."

"Let me talk to him," Dana ordered, stretching out her hand for the phone.

Stan didn't really mind handing over the phone since that gave him more freedom to watch Dana, but he wasn't sure he liked the idea of Dana talking to Slick. The bastard was a damned babe magnet. He could scratch his butt and women swooned at his feet. All he'd have to do is hear her voice and—

But then Stan remembered Reba was on that bus and that odd note in Slick's voice, and he grinned.

Dana, distracted, gave him a tentative smile back. "Unh huh," she said into the phone. "Yeah." The smile slid into a frown. She even looked good frowning. "Watkins Junction's about six miles from here as the crow flies . . . Yeah . . . All right . . . Okay. We'll see you then."

She snapped the phone off and handed it back to Stan. "We've got a plan."

So do I, Stan thought. He'd bet she wore lacy underwear even when she was out chopping down trees or hunting bears. Skimpy, sexy, lacy underwear in all sorts of ice-cream colors. The kind that you could see through. The kind that slid off with just a—

"We're going to meet your friends at Watkins Junction," she said.

It was Stan's turn to frown. "What's wrong with driving?"

"The roads are closed."

"You've got a snow plow on that old Scout."

"You want to plow the roads all the way to Maine?"

That Ice Maiden frost was back in her voice. Even that was sort of sexy. It made him think of all the different ways he could warm her up.

"I dunno. If it was just the two of us—"

The frost turned to icicles. "Forget it."

She crossed her arms over her chest. The movement did amazing things for that already generous bustline.

"I've got a better plan," she said.

"Yes?" said Stan hopefully.

"I've got this snow mobile . . . "

CHAPTER FOUR

SAM

Tuesday, evening, three days 'til Christmas Eve.

"Gotcha!"

With that single word, when her attention had wandered for all of a nanosecond, Sam cornered her in the back of the bus by sliding onto the bench seat next to her, thus trapping her against the window. What a tight squeeze it was, too, considering her bulk in the Santa suit!

"You are so juvenile," she said with a sniff.

"Yep," he agreed and adjusted his body closer to hers, something she would not have thought possible.

With all the movement he was making, he shook some of the boxes stacked behind. There was a chorus of "Suzie Gotta Pee," "Suzie Gotta Pee," "Suzie Gotta Pee," "Suzie Gotta Pee" from some of the gifts left over from the last shelter stop.

"What the hell?" Sam exclaimed as he turned to straighten the talking boxes.

"Samuel Merrick!" Emma Smith chided from the seat in front of them. Emma, a large, husky woman, much like Camryn Manheim, but older, and brusquer, was a retired eighth grade teacher, who had taught them all. The one thing she could not abide was bad language and she heard every bit of it with her trusty Miracle-Aid. "Tsk, tsk, tsk!"

Sam folded his hands in his lap and said, "Sorry, ma'am," batting his eyelashes with exaggeration. Once Emma turned around with a huff, he ruined the good little boy effect by winking at Reba. God, that wink went through her like an erotic current. The man was lethal. And way too close.

She doubted whether pushing him would do much good; the determined gleam in his eyes said loud and clear that no quarter would be given by this soldier, not after her having blocked all his previous moves. Plus, he had about seventy-five pounds on her. She supposed she could scream for help, but what a sight that would be . . . nine overaged Santas to the rescue . . . assuming they would come to her rescue, considering how Sam was charming the liver spots off of them all . . . *darn it.*

Yep, Sam had her right where he wanted her, apparently, after a day and some odd hours of the pursuit-and-avoid game they'd been playing. *Who am I kidding? It's exactly twenty-eight hours and thirty-five minutes since The Good-bye Kiss . . . not that I'm keeping tabs. And, heavens to Betsy, why am I feeling all melty inside at the prospect of the louse's having me where he wants me?*

"Hello," Sam said.

"Good-bye," she said.

He smiled.

She frowned.

He took her hand in his.

She pulled her hand away from his.

It was all so childish. But they weren't children anymore, and Reba couldn't risk the powerful wave of pain that would surely accompany any association with Sam. She didn't want to hear his phony excuses. She didn't want to discuss her long-standing anger toward him. She didn't want anything to do with the testosterone-oozing hunk. Stiffening her spine, she steeled herself to resist the allure he offered, and, yes, he was alluring, even as he merely sat beside her. Seemingly innocent. Never innocent.

He reached for her hand again, and she swatted him away, again, but harder this time. "Ouch," he said with a grin.

"Cut it out, Sam. Just cut it out."

The fury underlying her words must have struck a chord in him somewhere. He stilled. "What?"

"Don't touch me. Don't talk to me. In fact, don't even look at me. Don't think I haven't noticed the way you watch me all the time, just waiting for a chance to pounce."

"Hey, I do not pounce." He studied her carefully as if trying to figure out some puzzle. Then, he concluded in typical Dumb Man fashion, "You are being really intense here, sweetheart. That has got to be a good sign. If you didn't care, you wouldn't react so strongly, right? You must not want me near you because you fear the temptation. Yep, a very good sign."

"Either that, or you repulse me."

He appeared to give that serious consideration, then decided, "No, no, no! I won't consider that possibility."

"Stay away from me, Sam. I'm not one of your groupies. I'm not your . . . anything."

The vehemence of her response seemed to stun him, but then he immediately switched to irritation. "Groupies? Are you nuts? I have never been into the Blues' groupie scene."

"I wasn't talking about the Blue Angels. I was talking about you, Mister Egomaniac."

"Me? You are suffering from a huge misconception, honey. I don't have groupies."

"Oh, Sam, you've always had groupies."

He threw his hands in the air. "This is a ridiculous conversation. I don't want to talk about me. I want to talk about you. I want to talk about us."

"Here's a news flash. There is no us."

The sadness on his face tore at her soul, but at least he had the good judgment to say nothing for a few moments. He must have sensed her growing agitation and realized that the best thing he could do was sit silently next to her and let her grow accustomed to his presence. Which she would never do. Not now. Not ever. No way. *Please, God!*

When did it turn so warm in here? Betty must have jacked up the heat.

When did Sam start wearing aftershave, or was that tangy evergreen scent just a residue of soap on his skin? Heck it was probably just the greenery that decorated each of the windows in the bus. *How pathetic am I?*

When would she stop noticing every little thing about him? The intriguing laugh lines that bracketed the edges of his blue eyes and the corners of his firm mouth. Or perhaps they were sun crinkles, living in Florida as he did much of the year. Then, there was his rigid military demeanor, even when he stretched his long legs out into the aisle, or joked with the senior Santas, or, Saints forbid, gazed at her with a longing that was anything but soldierly. And, criminey, he had a body perfectly honed to suit the military and a grown woman's humming hormones.

She must have been more exhausted than she'd realized to have allowed Sam to slip past her watchful guard. It was only eight p.m. But she'd been up since five. In the midst of some stress over the weather conditions, they'd performed two shows today, in Sarasota Springs, New York, and Burlington, Vermont, after which they'd picked up Stan and his lady friend, Dana . . . rather, George's friend, Dana . . . or was it both? In any case, she was on the way to the wedding, too. That, on top of JD and the Amish woman, Callie, hopping onto the bus this morning. They were becoming a regular reunion commune. Right now, JD and Callie were sitting on the front seat of the bus, with Stan and Dana on the opposite side. The two men were chatting amiably across the aisle, while the women stared pensively out the darkened windows.

"That was not a good-bye kiss. No way was that a good-bye kiss!" Sam declared, out of the blue, jarring her out of her mental wanderings. Good Lord, the man was resuming a day-old conversation, as if it had never been interrupted.

"I am not going to discuss this."

"This?"

"Us," she said. "It's over . . . done with."

"No, it's not, Reba. God, I hate that song. I can't think when I hear that song. Can't you make them stop?"

"Huh?" Reba glanced up, realizing that her Santa crew had started caroling, as they often did, not just to practice for their homeless shelter events, but because they were, frankly, a cheerful group. It was the holiday season, for goodness sake. "What do you have against Christmas songs, Mr. Grinch?"

He poked her playfully in the arm, but the playfulness never reached his somber eyes. "I don't hate all Christmas songs, just that one," he grumbled.

She narrowed her eyes at him, interested, despite herself. "And why would that be? Too lower class for a hoity-toity celebrity pilot?"

At first, it appeared as if he wouldn't answer her, but then he disclosed something he hadn't shared with her in all the eight years she'd known him.

"My mother gave me up two days before Christmas when I was ten years old. Just walked into a police station, said she needed to find a home for me, plopped down a paltry little cardboard box with all my worldly belongings, and left. Just like that. In the background, that stinkin' 'Jingle Bells' song was playing. I'll never forget it. Me screaming like a banshee for my mother to come back, and Bing Crosby crooning away with those cheerful cornball lyrics."

Suddenly, a look of horror spread over his face as he realized how much he'd revealed. "Forget I said that. God above! Here I am trying to charm you into talking with me. Instead, you must think I'm downright pitiful."

Reba didn't think he was pitiful, at all. In fact, she was deeply touched. "You've certainly come a long way since then, Sam. Your mother would be so proud of you."

"My mother could have cared less."

Reba would have liked to argue that point. After all, she held a masters degree in psychology. Here was a man with major unresolved issues . . . and not just dealing with his mother. But it was none of her business, really.

He ran the fingertips of one hand over his forehead, an unconscious effort to smooth out the creases.

Reba had to make a fist to keep herself from reaching out and doing the smoothing herself.

"Tell me about The Santa Brigade . . . and Winter Haven. I never thought you'd follow in your Dad's footsteps with a nursing home."

"It just happened. I was in private practice . . . working for a Bangor psychological clinic when Dad got cancer. I took a leave to come home and care for him, which meant taking over directorship of the retirement community on a temporary basis. It hasn't been a nursing home for years, by the way. Dad was in hospice for a year before he died. By then I discovered that I liked the work, and I took over." She shrugged. What she left out was the agony of that year, caring for a loved one through that horrendous disease.

"It appears as if you've made the *retirement community* your own, though. Lots of modern ideas."

She tilted her head in question. "Oh, you mean The Santa Brigade?"

"That and the mandatory volunteer program and physical fitness regime you instituted. Maudeen told me about them while I was showing her how to reorganize some of her files this afternoon."

"You're a computer expert, too?"

He laughed. "Not quite a computer geek. Jets are all high tech today, though, and pilots are required to have advanced computer training."

"You? The person who took algebra twice?"

"Hey, I just wanted to be with you. I liked the way you tutored me." Reba had been a year younger than Sam, thus taking the same courses the year following him. She chose to ignore the eyebrow jiggling trick that accompanied his latter statement.

Now would be a good time to change the subject. "How about you? Do you intend to make the military a career?"

"If you'd asked me that a year ago, I probably would have said I'm destined to be a lifer. But I'm not sure now. At the least, this is my third and last year with the Blues. It's a policy to rotate squadron members every few years on a staggered basis, so there are always familiar faces. The Blues have never been a permanent career option. At the same time, I'm feeling burned out with the Navy these days. I've already served four tours in Iraq and Afghanistan, which is enough, but I have no idea what else I could do . . . in civilian life."

My goodness, Sam was opening up a lot today. He always used to keep his personal doubts inside, as if they signified weakness. It was probably a ploy, though she didn't think he'd go that far. "You could do anything you wanted, Sam."

"I don't know about that. I wish you could have seen me perform with the Blues, though, Reba. I'm a screw-up in lots of ways, but I'm a really good pilot. Hot damn, but I would have showed off for you."

"You always showed off for me, Sam. Whether it was skiing down Suicide Run, or diving off the high board." She shouldn't tell him, she really shouldn't. *Oh, heck!* "Actually, I did see you, Sam."

"You did? As a Blue Angel? When?"

"Two years ago, in Boston. You . . . the team . . . were great."

He took her hand in his and held tight this time. "You came to a Blue Angels show, and never contacted me? Why not?"

"What was the point?"

"The point? I'll tell you the point," he said hotly, squeezing her hand painfully. "We were friends. Good friends. Whatever else we might have been, friendship demands common courtesy. I can't believe you were so close and didn't even talk to me."

"I intended to, but there were lots of people surrounding you after the show."

"And you couldn't wait? Or yell out my name to get my attention?"

"There were girls there, Sam, and women. I wasn't about to become one of your groupies."

"Groupies again?" he muttered.

"What did you say?"

"Nothing, babe. Nothing."

"And stop calling me babe and honey and sweetheart."

He grinned, as if—*yep*—he was getting to her.

He was, but that was irrelevant.

"Are you involved with anyone? A relationship, I mean?" Another of those disarming, out-of-the-blue questions.

"No. Nothing steady."

"Good."

Good? What did that mean? It was not good with regard to him. Whether she had a boyfriend, or lover, shouldn't concern him in any way.

"And you?" she asked. *Jeesh!* Her brain must be splintering apart to be continuing this line of conversation.

He shook his head.

And she thought *good*.

"I've had lots of women—"

"No kidding."

"Would you let me finish, Ms. Smart-ass? I've had lots of women . . . well, not lots . . . but enough."

She barely restrained a sarcastic remark.

"But none of them ever lasted more than a few months. I never even lived with a woman. I certainly never loved any of them . . . not like I . . . "

He let his words trail off, and Reba just knew that the reason was because he wasn't sure what tense to use. Was it "not like I *loved* you?" Or "not like I *love* you?"

Not that it mattered.

"I told you that I wasn't going to discuss this, and I meant it." She stood up abruptly and yanked her hand out of his. "Golly, it's hot in here. Move, so I can take off my blasted Santa suit." Enough of hiding behind this disguise. If she didn't cool down soon, she was going to have a stroke, or something. Probably a hormone meltdown.

Sam stared at Reba for several long moments. He was about to resist her order, but then, a good soldier knew how to pick his battles.

"Act calm. Be in control. Never show emotion," he murmured the mantra under his breath.

He'd made some progress with Reba tonight. Best he step back and let her assimilate everything that had been said and the emotions that still sizzled between them. "Okay," he said. "I'll stop . . . for now. But I'm not going away, Reba. We have things that need to be cleared up."

"Like what, Sam?"

"Like why I never came back? Like why you got married? Like where we go from here?"

Before she had a chance to make some wiseacre comment about there being a snowball's chance in hell that they were going anywhere *together*, he stood up next to her, gave her a quick peck on the mouth before she had a chance to belt him a good one, then moved to the half-empty bench seat across the aisle. The window side of the seat was piled high with boxes of candy canes. All around him he heard people speaking in the deep Maine burr that was at once familiar, and oddly soothing to him.

Reba was already peeling off the Santa suit, as if it were on fire. He felt a little hot himself, but his body heat emanated from an entirely different source. Hey, maybe Reba's heat was the same as his. *Hmmmm.* How to capitalize on that?

"Would you like a little refreshment?" an elderly voice asked him. Actually, the offer was made by two elderly voices. One held a tray filled with paper cups of egg nog, and the other a tray of sliced fruitcake. It was the spinster twins, Maggie and Meg MacClaren. Their matching, perfectly coifed pinkish blond hairdos never seemed to lose their old-fashioned deep waves. They reminded everyone of those two elderly Baldwin sisters on *The Waltons.*

Since neither fruitcake or eggnog were his personal favorite, and besides, they'd just eaten dinner, if it could be called that, at the homeless shelter in Burlington, he shook his head, hard.

"That was a great show you ladies put on today."

Both sisters beamed.

"Well, thank you, Sam. I was most pleased by the reception Sister and I got for our reading of *A Christmas Carol.* I swear I saw a tear in the eye of that incorrigible lad . . . the one with orange spiked hair," Maggie said in her refined, soft-spoken voice. She leaned down and pressed her parchment-like skin next to his for a quick air-kiss.

Maggie and Meg were about five-foot tall, and tiny . . . and smart as whips. At their advanced age, they were better known to the general public as Dr. Maggie and Dr. Meg. Former Harvard professors of anthropology, they had developed a reputation late in life with their outrageous non-fiction books related to sex and aging . . . sort of a combination Dr. Ruth Westheimer and Margaret Mead. Although retired from teaching and the talk show circuits, they were still amazingly active. In fact, their most recent effort, *Super Sex After Seventy*, hit the NYT list for several weeks last year. The year before they had a runaway bestseller with, *Viagra: Why Is Grandma Smiling?*

"Would you like a little advice?" Dr. Meg offered then.

"About sex?" he choked out.

Reba, who was tossing pillows into a storage bin behind her seat, made a choking sound as well.

"No, dear, not about sex," Dr. Meg said with a soft laugh. "About love." But then, she quickly added, "Unless you need advice about sex."

"I could recommend a book," Dr. Maggie offered.

"Uh, I think I'll pass for now," he said, well aware that his face was flaming. "Maybe later."

"Maybe later," Reba scoffed, once the sisters moved back up the aisle, offering their refreshments to others on the bus.

He was about to tell Reba to be careful, or he would sic the elderly sex experts on her, but the words died in his throat.

Because now——*Holy hell, now*—Reba in a black turtleneck and a pair of tight black jeans was in the aisle, bent over at the waist, tying a pair of athletic shoes.

There were some things a woman should never do in front of a full-blooded male. At the top of the list was bending over in tight black jeans.

He wouldn't even bother trying to resist the temptation. Nosiree! He snaked a hand out and pinched her on the ass.

"Eeekkk!" Reba shrieked, jerking upright and pivoting on her heels to confront her attacker. "You jerk! I could have had a heart attack, you scared me so bad."

"Not to worry, sweetheart, I'm a certified EMT. You oughta see my killer technique for cardiovascular resuscitation?"

"Mouth to mouth, no doubt," she said as she rubbed her butt.

And a very nice butt it was, he noted, then frowned. "Hey, you look different. Have you lost weight?"

She grunted her disgust.

"Bend over again so I can check it out."

She had to laugh at that. "Not in this lifetime."

"It's good to see you smile again, Reba. Did you know, you haven't smiled at me once, since you saw me yesterday? I've missed your smile. I've missed you."

She straightened, giving him his first full view of the new Reba. She *had* lost weight, and she was in good physical condition. Really good. *Talk about eye candy!*

"Don't you dare stare at me like that." She practically hissed.

He tried, but could not suppress a grin. "How?"

"Like . . . like you really, really want me."

"Oh, baby, was that ever in doubt?"

"Do you do tricks?"

Sam choked on his coffee as the I'm-so-straitlaced-I-could-be-a-saint Emma Smith, who must be close to seventy years old, voiced her outrageous question. And she was looking straight at him. All six-foot, two hundred pounds of her.

He felt as if he were back in her class, and she'd just asked him what he was doing with that notebook in his lap.

"Why me?" He waved a hand to indicate Stan, who sat next to him, on the outside, and JD who sat across from him in the booth. They were indulging in catch-up conversation over cups of coffee in "Grease," the diner located next door to the Sleepytime Motel just north of Burlington, Vermont, where they would sleep that night. Some of the Santa Brigade members had gone off to their rooms, including Reba, while others still straggled behind, sitting in booths in front and behind them, and across the aisle. They were critiquing their latest shelter performances over tea, decaffeinated coffee and prune juice. With respect to that latter beverage, the one thing that Sam had learned while on the Santa bus was that the regular functioning of "plumbing" was of extreme importance to the elderly. They did not hesitate to talk about it, publicly, and give unsolicited advice to him or anyone else within their radar.

But that was neither here nor there. He was more concerned about JD and Stan who were both grinning like freakin' idiots at Mrs. Smith's question directed at him.

"Why not nab these other yahoos? Why me?" he repeated in a mortified whisper. Bad enough that he and his friends were privy to this conversation; he didn't want the entire senior citizen kingdom to hear as well. They probably heard anyway. Beside the bodily function obsession, he'd noticed another thing about seniors. They liked to mind everybody's business.

"I already asked them. They're gonna." Obviously, Mrs. Smith had no inclination for hushing, as demonstrated by her booming voice. She'd probably forgotten to put in her hearing aid, and didn't realize how loud she was taking.

Gonna? What kind of word is gonna for a former teacher? And, son of a gun, gonna what? "They are?" Sam was flabbergasted as he gazed at his two best friends in the world. Both of them nodded vigorously, barely stifling their laughter.

Well, he didn't think it was so damn funny.

"Yep. So, do you do tricks?"

"Not lately," he gasped out. *Not ever, actually.*

"Well, everyone on this bus earns his keep. Can't just stand around looking pretty, Mr. Hotshot Black Angel."

"It's Blue Angel, not Black Angel," he corrected her. He was beginning to get miffed with Mrs. Smith's abrasive attitude.

"Blue, black . . . whatever . . . you could be a purple angel for all I care." She glared at him. "What's your specialty, boy?"

Oh, my God! The old bat wants me to screw for money. Can my life go any further down the tube? I can't believe that JD and Stan agreed to this. And how the hell do I know what my specialty is?

Mrs. Smith had a clipboard braced against one of her forearms, and she was tapping a Scooby Doo ball point pen on it impatiently, waiting for his answer. The pen was probably one of the many donations made to the Santa Brigade effort. "*Tap, tap, tap, tap, tap . . .* " Mrs. Smith still waited for his answer.

"Do . . . do tricks with whom? Senior citizens? Homeless people? Isn't that sort of taking charity to the extreme?" He tried not to appear as revolted as he felt.

Mrs. Smith blinked at him rapidly, clearly confused. Then she reached over Stan and whacked him atop the head with her clipboard. "Once a moron, always a moron, Merrick. I was talking about magic tricks . . . to be performed at homeless shelters. Good Lord! What gutter have you been living in the past fourteen years?"

With that, she turned on her ample legs, knee-high stockings bunched at the ankles, and stomped away, muttering under her breath. Then, just before she reached the exit door, she tossed out, "I'll give you 'til nine a.m. tomorrow morning to decide what entertainment you'll provide, or you'll be off the bus. And don't think I can't do it."

"Way to go, Einstein," Stan said with a guffaw of laughter, clapping a hand on his shoulder so hard he probably bruised a shoulder blade . . . a hand which had, no doubt, been insured by Lloyds of London at one time when he'd been a star NFL quarterback. JD reached across the table, offering him a napkin to wipe away the coffee he'd apparently sprayed in front of him during his choking fit.

"I knew what she meant," he lied, hoping his heated face didn't give him away.

"Yeah, right!" JD and Stan hooted at the same time.

"Speaking of the Santa Brigade," Sam said, trying to change the subject, "It's as if I've fallen down the rabbit hole to an Alice in Wonderland Christmas mad house, but I've got to admit I'm really impressed with these characters and the shows they put on."

"Damn straight!" JD agreed. He'd witnessed two of the shows since he'd gotten on the bus this morning.

"You know, part of the success of the Blue Angels is the ability to put together and break down all the equipment necessary for an air show in the most efficient manner . . . day after day, city after city, for six months. To a smaller extent, that's exactly what this troupe does. Each person has a role, not just in the entertainment, but in packing up, soliciting gifts . . . " he shrugged, " . . . everything."

"Well, you have to give Reba credit for that," JD said.

"Speaking of Reba, how's it going between you two?" Stan asked.

"It's not."

Both of his pals laughed at his woeful tone of voice.

"Even his heroic skydiving caper didn't impress her," JD told Stan. He could tell JD was having a grand ol' time, at his expense.

"It impressed the hell out of me when I heard about it," Stan said.

"Where did you hear about it?" A sense of foreboding came over Sam.

Stan waved a hand airily. "Oh, everywhere. The radio, the *New York Post*, the *Today* show. Man oh man, you shoulda heard Meredith Vieira rave about how romantic you are."

Sam said a foul word, then confided sheepishly, "Reba called it a juvenile prank."

"Aaah, but I bet, deep down, she was all melty." JD smirked as if he'd just expounded some great wisdom.

"Melty? Melty? Is that a private eye word?"

JD wagged his eyebrows at him. "Slick, Slick, Slick, maybe I should give you lessons in charm since your legendary talents in that department have apparently worn out. In fact, some people lately have compared me to Harrison Ford . . . when he was younger."

"Are you delusional?" Sam scoffed. "What's next on your career agenda? Indiana JD?"

JD grinned and reached across the table to swat him playfully on the arm. "You're not the only one who can have movie star good looks, pretty boy." Both JD and Stan were laughing uproariously.

"Cut it out, you two. The manager is scowling at us," he

grumbled. "And the Senior Santas are getting an earful."

Stan started to tap his fingertips on the Formica table top, thoughtfully, then offered, "You wanna know what I think, Slick?"

Actually, no.

"I think you need to try a different tactic. It's like football, if one play doesn't work, improvise."

Hmmmm. One of the Blue Angels mottos is "Observe, Study, Adjust." Could that work?

"I think," JD added, "that charm works only when you're bulletproof, and, Slick, you were never bulletproof when it came to Reba."

That was really helpful.

"I don't give a rat's ass what either of you think. Unless you guys have some concrete suggestions, can the goofball opinions."

"Okay. How about this?" JD said, then made a suggestion that was so outrageous, and explicit, that Sam's mouth dropped open. He didn't look, but he could swear he heard the clicking of several dropped dentures, too.

"That could work, that could work," Stan remarked. And he was serious.

"By the way, do the Blue Angels allow you to skydive at will anywhere you want?" JD inquired. He batted his eyelashes at him as if he already knew the answer.

"Hardly."

"Yeah, I was wondering about that, too," Stan joined in. "I would think the Navy would be calling you in for a court martial, or at least some of that KP shit. Or is that only in the Army?"

"I'm in a little bit of trouble," he admitted. Actually, his superior had left three voice mail messages on his cell phone thus far, which he hadn't yet returned. "But I'll be okay. At the moment, they want me more than I want them."

JD and Stan frowned with confusion, but he didn't want to get into that career discussion just yet.

Seeing that he wasn't going to elaborate, JD said, "Back to Reba and how you can get her to talk to you. Before you proceed any farther with your charm assault . . . and don't tell me any different . . . I know you'll charm her over, eventually . . . well, I have to ask, are you thinking clearly?"

"Huh? You mean, about Reba?"

"Hell, yes, about Reba. I mean, she was a good friend to all of us when we were growing up in Snowdon. I'd hate to see her hurt by you . . . again."

"Hey, hey, hey! I was hurt, too . . . when she got married," he said defensively.

"Reba's married?" Stan was clearly shocked. "You're hitting on a married woman?"

"And no one, including George, ever bothered to tell me when she got divorced."

"Reba's divorced? No one even told me she got married," Stan griped. "What am I? The potted plant in this threesome? I thought we were best friends—for life."

Ignoring Stan, JD stared pointedly at Sam. "Bottom line, buddy, are you trolling for a little action here? Or something more?"

"I wish I knew. I've gotta tell you, I've been undergoing a severe case of career burnout lately. Good thing my tour with the Blues is just about over. It takes total dedication and concentration to fly those maneuvers, and I'm not sure I have it anymore. I know it sounds crazy, but suddenly I feel as if I've been running as fast as I could for the past fourteen years and only lately discovered that, in reality, I've only been running in place."

To his surprise, his two friends didn't look at him as if he'd gone off the deep end. In fact, they nodded their heads in understanding.

"You asked about Reba, JD. Well, all I can say is when George told me yesterday that Reba was the tour director of this Santa Looney Tunes Brigade and that she wasn't married, it was as if the blinders had fallen off my eyes. I felt happy and hopeful for the first time in ages." He shrugged. "What do you suppose that means?"

JD and Stan exchanged a knowing glance with each other, then turned to him. Simultaneously, they informed him, "You're in love."

Sam was going to protest, but he wasn't sure they hadn't hit the answer right on mark. The question was, What was he going to do about it?

Luckily, he was saved from having to answer that question, even to himself, by Stan. He was speaking to JD, "So, what's with you and the Amish chick?"

"Where is she anyway? I thought you were afraid she would run away," Sam added, glad to no longer be the center of conversation.

JD's face flushed a nice pink color before he murmured, "I handcuffed her to the bed back in our room."

"Holy shit!" Stan exclaimed.

"I've been meaning to give you some advice," Sam said to JD, his lips twitching with suppressed mirth. Time for JD to get a dose of his own medicine.

JD snorted with disgust.

"Really. You're screwing an Amish woman? For chrissake, JD, an Amish woman is just one notch below a nun. And handcuffs? Tsk-tsk-tsk! Even for you, that's kinda perverted." The whole time he spoke, Sam grinned, wondering if he might borrow the cuffs himself. That would be one way of getting Reba to sit still and listen to him. And after she talked to him, well, who knew what use they could be put to?

"Until tonight, Reba has been wearing that Jolly Ol' Fat Boy outfit," JD apprised Stan. Then he turned with seeming innocence to Sam. "Speaking of perversions, loverboy, where does having the hots for Santa Claus fall on the perversion scale?"

"I heard about this on the Internet," Maudeen, the Cyber Granny, piped in then. To the surprise of all three of them, her purple spiked head was peeping up over the back of JD's seat. She must be kneeling on her own bench seat, and, apparently, she'd been eavesdropping on their conversation. Surprise, surprise!

"Heard about what?" the three of them inquired at the same time. Which was a mistake . . . a big mistake.

"Sex perversions," she answered matter-of-factly. "In fact, I accidentally landed on a website yesterday dedicated to sex with dwarves. Can you imagine that?" She shook her head at them. "Nuns, Santas, Amish, dwarves, all the same fetish, I guess."

"Actually, in the Santooian Mountains, sex with the god of winter, which could be construed to be St. Nicholas, is considered a blessed event." Speaking now was Dr. Meg, expounding from her anthropologist role.

"Ah, I remember now," her sister, Dr. Maggie, said, "how icicles in the form of penises were used to decorate trees during their festivals. And they were flavored with herbs that the women sucked on to increase fertility."

"Where'd you say those mountains were?" It was Morey Goldstein speaking now, a former butcher from Bangor and the self-proclaimed stud muffin of the senior citizen community. He popped his bright red suspenders and winked jauntily at the two sisters. Morey had a collection of two hundred pairs of suspenders. Sam knew because Morey had regaled him for hours today with details about every one of them.

The twins reacted to Morey's question and his wink with soft giggles.

Now, I've seen it all!

"There's nothing perverted when two people love each other," the soft-spoken Ethel Ross remarked. She and her husband John were sitting in the next booth across the aisle, holding hands, as usual. If there were ever lifetime lovebirds, it was these two, who'd been married for fifty years. He knew because they'd regaled him for hours today with details about every one of those years.

"That's right, Samuel. Try anything you can, *anything*, if you really love Reba," John advised as he exchanged a look with his wife that clearly said they had personally tried it all themselves.

Oh, swell! I really need that picture in my mind. Two old people getting it on!

"What was that you were saying about landing in Alice in Wonderland's rabbit hole?" Stan asked him.

"I'm beginning to think we all landed there," JD said, "or else Bedlam."

The seniors began to exit then, waving cheerily to them as they passed by, and calling out, "Merry Christmas" to the diner staff. It wasn't surprising that the owner of the restaurant had packed up several cartons of nonperishable foodstuff for them to take to the next homeless shelter.

"They seem really nice," Stan observed when they were all gone.

"Wait 'til they start interfering in your life," Sam warned.

"Hah! They already have," JD said. "That bus must have passed by a half dozen towns with sheriff's offices today, but would Betty Morgan stop? Nosirree. She came up with more damn excuses why she couldn't veer off her scheduled route than Lucky Charms has marshmallows. There's no question in my mind that the ladies on this bus have been conspiring to protect Callie."

"From you?" Sam asked.

"From the law."

"Oh, that's right, you already told me she's an FTA. That means failure-to-appear," he told Stan, impressed with his own ability to have remembered that bit of bounty hunter lingo.

"Why would the members of the Santa Brigade want to protect a criminal?" Stan wanted to know.

"She's not really a criminal. At least, I'm not sure she is. She's a star witness in a federal racketeering case, and she disappeared the day her court testimony was due. But I think the Santa ladies have ulterior motives for harboring Callie. She's a famous designer, and they've enlisted her to help with dressing some old Barbie dolls they received yesterday. If they don't get them dressed, they can't give them out tomorrow, or Thursday."

Stan put his face in his hands, then shook his head like a shaggy dog. "Hold the train . . . uh, bus . . . here, JD. What does the Amish woman, sheriffs and FTA have to do with each other? Better yet, what dress designer?"

"Callie is *the* Callie of Callie Brandt Originals."

"Holy Smoke, JD! She's as famous as Donna Karan or Vera Wang."

"Who the hell is Vera Wing?" Sam was addressing Stan. "*You* know the names of women's dress designers?"

"It's Vera Wang, you lunkhead," Stan laughed. "And who hasn't heard of Callie Brandt? She designed a bunch of the gowns for the Oscars last year."

"Well, this just takes the cake! An ex-NFL football player who's into dress designs!"

"You wanna make something of it?" Stan growled just before poking him in the ribs with an elbow. Between the overhearty shoulder whack and this jab, not to mention Mrs. Smith's head bang with a clipboard, he was going to be black and blue.

Then he turned his attention back to JD "And you have *the* Callie Brandt handcuffed to your bed? For the love of Mike, JD, you are in big, big trouble."

Instead of disagreeing, JD nodded with a self-deprecating grimace.

It was Stan's turn to play catch-up.

"How you doing, buddy?" JD stared pointedly at the cane propped against the table, near Stan's knee.

"I'm okay," Stan answered, but the lack of enthusiasm in his voice belied his assurances. "With continued therapy, this gimp leg should be near perfect. Once I get this shoulder back the way it should be, I won't suffer so much pain, either. But my football days are over, guys."

A prolonged silence hit their booth then as each contemplated Stan's prognosis.

"Dammit, I'm thirty-two years old. I probably would have had to quit in a year or two anyway as these old bones grew creaky. But I always said I'd go out in a blaze of glory, not through the blaze of a distracted driver." The bitterness in his voice was telling.

"What will you do now?" JD asked.

"Hell if I know."

"Do you need any cash?" Sam inquired. "I have a little stashed away."

Stan laughed. "Thanks for the offer, but money is the least of my problems. Truth to tell, I've made a ton this past year, but not from football. It seems I have the Midas touch in picking stocks."

"Like how Midas?" JD wanted to know.

"Like one million profit on Dilly.com, alone. And another mil on some medical stocks. Like I said, I seem to have the knack."

He and JD just gaped at their friend. Who would have guessed it, when they were raggedy orphans back in Snowdon, that one of them would turn into a regular John Paul Kijewski.

"And the woman with you? Dana? Is she someone special?"

"Nah!" Stan said. "I mean, she's special, all right, with those great legs of hers." He smiled to himself as if picturing those very legs. Probably in some interesting positions. "She's a friend of George's. He asked me to pick her up along the way."

When Stan was done talking, a comfortable silence prevailed.

"No matter what our problems might be at the moment," Sam said suddenly, "you have to admit, we've come a long way from Snowdon."

"Yep," his two good buddies concurred.

Sam planted his elbow in the middle of the table, a signal for the multiple-handed shake that had been a symbol for their friendship from way back. The other two put their elbows on the table, as well, and all of them clasped hands, one on top of the other. Tears of emotion rimmed all three sets of eyes.

"Friends Forever," they said.

There was something missing from this picture, though. It was supposed to be a four-handed shake, not just three. Reba had been their best friend, too.

Sam vowed then and there. He was going to get Reba back, come hell or high water . . . or Santa Brigade. As a military man, he knew how to plan assaults. He had weapons. He was Slick. If nothing else, she was now his target. Let her just try to escape his cross-hairs.

Reba didn't stand a chance.

CHAPTER FIVE

KEVIN

Wednesday morning, two days 'til Christmas Eve

"This is just plain humiliating," Callie grumbled, sitting across from Kevin at a booth in the coffee shop. The diner was fairly full, mostly with members of the Santa Brigade, but a few other stragglers were also enjoying breakfast. All except for Callie Brandt, apparently.

"Hey," Kevin said, holding out his arms magnanimously, you're not in cuffs now!"

She shook her head, wrinkling her cute little nose. "What a saint you're turning out to be."

Inside Kevin bristled, but he kept his expression cheerful while he added more cream to his coffee and stirred. "Under the circumstances, I'm doing the best I can. If it weren't for you bribing the soft-hearted females on that bus, you'd be languishing in a sheriff's holding pen right now."

"I didn't bribe *anyone*."

"Lady, we probably passed within blocks of at least twenty sheriff's offices from New York to here, and somehow Betty kept managing to 'miss' every single one. Betty, the only person who *could* find a needle in a haystack within a minute." He looked down at her nearly untouched plate of pancakes. "Now eat up. You're already a little too skinny."

A small growl escaped her lips, but she dutifully began cutting into the hot stack with a vengeance that sort of worried him. He might have to frisk her again when they were done to make certain she didn't pocket that knife to use on him later.

Not that frisking her would be much of a chore. Under that mound of clothing she'd been wearing yesterday, he'd still managed to get a good idea where all the curves and hollows were located on this woman's body. Right where they were supposed to be.

He glanced across at her, as she now chewed furiously, and he had to stifle a grin. After she'd complained about the discomfort of traveling in Amish clothing—which had to be harsh punishment for a sleek and apparently famous fashion designer—he'd gone looking for a spare set of clothing for her. Reba and Betty and Stan's babe had all been way too tall for her. But Maudeen had been just the right size. So now Ms. hoity-toity fashion goddess was decked out in bright yellow spandex and a garish red, yellow and purple turtleneck sweater. With her wild black hair and apricot skin and pale green eyes, she looked much like a little fashion rainbow.

When he'd returned from borrowing the clothes from Maudeen, Callie had looked at him like he'd just beamed up from Fashion Hell. He'd shrugged. "Maudeen's a little flashy at times. She likes her outfits to match her hair."

She'd opened her mouth to protest, but then had pressed it shut and accepted his bounty with only a slight grimace. The fact that she hadn't complained in the face of Maudeen's *unusual* generosity had won her a few points in his book.

To be honest, several things she'd done had won some points he'd rather not be chalking up in her favor. Like the way she'd offered instantly to pitch in and help when Colonel Morgan had barked out that they needed dolls for their next stop, and the only dolls the Brigade could find among the boxes of inventory in the back of the bus were used, whose clothing had looked like they'd been made for Skid Row Barbie.

By the time Callie had finished poking through their scanty inventory of cloth and other miscellaneous items, did some quick stitching and adjustments, the dolls could have been strutting down a runway in Paris.

Kevin, while pretending not to be fascinated and impressed, had been both. And so had the rest of the Brigade, which had *oohed* and *aahed* over her handiwork as if she'd just personally painted the Sistine Chapel.

"Why are you grinning at me like that?" Callie asked, then brought her mug to her lips, eyes glowering over the top of it, even through the steam.

"I wasn't grinning," he denied, abashed that he probably had been. After all, the adorable way she'd frowned as she'd made tiny stitches in tiny dresses all the while grumbling about the relative breast sizes of the dolls had been really fun to watch.

"You look that goofy all the time, do you?"

Any grin that might have been lingering was surely gone by now. "I have it on good authority," he retorted, "that I bear an incredible resemblance to Harrison Ford. A way younger version, of course."

She practically snorted coffee out her nose. "An information clerk at a train station in Schenectady is good authority, is she?"

He waved that away. "She's not the only one who thinks so," he said, figuring that wasn't really a lie, as he was sure some person, somewhere, somehow had also made that observation. Just not to him directly.

Callie grinned her skepticism, which would have really ticked him off if he wasn't too busy deciding she was one hot tamale when she was amused, even at his expense. How he'd love to reach across the table and shove his hands through that wild black hair, pull her to him and kiss the cynical smile from her lips.

That thought made him clunk his coffee mug onto the Formica and lean way back in his seat. Kissing a fugitive from the law? He didn't think so. He'd come a long way from his street tough youth, prided himself on his upstanding citizen status these days. He fought for justice *within* the bounds of the legal system now. He wasn't about to stoop to getting personally involved with potential felons at this point in his life.

The niggling problem was, he'd called his secretary last night when he'd regretfully left Callie shackled in their room. He'd had Mrs. Boswell repeat the details of Callie's crime. What she'd run from didn't seem all that bad. She'd run from a subpoena to testify in a high-profile case. That would be bad if she'd been called to help put the bad guy away. But she hadn't. She'd been called to testify *for* the defendant, the weasel Dylan Morris. To his reluctant way of thinking, she was doing the public a service by not helping the thug beat the rap. But the fact was, somehow she'd been involved with the man to begin with, and that was almost unforgivable. Except he didn't know what that involvement was, and he also didn't like passing judgment without all the facts. Not to mention, he was curious as hell.

So he gave it another shot, not that it would do him any good. He'd tried a dozen times since picking her up, and she'd been stubbornly mute on the subject. Well, not exactly mute. "None of your damn business, you swine," was her standard response.

Still, he could be as persistent as a thirsty mosquito when he had to be. "So tell me, beautiful," he said, then almost choked on his own words. He hadn't meant to say that at all, hadn't said it as anything more than a spontaneous outburst. And the look on her face was at first shock, morphing fast into anger. Before she could blister him, he hurried on. "Just give me a good reason to let you go. Really. I'm not enjoying this anymore than you are."

Now there was a whopper. True, she was a pain in the butt, but a really fun one to observe. "One good explanation and I'll see you get safely back to your farm in New York."

She hesitated, which was the best sign he'd gotten from her so far. Then she looked around and shook her head. "Too many eyes and ears here, if you get my drift."

Kevin glanced around the diner, too, and realized she was right. A majority of Snowdon's finest were keenly interested in their every movement, most acutely, his old eighth grade teacher, Mrs. Smith, and the MacLaren sisters. And he knew from experience that Mrs. Smith could read lips, not to mention minds, so he didn't pursue his interrogation for now.

So he shrugged and asked instead, "So, you're a high-falutin' fashion designer, are you?"

"I do all right," she said, suddenly interested in her breakfast again.

"Right. The folks on that bus almost fainted when you arrived. They hardly blinked when Stan showed up, and that boy was *this* close to winning a Super Bowl ring." He chewed a forkful of scrambled eggs, then added, when she didn't respond, "Maudeen says you dress the stars. The really, really big stars."

"Some."

"That's why you looked so familiar. Living in New York, no matter how you try to avoid them, you can't help but catch all of those theater premieres and award shows. You go to a whole bunch of those, don't you?"

Her cheeks pinkened, and she still wouldn't look at him. "Only when I have to."

"You don't enjoy all that celebrity crap . . . excuse me . . . stuff?"

She set down her fork and studied him suspiciously over the top of a glass of orange juice. But he was truly interested, and it must have shown in his expression, because by the time she polished off the juice and set the glass down, she shrugged and stared at him straight on, eyes clear and gorgeous. "I love creating beautiful clothes," she said softly. "I'm lucky to make a good living doing what I love to do. Part of the process is public relations. If that means showing up at events where Suzy Superstar is wearing one of my gowns, that means I go. But I don't have to like it."

He believed her, dammit. Which shot her up another notch on that admiro-meter. And he was hating himself a little more and more by the moment. He was about to beg her to give him a reason to let her go when half the Santa Brigade—or so it seemed—suddenly appeared at their table.

"I hear you created that slinky number for Jennifer Lopez," Maudeen said.

"Not me," Callie replied, fast.

"Geena Davis?" asked Meg MacLaren. "Sister and I speculated on the possible anthropological reasons for some of her fashion choices."

"Not me, either."

"Madonna's pointy numbers?" Morey Goldstein asked, a whole lot of hope shimmering in his voice.

"Sorry to disappoint you."

Morey glared at Maudeen. "I thought you said she was famous."

Kevin watched Callie grow more and more uncomfortable, and waved over the waitress. "Check, please!"

Somehow, amid a barrage of other questions shot at Callie, he managed to pay the bill and get her into the Gore-Tex coat Maudeen had found for her in their stash of goodies, and get her out of there, holding fast to her elbow. After they'd strolled far enough from the diner, he lovingly grabbed her hand and intertwined their fingers, then slapped the cuffs on their joining wrists before she could say, "Boo."

She screeched at him and tried to kick his calf, but he sidestepped just in time. "Now, now."

"You are such a jerk," she said. "I thought you were actually trying to be nice."

That stung a little. He hadn't been *trying*, but he considered himself a naturally nice guy for the most part. Well, maybe not. Still, he was never intentionally a jerk unless someone pissed him off first. "I'm sorry. I'm not trying to be mean, either. I just can't take any chances." *And I don't want you to get away.* The scary part of that was, his reasoning had somehow slipped from justice to . . . something else.

He'd been irritated as hell last night as it became increasingly obvious that the Santa Brigade biddies were conspiring against him in favor of Callie. As much as he'd known how low their opinion of him had been when he was younger, a small part of him had looked forward to seeing them again, if nothing else, to prove to them that he'd grown into someone they could respect and proudly call one of their own once upon a time.

But no, once again, he'd been the bad guy, and the people in the only hometown he'd ever known had sided against him once more. It had felt like bitter bile in his gut, all over again. He'd made his Snowdon debut after all these years, and once more he'd been deemed a disappointment.

Still, he hadn't quite been able to bring himself to resent Callie as much as he should. She hadn't endeared herself instantly to those folks out of spite. She had no idea the baggage he and the good folks of Snowdon were carrying that went way beyond the millions of boxes in the back of that stupid bus.

And then, there were the hours he'd spent just watching her sleep in the motel room he'd insisted they share, much to her outrage. He'd kept staring at that dark, wild hair flared out starkly against the white of the pillow, her soft lips, slack and guileless in sleep, and something had stirred deep inside of him that he hadn't felt in a good long time, if ever.

Worse, he'd had to listen to a nightmare she'd had, which he just felt deep in his belly was a living one, and from there on, he started realizing that turning her in might become the biggest regret of his life. That was saying a lot, considering his life.

It had bothered him so bad that he'd gotten up and gently awakened her. No matter how slowly he'd tried, she'd come to consciousness whimpering, "Please don't make me lie!"

And his heart had nearly broken.

She was a famous fashion guru posing as an Amish woman who was wanted by the law. How much more of a lie was there than that? He was afraid to know, and dying to find out, at one and the same time.

"Damn you, Wilder, why won't you believe me that I won't try to run?" she asked now, yanking him back from the vision of her in her sleep, beautiful and tormented.

He tried to gather his wits, because at this single moment, he wanted to let her go so badly, he'd pay huge money for Betty to turn the bus around and take Callie anywhere she wanted to go. And at the same time, if he did that, she'd be gone. And that thought made him feel worse.

The analytical, systematic, judicial, prudent side of his brain had gone missing. Which meant he had nothing left to work with.

As they crunched through the new-fallen snow, that was getting deeper by the minute the way it was falling, he contemplated just giving her her freedom. The cold steel around his wrist was helping his decision. If it was freezing to his skin like that, it had to be doing the same to hers. And he didn't like that thought at all.

Up ahead he spotted Stan and his blonde goddess approaching, and he couldn't stand any more humiliation to Callie. "Promise you won't run?" he asked as he fished for the key to the handcuffs.

"Where am I going to go, you dolt?"

He looked down into her eyes and smiled, even as he worked the locks. "You are definitely not a New York native, if dolt is the best you can do."

He found out, in the next ten seconds, that dolt wasn't even close to the best she could do.

He's a kidnapper, he's a *skunk, he's a jerk, he's a scumbag, he's a rat, he's a slimebag, he's a dirtbag, he's an arrogant bastard, he's an unyielding tightass, he's a rat, he's a . . . a . . . jerk.*

Sitting on the bus as they chugged and jostled and stormed their way up the highways and small streets of the snow-bound Northeast, Callie was pretty sure she'd had to repeat herself a time or two there, because she'd run out of really nasty superlatives. But repetition was necessary if she wasn't going to delve into the good stuff.

Like that Harrison Ford in his early thirties would have been lucky to look like Kevin—JD, as his friends called him, for no reason she could figure—and be half as driven.

He was a bastard, and that was that. She wasn't even going to remember the good things, not a chance. Especially when last night she'd gotten an earful of just what a hellion he'd been in his youth. Who was he to judge her?

She tried to conjure up more outrage, but a lot of the stories Maudeen and the gang had related made it harder and harder to keep that self-righteous anger alive. If half the stories were true about his upbringing, the man should be doing . . .

"Jail time," Morey, the stud on a mission, said beside her, apparently reading her mind. "We were all sure he'd be in jail by now. All three of them, actually."

Callie was busy repairing busted stuffed toys, and didn't want to get too involved in this discussion with everyone listening. But as she glanced around, she saw that it seemed every single person was occupied digging through boxes, yelling out numbers and tagging toys for destinations. Even Kevin had his head in a box, and for some reason kept muttering, "I'm sorry, Miss Smith."

So it seemed they were alone. No time like the present to delve a little into the rat, the rotten jerk, whatever. "Why would Kevin be in jail, Mr. Goldstein?"

"Morey. Just Morey. No formalities here, especially with a cute young—"

"Morey Goldstein!" a voice admonished.

"Sorry, Emma," Morey yelled back. "Damn hearing aid of hers is lethal."

"I heard that!"

Morey rolled his eyes and lowered his voice to a whisper. "All three boys were throwaways. No one thought they'd amount to squat. I have to admit to doubts myself. But George—George Garrison, he's the vet in Snowdon—never gave up. Thought those kids had potential, no matter how many times they were dragged by their ears into the police station. George, he'd bail them out every single time. Ye-up. He'd give them the blistering they sure enough deserved, and then he'd kick 'em out into the world and say, 'Do better, now'."

"Why weren't their parents doing that?" Callie asked, fascinated, as she glanced back and watched all three of those huge men being blistered by the women, and taking it. It was cute, actually.

"Parents? You don't know anything about the boys, I see." He sighed. "They didn't have any to speak of."

"But, then who did they—"

Morey suddenly turned tight-lipped on her. "Didn't realize you didn't know. It's not my place to say."

Morey's reluctance to gossip reminded Callie that you didn't pry with folks in the Northeast. They were tight as New England clams when it came to their own. "I'm sorry, I didn't mean to pry."

Morey's tight expression softened. "I'll tell you a secret I shouldn't."

Calley planted her best smile on him. "Do tell. I'm great with secrets."

"That man of yours—"

"He's not—"

"Oh, don't worry, like I said, we keep our secrets. That man of yours . . . I admired the boy. He was an angry child, but determined. Every bad thing he whipped up, he did it outta anger for another. Never for himself." Morey lowered his voice even more. "Was a time when the mayor herself was being accused of stepping out, if you know what I mean. That boy was so mad that she—our mayors have been women since '76, you know—was being accused, he went and tracked down who'd be saying such a thing. Then he followed *her* for a few weeks."

Morey stopped for breath, but Callie was impatient. "And?"

"And let's just say that the "Happy Hour Motel" never got so many happy hours of free publicity in all its years. Room 6-B is now christened 'Sylvia's Sighs.'" Morey coughed a little and added, "I didn't have anything to do with that, you know. Just that the walls are thin and it was hard to get a decent night sleep in 6- A . . . so I heard."

"Morey, you've spent more time in 6-A than the maid," piped in Reba, who'd come up behind them.

Callie blushed at being caught gossiping, but Reba just grinned down at them both. All Callie could think about was tailoring that Santa suit so that it flattered the woman better. She was tall and gorgeous, everything Callie wasn't. And Callie had spied her out jogging the night before. Reba Anderson had a body Callie drooled to design dresses for.

The woman was tall and slender, but not skinny, by any stretch. She actually had a woman's body. As much as Callie enjoyed the money she made outfitting movie stars, she was getting just a little tired of trying to make pencils look sexy.

Morey slinked away, and Reba sat down in the seat across the aisle. "I can't thank you enough for pitching in."

"Oh, I'm happy to do it."

"So, was Morey regaling you with the legendary stories of the Three Hustleteers?"

Callie laughed. "Well, one in particular."

"I can guess which one. But trust me, all three were awful," Reba said, but her smile was soft and eyes limpid in remembrance.

"The entire town was certain they'd end up in a life of crime."

Since Callie had learned in the last twenty four hours she'd been among these folks what each of the Three Hustleteers had become, she smiled. "I guess they showed the town a thing or two."

"Or three," Reba said, nodding. Her eyes found each of the

former troublemakers, then turned back to Callie. "Everyone in Snowdon is happy with the way they turned out, but I'm guessing Sam and JD and Stan won't ever believe that. If it weren't for George's wedding, my guess is all of them would have been happy to live out their lives never stepping foot in Snowdon again."

Callie glanced up, but in the process pricked her finger on the needle. "Ouch," she said, then brought the injured digit to her mouth. "Who *is* this George person, anyway?"

Reba smiled at her. "Why don't you ask Kevin? He can tell you much better than I what George meant to him. To all three of them."

"Like I want to talk to that slug at all," Callie muttered, digging the needle into the cloth with a vengeance. Mostly because she was mad at herself for truly being curious about the man. "But tell me this. What does JD stand for? Obviously they aren't his initials."

"Juvenile delinquent," Reba responded. "He was called that so often by the adults in town, his friends began just shortening it."

"That's awful!"

"Oh, trust me, he earned the nickname." Reba grinned. "When you decide to ask him about his past—"

"I won't."

"When you decide *not* to talk to him about his past, make sure to ask about the Jamie Kellerman incident." She chuckled. "Here he comes. You can *not* ask him now, if you want." With that, Reba stood up and strolled forward.

For some reason, Callie's heart sped up like a race car. She tried to convince herself that it was irritation acceleration, but couldn't quite pull it off. Not to mention, as adamant as she'd been about denying any desire to hear about the Jamie Kellerman incident, she had to admit to a certain morbid curiosity. Not to mention, it might be a good thing. If she heard some awful stories about what a jerk he'd been as a kid, maybe she'd stop admiring some of the things she knew about him as an adult.

Like his reputation in New York was almost heroic. If prosecutors wanted to find that tiny piece of evidence or information about a criminal that would seal his or her fate during trial, they called on him to find it. And he rarely failed.

Like that as uncouth and uncaring as he tried to appear at times, he was unfailingly considerate, to her as well as to the people on this bus, who by all accounts had written him off as a no-good thug in his youth.

Like, that although he'd been rotten enough to force her to share a motel room with him last night, he hadn't once tried to ravish her, hadn't even made any suggestive remarks, hadn't attempted to take advantage of the situation in any way, giving her all the privacy she wanted. In fact, when she'd awakened from her now nearly nightly anxiety dream, it had been to him trying to soothe her, quiet her, then help her fall back to sleep by gently running his fingers over her forehead. Her last memory before succumbing to slumber was him whispering softly, "That's it, Sleeping Beauty, sweet dreams this time."

And funny enough, she'd slept like the dead the rest of the night.

None of the haunting nightmares that had plagued her the last few months. None of the fitful, worried sleep that had probably aged her five years in sixty days. She'd awakened refreshed, and for some insane reason, looking forward to the day spent with the Santa Brigade.

And to be honest, with Kevin—JD. Which was stupid with a capital S, considering he was hell-bent on turning her over to the authorities.

Or was he? As much as he grumbled about Maudeen and Betty's manipulation in getting as far away from law enforcement as much as possible, he wasn't actually complaining loud and hard, much less threatening them with obstruction of justice, or anything like that. He normally just rolled his eyes and kept his mouth shut. "Because Betty scares the beejeesus out of me," had been his explanation when she'd asked him about it earlier.

Somehow, she doubted that.

"Hiya, Stitch," she heard beside her, making her once again poke her poor finger.

"Ow!" she muttered, then forced herself to glare up at him. Her breath hitched, like it did just about every time his visage came suddenly into her view. She stuck her finger into her mouth again.

"I'm sorry," he said, scooching her over and sitting beside her. "Let me see that."

He forced her palm from her face and looked it over carefully, then dragged her hand to his own mouth, and placed the pad of her finger between his lips.

Her breath screeched to a halt and her nerves jangled like Christmas chimes. She'd protest, but her vocal chords decided to take a coffee break. She'd pull her hand away and slap his gorgeous face, but her mind wasn't sending the right signals. She couldn't even conjure up a scowl.

"Your hair is so beautiful," he said softly, around her finger.

"Uh . . . uh . . ." She regrouped in a few seconds, after enjoying the sensation for just a while longer. Tugging her hand back, she shot him a scorching look. "And yours looks like beavers had at it. A few years ago."

He ran a hand through his hair and shot her a rueful grin. "I've been kind of busy."

"Really?" She gave his head a once over, and tried to keep any sign of admiration out of her eyes. "Too busy terrorizing innocent citizens, hmm?"

"Oh, I don't know. Occasionally I get lucky and catch a live one." He had the most gorgeous chocolate-colored eyes she'd ever seen. Especially when they were crinkled in amusement.

She would have sat and stared at those eyes, that smile, if it didn't suddenly occur to her that he was actually laughing *at* her. She'd tried to zap him one, and he'd found it amusing.

Annoyed because she wasn't annoyed and she should definitely be really annoyed, she dragged her gaze from his, and attacked the cloth with a vengeance.

"You're pretty good at that, you know."

"At what?" she asked, not looking up.

"That fashion stuff. I don't know much about doll things, but the ones you cleaned up are really pretty."

The compliment zapped right at her, so much so, that she looked up. "You think so?" Then she almost bit out her tongue. She was a world-renowned fashion artist. Her dresses had graced the bodies of stars and royalty and . . . Maudeen—which was a sort of scary thought. So why his opinion—which probably meant zippo, and might even be BS—mattered, she couldn't figure.

He nodded, smiling. "I think you're going to make quite a few little girls happy today."

She wiped her itchy nose on her sleeve. "Too bad I won't be getting to see that, as I'll probably be locked in a . . . a jail cell by then."

Kevin had the grace to look pained at the thought. He glanced away, out the window, where snowflakes the size of small boats were falling. "Well, the thing is...," he started, then cleared his throat. "The thing is, Betty and Maudeen and the rest of the gang seem hellbent on keeping you out of jail. So it's a good bet you'll get to see the results of your efforts."

Oh, she hoped so. And not just because she'd give just about anything to avoid being forced back to a New York courtroom. She chanced a glance at Kevin, and sucked in a breath at the heat in his eyes. "That would be nice," she choked out. "I'd like that."

He coughed and mumbled something.

"What?" she asked.

"I said," he replied, looking away again. "Then count on it."

Callie stifled a smile and bent to her task again, and something that felt like a companionable silence fell between them, even as chaos reigned all around them.

"Maudeen!" Colonel Morgan barked from the front of the bus. He was busy organizing the Dear Santa Brigade letters piled in front of him, and checking off items on a clipboard.

"What?" Maudeen answered without looking up from her laptop.

"How many Raggedy Anns left in inventory?"

After a bit more clacking at keys, Maudeen answered, "Five."

"That's enough for our next stop," the commander said. Then he held up his clipboard and pointed at it. "But we'll need at least three more for the shelter in Fulton."

As was becoming routine, Callie watched as Maudeen went to work, scouring the internet sites for stores with Raggedy Ann inventories the Brigade could raid.

It was awesome, really, this philanthropic venture. And it warmed Callie's heart. As much as she hated the circumstances of her being forced to board this bus, she'd never forget these people, or their hard work, trying to bring as much joy as possible to people who for the most part didn't know the meaning of the word. Callie vowed right there and then to step up her efforts in the future to try to spread joy and cheer to the down and out.

Several minutes later, Maudeen stopped typing. "We're in trouble. There's not a store between here and Fulton with Raggedy Anns in stock. Most are so back-ordered, they'll be lucky to have them in by next year."

Callie set aside the cloth in her hands and stood abruptly. "Maudeen?"

"Yes, dear?" Maudeen said distractedly, chewing on her lower lip.

"I can make them."

"Excuse me?"

"If you get me to a K-Mart type of store, I can get the supplies and make them." She glanced down at Kevin, then back at Maudeen. "That is, if I'm not in jail by then."

Kevin made a choking sound.

"Oh, dear, that would be utterly *lovely* of you!" Maudeen responded, beaming underneath a mop of orange hair that would rival any Raggedy Ann doll.

A chorus of approving murmurs went up among the Brigade that had Callie's heart warming with pleasure.

"You will *not* be in jail by then," Emma Smith said, coming up the aisle. "Will she, Kevin?"

"No, ma'am," Kevin said, shaking his head rapidly. "She won't be."

"Good boy," Emma said, patting his cheek.

"I'll help too," Callie heard, and turned to see Dana standing. "I've got a little bit of experience with that sort of thing."

"A little bit?" Stan said, standing also. "The woman's awesome." Callie felt a sudden, real kinship with all of these people. "That would be wonderful, thank you," she said. "I'd welcome the help."

"It's settled then," Maudeen chimed in. "After the next stop, we go shopping."

Callie sat back down, unable to wipe the smile from her face as she picked up her sewing and dug back in. But she felt Kevin's eyes boring into her, so she glanced up. "What?"

"Lady, you are something else."

CHAPTER SIX

STAN

Wednesday morning, two days 'til Christmas Eve.

"So . . . you do this sort of thing often?" Morey Goldstein asked, leaning—*leering*—over the back of the seat in front of Dana, who was industriously mending doll clothes.

From his seat across the aisle, Stan glared daggers. Not five minutes ago the Brigade's resident Lothario had been putting the moves on Callie. Now here he was, patting his thick, white locks and making fish eyes at Dana.

It wasn't bad enough that he, Stan "The Man" Kijewski, millionaire football star and tax-paying adult, had Mrs. Smith correcting his grammar and the colonel ordering him around like one of the troops and over-sexed septuagenarian twins offering him advice on his love life. Now he had to put up with *this?*

Dana didn't seem to mind. She smiled up at the old goat just as if she were glad to see him. There wasn't even a touch of the Ice Maiden frost she used to drive *him* away.

"First time for me," she said in that husky, wet-dream inducing voice of hers. "Do *you* do this often?"

Stan squeezed his eyes closed against the disturbing visions her words conjured. He could think of lots of things he'd like to do to her and with her, but she hadn't invited him to try.

Not even twenty-four hours since he'd fallen on his ass in her front yard, yet already she'd taken up what threatened to be permanent residence among his most erotic fantasies. He wouldn't have worried so much if the first one hadn't hit him right there in her kitchen over ham and cheese sandwiches with milk.

Morey beamed and propped an elbow on the seat in front of her like a man settling in for a long flirtation.

"Every year," he boasted, proudly hooking a thumb in his suspenders. "The girls and me, we've been doing this for a long time. Years and years!"

"Six!" yelled Emma from the front of the bus.

Morey sighed, then brightened as a new thought hit. "Mind if I join you?" He gestured to the doll clothes and sewing supplies she'd heaped on the seat beside her.

"Please do." Dana smiled and shifted the stuff into a basket in her lap.

Morey slipped into the seat with the alacrity of a teenager. The movement of the bus didn't seem to bother him at all, which Stan resented since he had a hell of a time getting up and down the aisle with his cane and his bad leg.

Stan scowled at the battered Barbie doll he was supposed to be cleaning. That seat by Dana had been empty an hour ago. When he'd asked if he could sit there, she'd pointedly dumped all her junk in it and said, very coolly, that she needed the room for her work. And now she offers it to that smarmy old goat?

Growling, he scrubbed at a smudge of black on the doll's pointy bare breast. Skid Row Barbies, JD called 'em, but they were cleaning up amazingly well. Dana had shown him the first couple that Callie had dressed. The transformation was darned near unbelievable. JD's little spitfire had worked miracles. It wasn't hard to see why the woman was a world-famous dress designer. The little girls at the shelter would go ape-shit over them.

Not that he'd ever understood little girls or dolls, of course. Or grown-up women, for that matter.

Because he couldn't help himself, he glanced across the aisle. Morey and Dana were schmoozing away like long lost pals.

Resentment stung him again, harder this time. Dana had scarcely said a dozen words to him since they'd climbed—well, in his case, staggered—off that snowmobile and onto the bus yesterday afternoon. The woman seemed determined to plague him.

The torment went far beyond the additional aches in his shoulder, hip, and leg from that damned wild cross-country run yesterday. Two hours with his crotch pressed against her delicious backside had been about one hour and fifty-nine minutes too long for his self-restraint. Never mind that they'd both been encased in boots, helmets, and snowsuits that made them look like Michelin men. His crotch had known exactly where it was, and it had been troubling him ever since with eager suggestions of what he ought to do about it.

If Dana had suffered similar pangs, she hadn't given any sign of it. She'd climbed off that snowmobile as coolly as if she'd had no idea he was back there, then added insult to injury by offering to help him up.

He'd refused, of course, but not just to protect his masculine pride, as she'd assumed. No, the problem was he'd been darn near cross-eyed with mingled lust and pain. Who'd have guessed that two hours of being slammed around a Vermont mountain in weather cold enough to freeze rocks could leave you with a hard-on stiff enough to bore through wood?

Only Dana could have done it to him.

He wasn't sure he liked that thought at all.

Frustrated, Stan scrubbed harder. The black mark on the breast was gone, but there was this smudge on its leg . . .

His fingers tightened around the doll. The thing was like Dana— slim, leggy, and busty. The difference was, he'd much rather be rubbing Dana's leg. And her hip. And her back and belly and those incredible breasts . . .

Better not think about the breasts. He had enough problems as it was.

Thank God the doll was a brunette. But there was a blonde doll in the heap and—

It's a doll, he told himself firmly. *It's just a doll.*

But that didn't keep him from thinking of what it would be like if it were Dana, instead.

Gritting his teeth, he poured more of the citrus cleaner on the rag and scrubbed harder.

He might shut out the erotic thoughts the doll aroused, but he couldn't shut out Dana's voice or the irritating good cheer of Morey's.

"Been this way before, have you?" Morey was saying. Which was a polite, roundabout way of asking where she was from.

Dana nodded. Her hair—left free again, just the way Stan liked it—fell forward to hide her face behind a curtain of white-gold. She flipped it back, oblivious to the effect the movement had on his libido.

"I grew up near Snowdon," she said.

"That so?" Morey might not be one to share what he knew, but he was more than happy to pry into others' secrets Stan noted sourly. Gossipy old goose, that's what the fellow was. When he wasn't being a lech.

"Beerson Home for Girls, actually," she admitted—rather

reluctantly.

Dana had grown up at *Beerson's?* He had to force himself to stop scrubbing the Barbie before he scrubbed the plastic right off. He tossed the brunette in the bag with the other dolls that were ready for new clothes and new hairdos, then grabbed another out of the pile. *Not* the blonde. A redhead this time.

"That so?" said Morey.

She nodded again. How could such pale blonde hair have so many shades of gold and yellow in it?

"George used to take some of us hiking and camping. He taught me to love the wilderness."

"You're a forester, Reba says?"

"Wildlife management, actually."

Wildlife management. He could teach her a thing or two about wildlife, if she'd let him.

"Sounds interesting," said Morey.

"Hmmm," said Dana, concentrating on her mending.

Undeterred, Morey changed tack. "What're you going to do at our next performance. Reba asked you, right?"

Dana nodded. Stan gritted his teeth and forced his attention onto dirt, not gold.

"I'm going to tell stories to the little children. I do that sometimes at the schools around where I live. The children seem to like it."

What's not to like about an hour spent listening to that voice? She could read him the Manhattan phone directory and he'd get a hard-on.

The redhead joined the bag of clean, naked Barbies. The blonde was next on the pile. Yellow-head, actually, Stan decided, studying the thing. Not blonde at all, but definitely long, leggy, and busty.

He sighed and picked up a clean rag and set to work.

". . . especially animal tales from the Indian legends and myths. They really like those."

"Sounds good," said Morey. He propped his elbow on the armrest between the two seats and leaned closer. "I was thinking maybe you might like to help me out, too."

Stan's hand froze over the Barbie's right buttock.

"Oh?" said Dana, not looking up from her mending.

"I was thinking maybe you and me could put on a dance show. Of course," he added, blithely ignoring her start of surprise, "I'm already dancing with Maudeen, but I figured you and me, we could cut a little more modern number." He leaned closer still. "I'm a real good dancer."

And a good four inches shorter than Dana, damn him.

Stan blindly groped for the next doll. Two to go. He'd have to make them last because he was damned if he was going to walk away so long as Morey was there.

Dana blinked, opened her mouth, then closed it without saying a word.

"Whaddaya say?" Morey insisted, smiling wide so she got a good look at his well-polished dentures.

"I'm not much of a dancer, I'm afraid," Dana said apologetically, just as if she really were sorry.

I could teach you, Stan thought, then scowled when he remembered that he still had a hard time walking.

"Oh," said Morey, clearly disappointed.

Stan's annoyance changed to sympathy. He knew exactly how the old fart felt.

As if sensing Stan's change in mood, Morey glanced his way, then leaned across the aisle. "So, what are *you* going to do for the show?"

Stan kept his attention on the doll. "Nothing."

Morey frowned. "You gotta do something. Everyone does."

"Not me." Damned if he was going to admit that the only thing he'd ever done well was play football, and now he couldn't even do that.

Morey's frown deepened. "Reba won't like that." That in the tone of impending doom.

"Reba understood. I already explained it to her." He knew he sounded surly and, maybe, just a bit childish, but Reba's request had struck a raw nerve.

The question of what he was going to do with the rest of his life now that football was no longer an option had been troubling him for months. He'd had some offers to coach from a couple of NFL teams, but that route didn't really appeal to him. He loved football, but it was the physical game itself that drew him, not the more intellectual side that coaching represented.

The only other thing he'd managed well was his stock investments, but somehow he didn't think a homeless shelter was the place to be discussing tax-free annuities or the Dow Jones Industrial Average.

"Why don't you talk about football?" Dana leaned forward so she could see around Morey. "I'll bet a lot of people would like to hear about some of your games."

"Yeah, right," Stan mumbled. That red smudge on the doll's knee was never going to come out.

"No, seriously," Dana urged. She put down her mending. "Tell them about the game with Dallas in "97. You know, the one where you played with that cracked rib."

"You played with a cracked rib?" Morey asked with a look that said he thought that was the craziest thing he'd ever heard.

Stan shrugged. "Happens a lot. Guys play with cracked bones, strapped shoulders, sore muscles. You don't play football if you can't stand pain. Not the way the pros play it, anyway."

"But a cracked *rib?*" Morey insisted.

"Or how about that game with the Packers when the Typhoons were down twenty-two points in the fourth quarter and you had three long touchdown passes and a two-point conversion to force the game into overtime and a win? I know they'd like to hear about that!"

Stan and Morey both stared at her as though they weren't sure they were hearing right.

"You like football?" He'd never met a woman who really liked football. A lot who liked football players, but not one who really understood the game itself.

"Sure. Doesn't everyone?" A faint blush was beginning to color Dana's cheeks.

"Never watch it," said Morey with a dismissive wave of his hand.

Stan just stared. He was falling in love. He could see it coming, and there wasn't a damned thing he could do about it because George had set him up with the world's perfect woman.

"You like football," he said again in spite of a mouth gone suddenly dry.

"Well, some football, anyway," Dana said, sinking back in her seat. This time, when her hair fell forward to hide her red cheeks, she didn't bother to brush it back. Instead, she retrieved her mending and started working away as if a slave driver with whip were standing over her shoulder watching.

The next to the last Barbie lay in Stan's lap, forgotten.

Dana liked football.

"Lots of women like football," said Dr. Maggie, peering around the edge of her seat three rows up. Or maybe it was Dr. Meg. Stan got them confused a lot. "Women understand the symbolism of the battlefield quite well."

"And besides," added her sister, popping up from her seat, "we like those tight pants you boys wear. They're ever so much sexier than those awful basketball uniforms."

"Front *and* back," the first sister agreed, nodding happily. "I've often wondered about the protective gear you wear, though. They call them cups, don't they? It must be *very* uncomfortable."

Not as uncomfortable as having a three-hundred-pound defensive tackle slam into your unprotected balls. Stan didn't say it out loud. He could feel his own cheeks growing as hot and red as Dana's.

"He's got cups?" Ethel Ross poked her head into the aisle. "Coffee or bra?"

Unlike Emma Smith, who turned her hearing aid up so she'd be sure to catch every word, Ethel tended to turn her hearing aid off, too content with her own little world to worry much about what went on around her.

Her husband, John, dragged her back and discreetly explained about the cups.

"Really? Why, John, you never told me about *that!*" Ethel often, and unintentionally, compensated for her hearing loss by talking louder. "Will you show me some time?"

Again a whispered explanation. Ethel giggled, cuddling up against him. "Well, that's all right, then. As long as you don't forget!"

Fifty years of marriage, yet the two of them still billed and cooed like newly weds. Stan wasn't sure whether that was a good advertisement for marriage, or a warning to all sensible males to beware before rushing to shove their heads through the noose.

"That Packers game was fine," said the colonel, strolling back from the front of the bus where he'd been talking strategy with his daughter. "But I've always wondered what in hell got into you in that game against the Jets in '98. Three interceptions, two fumbles, both recovered by the Jets, once for a touchdown. Worst passing average of your whole career. And you can't tell me that broken finger was the only reason!"

The colonel had never been one to tolerate slipshod work. He'd retired from the Marines years ago, but somehow never lost the conviction that what the world needed was a little more discipline and a lot higher performance standards.

"I lost twenty dollars betting on that game," Emma called from the front of the bus.

Stan gaped. Emma Smith bet on *football?*

"Well?" barked the colonel. The man was in his seventies, but he was still so big and broad he filled the aisle. Judging from the muscles in those arms, he could bench-press two-fifty, maybe three hundred, easy.

He would have made a good offensive lineman, Stan thought, then hastily straightened in his seat under the man's disapproving glare.

"It was a bad game," Stan admitted. "That happens sometimes, and nobody really knows why."

"*Somebody* should know," snapped the colonel.

"Now, Colonel," said Dr. Maggie—or maybe it was Dr. Meg. She placed her hand on his arm and smiled demurely up at him.

The colonel actually blushed.

"You shouldn't be so hard on the boy," said Dr. Meg—or maybe it was Dr. Maggie. "I'm sure he did his best. Most men do, you know, even if they do come up a little short sometimes."

Stan watched, fascinated, as the red on the colonel's face deepened to a rich magenta.

Stan blinked and wondered if he was really seeing what he thought he was seeing. On the other side of the aisle, Morey snickered, then covered the sound with a fake cough. Dana still had her head bent over her work, but Stan could see her smile despite the curtain of gold that hid her face.

"Hrumph," said the colonel. "Humph!" He glanced at the ladies batting their eyes at him from either side of the aisle, swallowed, then executed a smart about-face and retreated up the aisle at double time.

The twins looked at each other and giggled. The one on the left— Stan was almost positive it was Dr. Maggie—slid out of her seat and set off after him. There was a determined set to her narrow shoulders that didn't bode well for the colonel's peace of mind.

"Those two *gotta* do something about their hair," said Maudeen. She was standing in the aisle behind them, hands propped on her hips, staring disapprovingly at Dr. Maggie's carefully marcelled pink hair. Her own bright purple hair seemed to glow in the overhead lights of the bus. "I keep telling 'em and telling 'em, but they never listen."

She glanced at Dana and her eyes lit up. "Now, you, honey—*you* I could do something with! How about a blue streak, say, starting at the top and working all the way down to the end? Or maybe three streaks, red, white, and blue? I could braid it special, if you like, maybe even tie in some little silver bells for Christmas?" she added hopefully.

Dana laughed and shook her head, making all that silk shimmer.

"I wouldn't have the nerve."

Maudeen sighed. "I didn't think so, but if you ever change your mind . . . "

"You'll be the first person I call," Dana assured her.

How come she never smiles at me *like that?* Stan wondered. He'd finished cleaning the last two dolls but hadn't put them in the bag. With his luck, if Maudeen knew he was done she'd bring him two dozen more. He'd had about all the naked Barbies he could take for one day.

It wouldn't have been so bad if he could have had a little naked Dana, too, but that didn't look any too likely. How did you make love to an icicle?

Fortunately, Maudeen had other plans. "Morey? I got some work for you."

Morey the perpetual optimist ran his hands over his hair to make sure everything was slicked into place, snapped his suspenders for good luck, then meekly followed her to the back of the bus where Reba and Callie were deep in discussion on something or other. Slick and JD were lurking two rows farther back trying to look as if they were watching the scenery and not the women, but any fool could see what—or, rather, *who*—really had their attention.

Stan sighed and slumped back in his seat. The only good thing about the whole damn mess was that Slick and JD didn't seem to be doing any better than he was. When it came to women, their pass completion stats were as deep in the toilet as his.

Slick, usually the smoothest guy in the lower forty-eight states, had been following Reba around like a love-sick puppy. The sexy star of the Blue Angels didn't look like the kind of guy who flew supersonic jets for a living. He looked . . . pathetic. Handsome, but pathetic.

Occasionally Reba took pity on him and patted him on the head when she walked down the aisle, but she was so busy keeping this Santa Brigade organized that half the time it seemed she didn't even know he existed. Or didn't want to know, which came to the same thing.

If it hadn't been for the occasional gleam Stan had seen in her eye when she looked at Slick—always when she thought Slick wasn't looking—he might have wondered if the world had turned upside down. Reba had been crazy about Slick when they were kids.

Unlike Dana, Stan thought morosely, who was not crazy about him at all.

Because he couldn't help himself, he glanced over at her. She didn't look up from her work—mending doll's underpants, he couldn't help noting.

Stan grimaced. The way things were going, the only underwear he was going to see in the next few days was his and a bunch of recycled Barbies' and Baby Snookums'.

JD wasn't doing any better. Half the time he was quarreling with Callie, the other half he was scowling at her, which meant he had it bad, poor bastard. So bad, he hadn't worked up the nerve to make a pass even though he and Callie were sharing a hotel room.

He could be sure about that, Stan thought glumly, because JD was still in possession of all his eyes, ears, and other essential body parts. If he'd tried to step out of line, that little firebrand he'd kidnapped would have done some serious damage even if she was half JD's size.

Dana, on the other hand, probably wouldn't have to resort to physical violence to defend her virtue. She could freeze him and all his essential body parts just by looking at him.

Only a besotted fool would risk it.

With sudden decision, Stan tossed the two remaining Barbies into the bag with the rest of them, then awkwardly shoved to his feet. He didn't need his cane to get across the aisle or to plop down into the seat Morey had vacated a couple of minutes earlier.

Dana looked up with surprise and a little thrill of terror as Stan settled into the seat beside her.

She'd been wanting him to do just that, of course, which is why she hadn't set her sewing there the minute Morey had walked away. The last time she'd set it there, she'd instantly regretted it, but she hadn't been able to figure out a way to retrieve her error without making it look as though she were throwing herself at him.

He cleared his throat and leaned toward her. "How's the sewing coming?"

"Fine."

"Need some help?"

She hesitated. "No. Thank you," she added a moment later, almost as an afterthought. Being this close to him did something to her brain and all those body functions she'd always taken for granted, like breathing and keeping her heart beating.

He leaned closer still. Was that aftershave, or men's cologne? The spicy, subtle scent of him teased her senses and made her want to lean into him and breathe deep. Real deep.

Which would make him notice her chest, which would be a good thing since he didn't seem to be noticing her at all. Well, not much, anyway. She'd seen him glance over at her a few times these past couple of hours, but he generally seemed to be scowling when he did, which was unsettling. Safe, but unsettling.

Still, she really wished he'd notice her chest.

It was the only thing about her men ever paid attention to. They took one look at her long, skinny body and her funny, round face, and her long, long, straight-as-string hair, and then they never bothered looking again because all they stared at was her chest.

As far as she could tell, Stan hadn't noticed much of anything at all. Or maybe he was always this grumpy. Maybe it was just the pain of his shoulder and leg. That would be enough to make anyone grumpy, especially if the injuries had cost them their career and their future. But that didn't stop her from wishing that he'd pay just a little bit more attention to her, and that she hadn't blockaded the seat like she had because then he would have sat down beside her a long time ago.

Dana frowned at the ruffly pair of pantaloons in her hands. If he'd sat down beside her earlier, then he'd have discovered just how dull and uninteresting a person she was all that much sooner, and he'd have forgotten about her chest because he was bored with all the rest, and then—

"Was it something I said?"

His question brought her head up with a snap.

He had the most beautiful eyes—that clear, clear green with short, thick, dark-brown lashes and—

"Something you said?" she said, dragging her attention back to the conversation.

"Or do you just not like football players?"

She could feel her cheeks start to heat. "I don't understand."

He reached out a hand and tucked her hair behind her ear and she stopped breathing again.

"I just wondered—"

She didn't get a chance to find out what because at that moment the bus rounded a curve and came to a sudden, heart-stopping, sliding halt.

Stan threw out his hand to keep her from falling forward. Her breasts smashed into his arm before she got a hand out to brace herself against the seat in front of her. At the impact, he gave a little grunt of pain and let his arm drop.

"You okay?" she said, torn between worry for him and the unsettling, slightly breathless feeling that that brief, violent contact had started in her.

"Yeah," he said, grimacing and rubbing his shoulder. "You?"

"Fine. Thanks." Because she was afraid she wouldn't be able to resist rubbing his shoulder, too, she angled up out of her seat to see what was going on ahead. "What happened?"

"I don't know, but it looks like we're going to find out."

The cries of alarm and babble of exclamations swirling around them was almost buried under the sound of everyone rushing to the front of the bus to see what was going on.

"Snow slide!" someone called cheerfully from up front. "It's blocked the road."

The babble got louder. Nothing like a disaster to brighten everyone's day.

Through it all, Dana could hear the colonel barking orders and Reba's calm, confident voice bringing order to the confusion. Which wasn't surprising, since the only thing that seemed to fluster her, as far as Dana could tell, was the extraordinarily handsome Navy pilot who followed her around like a dog on a leash.

"Are you going to get up?" Dana asked when Stan didn't move.

"In a minute." His gaze was fixed on her with an intensity that took her breath away.

With everyone at the front of the bus, crowding each other in their hurry to get off and inspect the snow slide, Dana had the oddest feeling that they were suddenly alone. *Really* alone, just the two of them and this sudden heat between them that couldn't be her imagination only.

"I—I think we'd better go see if they need any help," Dana said. She was having a hard time getting the words out because her brain didn't seem to be able to think about anything except how close he was and that spicy aftershave and how inviting his mouth looked and—

"You are so beautiful."

He said it so low that for a minute she wasn't sure she'd really heard it, and then she couldn't hear anything except a roaring in her ears because he'd closed the gap between them and kissed her.

It wasn't a hot kiss. Well, not too hot. Still this side of blistering, anyway. And it didn't really last that long. A year or so, maybe. Just long enough for her lungs to start screaming for air and her pulse rate to rocket to dangerous levels, but that was okay because her brain had stopped working while the rest of her body started screaming for more and in the resultant confusion she couldn't do anything but moan and lean into him and wordlessly ask for more.

She wasn't sure which of them broke off first. They were both flushed and breathing hard, even though nothing except their lips had touched.

The kiss had surprised her, but the stunned look on Stan's face confused her completely. She wasn't much of a kisser, of course, and he couldn't have expected much, but it definitely wasn't disappointment that had him looking so flustered. And that flustered her, because she wanted to think it might be because he'd really *liked* kissing her, which was stupid and ridiculous . . . and . . . wonderful.

Even though she knew she shouldn't, that it was dangerous to give him an inch, she could feel the ice she'd set between them beginning to thaw.

"Uh," he said, and took a deep breath, then licked his lips nervously. "Maybe we'd better go see what's going on out there."

That was definitely the safer thing to do, but for a moment, there, she didn't want to try safe at all.

And then he grinned and she'd swear the sun came out even if the rest of the world thought it was still hiding behind thick gray snow clouds.

He was awkward getting out of the seat, but he wasn't at all awkward when he grabbed her coat off the overhead rack and held it while she slipped her arms in the sleeves. And this time when he followed her down the aisle, she could still hear the way his cane knocked against the seats, but all she could think about was the way his lips felt when they were pressed against hers.

The icy air and the falling snow were welcomingly chilly against her hot cheeks when she stepped off the bus. Fortunately, no one seemed to notice they were late joining the party. Everyone's attention was fixed on the mountain of snow that had slid off the steep hillside, burying the road under a ton of white that was going to take a *big* snowplow to move.

Betty Morgan, NASCAR racer and bus driver extraordinaire, was already lining up the plows. While the Brigade poked at the snow and exclaimed and fretted over whether they'd make their next show in time, Betty was on her cell phone calling in favors. Dana could hear her clearly, even over the chatter.

"Joe? Betty Morgan here. How ya' doin'? . . . Good, good. Listen,

I got a problem here . . . Yeah, I know the roads are closed. That's why I need your help."

"Maxie? Hi! Betty Morgan here. How are you and the family? No kidding? Six, already! That's great! Hey, I need some help . . . "

She'd hardly hung up on the last call when a monster truck with a huge snow plow on the front came roaring up the road behind them. The driver, a beefy, bald-headed guy named Frank who sported an eagle tattooed on his forehead, climbed down from the cab, readjusted his substantial beer belly, and strolled over to inspect the problem.

"Got yourself a little problem, here, Betty," he said after a moment's judicious consideration.

"That's why I called you," said Betty, beaming up at him. "Joe's bringing his backhoe and Red Dog's coming with his plow, but I knew we couldn't do it without you."

Dana, Stan, Reba, Slick, Callie, and JD watched with interest from a safe spot to the side and out of the wind.

"He's blushing," said Stan with awe. "That guy is actually blushing."

"Probably one of her old boyfriends," Reba said. "Betty's had more offers of marriage than any woman I've ever met."

"Bad-Ass Betty?" said Stan and Slick and JD in disbelieving chorus.

Dana could feel herself stiffening instinctively, even though she knew it wasn't directed at her.

"You're kidding." Slick watched the wiry little woman herd the Brigade out of the way so Frank could bring his truck up. "That lady's as tough as they come and—what?"

Reba poked him in the chest again. "You think just because women are intelligent and strong and capable that they're not desirable, too? Is that what you think?"

"No! Hey, did I say that?" Slick protested, backing up a step, hands up, palms out in surrender. "I didn't say that."

"That's what you meant. I'm not dumb, you know."

"Don't say it," Callie added, glaring at JD with a dangerously martial light in her eye. "Don't even think it."

"What the hell? What'd I do?" said JD, looking hurt. "I didn't say anything."

"You were thinking it. I could tell. And don't *you* say anything, either!" she added, turning on Stan.

Stan was twice her size, but he just stood there, staring down at her and blinking a little like a bewildered sheep.

Dana didn't know whether to feel sorry for the three guys or grateful for Reba's and Callie's defense of Betty. They didn't know it, but she felt as if they were defending her, too. She'd never had a lot of boyfriends and she'd never had even one offer of marriage, but she knew what it was like to be considered unfeminine and undesirable. It hurt, that's how it felt.

Maybe if she'd been more like Reba and Callie, pretty and confident and utterly sure of herself, it would have been different. But she wasn't and never had been. Both of them would have known what to do if JD or Slick kissed them as Stan had kissed her, and neither of them would be walking around ten minutes later still dizzy and trembling and elated and scared like she was.

The arrival of Joe on his backhoe, immediately followed by Red Dog and his plow broke up the group. Reba, with Slick trailing in her wake indignantly trying to explain, went off to make sure all the Brigade members were warmly bundled against the snow. Callie and JD stalked off in the other direction, still arguing.

"Whew!" said Stan. "Women!"

"What do you mean, *women*?" Dana demanded. Reba and Callie's example made her feel just a little bit bold.

"See! Now you're doing it, too! A fellow doesn't stand a chance when you guys gang up on him."

Dana could have cheered when Maxie roared in right then with a car full of kids and the biggest thermos of hot coffee she had ever seen.

"I'd better go see if I can help," she said, grateful for the excuse to flee. It was easier and a whole lot safer than staying to argue.

Stan just stood there watching her walk away without saying a word.

Slick and JD, she thought sadly, had at least cared enough to chase after Reba and Callie so they could keep on arguing.

Maxie turned out to be a cheerful redhead who had happily abandoned her little eatery when Betty called.

"Brought donuts, too," she said, whipping out a folding table and setting up a coffee bar right there in the middle of the road.

The Brigade flocked to her like pigeons to a peanut vendor, arguing over who got the Boston cremes and who got the chocolate frosted as they cheerfully fixed cups of steaming coffee for Betty and the men clearing the road.

Betty was too busy supervising the snow removal to notice.

"Isn't she great?" said the colonel, almost bursting with fatherly pride as he watched his daughter shout orders.

"She's incredible," said Dana with sincerity. "More coffee, Colonel?"

"Don't mind if I do." The colonel beamed, holding out his cup.

"We have to talk."

Dana jumped at the feel of Stan's warm breath on her ear. "I can't. I—"

"Now!" said Stan, passing the colonel his cup, then grabbing her hand and pulling her away from table.

One look at his face convinced her to stop arguing and go along, even if her heart was suddenly threatening to pound its way out of her chest.

They were almost to the bus and safely out of sight of the others when he slipped on the icy road.

Without thinking, Dana grabbed him, wrapping her free hand around him and bracing her body to prop him up. She was strong and fit, but he was a big man. If he hadn't let go her other hand so he could grab her shoulder and she could wrap him in a bear hug, they would both have gone tumbling.

"You all right?" she said, when she was sure he wasn't going to slip again.

"Yes, damn it," he snarled, "I'm all right."

She tried to move away from him, but he tightened his hold on her shoulder and dragged her back. This close, the heat of him and the scent of that after shave made her dizzy.

She didn't like dizzy.

"You wouldn't be slipping if you'd worn more sensible shoes," she said.

His shoulders went rigid.

"I suppose, living in San Diego like you do, there's not much need for good walking shoes."

"I can't wear anything else." The words came out sounding strained, as if he'd forced them past throat muscles that were strung too tight.

Embarrassment flooded her. Given the damage to his hip and leg, she should have thought of that. So much for being mature and confident.

Evidently mistaking her silence for incomprehension, he added, "I can't bend too easily these days. Pulling on a pair of socks can take me ten minutes, so loafers . . . " He shrugged, as if it didn't matter. She knew it did. "I can't use anything with a sole that grips, either. My left leg drags a bit, and rubber soles catch too easily."

"Oh," she said.

And then, through her embarrassment, she realized that his arm was still around her shoulder and she was still pressed tight against him.

"I guess you can stand on your own now, then," she said, and tried to pull free.

He wouldn't let her.

She looked up, startled, and found him staring down at her with an odd, dangerous little glint in his eyes. There seemed to be a bit of a harder line around his jaw, too, as if he'd made up his mind to something and he was determined to follow through, come hell or high water.

"Stan?" she said. Her chest felt tight. For lack of air, no doubt, because she was having a hard time breathing . . . again.

"Dana," he said, and then he lowered his head, and kissed her . . . again. And this time he really put some heat in it.

CHAPTER SEVEN

SAM

Early Wednesday afternoon, two days 'til Christmas Eve.

"Who'd have ever thought that a homeless shelter could be so . . . happy?"

"Happy?" Reba laughed at Sam's observation.

God, he loved the way she laughed . . . soft and sexy. He wished she'd do it more often. But she hardly ever did . . . *around him.*

What would she do if I leaned forward and planted a big one, right on her laughing mouth?

Hit me over the head with her Santa sack, he answered with a laugh of his own.

And—*my, oh, my*—after getting a brief glimpse yesterday of Reba's new and improved shape—not that her old one hadn't been pleasing to him—he would really, really like to check out the changes some more. Up close. Sans Santa suit. Hell, sans underwear, too.

"Why are you grinning?"

"Am I grinning?"

She shook her head at him. "I'm not sure I'd go so far as to describe this place as happy," Reba went on, even as she unconsciously hitched up her Santa belly, which kept slipping under the wide belt. His, on the other hand, stayed in place because he'd had the foresight to employ a little of modern man's miracle tool . . . duct tape. It was amazing what they carried on that freakin' bus.

He and Reba, both dressed in St. Nick attire, were leaning against the wall, sipping at paper cups of coffee. They were taking a break from the Santa Brigade's entertainment program at the Good Samaritan Refuge in Littleton, New Hampshire. In the short silence between them, he soaked in the whole raucous scene before them. Strings of blinking lights and holly decorated practically every wall of the huge assembly room. There were artificial trees placed in each of the four corners, and an enormous fresh-cut fir tree—at least twenty feet tall—in the center. All bore homemade ornaments and strings of popcorn and holly berries. Christmas music played in the background. Refreshment tables practically sagged with the amount of donated food and sweet treats.

"Oh, yeah, this is happy," he said, as much to Reba as to himself. "Believe me, I've seen more than a few charity shelters in my younger days, and most of them reeked with sadness, bigtime. As I recall, they reeked, period. I don't think I'll ever forget the odors . . . canned soup, sour milk, stale booze, and . . . despair."

Actually, his experiences had been more with flophouses . . . places he and his mother landed in occasionally when the drugs ran out and they were, literally, down and out. In sharp contrast, there was an air of hope here at Sammy's, as Good Samaritan was called, thanks to the tireless efforts of its director, Jane Justiss, and her troop of volunteers.

His early childhood had always been a taboo subject even with the best of friends. Reba looked as if she'd like to grill him about the background he'd revealed with that careless comment about younger days. Instead, she said, "They try hard to achieve that effect. So, maybe you're right. And, if only a few people come away a little happier . . . well, that's the point, isn't it?" A pensive expression crossed her face before she put a hand on his forearm. "It never occurred to me, when Emma commandeered you into helping out, that homeless shelters might bring back bad memories. You don't have to do this, Sam."

"Yeah, I do. You can say lots of things about me, but I always pull my own weight."

"Well, it's appreciated. No one expected so many people to show up. We need all the help we can get."

He nodded, gazing about at the large number of people who swarmed around the converted lumber mill . . . at least a hundred, not including the workers and the Santa Brigade. Not all of them were residents of the facility. Some were poor families who had their own homes, but were in need of Christmas gifts for their children. An alarming number were individuals wanting a hot meal and a dash of holiday cheer.

Suddenly, he thought of something. "The Brigade is going to run out of its stash of gifts even quicker than anticipated, isn't it?"

Reba nodded, nibbling her bottom lip with worry. Geez, he hated it when she did that. He wanted to be the one nibbling her bottom lip. "And we still have three more shelter stops to make, tonight and tomorrow, before heading home to Snowdon."

"If transportation weren't a problem, I could call some of my buddies in the Blues. There are only six Blue Angels in any one squadron, but eighty back-up personnel. And lots of formers. They'd gather whatever you need in no time, but I doubt whether they could fly in anything with weather conditions as they are."

"I know. The same is true of our Brigade angels, those people and businesses who can always be relied on in a pinch. Maudeen's in one of the back rooms on her computer right now, seeing what she can drum up." She shrugged. "It'll work out. It always does."

"Like how Callie is whipping out designer fashions for those Skid Row Barbies."

Reba tsk-ed at his calling the dolls by the nickname that JD had coined when first spying the dolls in tattered attire in a refuse box in the back of the bus, but she had to agree. They both glanced across the room where a Callie/Santa was doing just that with scraps of material and yarn she'd found about the bus—a far cry from her high-fashion designer business. Callie had enlisted some of the homeless shelter women to help her. In fact, with all she was teaching them, some of the women were talking about making the custom Barbie outfits after Christmas, as a year-round, moneymaking enterprise.

Dana, also a Santa, sat a short distance away, showing another group of women how to do needlepoint. Sam didn't know much about sewing crafts, but she appeared to be as skilled as Callie, in her own way, although it was just a hobby for her. While Dana stitched, she told Indian folk tales to some of the young people, interspersing her stories with actual anecdotes of things that had happened to her in the woods as a forest ranger. As an avid environmentalist, she gave great credence to the practices of Native Americans who had cherished the land, just as she did. Dana had a calming voice and a soothing demeanor, not to mention a sensational figure. He could see why Stan was attracted to her.

Meanwhile, JD, also in Santa costume, was sticking close to Callie—his prisoner, so to speak. The big bad bounty hunter— biting his tongue with concentration—was sitting on the floor at her feet, rolling skeins of red yarn into a ball the size of a basketball. JD had just completed his talent program . . . a wildly popular card trick event that had had kids alternately slack-jawed with incredulity, then rolling on the floor with laughter.

"Between Callie and Dana, we're going to have a nice supply of dolls and embroidered pillows for the remaining shelters. But we need so much more to fill our inventory. Christmas candy. Items of clothing, especially socks and gloves. Baby items. Toys for boys." She grinned at him. "More Chia pets."

Sam groaned. At one time—probably in the middle of the night when he couldn't sleep and was watching a really educational program, like an infomercial—he would have sworn there had to be a special place in hell for the manufacturer of those ludicrous plant containers. But the shelter residents seemed to love them. *Go figure!*

"It's your turn, Mr. Merrick," a cheery voice said.

He and Reba turned to see Jane motioning him to come toward the center of the room where a group of kids, and adults, too, were gathering to hear his part of the entertainment program.

"Oh, swell!" he muttered under his breath.

"You'll do fine, Sam," Reba encouraged with a squeeze of his arm. Hey, had her hand been there all the time? And he hadn't taken advantage of it? He must be slipping.

"I don't suppose you want to give me a bit of motivation?"

"What? You want me to come with you?"

"Well, that's not quite what I had in mind." He pulled a straggly bit of mistletoe out of his pocket and held it over her head. "Merry Christmas, honey."

"Saaaammmm," she chided, but she didn't seem mad, or overly annoyed, which he took for a green light.

He leaned forward and pressed his lips lightly against hers, Santa beard against Santa beard. She tasted of coffee and Christmas and everything wonderful that Sam had missed all these years, without even realizing what a hole there was in his life. Perhaps being burnt by the flame wouldn't be such a bad thing.

It was a fleeting kiss, barely a whisper of a caress, but both of them stared at each other, unable to break eye contact. Reba was equally affected by the kiss, he could see that.

What would it be like to make love if just a kiss ignites a flame between us?

We'd probably set each other afire, that's what.

Holy smoke! Doesn't that pose some interesting possibilities? I can't wait.

"Dawdling again, Mr. Merrick?"

He and Reba jumped apart, although they hadn't been all that close. It was Emma Smith, of course, with clipboard in hand. And—

Lordy, Lordy—she was one big Santa . . . the frowningest one he'd ever seen. If anyone could whip a team of reindeer together, or a Santa Brigade, it was this woman.

"I'm on my way, Mrs. Smith."

He grabbed Reba's hand, taking her up on her offer to accompany him. He couldn't believe he was going to entertain a bunch of kids. They passed Stan on the way, encircled by a group of young boys who were obviously entranced by his instructions on the correct way to hold a football and pass the bomb for a sure touchdown. Stan was a gifted teacher, that was clear, though he might not be aware of the talent. Sam, on the other hand, had no such delusions about his gifts. He could fly jets, yeah, and he'd been told he could charm the hair off a hog. Those were the only things he had going for him.

Instinctively, he squeezed Reba's hand, seeking reassurance. "Ouch," she said.

He loosened his grip, but still held on. No way was he letting her go.

"Maybe I should go over and help Morey and Bob set up for their dance program."

"Uh-uh!"

She arched an eyebrow at him.

"If I'm going to make a fool of myself," he said. "I want company."

Reba had no right to be so proud of Sam, but she was.

She'd sensed his nervousness about participating in a solo Santa Brigade event, but he had no need to worry. His natural charisma came through, no matter what he did . . . always making eye contact with the people he addressed . . . always making them feel, each and every one, as if they were important to him. He'd said yesterday that he wasn't sure what to do with his future, career-wise. Well, she for one believed that he had unlimited opportunities if he channeled that charm.

Sam was perched on a high stool with bunches of young people scattered on the floor around him in a wide half-circle. Stan's demonstration had ended, and he and his group had ambled over, too. J.D. was there, as well, apparently chastised by Callie for having made such a big yarn ball. There were also some parents in the audience, shelter volunteers, and a few young women, attracted by the good-looking man and not necessarily the talk.

He'd removed his Santa outfit, contending his program would have more authenticity that way. He was right. But did he have to look so drop-dead gorgeous in a uniform?

Using only a Blue Angels brochure he'd pulled from his duffel bag and a cardboard model airplane he'd put together from a kit he'd found on the bus, Sam talked informally about airplanes, their parts, how they worked, modern technology, and how he'd first become interested in flying. It could have been boring, but it wasn't. Sam interspersed his narration with self-deprecating humor and interesting stories, especially relating to stunts performed by the Blue Angels . . . Barrel Rolls, Loops, Splits, High Alphas. He also peppered his talk with smiles, and when Sam Merrick smiled, the world tilted on its axis. At least, Reba's did.

"He is some kind of hunk," Jane remarked to her.

Apparently, Reba's world wasn't the only one being rocked by Sam. She hadn't realized that the shelter director was standing next to her. This was the third year that they'd stopped at Sammy's; so she knew her fairly well. "Yep. *Hunk* about says it all."

"Is he yours?"

"Huh?" Reba studied Jane, normally a ball of energy around the shelter, to see where that question had come from. No more than thirty years old, she was an attractive, no-nonsense woman with plain clothes and a clear vision of life. She was also red-faced, but unabashedly interested. "No, Sam doesn't belong to me." *Darn it!*

No, no, no! Not "darn it." I meant, "Thank goodness."

"Are you sure about that?"

"Absolutely." *Oh, all right. I do mean, "Darn it."* "Why do you ask?"

"The way you two look at each other, it's as if you're the only two people in the universe."

Pleasure rippled through Reba, despite herself.

"And sometimes when you're not looking, he stares at you with what can only be described as . . . well, hunger."

Oh, good heavens! The ripples turned to waves. Hot waves. "Of course, you look at him the same way."

Do not!

"Do ya hafta be rich to become a pilot?" a little boy in front of them asked, thus jarring Reba back to Sam's presentation. *Thank goodness!* The half-pint wore a faded plaid shirt rolled up at the cuffs, jeans rolled up at the hems—both probably courtesy of Goodwill— and red basketball shoes with lots of holes in them. His black hair was slicked back wetly . . . obviously from a recent bath for this special Christmas event.

"That's Richie Taylor. A sad case. He's nine years old. His mother's a cocaine addict. They live here most of the time," Jane whispered in Reba's ear. "God only knows where they live the rest of the time."

Reba's heart about broke when she gazed at the boy. He, and children like him, were the reason the Santa Brigade worked so tirelessly. Their piddly gifts probably didn't make that much difference in the scheme of things, but if all they showed was that someone cared . . . well, that was enough, she supposed.

Sam shook his head. "I was an orphan. If being a pilot . . . or a Blue Angel . . . called for money, I never would have made it. Nope, I got a scholarship to the Naval Academy. That's where I first learned to fly."

The little boy didn't seem heartened by that news. He raised his hand again. "Betcha have to be super smart, then."

Sam laughed. "Nope, again. You don't have to be super smart, but you do have to work hard."

Another child . . . a girl this time, wearing long blonde pigtails and minus two front teeth . . . asked, "Can girls be pilots, too?"

"Of course," Sam said, "but only if they're as pretty as you are." The little girl beamed.

Someone else was waving a hand wildly. It was the Stan Santa. "Do ya get lots of girls, wearing a fancy uniform and all? Do the females, like, fall at your feet? Huh? Huh? Huh?"

Sam flashed another of his rock-your-world smiles and pretended to visually search the floor at the base of his stool for piles of babes. "To tell the truth, *sir*," he told Stan, "most of the fallen women get taken by celebrity sports heroes. Pilots and lesser beings get the leftovers."

Everyone craned their necks to gape at Stan at the back of the circle, some of them even examining his feet to see if there was perhaps a fallen woman or two. Stan had the grace to blush and raise a two-fingered salute to Sam in a "checkmate" fashion.

Lots of other questions followed, many involving pilot training, the kinds of planes he'd flown, where he'd traveled, but mostly regarding the intricate, dangerous aerobatics he performed in supersonic jets.

"Actually, we've been trained so well that many of the maneuvers are routine to us. Doesn't matter if I'm doing triple loops. Doesn't matter if I'm flying jets, upside down, at five hundred miles a minute. Doesn't matter if my fellow Blues are flying jets which are really only an arm's length from mine. None of these stunts seem any more dangerous to me than driving down a highway in a car."

"Could someone become a pilot if they . . . uh . . . didn't go ta school everyday? Uhm . . . uh . . . like maybe they had ta stay home sometimes and . . . you know . . . take care of . . . uh . . . someone." It was Richie again, and the boy's eyes darted with concern, that he'd said too much, across the room to where an extremely thin, limp-haired woman in denim coveralls leaned against a wall, her eyes bloodshot, her hands trembling with the need for a fix. Richie's mother. She was probably twenty-five but looked no more than fifteen, malnourished as she was. Shit! Fifteen was probably the age when she'd become pregnant with the boy.

Sam's gaze, like Reba's, had made the connection with the young woman. Except that his expression was horrified, then angry, for a brief moment before he masked it over. Reba knew that he'd made a connection between Richie's background and his own.

"Son," he said, after gulping several times, "you can do anything you want in life. Anything. If you can't make it to school everyday . . . big deal! Study at home. If you don't have the money for books, find a library. And ask an adult for help, if you need to. There are lots of people out there who are dying to help a bright kid like you."

The kid brightened on being referred to as bright.

"And, remember, no matter how bad things are around you, you can rise above it. I did."

Jane started to applaud, and everyone joined in.

Sam seemed stunned. He hadn't realized that he was done. He glowered at Reba, as if to say, "See what you got me into?"

Then, he stood and walked resolutely away, nodding and shaking hands as he wended his way through the crowd. One thing she noticed. Distracted and anxious to get away as he obviously was, he took the time to hand the Blue Angels brochure to Richie and patted his head as he passed by.

It took twenty minutes for Reba to find him. He should have known she'd follow him. As much as he adored her, she could be a real pest sometimes.

If I'd asked her to come with me, she'd have probably refused, but when I want to be alone, she suddenly becomes my shadow. Jeesh! Doesn't she know there are times when a guy needs to lick his wounds in private?

"Sam, are you in there?"

Yep, a pest.

Noticing that he was, indeed, inside the storage room, she closed the door firmly behind her, not even asking if she could come in. *Pest, pest, pest!* "You left in such a hurry, JD and Stan were worried about you . . . I was worried about you."

JD and Stan always worry about me. We worry about each other. Big deal! If I stubbed my big toe, they'd be on me like regular Floyd Nightengales.

Because there were no chairs, he was sitting on a long oak table, where they probably sorted groceries. His legs dangled down to the floor. On both walls, he was surrounded by industrial sized cans of everything from catsup to chocolate pudding. There was a whole ten-foot shelf for toilet tissue alone . . . enough for a small army.

"I'll be out in a few minutes. Go away, Reba."

Did she listen to him? No. Just like always, she had a mind of her own. Coming closer, she questioned, "What's the matter? Why are you hiding out in here?"

"I'm not hiding. Go away, Reba."

She made a small sound of skepticism. "Meditating then?"

"Don't be a smart mouth." He sighed deeply. Reba clearly wasn't going to go away without an explanation. "Look, if I'd stayed out there, I probably would have strangled that woman."

Reba didn't even bother to ask who he was referring to. She knew. The little boy's mother. "You can't blame her for—"

"Can't blame her? I sure can blame her, and I do. What the hell business does she have bringing a kid into the world if she doesn't plan to care for it? She doesn't give a damn about that boy. All she cares about is sucking more shit up her nose . . . or pumping it into her veins."

"Jane told me that Richie . . . that's the boy's name . . . is permitted to stay at the shelter anytime, but addicts are not allowed in unless they're clean. His mother is trying. She's been clean for several weeks."

"Weeks!" Sam scoffed.

"Sam, addiction's an illness."

"Bull!"

"You have no right to say she doesn't love her son."

"Yes, I do. I have every right. If she loved that boy, she would give up the drugs. The child should be more precious to her than the high."

Reba shimmied her fat Santa behind up onto the table beside him. Apparently, she was planning to stay. The word *pest* came to mind.

"Sam, I worked with some drug addicts when I was in practice. I can't begin to understand how it would feel to have a druggie for a Mom, but I do know this . . . drug addiction is a sickness that supplants everything else in a person's life . . . even family ties. It's not an excuse, but an explanation." On and on she went trying to convince him he was wrong.

The explanations were logical, but it was hard to take them seriously when they came from a Santa Claus. Still, he found himself listening. In the end, he wasn't convinced. "People like that should be put in jail."

"Or forced to go into rehab programs," she argued, taking his hand in hers—a first since he'd met up with her two days ago—and twining her fingers with his. "I'll tell you one thing. Your mother must have loved you a great deal."

So that's why she'd taken his hand? So he couldn't escape her clutches. He tugged, anyhow. But she was determined to tell him something he just knew he wasn't going to like. Dangerous territory Reba treaded here. If she was a man, he'd probably punch her in the nose for the nerve. He restrained himself, barely. "I . . . don't . . . want . . . to . . . hear . . . this."

"Well, you're going to hear it. Think about it, Sam. Your mother knew her habit was out of control. Did she o.d. on the street, uncaring of your welfare? Did she sell you to some pimp for drug money? Did she walk off and leave you to fend for yourself? No, she took you to the safest place she knew . . . a police station . . . and asked them to find a home for you. I can't imagine how that tore her heart out. What greater love could she have shown for you than to give you up?"

What greater love could she have shown for you than to give you up? The words repeated themselves over and over in Sam's head. *Impossible! They couldn't be true. Could they?*

"Don't you have any good memories of your mother?" Reba persisted.

He squeezed his eyes shut tight, trying not to hear, trying not to remember his mother in the earlier non-drug days. "Laughing. She used to laugh a lot," he revealed before he had a chance to curb his tongue. "And jumping rope . . . I have a vivid mind picture of her jumping rope with me. She loved jelly beans and chili hot dogs and pink lipstick. And Saturday morning cartoons. How could I have forgotten those? The two of us . . . me only three or four . . . and she . . . hell, she must have been only seventeen or so . . . lying on a tattered sofa watching marathons of Scooby Doo and Bullwinkle and Roadrunner on that old black and white TV."

"My God, Sam! She must have been a kid herself. A teenager with a baby. And no husband or family to help her out.

There was a long silence between them before he spoke again. "Thank you," he said, squeezing Reba's hand.

She cocked her head to the side to see him better. "For what?"

"For making me see that *maybe* I've been wrong about my mother. Well, not wrong exactly . . . just not seeing the whole picture. I'm not saying I forgive her or anything like that. It's too soon. I might not ever be able to go that far. But you've given me some things to think about."

"That's a start," Reba said softly.

Now seemed like a good time to change the subject, in Sam's opinion. "You look sexy in that Santa outfit."

"I do not. I look silly." She ripped off her mustache, beard and hat. About a yard of silky gold strands billowed out in the process. "Oh, definitely sexy."

"You look pretty sexy yourself . . . in that uniform."

"You think?" He smiled. Man, she had to be the only woman in the world who could take him from depression to happiness in a matter of seconds. "That's what all the girls say."

"I'll bet they do."

"Reba, I've never been as promiscuous as everyone thought."

"I know."

Yep, now that he thought about it, Reba had never believed all the wild stories about him. She'd been like a pit bull to his rescue anytime accusations had been made. Always, she'd taken his side, without question. He wanted that pit bull back. He wanted Reba back.

Glancing down, he realized that they were still holding hands. It felt so very, very good, just sitting there with Reba in companionable silence. Like old times.

After a while, though, it wasn't enough.

"I've never made love with a Santa before," he said tentatively. He braced himself, in case Reba decided to bop him over the head with a five-pound can of stewed tomatoes.

Instead, a mischievous gleam entered her eyes . . . eyes which he suddenly noticed were smiling again. "Yes, you have, Sam. Remember the boat house at the point . . . and the picnic table at the beach . . . and the back seat of George's Oldsmobile and—"

He put the fingertips of his free hand to her lips for silence. To her he sent the silent message, *Remember? Oh, baby, every male cell in my body recalls those events in testosterone-screaming detail.* Then to himself he sent a different message entirely, *Slow down, buddy. Take it easy. Don't jump the gun. Just because she's being nice doesn't mean she wants to jump my bones. Does it?*

When he could finally speak above a gurgle, he said, "Reba, not only can I remember every single one of those times . . . twelve to be exact . . . but I can name times, places, colors, smells. Hell, I've been replaying them in my mind for fourteen years."

She waved her free hand in a halting fashion at his last words. "I don't want to talk about the past fourteen years. Not right now."

He nodded. "So, what does a female Santa wear under all that padding? Frederick's of the North Pole? Santa's Secret? Elfin Magic Bra?"

She looked him directly in the eye and said, "Nothing."

"Oh, geez! Oh, damn! Oh, man! Christmas is coming early this year . . . I think." He remained calm, on the outside, but his heart was racing a mile a minute.

She ignored his presumptuous remark. Instead, she came up with a presumptuous remark of her own. "So, what does a pilot wear under that fancy-pancy uniform?"

"Yep, Christmas has arrived, and I'm about to open my present . . . I think. That *is* what you're implying, isn't it?" On the other hand, who was it who said that assumption was the mother of all screw-ups? Was he making major leaps into Assumptionville?

"Well, that depends, Sam. What kind of boy have you been . . . what kind of *man* are you? Naughty or nice?"

He thought a moment, thanking the heavens that he hadn't assumed too much. "Definitely naughty."

"Bingo! Good answer," she said. "But back to my question. What *does* a hot-shot flyboy wear under that babe-magnet uniform?"

He smiled then. "Nothing, babe. Not a thing."

For several long moments, they just stared at each other.

Somehow . . . she didn't recall when or how . . . Sam had pushed himself off from the table. He stood in front of her now, close, between her outspread Santa legs.

And still they just gazed at each other.

Memories and long-suppressed emotions swirled between them, growing and growing, like a storm which churns and brews 'til it finally explodes in a rush of wind. Would they explode? Oh, surely they would, but it would be a good thing. A very good thing.

Sam put a hand to her cheek, almost with reverence, and whispered, "Reba."

She leaned into his hand and could have wept with all her feelings. There was so much she wanted to say, but only one word came out, "Sam." It was enough.

Reba acknowledged to herself that she'd crossed over some mental line in the sand within the past five minutes or so. But, no, that wasn't quite true. The line had been crossed gradually over the past two days, perhaps even when she'd first seen Sam skydiving down to her, but definitely when she'd heard him speak to the shelter audience and most particularly, young Richie.

The line did not represent love because Reba, even in her most angry moments, recognized that her love for Sam had never died. Instead, the line represented surrender . . . a giving up of herself to the fates . . . or God. A willingness to be carried along with what would be. Or maybe even what might *not* be.

"I am so sorry." Four words, but so powerful, coming from Sam's lips.

She nodded her acceptance of the apology and looped her arms about his neck. She didn't have to ask what he was sorry for. She knew best how much he had hurt her. But she was going to trust Sam, she decided then and there, as she always had long ago, but had regretfully stopped years ago. There was an explanation. She would hear it when the time was right.

She had things that needed to be said, too. Explanations. Bones to pick. But not now. Not now.

"I love you," she said.

He closed his eyes for a brief moment, overcome. She saw the effort he made to try swallowing. Then, he, too, said, "I love you." His blue eyes held hers as if trying to convince her of his sincerity. "I never stopped loving you, Reba. I never did. Never."

He spoke those last words against her mouth, even as he took hers in a hungry kiss. Sam could be a gentle lover, when he wanted, but he was beyond gentle now. He devoured her with kisses so deep and demanding, she could only open and go with the flow of his passion. A journey that already had her whimpering. It was too much, and not enough.

She ran her fingers through his short hair. She nibbled at his chin line. She spread her legs wider with a surging need to get closer to him, which was impossible with her Santa pillows.

Sam laughed softly and nipped at her upper lip with his teeth. "Reba, honey, I could be out of this uniform in two seconds flat, but how are we ever going to get you out of that damn Santa suit? And then back in it, to finish the brigade program?"

In between those two long sentences, Sam was doing incredible things to her ears, which he'd exposed by pushing her hair back off her face. Things involving the tip of his tongue and wetness and sexual simulation. *Oh . . . my . . . God!* She felt the effects of his tongue in her ear ripple to her breasts and between her legs.

But Sam had said something that called for a response. At least, she thought he had. *Oh. That's right. The Santa suit.*

"I guess we better wait," she said, "for a better time."

"I don't want to wait," he said and already, somehow, while her mind had been wandering . . . in the most delicious way . . . Sam had managed to open the front of her Santa jacket, revealing the pillow tied over her belly and her red lace Christmas bra. The pillow, which was belted around her waist, garnered a grunt of disgust, but the bra didn't disgust him, she could see that in the widening of his eyes and the slight hitch in his breathing.

"You lied," he noted in a grainy voice as he undid the front closure. When she spilled out before him, his slight hitch turned to a gasp.

She closed her eyes, suddenly shy before his perusal, embarrassed by the hardening of her nipples and the rhythmic pants which escaped her lips.

"Reba, you are so beautiful," he murmured, touching the tips of her breasts with his fingertips.

"No, you're the beautiful one," she said, or at least she thought she said it. She couldn't be sure because the erotic shock of his light caress caused her to arch her breasts forward and throw her head back. She wanted more. Much more.

And it appeared she was going to get it because, when she opened her eyes drowsily . . . drowsily was all she could manage since her lids drooped with heaviness . . . she saw that Sam hadn't been lying. He could, indeed, remove his uniform in two seconds flat. Well, at least down to the waist. His chest was bare, from wide shoulders down to the sinfully narrow, belted waistband of his slacks. And he was busy removing her pillows as well.

In no time at all, she felt the delicious sensation of his chest hairs brushing against her nipples. And she, in her Santa trousers, and he in his Uncle Sam trousers, found a way to fit his erection against her arousal. Not perfect, considering the fabric between them, but satisfactory. Oh, definitely satisfactory. Especially when Sam placed his hands on her behind and moved her forward so that she barely rested on the edge of the table and had to wrap her legs around his hips for balance.

"So sweet, so sweet," he said against her breast as he took one nipple, then another, between his lips and suckled hard.

She couldn't help herself. She bucked against him, trying to rub that engorged part of her against that engorged part of him. She must have succeeded because he moaned and took her breast harder and deeper.

Alternately, she mewled and whimpered, begging, "Please, please, please." She was coming, much too fast, much too soon. Which wasn't helped at all when he slipped a hand inside her Santa trousers, against her belly, under the waistband of her panties, where he found her wetness. He smiled . . . or tried to smile . . . through gritted teeth.

In her mortification at being aroused so pathetically soon, she tried to shimmy back on the table, away from him.

He allowed it, but only for a second. With expertise born of years of experience, no doubt, or maybe inventiveness spurred by desperation, Sam pushed her back and arranged her flat on the table. Then he climbed up and settled himself over her. She was going to have splinters in her butt, and he was going to have splinters in his knees, but who cared!

Sam had learned lots of tricks over the years . . . things to hone his sexual expertise . . . she would bet her Santa suit on that fact. After all, they'd been bumbling virgins, learning together all those years ago. But he wasn't employing any out-of-the-ordinary techniques now.

It was all too fast and frantic. And, yes, dammit, it *was* out-of-the-ordinary, because it was her and Sam. That was the magic ingredient.

With a whooshy exhale, he braced himself on straightened arms, his neck straining with restraint. No more preliminaries. The foreplay would have to come later. Afterplay. Yeah, she liked the sound of that. In fact, she liked everything Sam did. Even . . . *oh, my God!*

He didn't do that!

Did he?

He did!

"I hope to God you're on the pill, Reba, because my trembling hands couldn't find a condom right now if my life depended on it." How he managed to say all that, she couldn't imagine. The man was a wonder, no doubt about it. Multi-talented. Definitely multitalented.

She nodded that she was on the pill. Thank God for irregular periods that required that medical intervention. She couldn't have waited for a condom, either.

He smiled then. A genuine, stop-your-heart Sam smile. Then, the unthinkable happened.

"Reba! Where are you?" It was Maudeen calling to her in the hallway. There was a jiggling of the doorknob. Luckily, she'd had the foresight to lock the door when she'd discovered Sam in here. "Where are you, Reba? It's time to start the final Santa gift-giving part of the program." Maudeen's voice got increasingly more faint as she travelled down the corridor.

"No, no, no, no, no!" Sam protested in a horrified whisper. "We can't stop now."

Reba felt the same way, but, really, time for a reality check. They were in a public building, a store room, for heaven's sake.

"Don't move," Sam ordered through gritted teeth. His forehead was pressed against hers as he labored to get his breathing back to normal. She was making some puffing noises, as well.

Finally, they were able to look at each other without crossing their eyes. They were only half-aroused now.

"Whew! That was a close call." He rolled to his side, tucking her under his shoulder, and winked at her.

She laughed softly. The table was barely wide enough for one of them, but managed to hold the two of them as long as they lay really close, which they did. It was a good thing they hadn't fallen off the table in their frenzied actions of just moments ago.

"I'm sorry," he said.

"For what?" she inquired, running her fingertips over his brow in an attempt to erase the frown lines.

"For being too quick. For rushing you. For bad timing. For almost having sex in practically a public place. Holy hell, I behaved like . . . "

" . . . a teenager?"

"Yeah, a horny, inexperienced, overeager kid with his first girl."

"I remember our first time, together, and it wasn't all that bad."

He made a snorting sound of disgust. "I should have gained a little control over the years."

"Me, too."

"No, no, no," he said, shaking his head vigorously from side to side. "You should have no control when you're around me, but I'm the man. I should have control."

"That is so sexist it doesn't even merit comment. But, really, we better go." Her remark was half-hearted, seeing as how she was so relaxed and happy right where she was.

"Yeah," he said. Then, "Look at us . . . at me." Sam was staring downward where his Navy trousers and her Santa pants were gathered at their knees. "We're pitiful."

She thought they looked rather nice. With an odd irrelevance, she remembered reading one time about some famous English lady who said something in her diary to the effect, "Lord Samuel came home from the wars today and made love to me with his boots on." Rather like her and Sam, making love with their boots on.

"Sam, there's one thing I want to say."

His body went rigid with foreboding. "It better be, `I love you'."

"Of course, I love you. I already told you that."

"Not enough. Not lately."

She gave him a playful tap on the chin with her fist for interrupting. "I just wanted to say that what we just did . . . *almost* did . . . doesn't carry any promises."

Sam sat up abruptly and stared down at her. "Don't you dare say you're regretting what *almost* happened. Don't you dare."

The hurt in Sam's voice tore at her, but there were some things that needed to be clear between them.

"Listen, Sam, when I gave you the Good-bye Kiss back in Allentown—"

"It was *not* a Good-Bye kiss," he asserted.

"Okay, when I gave you *that* kiss, I implied that since you wouldn't be coming back to Maine *for good*, then there could be nothing between us. Well, I changed my mind. Remember what I said about your mother?"

"My mother again?" He groaned.

"Yes. I said that your mother must really have loved you if she was willing to give you up."

"Uh-huh," he said, confused.

"Well, can I do any less?"

When understanding hit, he stood abruptly and was already yanking up his pants. "You are not giving me up. No way, no time, no where, no how."

"Think about it, Sam. I'm giving you what you want. Freedom. Just what you want."

"Who says I want freedom?"

"You don't want your freedom?"

"Yes . . . I mean, no. Hell if I know." He glared at her. "Did I just get laid here?"

She laughed at his bluntness. How like a man to take that conclusion from everything she had said! "We almost made love, Sam. Whether we completed the act or not is irrelevant. I love you. You love me. But there are no commitments."

Just as Sam had said he could remove his clothes in two seconds flat, that's about how much time it too him to re-dress himself, to a perfect tee. Anger hastened his actions. Suddenly shy under his scowling scrutiny while he dressed, Reba began to cover her nakedness, too, though not as quickly.

"This conversation is not ended." Sam walked over to the door, unlocked it, ducked his head out and glanced both ways before closing it again and telling her, "All clear."

She nodded, already with her trousers raised and pillows in place. He came back and burrowed his fingers in her hair on both sides of her face. Then he kissed her . . . a long, lingering kiss full of just what she'd said she didn't need—promise.

Then he walked away, closing the door behind him.

Moments later, he returned, opening the door just enough for his head to peek in, "You better hurry up. Everyone's waiting for you. I told them you'd been in the ladies room, trying to seduce me. Everyone wanted to know if you were crying with frustration, seeing as how I'm so hard to get."

She made a clucking sound of disapproval at his teasing.

"Just kidding. Everyone thinks you went jogging."

"In a Santa suit?"

He shrugged, as if her jogging habits might be a bit weird. "One last thing, Reba . . . "

"Yes . . . ?" She couldn't wait to hear what his exit line would be now. What was he going to tease her about? Her less-than-spectacular new body? Her lack of skills in the sex department? The way she was screwing up her Santa suit as she hurried to dress?

"You were beautiful, Reba," he said in a voice thick with emotion. "So beautiful you took my breath away. I'll probably have a heart attack when we do make love, and mark me well, babe. We *will* make love."

Then he was gone.

Talk about exit lines!

Talk about charm!

Talk about Sam!

Talk, talk, talk! Sam was sick to death of all the talk.

Morey in a Santa suit with candy cane suspenders wanted to talk to him about the soft shoe dance program he'd just completed with Bob, also in a Santa suit. Bob—or the Colonel, as he was called— had a "super keen" exercise proposal for Winter Haven that he'd like to discuss with him. Jane wanted to talk to him about the offer he'd made to sponsor that kid Richie with some anonymous monthly checks. Dr. Maggie and Dr. Meg wanted to talk with him about sex practices in military installations for a study they were contemplating. And he'd barely escaped Betty who'd been approaching him a few moments ago with a dogged jut to her chin that he suspected meant an update on her contraception lecture.

He was back in his Santa attire, as ordered by Mrs. Smith when she'd caught him coming back from the store room. Then Mrs. Smith had commenced talking with him, as well, about every blessed thing under the sun. If he ever heard the recipe for Plum Pudding again in this lifetime, it would be too soon.

He wanted this whole Santa Brigade program to be over so that he could be with Reba again. And it wasn't talk he had in mind, either.

Unfinished business was the name of the game.

Reba, Callie and Dana were seated on high stools in the center of the room, near the giant fir tree, dispensing gaily wrapped presents that had individualized tags on them for all the kids. Maudeen and her computer were responsible for that amazing feat . . . coordinating each kid's wish with a specific gift. By the time they arrived at the shelters, they had detailed wish lists and gifts that matched or closely approximated the requests.

He knew Reba wasn't ignoring him, precisely. But it felt that way nonetheless. After what had just transpired between them, he wanted desperately to recapture the closeness. But how could he do that when everyone kept talking to him? And she kept doing Santa things?

JD and Stan didn't seem to be faring any better with the two women who had caught their attention.

Just then, a new song came on the sound system. It was loud and it was joyful and it was freakin' "Jingle Bells."

"Not a chance in hell!" he said, storming toward the side of the hall where he'd spied the music turntables on a small stage. "If I have my way, that song is banned forever . . . in my hearing."

Flicking through the stack of CD's on the table, he stopped at one in particular. And laughed. "Oh, Reba, you are going to be soooo surprised."

"What's up, Slick?" Stan said, coming up the steps to stand beside him.

"You were talking to yourself," JD remarked with a smirk. He had followed after Stan.

"It's like this, boys," he told them with a slow drawl, "I've been noticing that you two are batting zero where Callie and Dana are concerned. I think you need a lesson in smooth."

"Hey, Slick, I don't see you chalking up any major carnal points with Reba," Stan added with an exaggerated sniff of affront.

Sam ignored their comments and showed them the CD. Both JD and Stan groaned.

It was the soundtrack from the movie "Top Gun," which had come out during their senior year in high school. Ironically, the movie took place in a jet pilot training center in Florida, just like the one Sam attended a few years later. JD and Stan were trying to ignore the CD he was waving in their faces. Not only had the three of them watched the movie a zillion times, but they'd become adept at reenacting the famous bar scene in the movie where jet pilot trainees, Tom Cruise, and his buddy, Anthony Edwards, serenaded their superior officer, Kelly Preston. Usually, Reba had been the one that the three of them had practiced their hokey routine on, but now . . .

"You know what I think?" Sam said, grinning widely at JD and Slick. "I think they've lost that lovin' feelin'." He put emphasis on *they* and looked toward the three female Santas sitting appropriately on what could have been bar stools.

"Oh, no, they definitely have not lost that lovin' feelin'." It was JD speaking, and he was shaking his head like a shaggy dog, except that he was a shaggy-haired Santa. They all were.

"I hate it when she does that . . . loses that lovin' feelin', I mean." Stan had a decided glimmer in his eyes as he stared at Dana, as if he had something special in mind for her. *Man, oh, man.* If Dana had, in fact, lost that lovin' feelin', he could tell that Stan was bound and determined to get it back for her.

"Hey, Richie," Sam called out to the little boy, motioning for him to come over. "Can you hit the play button on this CD player once you see us get close to the Christmas tree over there?"

"Sure." Richie puffed out his chest with pride that Sam would have entrusted him with an important task. Sam was definitely going to have to do something for this boy . . . and not just a check a month.

The three of them stepped off the small stage then and ambled toward their three "victims."

"I can't believe I'm doing this," they all said simultaneously. Then the three of them grinned and gave high fives to each other.

The Snowdon version of the Righteous Brothers were officially out of retirement. Reba was almost at the bottom of her Santa sack, and so were Callie and Dana.

That's when she noticed three large Santas ambling toward them with the most peculiar twinkles in their eyes. They were up to no good was her guess. Just before they got there, the Sam Santa called out, "Oh, Reebbaa!"

And the JD Santa followed suit with, "Oh, Caaalllie!"

Followed by the Stan Santa with, "Oh, Daaannna!"

"Oh, good grief!" Reba muttered.

"What's going on?" Callie asked.

"You don't want to know," Reba answered.

"I think they look cute," Dana remarked. The woman was obviously besotted with Stan. Either that or she blushed every time he got near her for some other reason.

Actually, they did look kind of cute as they walked toward them with a rhythmic spring to their steps and started snapping their fingers and singing, "Boom da boom da boom." My God, they were about to get "the treatment" from the three hunkiest Santas in the world.

"Is this a new routine for the Santa Brigade program?" Jane wanted to know.

"You could say that."

Just then, a new song burst out over the PA system. That old

Righteous Brothers song, "She's Lost That Lovin' Feelin'," which became immortalized in the bar scene from Top Gun. And Reba knew just what "treatment" this newest and unexpected segment of the entertainment program was going to take.

Sam leaned in close to her and crooned, along with the sound track, something about her never closing her eyes anymore when he kissed her lips.

And JD sang out to Callie in his off-key baritone complaining that she tried hard to hide it, but baaabbbyy, baby, he knew it.

Stan completed the set of stanzas by singing to Dana that she'd lost that lovin' feelin', and now it was gone, gone, gone.

They all joined in with a loud, "Whoo ooh ooh! Whoo ooh ooh!"

The guys danced around them. They shimmied. They strutted. They shook their fat Santa behinds. They sang their little hearts out.

Everyone in the crowd was laughing and clapping, especially when Sam got down on one knee at the end, put both hands over his heart, and avowed, musically that baby, baby, he'd get down on his knees for her.

It was a wonderful grand finale to what seemed like the best Christmas show the Santa Brigade had ever put on.

CHAPTER EIGHT

KEVIN

Wednesday Afternoon, Two Days 'til Christmas Eve

Colonel Morgan shook himself like a dog as he climbed the bus steps. "The store's closed due to weather," he announced in a commanding military voice that brooked no argument.

Of course, he got plenty of argument.

Straight from Callie, Kevin noted. The woman would fight a dog over a bone. She was a pain in the ass that way. A cute pain, but a pain nonetheless.

"Let's break in," she offered. "We'll leave money. Who'd convict us?"

Kevin was quickly learning that the woman with the bed-me wild hair owned a larcenous little heart. First she jumped on a subpoena, then she'd pick-pocketed him, now she wanted to break and enter.

Funny enough, she got a rousing answer to that. All of these philanthropist Santas considered this a *good* idea.

Kevin made his way to the front of the bus and turned to the crew. "This isn't a smart idea. Really. We need a better plan."

"We need to make those kids happy," Meg and Maggie said simultaneously.

"We'll pay them back," Mrs. Smith—who'd faint if she ever got a parking ticket—agreed.

"Let's storm the store!" Morey cried, pounding his fist on the seat in front of him. "We'll get toys and more!"

It became a battle cry. "Let's storm the store! We'll get toys and more! Let's storm the store! We'll get toys and more!"

Kevin stalked to the back of the bus, and confronted his supposed friends, who were standing oh-so-casually and smirking too much for his liking.

"Are we going to stop these fanatics from breaking the law, or what?" he asked, crossing his arms.

Stan lifted his hands helplessly. "I learned a long time ago not to mess with the Snowdon seniors."

Sam nodded toward the front. "Don't look now, but your little hellion is raiding your backpack."

Kevin whirled in time to catch Callie lifting out handcuffs with a snort, and tossing them down. She then continued digging in his pack.

"Hey!" he yelled. "Get out of there!"

"The man fancies himself some kind of James Bond," Callie informed the group. "He's gotta have some lock picks in here somewhere."

Kevin stormed up the aisle. "Give me that."

Callie ignored him. "How many pairs of handcuffs does one private investigator need?" she asked, her tone dripping with disgust.

"He's got more than one pair in there?" Slick asked, coming up behind him.

"I have to take in more than one perp, occasionally," Kevin tried to explain to the suddenly interested crowd. "Give me my backpack, woman."

"Oh, and look here!" Callie said, pulling out a box of condoms. A chorus of "ooohs" reverberated throughout the bus.

"Give me those," Kevin demanded, trying to grab for the box. Callie evaded him. "What, hotshot, planning on scoring big in Maine?"

"It's a gag gift for George's bachelor party," Kevin said, indignant.

"And look," Callie said. "Glow in the dark! That should be fun."

"Oh," Morey said. "Can I borrow a couple of those?"

"To use on what, Morey?" Mrs. Smith asked. "Your breakfast banana?"

"I'll have you know—"

"Stop!" Kevin said, finally managing to wrestle the condoms and his backpack away from the woman who he was going to turn over to the police at his next possible opportunity. To hell with the lust he was beginning to feel just looking at her. She was trouble, and she deserved to be locked up.

In fur-lined cuffs. And chain-encrusted teddies. Were there such things? He didn't know, but if there were, he'd love to have her wearing them so he could tie her up and—

He stuffed the condoms back into his pack. "We are *not* going to break into anything."

"What?" the little felon wannabe snapped at him. "You have a better idea?"

He shook his head to banish the images shimmying from one side of his brain to the other. "Oh, I don't know. How about, say, something *legal*?" he suggested.

"That doesn't sound very exciting," Morey commented.

"Legal's not going to get us supplies," Callie retorted.

"Leave everything to me," Betty boomed from the driver's seat. "I've got a favor or two I can call in."

Kevin could swear the majority of the senior Santas looked utterly disappointed.

Everyone watched as Betty punched a number into her cell phone. An almost eerie silence filled the bus. Between the constant chatter among the busy elves and the barked orders from the Colonel and Betty's whoops of joy as she defied driving logic and the ever-present, concocted-to-drive-any-person-insane Christmas music, noise was a given on this bus.

The sudden silence, along with the blinding snow, gave Kevin a strange sense of being stuck in a cocoon. In a cocoon with over a dozen crazy people.

"Farley! How's it hanging, sweet stuff?" Betty practically whispered into the stillness.

Betty? Whispering?

"Yep, it's me." She paused for a second, then laughed, a low throaty sound that spelled "intimate past." Stan, Slick and JD exchanged glances. The image of Betty Bad-ass in *any* kind of intimate situation was close to incomprehensible. In fact, downright spooky.

"She's done more than the Texas two-step with that one," Maudeen decided.

"We'll talk about that later," Betty said into the phone.

"I bet they will," Morey opined. "I could use a little talking like that myself." He glanced at Maudeen who didn't even bother to take her eyes off her computer.

"I need your help, sugar," Betty continued. "Who's the manager of the Big-Mart these days?"

Kevin was having trouble concentrating on the events going on around him, seeing as Callie took that moment to shake her come-and-get-me hair right in damn front of him.

Okay, so she wasn't doing it on purpose just to lay a hard-on that wouldn't quit between his thighs, but she was having that effect on him regardless. And it made him kind of mad because she was supposed to be his prisoner and a really rotten one at that, and instead he was starting to like her. Not to mention lust her. Even if she *was* willing at a moment's notice to break the law.

He growled in self-disgust. This was crazy, all of it. Here he was stuck with a bunch of people he'd never wanted to see again in his life, and he was *enjoying* himself. He was watching his childhood delinquent pals, who'd somehow—against all odds—grown into successful men. Men only too happy to be reaching out to kids in the touchy-feeliest types of ways.

And worse yet, Kevin felt himself falling for a woman whose only goal in life was to clothe rich people.

And to clothe Barbies for poor kids. And to make dolls for kids who didn't ask for much. And to embrace those kids and give them hope and laughter.

She was also a fugitive of sorts who'd robbed him, Kevin decided to remind himself. It helped in the scheme of things to control his raging lust. Well, actually it didn't help a whole hell of a lot.

Even sporting the Maudeen fashion blasphemy, the woman was hot. And beautiful. And in need of all the Christmas spirit a man could dish out.

Too bad she was as receptive as the Grinch.

Ten minutes after Betty hung up the phone, the cavalry arrived in the form of a truck with a snow plow, followed by a Sheriff's car. Callie swallowed hard, even as she continued to pass out lists of supplies she wanted each of the Santas to gather.

Would Kevin turn her in? She didn't know, and was horrified to realize that her heart would be broken if he did. And not just because it would ruin her plans. It would also ruin any barely acknowledged hopes she'd been harboring that he was beginning to feel something for her besides exasperation.

Which was stupid. But back at the shelter she'd watched as he taught spell-bound children various card and magic tricks and she'd been fascinated by his hands, by his shaggy hair, by his patience and his smile. Hell, she'd even been mesmerized by his laughter. She'd never been mesmerized by a person's laughter before.

And something weird had squeezed her insides as she'd surreptitiously followed his every movement, and she'd realized that as much of a pain as he was, she really, really liked him.

Incredibly stupid, considering she'd done nothing but give him a really hard time about almost everything. So he had not a single reason whatsoever to even tolerate her, much less learn to like her as well.

Which meant the moment he realized the heat had arrived, he'd gladly dump her on them.

And, unfortunately, the heat had landed right on their bus step. Callie swallowed back a small sob. Not only would her father's Christmas be ruined, some of the kids on their next stops probably would be disappointed, too. Not that Dana and the rest of the gang weren't doing a fabulous job of helping out—in fact Dana was about the most talented woman with a needle and thread Callie had ever met—but they needed so many toys and they needed them fast.

"What's wrong, Ms. Brandt?" Mrs. Smith asked, as she took the shopping list with her name on it from Callie's suddenly boneless fingers.

All Callie could manage was a shake of her head, while she blinked back tears. In the short time she'd come to be with these folks, she'd really grown to adore them, their eccentricities, and most especially their hearts. Hell, they'd been willing to break and enter with her, just to ensure that they didn't leave a single child toy-less at this time of year.

She chanced a glance out the window, and through the thick snow watched as the cop car's lights bounced all around it, coloring the snow, the store, and the people.

People. One of them was Kevin. He was probably, right this moment, discussing the logistics of handing her butt over to them, to be hauled back to New York and to hell.

Her lips and cheeks seemed to go numb, along with her brain. She didn't know how she managed to keep working, to keep handing out assignments, to keep smiling as if she didn't have a care in the world.

Would the cops let her hug these people one last time before they hauled her away in disgrace? Would they give her time to beg Reba and Dana to keep in touch, to write to her occasionally?

Although she'd only known the two women such a short time, she felt a bond with them as if they'd been friends all their lives. Reba, so compassionate and dedicated, Dana, so unaware of her beauty, inside and out.

It hurt like hell to think that she was about to tarnish the hard work and dedication this bus and its mission represented. These people, who'd accepted her unquestioningly, didn't deserve to have their higher cause blemished by the tawdry arrest of a woman in their midst. When she got finished doing hard time, she vowed silently, she'd make it up to all of them.

"Put this on."

Callie whirled to find Kevin, looking grim, shoving Morey's monstrosity of a fur cap at her. "What?"

"I said," he repeated slowly, as if to a dimwit, "put the hat on. And tuck that hair under it already."

"I don't think—"

"That's true, you usually don't," he said, pretty rudely. "But if we're getting you into that store without the sheriff recognizing you, you need to hide that hair." He paused and his eyes raked over her face. "Why are you looking like someone just kicked your dog?"

"I thought—" She choked over the sob that had been threatening for minutes now. She felt moisture on her eyelashes.

Kevin looked at her in horror. "Don't you start crying. I mean it. Don't even think about it."

Callie blinked, trying to cooperate. "You're not . . . turning me in?"

His face took on the aura of a thundercloud. "Hell, no! What do you—"

Callie couldn't help it. She threw herself at him, her arms around his neck in a death grip. "Oh, thank you! Thank you, thank you! I know you're a big jerk and everything and that it's your job and you have this really stupid sense of justice and that it probably kills you not to get your fee for finding me and everything and that I've been pretty much of a thorn, but this is the *best* Christmas gift you could give me!"

"You had me at the 'thank you' part, but you kind of lost me after the 'big jerk' bit."

Callie let him go, even if she'd *really* enjoyed feeling his chest against her body. "Well, you have to admit, your head's about as hard as—"

"Shut up and put on the hat," the entire brigade said in unison. Callie shut up and put on the hat.

"Was it my imagination, or did the sheriff look at me funny?" Callie asked, as Kevin dragged her into the store behind a bunch of the Santas.

Kevin, still reeling from the feel of Callie's breasts pressed against him, tried to gather his scattered thoughts. One of which was how scared he'd been that the sheriff would recognize her and rip her away from him.

He could easily argue to himself that he might lose the commission if it were learned that he'd had her in his custody for a long time without dragging her into authorities himself, but he saw no reason to start lying to himself at this point. He'd been utterly terrified to let her out of his sight.

The woman was a pain, but somewhere along the line she'd become *his* pain, and he reserved the right to decide when and where his sense of duty and justice kicked in.

Somehow he had the feeling that his marbles had completely tumbled from the bag in the last two days, but he wasn't in the mood to think about it now. She was here and she was safe and he wasn't letting her out of his sight.

"Well," he told her, at least half truthfully, "he was most likely fascinated by your overall fashion statement. He probably hasn't seen anyone wearing a lime green biker babe number and beaver hat together before."

Callie grabbed his arm and spun him toward her in an impressive show of ferocity. "Clothes!"

"Excuse me?"

She released him and spun around, her arms wide in a *Sound Of Music*, "The Hills Are Alive" exuberance. "This is a store! It has clothes! Normal clothes!"

"The manager said he'd donate the supplies for the dolls, honey, not clothing for the not-so-needy."

She kept her arms outspread. "Do I, or do I not, look needy?"

Kevin couldn't argue that. At the moment she looked like a bright green Smurf with an animal on her head. He'd never seen anything sexier in his life, which just went to prove that his life was sorely lacking and his hormones had hit the skids in the taste department.

"What I'm saying," he replied, employing tact by not answering that question directly," is that the donation the manager so kindly offered was for truly needy people. I don't think badly-dressed fugitives are what he had in mind."

Callie plopped her hands on her luscious hips. "What do you take me for? Whether your Neanderthal brain can figure this out or not, I'm a normally law-abiding citizen. I'm going to pay for the clothes."

"With what? You're broke."

She pulled his wallet out of a pocket in her coat and leafed through it. "Nope, I have plenty of cash."

"I think we should talk about this penchant of yours to scarf other people's wallets," Kevin spoke to the curtain between him and his prisoner.

"I have never stolen a wallet in my life," Callie retorted, "before yours. And it was completely out of desperation."

"You weren't desperate today."

There was a pause. "No, that's true. I was just mad over those condoms."

If he hadn't been leaning against the wall, he'd have fallen over. "You were mad over the condoms?" This was a really hopeful sign. "Well, they were just so tacky," she said after a bit.

"I *told* you they were a gag gift."

"Yeah, right." The curtain swung open for a nanosecond, just long enough for her to fling jeans at him, and not nearly long enough for him to enjoy the view of her in her skivvies. "Can you find those in a six, please?" she asked.

Jake stalked back out to the women's clothing section. It offended his righteous male sensibilities that he was having to do clothes shopping. But he couldn't leave Callie alone. She wasn't trustworthy.

Well, maybe that wasn't exactly right. He'd watched her on the bus and at the shelters and he'd been wildly impressed with her passion and compassion. He'd witnessed her smiling radiantly as the little girls who'd received her re-vamped Barbies jumped up and down with excitement. He'd seen her slip dollar bills into the hands of little kids who'd already seemed ravaged by life.

Then again, those had probably been *his* dollar bills.

"Need help?"

Kevin swung around to find Dana standing there, a booty full of yarn and fabric and a bunch of other stuff in her cart.

Having lost his mind some time between Monday and now, he said, "Do I look like Harrison Ford? The younger version, of course."

Much to her credit, she didn't immediately consider calling medical personnel and having him committed. She just looked him over and said, "Harrison should be so lucky."

At that moment Kevin decided Dana would be one of their kids' godmothers. She was just that kind of sweet-with-great-taste type spirits. He was sure Callie would agree.

And then his senses stopped swimming in the shallow end of the sanity pool, and he realized what he'd said and where his mind had gone. "I'm sorry. Really. It was just a mini-survey on the Harrison Ford thing. Callie doesn't seem to appreciate the resemblance."

"I'm sure she appreciates your looks a lot. She's probably just shy about admitting it."

Callie, shy. Now that was a laugher if he'd ever heard one.

Over the PA system, a voice that sounded suspiciously like Maudeen's, rang out, "Morey Goldstein, your presence is required in aisle nine. Morey Goldstein, aisle nine."

"Isn't aisle nine the ladies lingerie?" Kevin wondered out loud, seeing as he'd visited that part of the store himself. Kevin had to wonder what Santa supplies were needed from aisle nine. Then again, considering it was Morey and Maudeen, he didn't want to wonder too hard.

Maudeen continued, "Oh, and by the way, Stan needs Dana to help him in sporting goods. Dana to sporting goods, please."

Dana attempted to look irritated at the summons, but Kevin noted that a certain heat shimmered behind those blue eyes. She shrugged. "Looks like they're calling my name."

"If he gets out of line, you have my permission to pelt his hide with a BB gun," Kevin told her.

Dana shot him a grin over her shoulder, but hustled away with what one could only call exuberance.

Kevin headed to the shelves of jeans and waded through them until he found a pair labeled as a size six. He held them up in front of him, marveling that anyone could fit into that itty-bitty piece of fabric. But picturing Callie's body filling them out in all the right ways was no trouble at all.

As he made his way back to the dressing room, he pulled a couple of pretty looking shirts off racks. He figured if Callie wanted clothes, she'd get clothes. And if she was grateful enough—

No, he didn't think he'd better go there. Somehow he had the feeling that Callie would consider the thought of payback in the form of de-clothing somewhat seedy.

Too bad.

"Incoming," he called in warning as he walked into the dressing area.

Callie peeked out from behind a curtain, and lust hit him like an A-bomb to the gut. That hair of hers should be illegal. The lips should be outlawed, too. In fact, everything about her radiated S.I.N. in big, neon letters.

Kevin swallowed and held out his offerings. "I brought you some shirts, too."

She looked at them dubiously, but then broke out in a reluctant grin. "Not bad, JD."

Kevin winced, but didn't argue her use of his nickname. Just so long as she didn't ask—

"What does JD stand for, anyway?" she asked, as she grabbed the clothes from his hand, then whisked the curtain closed.

Figures. "You don't want to know."

"Sure, I do," she said, and he could hear the rustle of clothes as she undressed.

Just the *thought* of Callie taking off her clothes behind a curtain that could be flung aside with the flick of his wrist was enough to practically lay him low. Hormones began ricocheting through his lower body.

"So," she said. "What does it mean?"

"Huh?"

"JD, what does it mean? Obviously it's not your initials."

"Just an old nickname from Snowdon days."

"And it stands for ... ?" she persisted. "It has to stand for something."

Damn. "Well, I was ... rambunctious in my youth."

"And?"

"And some of the adults around town called me 'that juvenile delinquent.'" He ignored her snort of laughter. "Slick and Stan thought that was real funny, so they shortened it to JD."

"So the big and bad law and order guy used to be a hell-raiser, huh?"

"I wasn't *that* bad. In fact," he said, employing a phrase he thought might win him woman points, "I was misunderstood."

If woman points included making a person break out into peels of laughter, he'd just scored big. Somehow, he wasn't feeling all that victorious, however.

"That's cute," she finally responded, after practically busting a gut. But to her credit, she sounded sincere about it. No sarcasm, no cutting remark. This was progress.

"How about you?" he asked. "How does Cassandra become Callie?"

"Well," she said, her voice sounding muffled, "That came from my little sister. When she was just learning to talk, she couldn't quite handle Cassandra Lee. About all she could manage was Callie, so it stuck."

"That's kind of neat, too," he conceded.

"Damn, it's stuck!"

"No, really, Callie's a pretty name."

"Not my name, dummy. The zipper on these jeans. It's stuck."

"Oh." He swallowed again. "Need some help?"

"Yeah, right," she said, huffing and puffing a little with the effort to work the zipper.

"Hey, I was just offering to be nice!" he lied.

"Uh-huh," she grunted.

Kevin frowned, but seeing as he couldn't truthfully deny ulterior motives, he said nothing.

The PA system once again squawked on. "Colonel Morgan, Maggie needs you in health and beauty aids. Please go to health and beauty aids." This time the voice sounded more like one of the twins.

"I'm still stuck," Callie said behind the curtain. And she sounded defeated and near to tears, which just about broke Kevin's heart. "Honey, let me help," he said. "I'll be good, I promise."

"That's what I'm afraid of," she whispered.

That was enough for him, no matter which way she meant that. "May I come in?"

"Yes, please."

He took a deep breath before shoving the curtain aside, because he thought he'd need the fortification of oxygen just in case his breathing malfunctioned.

His breathing malfunctioned.

Her black and curly hair was wild around a face that signaled utter distress, eyes hurt, damp and defeated. She was half-in, half-out of a forest green shirt, and the jeans she wore were peeled back away from her belly to expose a stomach that was too gorgeous for words.

"Help me, JD."

Kevin dragged his gaze from her belly button, feeling helpless and ready to pounce at once. And his heart cracked. "What's wrong, sweetheart? It's just a stuck zipper."

"Everything," she said, her voice hoarse. She dropped into a plastic chair in the corner. "I'm a wanted fugitive, it's Christmas, and I can't be anywhere near my family, I've resorted to pick-pocketing, and now . . . now the zipper won't . . . work."

Kevin hunkered down in front of her. "First of all, I pretty much admire that you skipped out on a date with testifying for the scumball."

"You do?"

"Yes. I don't know the details, but I have to believe you have good reason."

Her damp green eyes blinked. "I really do. I think."

"Tell me, Callie."

Once again, the PA system kicked in. "Kevin Wilder, you're not pulling your load."

Kevin groaned at the sound of Mrs. Smith's admonition. "I guess you need to go," Callie said, then sniffed.

"No way, fashion babe. I need to be here. You have zipper issues."

"I'm a mess."

"You're the most beautiful woman I've ever seen. Now stand up. Let me fix those jeans."

She began to stand, but then Kevin thought better of it, and dropped her back down into her seat. "Wait. I'm kissing you senseless first, okay?"

And he did, although who went senseless first was a matter of debate. All he knew was that her lips cooperated in the most carnal way.

Somehow he stood her up and turned her to face the mirror. As he kissed and licked her neck, he raised her blouse and snapped her bra, revealing breasts that God must have had in mind when he created woman.

"JD . . . uhhh, Kevin,—"

"You can call me JD."

"Really?"

"Really. It's faster."

"JD, you're touching me."

"Not enough."

"My breasts," she said in a whisper, "aren't anywhere near my zipper."

"Your breasts are so beautiful, I can hardly stand it."

"My zipper?" she said, but her words came out in a breath smaller than a whisper.

"I'm getting there."

He couldn't keep his hands off of her, couldn't stop himself from inhaling her scent, couldn't stop himself from wanting her beyond belief. She was beautiful, and she was in his hands right now, and she was responding to his touch.

"Kevin Wilder, right now!" the PA system boomed. This time it was Betty, and that was almost scary enough to stop, but not quite.

"You need to go," Callie said, her voice softer than snowfall.

"I need to be here with you. You've got a fashion dilemma."

"Yes, I have a fashion dilemma."

He let his hand drift down between the stuck jeans, and touched her. He was shocked at her reaction, not to mention how wet and needy she seemed to be. And it fed his need for her.

"Wild Child, get your butt out here now or we're leaving without you!"

"Damn."

CHAPTER NINE

STAN

Late Wednesday afternoon, two days 'til Christmas Eve.

"I don't *believe* this!" Reba punched the off button on her cell phone and banged her forehead on the seat back in front of her. Twice. "Things were starting to go right again, now *this*!"

Dana looked up from her mending, startled.

"Reba, honey? What's wrong?" Slick patted Reba's shoulder soothingly.

"Noooo!" said Reba, and pounded the cell phone on the seat back, too.

"How about if I take this?" JD said, slipping the phone out of her hand.

"Reba?" said Callie anxiously, bending over her.

Bits of colored silk were tangled in her hair—a sudden blast from the bus' fans had caught her when she was tossing sewing scraps in a trash bag—and a long swath of multi-hued silk was draped over her shoulders, accenting her delicate beauty. Her nearness distracted JD for a moment, leaving Slick to press Reba for an explanation of this sudden outburst.

"Our hotel collapsed!" she said, angrily flinging herself back in her seat. "The roof caved in under the weight of all the snow and now we don't have anywhere to stay tonight."

"Surely there are other hotels—"

"Nothing. Our hotel's manager called every decent place around. They're all either closed for the winter or booked solid with other travelers who've gotten stuck in this damned storm."

"Well, shi—darn it!" Slick cocked a wary eye at Emma Smith six rows ahead. "There must be someplace around that can fit in a few more strays."

"Maybe if we swung farther east," JD suggested, frowning out at the still falling snow.

Reba shook her head. "We're behind schedule now. If we have to go too far out of our way, we'll never make it home in time for George's wedding." Her eyes narrowed as she chewed on her lower lip, thinking hard. The woman didn't know the meaning of the word *defeat*.

The four put their heads together, discussing possibilities.

Dana watched it all helplessly. She wished there were something she could do to help besides mend doll clothes and tell stories to children. The people on this bus were like a family, and she badly wanted to belong.

Not that everyone hadn't welcomed her as warmly as they'd welcomed Stan and Slick and JD and Callie, but she still felt like an outsider in spite of their generosity. Granted, the kids at the shelter this afternoon had enjoyed her stories almost as much as the older kids and the adults had enjoyed Stan's good-humored, self-deprecating tales of all his fumbles and bloopers during his career, but being accepted wasn't the same as belonging. And, all right, Callie was an outsider, too, but she was so vivacious and sure of herself that she'd fit in anyplace.

Besides, there was definitely something going on between her and JD. He might be threatening to turn Callie over to the police, but nobody really believed he'd do it. After all, he certainly hadn't tipped the police off at the Big-Mart. No, something was definintely heating up between them. Sparks flew every time they were close.

The same sorts of sparks seemed to be flying between Reba and Slick, though in their case both of them seemed intent on pretending the other didn't exist. Well, Reba did, anyway. Slick hadn't managed to hide the fact he watched her every chance he got. Everyone had noticed. Dr. Maggie and Dr. Meg had a private bet going on how long it would be before the two gave in and admitted they'd been crazy about each other for years.

Dana sighed. It must be wonderfully comforting, being so much a part of a community like that. Reba belonged and Callie fit in, but she'd never found it that easy. And then there was Stan . . .

Troubled, she tucked her mending back in the basket. She was almost done, anyway, and the dull gray daylight was beginning to fade. She couldn't see how they were going to make all those Raggedy Ann and Andy dolls by tomorrow, but both Callie and Reba seemed to consider that a done deal, so she'd given up worrying about it.

She couldn't help worrying about this new kink in their plans, however. Surely there was something she could do to help the Brigade out now. Her first job had been in this area. There had to be *someplace . . .*

An idea stung her, shooting her upright in her seat. Before she could convince herself it would never do, she slipped out of her seat and headed up the aisle toward Stan.

Most of the Brigade were napping. Stan had claimed two unoccupied seats and stretched out as far as he could, propping his bad leg on a pillow and cramming another pillow against the window to support his head. He looked, Dana thought, about as comfortable as an elephant in an ice box.

He also looked extraordinarily sexy and dangerously tempting. There was something so very intriguing in watching a strong, competent man suddenly turned vulnerable in the throes of sleep.

And that, of course, was ridiculous. Stan Kijewski was anything but vulnerable.

Ever since that hot, disconcerting kiss in the snow and the teasing, deliberately tormenting exchanges he'd instigated since, she'd been fighting against the urge to make the next kiss something more, to let down her defenses and give free rein to her desire. She didn't have much experience in this sort of thing, but she was quite sure Stan would be willing—more than willing—to go as far as she wanted, if not farther.

Yet as many times as she'd let that particularly enticing scenario play in her dreams, she couldn't quite work up the courage to try it. Wrestling a bear would be a hell of a lot safer than letting her heart lead her down such a dangerously slippery path.

The trouble was, he saw their little exchanges as harmless flirtation. If the flirtation led to sex, she had no doubt he'd enjoy every minute—and make sure she did, too—but once George's wedding was over, Stan would go back to San Diego and she'd be left with a broken heart.

She'd had her heart broken too many times as a child to want to risk it now.

With that stern reminder, she leaned down and poked his thigh to bring him awake. She immediately wished she hadn't—just touching him was enough to set her nerve ends tingling.

"Give me your cell phone," she said when he opened one eye to glare at her. "Please."

He grumbled and awkwardly shifted around to dig through his jacket pocket.

"Thanks." She slid into the half-vacated seat—even sitting up he took up an awful lot of space—and punched in a remembered number.

"You'd better not be calling a boyfriend," Stan growled.

"Michael?" she said hopefully when a male voice answered. "Mike Parker! How are you?"

"Dana?" The familiar voice brought fond memories rushing back. "Where in hell are you?"

"I'm on a bus in the middle of a snowstorm," she said, grinning, "and I hope you can help me out."

"For you, anything . . . if I can." She could hear the wariness in his voice.

"Is Moose Lodge still open? Can you take in"—she counted hurriedly—"fifteen weary travelers for tonight?"

"Fifteen? Don't tell me you're camping out with a bunch of crazies in *this* weather!"

She explained quickly, conscious of Stan watching her, straining to catch Mike's end of the conversation. She tried to pretend she didn't notice, but it was hard when she was so intensely, achingly aware of him and of his thigh where it pressed against hers.

The silence on Mike's end of the line was deafening.

"Mike? You still there?"

"I don't know, Dana. I'd like to help you out, really I would, but . . . "

Dana's shoulders slumped. "But you're all booked up. I understand, Mike. Honest."

"No, it's not that." Another pause. "The trouble is," he continued at last, reluctantly, "we're shutting down the place, Dana. God knows we've tried. Penny and I have worked our fingers to the bone, but we just haven't been able to make a go of it. Right now it's just us and the kids. No maids, no cooks, no waiters. Just us. Most of the rooms aren't made up, whatever food's left is in cans or the freezers, and we haven't dusted the main lodge for weeks. We figured we'd stay through Christmas, then pack up and let the bank have the place."

His despair came through loud and clear.

"Oh, God, Mike! I'm so sorry. I know how much you and Penny love that old place."

"The kids, too, but . . . well . . . " She could almost hear him shrug, defeated. "That's the way it goes sometimes."

"Give me the phone."

Dana blinked at Stan's outstretched hand.

"Give me the phone," he insisted. "I heard enough and I think I know how we can fix this."

She gave him the phone. He settled back against his pillow so she couldn't hear Mike's part of the conversation.

"Hello, Mike? Stan Kijewski here . . . Yeah, that Kijewski. Thanks. I appreciate that. Unhuh . . . Yeah . . . Listen, I don't mean to butt in but I caught some of your conversation with Dana . . . Unhuh . . . Unhuh . . . Why not give it one last try? You haven't lost until the clock runs out, you know . . . Yeah, that was a good game, wasn't it? And I was sweating it, let me tell you. We barely got that last play in before the clock killed us, but it was a touchdown and that's all we needed, just one point ahead to win . . . Yeah . . . Unhuh . . . Ummm . . . Betty can fix that . . . Yeah, but—How about if we paid for a couple of local folks to come in and help you, then? Could we do that? . . . Sure, no problem . . . No, really . . . We'll put Dana in the kitchen. I'll bet she's a great cook."

He winked at her. "Nope, that's fine . . . No, really." He grinned. "I'm assuming you'll still take a credit card . . . Yeah . . . Yeah . . . Great! You want to talk to Dana? Okay, I'll tell her. Believe me, anything's better than sleeping on this bus. The seats are waaaay too small for anyone larger than a midget. And, Mike? Thanks."

He flipped the phone off before she could protest. "You can call him back as soon as you clear it with Reba."

"What, exactly, am I clearing with Reba?" she demanded, suspicious.

"That your friend Mike will put us up for whatever she was going to pay that other hotel. Providing, of course, that Betty can get us there in the first place. He says the road to the place is knee deep in snow."

"Betty can get us anywhere," said Dana with conviction. "But Reba was paying that hotel peanuts, from what I heard. The owner was a friend of Betty's."

"Isn't everybody?"

"Stan!"

He grinned and batted those beautiful green eyes at her. "That's me. Care to do anything about it? I've got some great ideas if you're interested."

He'd been obnoxiously cheerful ever since that kiss in the snow. She shoved aside the memory of that long, hot, troublesome kiss.

"What did you and Mike agree on?"

"You," he said, shoving her out of the seat. "He said you had a great ass."

"He did not," she objected, getting to her feet. "Did he? What did you say?"

"I agreed." He made shooing motions with his hand. "Now, go on. Git. Go tell Reba we've got a place to stay tonight after all and let me get back to my nap. And take that damned phone with you. I don't want anyone else ruining my beauty sleep."

Betty's friend, Wolfman Woody, had plowed the road into Moose Lodge, just as he'd said he would. There were already at least two and maybe three tracks of cars headed in—the employees Mike had called back on Stan's say-so. Probably with the promise of double or triple wages for the one night's work, Dana thought. Wages she suspected Stan had agreed to pay out of his own pocket.

When she'd asked Stan about it, though, he'd just grinned and tried to kiss her. She'd evaded that kiss, then spent the next hour wishing she hadn't.

It was all so darned confusing! Okay, she'd had a crush on him for years, but that wasn't the same as falling in love. And she was very much afraid that this was really, truly love.

Loving Stan Kijewski was not a good idea. They lived in different worlds, wanted different things. He was gorgeous, confident, and wealthy. She was none of those things. He was . . . *oh, hell*. What did it matter? He was the man she'd fallen in love with, and that, unfortunately, was that.

Thank God he'd never know about all those posters hanging in her bedroom.

Her gloomy thoughts were interrupted by a cheer from everyone on the bus as Betty pulled into the big drive in front of Moose Lodge. The place was a sprawling, two-story log building that had originally been built in the 1890s for wealthy hunters who wanted to spend a few weeks roughing it without having to do forego hot water, servants, and good food.

There were lights in the windows of the dining hall on the left, but the windows of the two floors of guest rooms on the right-hand wing of the central lodge were depressingly dark. Individual cabins tucked back in the trees were barely visible through the falling snow, their windows just as dark.

Despite the dark logs of the buildings and the unlit windows, there was something comfortable about the place, something warm and friendly and welcoming.

Dana stared at the place, remembering. Mike and Penny Parker were old college friends. Even back then they'd talked of buying the lodge and restoring it to its former glory. It was a pity the dream hadn't worked out the way they'd wanted.

Nothing of their troubles showed on their faces when they emerged to welcome their unexpected guests, however. Mike was his same slender, smiling self, Penny a little dynamo at his side. Taylor and Tyler, the six-year-old identical twins who'd been born just after their parents bought Moose Lodge and who'd never known any other home, raced down the broad steps, whooping in excitement.

With the twins as their talkative escort, the Brigade piled off the bus and swept into the lodge, chattering and gawking and asking questions a mile a minute.

"You coming? Or are you planning on camping on the bus tonight?"

The question brought Dana out of her thoughts with a snap. Stan was standing in the aisle, grinning down at her. A frisson of sexual awareness shot through her, making her blush.

"Yes, of course. Right away," she said, grateful for an excuse to hide her face as she fumbled for her bag under the seat.

Stan followed her down the aisle, grinning. She was thinking about sex. She'd deny it, of course, but he could tell. Fair skin or not, Dana Freeman wasn't the kind of woman who blushed for much of anything else.

"Hey!" he called as she started toward the broad front steps. "Aren't you going to help me across the ice? Make sure I don't fall and hurt myself?"

She stopped, then swung back to face him, hands fisted on her hips. "I helped you when we were stopped by that snow slide, and you took advantage of the situation to kiss me. I helped you at the shelter and again at Big Mart, and both times you took advantage and kissed me again. I don't trust you."

He tried his best to look innocent and hurt and needy, all at the same time.

"Besides," she added, gimlet-eyed, "You don't need my help."

"Sure I do. Who else am I gonna lean on? Dr. Meg?"

"How about Slick or JD?"

"Nah. They'd think it was funny if I ended on my ass in the snow."

"The Colonel?"

His eyes went wide in mock horror. "You're joking, right? The Colonel would seriously question my manhood for anything less than major injury. Preferably one with blood and a loss of limbs."

"Yuck."

"Come on, Dana," he coaxed, trying to look innocent and pathetic and needy. Just looking at her made him grin like a fool and think lustful thoughts. He held his hands wide. "It's just a few feet. Think how bad you'd feel if I slipped and really hurt myself."

Her gorgeous eyes narrowed to shards of ice.

"No kisses. I promise." He mentally crossed his fingers. She shifted uncertainly.

"Please?" he said. Dana was a sucker for "please."

Heaving a sigh of long suffering, she trudged back to him. "All right. But from now on, you're on your own."

She fit against him perfectly, just as he'd known she would. When she slid her arm around his waist at the back, he draped his arm over her shoulders and pulled her closer.

"Oof! Don't squash me, you big lummox." She punched him in the ribs. "I said I'd help you. I didn't say I'd *carry* you."

"You didn't say you'd kiss me, either, but a fellow can't help hoping," said Stan cheerfully. She was crazy about him. The punch in the ribs proved it.

She didn't give him a chance to snatch a kiss, though. Not even a quick one.

A minute later they walked through the broad double doors and into the lodge's massive great room. Stan stopped short, surprised. "Hey! This place is great!"

When she pointedly slipped away from him, he let her go. She wouldn't go far, and there wasn't much he could do when the entire Brigade was milling around admiring the place.

There was a lot to admire. Moose Lodge was straight out of a history book. The walls and rafters were constructed of massive pine logs that these days would cost a king's ransom. Broad stone fireplaces filled the walls at either end of the room, a cheerfully crackling fire in each to welcome visitors in from the cold. The floors were of broad pine planks that would cost another fortune to duplicate, the furniture comfortable rather than stylish. At the opposite side of the room, a wall of multi-paned windows looked out on a snow-covered clearing surrounded by pines and winter-bare trees. To the right, a broad stairway crafted of pine-logs led to a second-floor gallery and a hall to the guest rooms. On the main floor, broad hallways at either end of the room led to what looked like a dining room on one side and more guests' rooms on the other. Two mounted moose heads, one on either fireplace, stared glassily across the room at each other.

On closer inspection, the furniture was worn and often saggy, the moose heads looked slightly moth-eaten, and dust was everywhere. Judging from the looks of it, the last real fix-up on the place had been at least thirty years ago. At today's prices, it would take a fortune to do the place up now.

God knew what the guest rooms looked like.

Stan spotted Dana across the room and felt an increasingly familiar surge of heat and hunger deep in his belly. With the right company, he'd never notice the furnishings.

"Great place!" Slick stopped beside him, with JD right behind.

"Shame it's been let go." JD scanned the room, then glanced toward the chattering crowd that had congregated around the coffee pot the Parkers had set out. Callie was safely behind the coffee pot, handing out cups and packets of sugar. Obviously reassured, JD turned his attention on the nearest moose head. "Remember that old deer head at the Home?"

"Who could forget?" Slick wasn't looking at the stuffed moose. His attention was fixed on Reba, who was comparing a checklist with the luggage that was being set down at the far side of the room by two cheerful, jeans-clad teenagers who'd braved the storm to get here, drawn by the Parkers' call for help and Stan's promise of triple wages for the two days' work. Either the woman didn't know how to stop working, or she was making damned sure Slick didn't get any time alone with her.

Stan's gaze flicked to Dana, who was standing at the window, her back to the room and everyone in it, staring wistfully out at the falling snow.

Something that wasn't lust, something unfamiliar but potent, twisted within him at the sight. He'd taken two steps in her direction when JD pulled him back.

"Whoa, boy. You'd better be damn sure you've got a clear view down field before you throw that pass."

Stan snorted and pulled free of his friend's hold. "You're a fine one to talk."

JD's face darkened. "I don't know what you mean."

"Oh, yeah?"

"Now, children," said Slick.

Stan and JD turned on him.

"Butt out, Slick," said JD between gritted teeth.

"Yeah, butt out," Stan chorused, scowling.

"What the hell?" Slick stared at them. "Have you two lost your minds?"

JD glared at him. Then he sighed. "I'm not sure I've got much of a mind left to lose," he admitted, once more glancing in Callie's direction.

"Hey, I understand." Slick pointedly did *not* glance toward Reba. "Believe me, I *do* understand."

"You two are pathetic," Stan said, smugly pleased that he could enjoy the game without risking the miseries his friends were enduring. Dana was tempting, but he wasn't thinking *serious* here.

No dangerous life-time commitment stuff. Not for *him*.

"I'd deck you for that," JD growled, "except for the fact you're right. Definitely pathetic."

"At least you have someone pretty to look at in the other bed." Stan regretted the words the minute they were out. He was, he realized suddenly, feeling more than just a little jealous. It was a very strange feeling. A very *dangerous* feeling.

"For a while there, I thought you two had actually clicked." Slick studied JD, eyes alight with speculation. "What happened? Did she object to the handcuffs?"

"Don't ask." JD's shoulders slumped. The man who tackled the most dangerous murderers without breaking a sweat had been felled by a pint-sized felon with a flair for fashion.

"Still, proximity and all that . . . " The words trailed away as Stan considered the idea that had suddenly hit him. He glanced at the long halls that led to the guest rooms on the first and second floors.

"He's thinking," said Slick.

JD's eyes narrowed. "*What* are you thinking, Stanley, old boy?"

"Don't call me Stanley."

"Come on, out with it," Slick ordered.

"I was thinking that there are a lot of rooms in this lodge," said Stan, rather dreamily. "A lot of *empty* rooms."

"And cabins," said Slick, beginning to smile.

"And cabins," Stan agreed. He wasn't interested in cabins. If he tried to chase Dana through the snow, he'd fall on his ass for sure. But on nice, solid wood floors . . .

"So?" JD, already paired with the woman of his dreams—or his worst nightmares, depending on the moment—was a little slow on the uptake.

"So we don't have to share rooms like we did last night," said Slick with satisfaction.

"Good thing, too," Stan said. "You snore."

"You ought to hear the noises you make!"

"You were worried about Slick's snoring?" said JD, bewildered. Stan glanced at Slick.

Slick tried to look mournful. "It's the sex. It's done something to his brain."

"He doesn't have a brain."

"True."

"Damnit," JD growled. "If you bastards—Oh! I get it!"

"He got it," Slick informed Stan.

"Her," Stan corrected. "Not that it did him any good."

JD's hands balled into fists. "Don't say it."

Slick grinned. "Sorry. It's just—"

"We're jealous," said Stan.

"And we want a little equal opportunity."

"Ahhhhh," said JD. "You two want your own rooms and you want to make sure Dana and Reba get separate rooms, too. Like, maybe, right by yours."

"Very good!" Slick lightly punched Stan's arm. "See? He's not totally stupid."

"Not usually," Stan agreed.

"Go to hell," said JD, grinning.

Slick was automatically elected to convince Emma and Maudeen that a little adjustment in the sleeping arrangements was in order. Since it was Slick that was doing the convincing, the results were a foregone conclusion.

Half an hour later Stan followed Dana and one of the lodge's teenage employees down the main floor hall to the two doors set side by side at the far end.

The teen, David, set down the bags he was carrying and unlocked the doors. "You're in this one, ma'am," he said, gesturing to the room on the left. "And this is yours, sir."

He smiled hopefully up at Stan. "I'm not supposed to bother you, Mr. Kijewski, sir, but if you have a few minutes, could you give me some pointers on throwing a football?"

"Sure. A little bit later, though, okay? And don't expect any demonstrations. I'm not much of a passer any more, either."

Stan was so intent on Dana that even the admission of his lost abilities didn't bother him like it used to.

She looked so damned delectable. Even when she deliberately turned frosty and distant, like now. The heat she generated in him was more than enough to warm them both, anyway. All he had to do was figure out a way to convince her of it.

"... there's matches for the fireplace here, and extra logs are stacked over there. There's candles, too, in case the power goes out."

Stan dragged himself back to attention while David went through his spiel.

"And this door joins the two suites, if you want," David added, trying to look innocent.

Stan's smile vanished. If the boy had been over twenty-one, he'd have decked him for the glance he shot at Dana. The kid had been studying waaaay too many of those swimsuit issues.

"Great. Thanks." He handed the boy a tip that had him stuttering, then deliberately shut him out of the room and propped his shoulder on the frame of the still-open door between the two rooms.

Dana was bent over trying to open a drawer on a night stand that looked like somethings out of a Fifties designer magazine. The view was delectable. Her rump made a nice, curvy upside-down heart, with the point of the heart there in the middle of her spine where her hips curved into that tiny waist.

He couldn't wait to take a closer look.

"Nice place," he said, deliberately casual.

She straightened and turned, hackles up and ready for a fight. Unfortunately, it wasn't for the kind of wrestling match he had in mind.

"Mike and Penny have done the best they can," she snapped.

"Hey! I don't have any complaints. I *like* the place."

She eyed him doubtfully. "You do?"

"Yeah. I think it's great. Which doesn't mean it couldn't use a bit of a fix up."

She sighed and slumped onto the bed, making the wooden bed frame creak.

The mattress, Stan couldn't help noticing, dipped a bit in the middle. The bedspread was one of that fuzzy kind that his grandmother used to have. Those bedspreads had been old when he was a kid. What did they call them? Chenille? The one on Dana's bed looked like the fuzz had been worn off right there in the middle where the dip in the mattress was.

"I didn't realize the place was quite this . . . *old*," she admitted, looking around the room. "I knew Mike and Penny had run into a lot of expenses they hadn't counted on, like having to replace the roof and installing a new boiler, that sort of thing, but I had no idea . . . "

She scowled at the drawer pull that had come off in her hand, then tossed it on top of the night stand.

Stan stifled the urge to take her in his arms and comfort her. It wasn't comfort he wanted to offer her, he reminded himself, and it wasn't smart to let himself get confused about that sort of thing.

"The way things are these days," he said, "some big developer will buy the place and turn it into a getaway for the rich."

Dana nodded. "Or tear the lodge down and sell the land for luxury homes."

At the thought, they both stared glumly out the window at the shrouded trees and the silently falling snow.

"Well, that's the way things go sometimes," Stan said gruffly, straightening. Life had a way of slamming you when you least expected it, and there didn't seem to be a damn thing you could do about it.

"Yeah, that's the way it goes." Dana shoved off the bed. The wooden bed frame creaked again, louder this time. The kind of annoying creak that would wake up half the people in the lodge if anyone tried anything athletic on that dippy mattress.

Dana didn't seem to notice. After a moment's hesitation, she crossed to where he stood and grabbed the edge of the open door, which opened into her room. "If you don't mind, I'd like to change."

Stan relaxed, grateful for the change of conversational topic. This was sex. He understood sex. This was like playing at home with the home field advantage.

He smiled down at her. "I don't mind."

Her delectable Madonna's mouth curved into a frown. "*After* I shut the door."

He stepped forward, into her room.

"Oh, no, you don't!" Her hand, palm out, slammed into his chest. "*You're* staying on the other side."

"Sure you don't need any help? I'm real good with zippers."

"Out!" She pushed. He backed up.

"Just say the word and I'm your man. Zippers. Shoes. Stockings." He gave her what he hoped was an encouraging leer. "I give *great* back rubs." She pushed harder. "Shoulder rubs, too. Belly rubs. Foot rubs. Rub rubs?" he added hopefully as she shoved him back onto his side of the doorway.

She started to swing the door shut, then froze. "There's no lock on this door."

"All *right!*"

Those ice blue eyes hit him.

"I mean, that's too bad. Really."

She slammed the door in his face.

Stan grinned at the unlocked slab of pine, then turned, whistling, and went to check the mattress on his bed.

To Dana's immense relief, Reba drafted Stan to help Emma and Betty in the kitchen—Mike hadn't been able to get a cook on such short notice—and assigned her to help with the Raggedy Ann and Andy assembly line Callie had organized in the dining hall.

However much the Brigade might enjoy their adventure, they took their responsibilities seriously. Work before fun. Or rather, *with* fun. Even as they worked, the Brigade was chattering and laughing and quarreling. They were like a family, Dana thought wistfully, scanning the room, only they had come together out of a shared concern for those less fortunate than themselves rather than by the chance that threw families together—or tore them apart.

Reba and Ethel were busy digging through the boxes of stuff the Big-Mart manager had donated, sorting out what could be given away into their appropriate piles—cosmetics, toiletries, clothes, toys, and household gear—and setting the rest aside for future use or for the yearly rummage that helped fill the Brigade's coffers.

Maudeen was madly clicking away on her computer, figuring out what they had and what they'd need and for whom, while Dr. Meg and Morey—who was sporting an impressive pair of suspenders with fat Santas dancing up and down their length—busily wrapped the gifts and labeled them. The colorful pile of finished packages already buried one table and threatened to spill onto another. They'd had a last-minute request that they make a second stop at a shelter near Snowdon, which had had an unexpected influx of new people who'd been stuck by the storm, so Maudeen was having to do a bit of juggling. The Big-Mart donations were going to come in handy.

"My, my. Look at this." Ethel held up a hideous plaster parrot in brilliant shades of purple and pink and puce. "What do you think?"

"Rummage sale!" everyone chorused.

"And this?" She dragged a soiled and slightly tattered floral wall hanging out of a box and held it up for inspection.

"Rummage sale!"

"No, wait!" Maudeen cried. She pounded the computer's keyboard, squinted at the screen, then pounded some more. "Yes, here it is," she said, beaming in satisfaction. "Mrs. Shirley Eisenstock. She's one of the newbies at the Snowdon shelter and the manager there thinks she'd really enjoy something pretty to brighten up her family's cubicle."

"I can fix it," Dana offered. "A little cleaning and ironing and a bit of mending and it will look good as new."

"You're going to clean the cubicles?" Ethel asked, puzzled.

"She's going to fix the hanging *for* the cubicle," Reba said, enunciating clearly. "Turn up your hearing aid, Ethel."

Instead, Ethel dived back into the boxes. "Oh, goodie! Shoes!"

Maudeen rolled her eyes heavenward, then went back to pounding the keyboard.

In the main lobby, clearly visible through the open doors of the dining hall, John and the colonel, with the twin's enthusiastic if slightly less than helpful assistance, were wrestling with a tall, rather scrubby pine tree that JD and Slick had chopped down earlier.

Mike, in a bold effort at optimism, had sworn he chose that tree because he needed to clear it out so several younger, stronger trees would grow better next summer. Everybody had carefully avoided mentioning that he wouldn't be here next summer to see them grow. Penny had broken down at the thought of this last Christmas tree at Moose Lodge, then laughed through her tears when Morey had stuck an enormous red bow behind his ear and swept her into a whirling waltz across the floor.

Brave soul that she was, Penny had immediately put aside her own pain and dredged up two sewing machines for the doll manufacturing.

Callie and Dr. Maggie were making the old Singers roar as they stiched up arms and legs and a small mountain of doll clothes. Dana was embroidering faces and doing any hand sewing that was needed.

Despite their pleas of ignorance when it came to sewing and dolls, Slick and JD had been drafted into the doll brigade, too. Under Callie's sharp-eyed supervision, they were cutting cloth and yarn and stuffing the finished dolls as fast as they could go. To Dana's amazement, the five of them had already produced seven good-sized dolls and promised to have the rest finished long before bedtime tonight.

But not before supper! Tantalizing smells of chili and cornbread and a chocolate cake baking in the oven wafted from the kitchen where Stan was slaving away. The promise of supper made Dana's stomach growl.

The thought of Stan made her ache.

Thank God she hadn't gotten assigned to the kitchen, she thought, scowling at the pile of doll faces she still had to embroider. She was really very pleased she was out here working on the dolls. Absolutely, overwhelmingly delighted.

For the fifth time in as many minutes, she glanced up when the double doors to the kitchen swung open, only to droop when it wasn't Stan who walked through.

Irritated, she stabbed her needle into the doll's face she was embroidering. Right into the eye.

She was *glad* he was in the kitchen and she was out here. Glad, glad, *glad*! Yessirree, GLAD!

"You look like you could strangle someone if you got half a chance."

Dana looked up, startled, to find Reba standing beside her, smiling.

Reba set the furled wall hanging on the table, then gestured to the chair beside her. "Mind if I join you?"

"Oh! No. No, of course not. Please." Dana swept her sewing stuff off the chair and onto the table in front of her.

"I just wanted to thank you for all your help," Reba said, settling into the chair as gracefully as she did everything else. "We're all very grateful. For the mending and the entertainment for the kids, and especially for finding this lodge. I don't know what we'd have done if you hadn't. The Parkers are absolutely wonderful."

Dana ducked her head to hide the sudden blush. "Actually, it was Stan who made it possible. If he hadn't agreed to pay all the extra costs, and triple time for the kids who are helping Penny and Mike—"

"Stan's doing all that?"

Dana nodded, suddenly worried she'd said something she shouldn't have. "Mike told me. I don't think Stan wants anyone to know."

Reba smiled. "I suspected he might have done something like that. It's just the sort of thing he would do."

"It is?" Dana asked blankly, then wondered why that surprised her. She'd read those articles about all his volunteer work with kids.

The trouble was, whenever he looked at her, everything went out of her head except the charged sexual awareness between them and the knowledge that she could have him if she would just let down the barriers she kept between them. Not for long. Not for forever. But she could have him for awhile. And wasn't that better than never having him at all? She wished she knew. Things would be a lot easier if she did.

"Stan said you'd never met before yesterday," Reba said. Not prying, exactly, but clearly curious.

Dana frowned, then turned the doll's face over and knotted off her thread. "That's right."

"Somehow, I find that hard to believe. You seem so . . . comfortable together."

"We do?"

Reba nodded. "I know you're always quarreling, but that doesn't mean anything. Stan obviously likes you. A lot."

He wants me, Dana silently objected. *But only for now.* It wasn't the same thing at all.

Rather than reply, she changed the topic. "Slick's very nice."

Reba flinched, then forced a smile. "Yes, he is. Just ask any woman who's not deaf, blind, and senile."

For a moment, Dana wasn't sure she really heard the doubt in Reba's voice that she thought she heard. But then she looked into the other woman's eyes and realized that, in her own way, beautiful, cool, calm Reba, who was never uncertain about anything, was just as uncertain about Slick Merrick and her feelings for him as Dana was about Stan Kijewski.

The insight was so unexpected, so stunning in its impact, that Dana almost stopped breathing.

"Guess I'd better check on things in the kitchen," Reba said, pointedly getting to her feet.

Callie, who was working at the next table, had been listening to the conversation. She glanced at Reba's retreating back, then at JD, who was unrolling the enormous ball of red yarn he'd made that afternoon and cutting it into the prescribed lengths for the dolls' hair.

"I can't believe you're making me destroy this work of art," he grumbled. "Look at it! Round! I got it *round*, not lopsided. Do you know how hard that is to manage? And now you want me to cut it up?"

"Yes, I want you to cut it up," Callie said, ignoring his grumbling.

"Round and firm and fully packed." He patted the ball of yarn lovingly, like a lover pats a loved one. He was looking straight at Callie when he did it. "I'm telling you, it's a work of art. The Sistine Chapel of yarn balls. You should be more appreciative."

Callie snorted. "I'd appreciate it cut up. *Properly* cut up! Don't just whack it off like that," she added, leaning across the table to slap his hand. "Measure it! You cut it wrong and we'll have to trim everything."

JD heaved a huge sigh and reluctantly turned back to his measuring. "Women!"

"Men!" Callie shook out the red-and-white gingham fabric with a snap.

"You can say that again!" Penny Parker walked up right then. Mike, laden with boxes and covered in cobwebs, was three steps behind.

Seeing him, John and the colonel abandoned their efforts with the tree and came bustling into the hall with the twins hard on their heels.

"Did you find them?" the colonel asked, beaming like a schoolboy. "Did you find those ornaments? And the lights?"

Mike nodded, setting the boxes he carried on a nearby table, then brushing off the dust and cobwebs that covered him. "The lights were new last year, but I think some of those ornaments go back to the thirties, maybe earlier."

"We've never used them," Penny explained, "but we thought, since this is the last year . . . "

She deliberately shrugged off the thought, then glanced at the tables covered with dolls in various stages of construction. She shook her head in amazement. "You guys are incredible."

"And we're all grateful you and Mike could take us in." Whatever lay between her and JD, in the short time she'd been on the bus, Callie had made the Brigade's mission her own.

"Besides, I'm delighted to meet someone who's my size," she

added, laughing. "Reba and Dana could have been models, they're so tall and slim and gorgeous. I was beginning to feel a little lost in their shadows."

Dana blinked in surprise at the unexpected compliment.

Penny, as confident in her own way as Reba and Callie were in theirs, smiled back. "I know just what you mean. Whenever Mike and I fight, he's always accusing me of hitting below the belt, but I just tell him I'd have to stand on a stool to reach anything higher."

She flashed a wicked look at her husband, who laughed. "Leave me out of this! A man hasn't got a chance, *especially* not when you women aim below the belt!"

Penny wrinkled her nose at him, eyes alight with laughter, totally unfazed by the sexual innuendo.

Dr. Maggie beamed approvingly over the wild thatch of red yarn hair she was sewing for a doll, then glanced at the colonel, who was looking at her with an odd light in his eyes. The minute he caught her glance, however, his attention snapped back to the dusty boxes of ornaments that Mike was opening.

Dana, who'd been following the exchange with fascinated interest, would swear he was blushing under that tan.

At that moment, Ethel emerged from her boxes to hold up a pinkish plastic tube with a rounded tip. "Now, whatever in the world is this?"

Morey giggled and snapped his suspenders. Dana blushed. JD and Slick grinned.

Maudeen glanced at the twins, then leaned across the table and, in a low voice, tried to explain.

"What?" said Ethel. "What did you say?"

Maudeen tried again, a little louder this time.

"A grater?" Ethel frowned at the thing. "Doesn't look like any grater I've ever seen.

"I said, it's a *vi*brator," Maudeen roared, frustrated. "Damn it, Ethel! Turn up your hearing aid!"

"What's a vibrator?" one of the twins asked, craning for a better look.

"It ... errr ... " said their father. "Ask your mother. She'll explain."

"It's something for ... uh ... old people," said their mother. She snatched one of the boxes of ornaments off the table and handed it to the boys. "Here. Why don't you see what's in here. And don't drop anything!" she added as the twins, the plastic thing for "old people" already forgotten, began ripping at the tape sealing the box.

"Three D batteries," Ethel murmured, squinting at the fine print on the side. "Say, Maudeen. You wouldn't want to sell me this, would you? This and three good, strong batteries?"

Morey, eyes sparkling wickedly, said, "You know, I was gonna suggest we each make a bow for the tree and hang our wishes on it, but by the look of things, John isn't going to need to. He just got his wish answered early."

Dana watched as John Ross turned three shades of crimson, then, grinning, winked at his wife.

It was all a little too much for her to take in—the laughter, the closeness, the teasing. The constant noise. She was accustomed to the muted sounds of the forest and the silence of her own house. There'd been times during the course of the day when she'd wanted to clap her hands over her ears and run for the hills. And yet the energy, the human warmth, were a welcome balm, too.

She'd never realized just how alone she really was . . . until now.

Her thoughts were interrupted by the sudden appearance of a small, black-haired boy at her elbow.

"Are you the story lady?" he asked, gazing up at her hopefully, the box of ornaments already forgotten.

"Well, I—" She smiled. "Yes, I guess I am. And you're . . . Tyler, right?"

"How'd you know?"

"Most folks can't tell us apart," Taylor informed her, magically appearing on her other side. "Sometimes not even Mom and Dad."

"I guess I'm just used to looking for all the little signs that others miss," she said. "You have to, if you're going to work with forest animals."

"Real animals?" Tyler asked. "Like deer and moose and stuff?"

"Like lions and tigers and bears?" his brother added, wide-eyed.

"Well, deer and moose, anyway," Dana said, smiling. "I'm afraid New England's a little short of lions and tigers."

"Reba says you know lots of stories," Taylor said.

"Lots and lots of stories," Tyler added hopefully. "About bears and wolves and stuff."

"And stuff," Dana agreed. "Would you like me to tell you some?"

Two dark heads nodded in unison.

Stan gave one last, vigorous stir to the huge pot of chili he'd made under Emma Smith's stern supervision—she'd disapproved of the way he chopped the onions—then set down his spoon and pulled off his apron. Mrs. Smith would never notice he was gone. She was too busy fussing over the cake she and Betty were whipping up.

He had to go find Dana. He'd iron or sew on buttons if he had to—he was pretty sure he remembered how to sew on buttons—but he was not staying in that damned kitchen one more minute. Not when Dana was out there instead of in here with him.

He'd thought he'd had it all worked out. She'd help him with the chili, which would give him an excuse to get close to her and to feed her and watch the way that little crease formed on the bridge of her nose whenever she was thinking hard. He'd ply her with wine then maybe, just maybe, convince her to sneak away to the pantry, where they could try out a couple of wild little fantasies he had about her and him and those long, long legs of hers wrapped tight around him.

But somehow it hadn't worked out that way and he couldn't bear to spend another minute with the chili when he could have all the spice a man would ever need with her.

He got as far as the door to the dining room when he was suddenly brought up short.

Two handsome, tousle-headed males had gotten to her first. One of the twins was sitting on her lap, gazing up at her with adoration, while the other was resting, knees tucked under his chin, on the dining room chair beside her. Both boys were perfectly still and quiet, so entranced by whatever tale she was telling that they'd stopped wiggling and talking and were just sitting there, hanging on her every word.

Stan blinked. Then he grabbed the edge of the door for support as a hunger that wasn't sex but that was as sharp and hot and demanding as anything he'd ever felt damn near drove him to his knees.

CHAPTER TEN

SAM

Wednesday night, two days 'til Christmas Eve.

"Holy hell, Slick! Where'd you get all these candles?"

Where'd you get all these candles? Sam mimicked JD's words to himself, silently, but out loud all he said was, "Go away, JD."

"Is that any way to talk to a friend?" JD tsk-tsked a few times before he added, "Are you making a shrine here? Like, uh, are you gonna be prayin' or somethin'?"

Hardly! Well, maybe, but not for peace and goodwill toward all men.

"I don't think I've ever seen you down on your knees."

Oooh, I intend to be down on my knees, all right, but I won't be praying. Sam had been arranging some pillows he'd filched from the lodge. He turned around, intending to set JD straight, only to see him grinning like a Cheshire cat. The bum hadn't meant praying with the knees remark, after all.

His good buddy was leaning casually against the jamb of the open doorway of his cabin, legs crossed at the ankles. The problem was, Sam wasn't in the mood for buddying around right now, and he'd deliberately chosen one of the cabins farthest from the lodge to ensure his privacy. He'd left the door open, temporarily, to create a draft for the fire which now roared in the stone fireplace.

"So, do you carry candles around with you all the time? Are they, like, ingredients for smoothness? I mean, do you have an actual smoothness kit?"

Sam made a snorting sound of disgust. "I bought them from Maudeen."

"Maudeen had . . . " JD made a great show of pointing to each of the candles and counting, " . . . *twenty-three* candles on her person?"

"Not exactly on her person. They were donations to the Santa

Brigade . . . leftovers," Sam explained defensively.

Hell, it should be obvious, considering the condition of the candles. There were thin tapers and fat candles that gave off holiday scents. Some were in the shape of objects, like Santas or Christmas trees, and some were in cheap holders. One of them might even be a menorah. But all of them were scratched or bent . . . damaged goods donated by some business. "Don't worry about the Santa Brigade's depleted stock, though. The old bird ripped me off big time before she dug into her Santa goodie bag. She charged me a hundred bucks, which she'll use to buy more stuff."

JD's jaw dropped open. "Why?"

"Why what? Why did Maudeen take me to the cleaners?"

"Why did you want so blinkin' many candles?"

Sam quirked one eyebrow at his friend, as if he were dense as a doorknob . . . which he was not.

JD scanned the small cabin, which consisted of the main living area where the fireplace was located with two big easy chairs, some kerosene lamps, and a big ol' bear rug on the floor. Frankly, it was the big ol' bear rug that had sold him on this particular cabin. Man, did he have plans for Mr. Grizzley! Wide archways opened off two sides, one leading into a kitchenette and the other into a small bedroom where already the high bed had been made up with linens, wool blankets and a brightly covered patchwork quilt. Under the candle light, the worn fabrics and carpet and the dingy log walls were invisible. You could hardly tell that the random plank pine flooring had needed resanding for at least twenty years. Instead, the cabin looked charming and warm and . . . romantic.

"Oh," JD said as understanding dawned. "Golly gee, Slick, you are one smooth sucker. I never would have thought of this kind of thing . . . ahead of time."

That remark didn't ever merit a response. "How'd you find me anyhow?"

"Followed the wheelbarrow tracks."

That made sense. No way had Sam been going to make multiple trips up this mountainside from the lodge to cart all the things he'd needed to clean and spruce up the cabin. He'd found one of those old-fashioned, deep wheelbarrows in a tool shed.

"Those tracks aren't going to be visible for long, though. The snow's coming down thicker'n thieves now."

Sam nodded, discerning JD's hidden message. They were going to be snowbound here for awhile, and there was a chance they might not be able to make George's wedding. He would hate for that to happen. They all would.

"So, are you staying in the lodge then?"

"Nope," JD answered with a wide grin. "I'm your neighbor. Next cabin down."

"Great! Maybe I can borrow a cup of sugar, or something."

"In case you want to bake a cake, or something?"

"Go away, JD."

Of course, JD did just the opposite. He entered the cabin, closing the door behind him. "So, what else did Cyber Granny have in her goodie bag?"

Sam pointed to a small tape player, punched a button, and out came Chris deBurgh with his hot, sexy rendition of "The Lady in Red." Sam thought that song was particularly appropriate since his lady was most often seen of late in a red Santa suit. But then, the only other choice Maudeen had offered him was Sam Cooke's Greatest Hits.

JD's jaw dropped another notch.

Then Sam showed him the small table in the kitchen area covered with a red and green plaid tablecloth. You could hardly see the chips in the ironstone china for all the sprigs of holly, interspersed with mistletoe, that surrounded the plates and the candle centerpiece. He'd declined Maudeen's offer of fruitcake and eggnog, but there was an assortment of plastic-wrapped cheeses, crackers, a can of caviar, a mini rum cake, and even a bottle of wine.

"For later," he explained since they'd all just eaten a hearty potluck meal down at the lodge.

JD's jaw dropped yet another notch.

"And here's the coop de grass," he said, deliberately misspeaking the phrase, as he and the guys always used to do following high school French classes. He opened a gift box and took out an object, which he held in the air by two thin straps. It was a black lace teddy. What Maudeen had been going to do with it, he had no idea . . . and he didn't want to know. "Y'know what the best thing is about this . . . thing?" Maudeen had called it a teddy . . . a "Freddy Teddy," to be precise . . . from Frederick's of Hollywood. But he'd be damned if he'd tell JD that.

"The strategically placed red bows?"

"Nope. It's heat sensitive."

"I . . . beg . . . your . . . pardon."

"See, whenever these little bells in the front get warm, they play music." He held the cluster of tiny bells tightly in his fist for a moment until they began playing, "Jingle Bells." Sam thought this was one instance when he might be able to put up with that stupid song.

JD grinned as he considered all the ways that enough heat could be generated to jumpstart the bells. Then he demanded, "Give me some of this stuff."

Sam laughed. "Not on your life."

"Sell me some stuff then."

"No. Besides, I doubt if you have enough money. Callie probably pickpocketed you again."

JD made a scoffing noise at that prospect. Still, he patted his jacket pocket, just to make sure his wallet was still there. "C'mon. For old times sake."

"You've played the old times sake card too many times over the years. Time for you to go away and play with your . . . uh, handcuffs," he advised, shoving JD toward the door. Then he stopped in his tracks. "On the other hand, I might consider trading a half dozen candles for . . ."

JD laughed, knowing what was coming.

" . . . a set of handcuffs."

JD laughed some more. But he didn't say no.

Oh, boy, oh, boy, oh, boy!

After JD was gone, Sam leaned back against the closed door, twirled a set of handcuffs like a lasso, and smiled to himself. *Mistletoe, a bear rug and handcuffs! Is this a man's idea of the perfect Christmas, or what?*

Now, next step on his agenda. How to lure Reba to his bear lair?

Man, oh, man. it was creepy, tiptoeing down the eerily silent, deserted hallways of the second floor at the lodge, searching for Reba's room. It was almost like the horror movie, *The Shining* which took place in an empty, off-season lodge. If anyone even remotely resembling Jack Nicholson wielding a knife popped out of one of these doorways, Sam swore he was going to have a heart attack.

"What're you doin', skulking around?" a crotchety old voice inquired behind him.

Sam's heart bungee-jumped up to his throat, and, yep, his body was on autopilot and he was approaching heart attack city. "Jeez, Maudeen! Couldn't you give a guy warning before sneaking up on him?"

"Seems to me, you're the one sneakin', buddy boy."

He turned around and felt himself go bug-eyed at what he saw. Maudeen in a calf-length, two-piece outfit that he thought was referred to as a peignoir set. It was made of some thin swishy material in bright pink. On her feet were backless high heels covered with feathery puffs in matching hot pink. Her hair was also pink tonight. She looked like a big fluff of candy cotton.

"Where are you off to in that get-up?" he finally managed to get out.

"Morey's room. We have a date."

Oh . . . my . . . God!

In one hand, she carried a bottle of champagne. In the other, a jar with a small paint brush attached.

"And that?" He pointed at the jar.

"Chocolate body paint."

Oh . . . my . . . God! Then he thought of something else. "How come you didn't offer me *that* when you sold me all those freakin' candles?"

"Watch yer language, sonny. And the reason is, you didn't ask. You should be familiar with that drill, being in the military and all. 'Don't ask, don't tell.' Ha, ha, ha."

Her little joke didn't merit even a chuckle from him. So, he threw a twenty dollar bill at her and grabbed the jar, stuffing it in his jacket pocket.

"I suppose you're on the prowl for Reba," Maudeen said. "Big plans, huh?" No beating around the bush with this senior babe.

He nodded. Being busted by a Pretty-in-Pink Cyber Granny sort of paralyzed a guy's tongue.

Maudeen motioned with her thumb toward the next doorway, then continued down the corridor where Morey opened a door before she even knocked. In that brief moment before he whisked Maudeen inside, Sam saw Morey, in all his glory. No suspenders this time! Nope, the old goat wore a long silk robe, belted at the waist, and a jaunty cravat tied at his neck. Just like an old 1940's David Niven movie, minus the thin mustache.

With a shake of his head to clear it of that image, Sam walked over and knocked softly on Reba's door. Reba cracked the door open almost immediately.

"Sam! What are you doing here?"

"Let me come in."

"I'm not dressed," she said.

"Good." He pushed his way in, not wanting to gain the attention of any more seniors lodging on this floor. Lord knows what they were up to! Then, he observed, "You are so dressed."

Unlike the hot-to-trot Maudeen, Reba was wearing a long flannel nightgown and big wool socks. Her hair was pulled back into a pony tail, and her face was scrubbed free of make-up. In other words, she looked adorable.

"Nice duds!" he commented, walking further into her room . . . a suite, actually. Or it would have been a posh mountain suite at one time . . . about a century ago. Now, suffering from severe neglect, it was just a big old log-walled room with a cold fireplace, faded furniture and threadbare carpets. Its one redeeming value was the wide sweep of windows that covered one wall, looking out at the mountains. A spectacular view right now, with the snow coming down heavily like a wispy white lace curtain, underlit by the warm glow of an old fashioned gas lamp.

"It's cold. And I wasn't expecting company tonight." Reba crossed her arms defensively over her chest. As if he could see anything under that L.L. Bean version of a negligee!

"Let's go for a walk," he suggested suddenly.

"A walk? Are you nuts? It's about ten degrees outside. And snowing to beat the band."

"I want to show you my cabin."

"Uh-huh. Not tonight, Sam."

"You and I have unfinished business," he told her, walking up real close. With the fingertips of one hand, he traced her lips which parted as she gazed unblinkingly at him. But forget about the parted lips; there was a stubborn jut to her chin, as well. "You and I have unfinished business," he repeated, this time in a more insistent tone.

"I know, but I've been thinking . . . "

Uh-oh! Always a bad idea when a woman starts thinking! " . . . perhaps we should wait 'til after George's wedding. Decisions shouldn't be made in the heat of passion."

Heat of passion? He liked the sound of that. "On the other hand, sometimes people wait too long, and the opportunity gets lost. You and I do not want to lose each other again, Reba."

"Sometimes it's best to wait for the right time . . . ," she countered, ". . . to see what God . . . or the fates . . . have in store for us. If it was meant to be, it will be."

"Haven't you ever heard the expression, 'God helps those who help themselves.'?"

She laughed at his perseverance.

"You said you loved me."

"I do."

"Well?"

She sighed deeply. "Sometimes love isn't enough. Oh, don't go frowning, Sam. I'm not saying I want to end anything. I just don't want to begin anything hastily, either. Everything has happened so quickly these past two days. We need to slow down and act like adults, not teenagers with raging hormones."

"You know what I think, Reba? You think too much." With that, he reached down and took one of her hands in his. Raising it to his mouth, he kissed each of her knuckles . . . just before he clicked a handcuff to her wrist. She barely had a chance to register what he'd done when he snapped the other metal bracelet on her other wrist.

She stared, flabbergasted, at her shackled wrists, then raised her eyes to his.

"Are you coming willingly, or do I have to carry you?"

"You couldn't carry me, even if you were going to try, which you're not." Same old Reba. Even when she was thin, she thought she was fat. Even when she was practically hog-tied, she still argued with him.

"Wanna bet?" He'd had enough of talking. Time for some action. Sam lifted Reba by the waist and stomped over to the bed where he threw her onto a chenille bedspread. Then, quickly, he rolled her up in the bedspread 'til she formed a big chenille tube. There were a lot of muffled words coming out of the tube, most of them swear words, he would guess, but one sentence did emerge intact. "What . . . are . . . you . . . doing?"

He had the answer to that one, and it just came to him in that instant. He would have patted himself on the back for the inspiration, if he'd had a free hand. "You're going to be my love prisoner."

As he slung her over his shoulder and proceeded toward his waiting chariot . . . uh, wheelbarrow, there was only stunned silence coming from Reba. He was a bit stunned himself. First, he skydived to Reba. Then, he joined a Santa Brigade to be with Reba. Finally, he captured Reba.

He couldn't wait to see what he would do next.

"Don't be mad, Reba."

"Oh, I'm mad, all right," she said, but only half-heartedly. She couldn't help but be flattered that Sam would have gone to so much trouble for her. The candles. The fire. The clean cabin . . . she could only imagine how much work that had taken. The Christmas decorations. The food. Heck, even her "kidnapping."

Just moments ago, he'd dropped her unceremoniously on the floor of his cabin and unrolled her from the bedspread . . . following a bumpy ride in his wheelbarrow. While entubed, she'd rehearsed lots of things she was going to say to him once she was free, all of them starting with an expletive. But now that she was free, she found herself speechless.

Sam stood before her, shivering. Even though he had on his aviator's jacket and leather gloves, he was covered from head to toe with at least an inch of snow, including his white eyebrows and eyelashes. The way the storm was hitting full-force now, they would all be snowbound by morning.

"Take off those wet clothes and sit down in front of the fire before you catch pneumonia," she snapped, finally regaining the ability to speak.

He smiled, or tried to, through chattering teeth.

"Don't go thinking you're off the hook. I have lots to say to you, mister, but I don't relish talking to a corpse." Well, that certainly sounded tough . . . she hoped. The one thing she didn't want to sound was easy. *Tough, yes. Easy, no.* She kept repeating that refrain to herself as Sam pulled a pair of sweat pants and a tee shirt out of his duffle bag near the door and went into the bathroom to change.

While he was gone, she shuffled around the room in her wool socks, examining everything with her handcuffed hands. The cabin would have been really comfortable in the lodge's heyday . . . the late 1890's. And it must have been renovated at some point . . . perhaps the 1950's . . . because there was a kitchen with appliances and running water, although the electricity had been cut off for some time. She tried to avoid peering into the bedroom with its high, country style bed and soft quilt; so, she sauntered into the kitchenette. Nibbling on a cracker, she managed to open a gift box, even handcuffed, then exclaimed, "Samuel Merrick! You are the biggest dope in the world!"

"Were you talking to me?" he said, coming out of the bathroom and neatly laying his wet clothing over a chair near the fire. As Reba recalled, Sam had been a neat-freak, even before he went into the military.

"Yes, I'm talking to you, Dope-of-the-Month." She held up a black negligee, as if that said it all.

Sam's face turned red. And, criminey, how could a man look so handsome in faded sweats and a white tee shirt that proclaimed, *I'm Blue. Are You?* Affronted, he put one fist on a hip and asked, "What? You don't like it?"

"Sam! Maudeen's been trying to pawn this outfit off on every woman at Winter Haven for the past two years. I hope you didn't give her money for it."

His face turned even redder. Then, with a grunt of disgust, probably at himself, he dropped down on his knees to a bear rug before the fire, threw on another log from the big pile stacked against the wall, and motioned for her to join him.

She did, but almost immediately held out her hands. "Game's over, Rambo. How about unlocking me now?"

He shook his head. "Not yet."

"Why?"

"Because I have plans."

She knew what plans he had. And so did her suddenly achy breasts and that place between her legs. Both were hard to ignore. Even when she was mad at Sam, he could still turn her on. Some things never changed.

Because she didn't immediately protest his "plans," Sam must have taken her silence for acquiescence. "The question is, honey, do we make love first, and talk later? Or do we talk now, and make love later?"

"Or do we do neither?" She'd just tossed that in to be obstinate . . . so she wouldn't appear easy.

Sam seemed surprised. "Is that what you really want?"

She thought for all of a nanosecond. "No."

He let out a whoosh of relief. It was hard to believe that Sam, a world-famous Blue Angels pilot, could be so unsure of himself . . . when around her, anyhow.

"Come here, you." He put a hand on her nape and tugged her closer. Then he settled her between his bent knees so that they both faced the fire. Her back was to him, her legs outstretched. When he had her situated the way he wanted, Sam crossed his arms over her chest and rested his chin on her shoulder.

For long moments, they both just stared at the fire, letting its warmth seep into their bones. A relaxed tranquility lay between them in a room bright with light from the fire, the many burning candles and the pristine snow which showed through the two living room windows. When Sam finally began to speak against her ear, she realized there was another reason why he'd wanted them in the position they were in . . . so she couldn't see his face when he spoke of things that only he, in his misplaced masculine pride, considered embarrassing.

"I have never been good enough for you, Reba. Shhh. Let me speak, or I'll never get the words out. 'Bad boy!' 'Troublemaker!' 'Rotten seed!' 'Blood of an addict running in his veins!' 'He'll never amount to anything!' 'Jail's the best place for his kind!' 'Inner city trash!' 'Worthless!' I heard those descriptions of myself, nonstop, from the time I was a little kid. And make no mistake about it, adults can be just as cruel as kids. Their words bite just as hard. Police, teachers, social workers, grocery store clerks, whatever. It wasn't 'til I left Snowdon that I realized I could start over with a clean slate. I didn't become different. I was still bad inside, but no one knew my past. I worked hard to keep it hidden."

Reba's heart broke for Sam, for the little boy who never thought he was good enough, for the young man who'd apparently felt the same way, even for the adult who must, unbelievably, still carry some of those insecurities. She raised her cuffed hands and squeezed the forearms crossed over her. "Sam, I never judged you that way. George never did, either. And I have to believe that lots of people in Snowdon were nonjudgmental."

"Maybe, in hindsight, I put more weight on the negative remarks. And, in their defense, I have to admit I played the bad boy role to the hilt at times. The old, 'If I've got the name, I might as well play the game' scenario. A vicious circle."

"I do remember, now that you mention it, how you and JD and Stan often said you were falsely accused of stuff . . . just because you were from the home . . . or just because your reputations preceded you."

"Yep! Why do you think we stuck together all the time?"

"Do JD and Stan have these same feelings?" She frowned, finding it hard to believe there was so much she hadn't seen.

Sam shrugged. "We never talked about it, but, yeah, I guess we all carried some baggage when we left Snowdon, to one extent or another."

"I had no idea that it was that bad."

"I didn't tell you this to get your sympathy. I'm trying to explain why I acted the way I did after I left Snowdon. If I'm bungling the job, it's because I don't understand it entirely myself. It's not a problem anymore, though. Really. So, don't go putting your psychologist hat on and trying to analyze me. I put this all behind me a long time ago. The only reason I'm bringing it up now is that you deserve an explanation."

She nodded. Then something occurred to her that never would have entered her mind before. "Did my parents ever say anything to you? My mother died a year or two after you came to Snowdon, I think, and she was sick most of the time by then. But my Dad? Oh, Sam! Please don't tell me that he hurt you, too."

"No, he never said anything . . . not outright. But he thought it, Reba. And it was in his eyes every time he looked at me. He never considered me good enough for you."

Reba swatted his forearm with one palm. "You fool! My father never thought anyone, boy or man, was good enough for me. You know zippo about fathers and daughters if you took that attitude personally."

"Okay, I'll concede that one," he said. "But we're getting off the subject. I didn't really care about the opinion of the Snowdon residents. It was you, Reba. I had to do something to make myself worthy of you. I needed to *earn* you. First, at the Academy. Then, in the Navy when I was flying Jets. Even in the Blues. Oh, by then, you were already married . . . or I thought you still were . . . but, always, when I would reach some new level, I would think, 'Reba would be proud of me now.'"

She was angry now and tried to turn around and face him. He wouldn't allow her to. So, she spoke her furious words to the fire. "You make me so mad I could spit, Samuel Merrick. I was always proud of you . . . the you I knew and loved. I never needed football touchdowns in high school, or show-off skiing exhibitions, or academic honors in college, or military medals, or high-in-the-sky daredevil flying tactics. You were always perfect to me."

"Me? Perfect? Now you're going too far." Sam's words were doubtful, but she sensed that he liked what she'd said.

The male ego never ceased to amaze her, always needing to be boosted and soothed . . . especially Sam's. Well, it was a small thing to do, she supposed. "Not perfect as in never making a mistake, but perfect as in a good human being, with a heart of gold. You're loyal, and fair, and kind, not to mention too gorgeous to live." She chuckled on adding that last characteristic.

Instead of laughing, as he usually would, Sam was quiet. "Lots of people, especially females, like me because of how I look, Reba."

That was the last straw. She squirmed out of his arms and turned so that she was kneeling between his legs, facing him. Wagging a forefinger in his face, she said, "Don't you dare imply that I ever, *ever*, cared about you because of your appearance."

"I'm not . . . I didn't . . . I was trying to say that you're the only one who cared about *me*. Sometimes I think you would have loved me even if I were homely as a hog."

"Well, maybe not hog-homely," she teased. "And I'm no different than everyone else. I do like looking at you, Sam."

He smiled . . . that wonderful, beautiful smile that was pure Sam . . . the one that melted her bones and tipped her world on its axis. But there was one more hurdle that had to be crossed.

"Bottom line, Sam, you never came back. You broke my heart. Not all at once. No, in a more painful way. Little by little . . . day by day, month by month, year by year. I kept hoping, at least in the beginning that you would come back. Even when the letters grew farther apart, and the phone calls stopped."

"It was hard work at the Academy . . . harder than I'd ever imagined it would be. And it required focus almost twenty-four hours a day. A seventeen-hour-a-day, endless treadmill of physical exercise, classroom lectures, marching drills and late night studying. Later, there was summer duty aboard carriers. And then flight training. I kept asking you to come visit, and when you didn't, I probably dug in my heels. I guess I thought there was all the time in the world for us to get things right. I never expected you to get married, Reba. Stupid of me, I suppose, to presume that you would wait 'til I got my act together. You talk about me breaking your heart, little by little. Well, honey, you broke my heart in one fell swoop. I went off the deep end for awhile. I even . . ." He waved a hand as if it didn't matter anymore and the memory was too painful to recount.

"Oh, Sam."

"You should have told me yourself, Reba."

"You should have told me why you stopped writing, Sam."

"I thought you stopped loving me, babe."

"I thought the same."

"I'm sorry. Can you ever forgive me?"

Tears welled in her eyes. All she could do was nod.

His back was propped against the side of the chair, and she still knelt between his outstretched legs. He reached a hand up to caress her hair, trailing his fingertips along her jawline and over her lips.

She would have liked to do the same to him, but her hands were still cuffed together.

"So, what do we do next, Sam?"

Sam grinned then. "Oh, sweetheart! I thought you'd never ask."

In the back of Reba's mind, a little niggling thought intruded, reminding her that nothing had really been decided between her and Sam. The past had been explained, but what about the future?

Not now, she decided. Whatever would be would be. For now, she was going to grasp the gold ring and hold on tight for as long as she could. If the ring slipped out of her fingers, eventually, well, at least she could say that she'd held it for awhile.

Sam was kneeling now, too. He took both of her hands in his, then asked an unexpected, loaded question. "Which do you like best? The nightgown or the handcuffs?"

Reba had to think for a minute before she understood his meaning. "Oh, definitely the handcuffs."

"Oh, I like your answer." With that, Sam reached into a side pocket of his sweat pants, pulled out a pocket knife—this boy scout was always prepared—and proceeded to cut a seam down one outside arm of her nightgown from neckline to wrist, then the other. The flannel fabric fell off her shoulders, down her back, over the front, baring her breasts, caught by her handcuffed arms. Within seconds Sam had the rest of the gown pulled down and tossed aside so that she knelt before him, naked except for her wool socks, which he also removed.

Reba did feel like a love prisoner then, just as Sam had said she would be. And she liked it. A lot.

Then Sam quickly removed his own clothing, and in the process, Reba had to blink several times at the sheer beauty of the man. Perfect proportions. Tan skin. Muscles. Sculpted features.

That was her last coherent thought for awhile.

"I want to do everything the first time. You just lie still. Please. I'm been dreaming about this for so long . . . fantasizing. Okay?"

What could she say except a barely audible, "yes"? Who wouldn't want to be the fulfillment of a man's fantasy . . . of this man's fantasy? Truth to tell, she had a few fantasies of her own; maybe she would tell him about those . . . later.

Sam, sitting on his haunches to her side, arranged her on the bearskin rug to his satisfaction . . . her cuffed hands raised overhead, the metal links caught in the bear's open jaw.

"Raise your one knee a tiny bit, honey."

She did.

"Spread the other leg . . . just a little . . . oh, yes. Just like that."

When he leaned forward to release her hair from its rubber band, his hardened penis brushed against her hip. She wanted very much to touch him.

Sam chuckled. "Keep on looking at me like that, babe, and this game will be over before it begins."

Reba felt her face heat with embarrassment.

"Gee, Reba, I didn't know you could do that. Blush all over." While he spoke, teasingly, he was spreading the long tresses released from her pony tail out to the side and over her shoulders.

She blushed some more.

Sam spent a long time then, examining her body, remarking on every little change, comparing the "Old Reba" to the "New Reba." Everything was worthy of comment, from her fresh-scrubbed face, which he seemed to like, to her flame-painted toenails, which he did not. The things that pleased him most were parts of her anatomy which had not changed.

"Your nipples are pointy. Did you know that, Reba? God, I love pointy nipples.

"You still have dimples behind your knees," he announced with such glee you would have thought he'd discovered a new planet.

"Your lips part when you're aroused, did you know that? And you make these little breathy sounds that turn me so hot I can't stand it. You're aroused now, baby. And I'm hotter than a firecracker."

Sam especially admired the hair between her legs, which he petted . . . and petted . . . and petted. And referred to in a wonderfully rough voice as "silk," and "spun gold."

When he encouraged her to spread wider, she moaned, but acquiesced. "Sam, I'm ready now. Don't make me wait."

"Oh, baby, it's much too soon. You have to wait. I promise I'll make it worth your while." He arranged himself between her legs and lay atop her so that his erection nestled along her woman channel, perfectly. She had the coarse hair of the bearskin rug abrading against her back, and Sam's furred chest and legs abrading her front. Then he took her face in his hands and kissed her, first soft, with reverence, then hard, with hunger. He showed her with his mouth and teeth and tongue how very much he wanted her, even if his mind was holding back.

Before he ever pulled away from his assault on her mouth, and moved lower, Reba was whimpering with desire. She tugged her hands, trying to get free, but the loops of the chain were indeed caught in the bear's teeth by now. She rolled from side to side and tried to buck Sam off.

Sam laughed his triumph at her hopeless struggles. "You are my love prisoner," he murmured against her ear, "to do with as I want."

The words thrilled, and annoyed her. She tried to turn her face away.

"Tell me that you like being my love prisoner. Tell me, Reba. Tell me." The whole time he entreated her, he was doing incredible things to her breasts with his talented fingers. Very talented fingers.

"I like being your love prisoner," she finally admitted half-coherently.

Reba discovered a talent of her own then. By undulating her hips, she was able to rub that engorged part of herself against that long column of his own engorgement. The slickness . . . the friction . . . the rhythm were delicious agony . . . tortured excitement. To both of them, apparently, because Sam moaned and gritted his teeth.

"I can't wait, baby. I wanted to wait . . . to make it so good for you . . . but I caaaannnn't wait." With that, Sam plunged himself into her wetness with a masculine howl of primitive pleasure. He was embedded in her, unmoving. And yet a part of him did move . . . a subtle throb . . . throb . . . throb.

Or, criminey, could it be that she was the one throbbing around him?

Even as Reba was momentarily dazed by what was happening inside her, Sam began to move, and she couldn't help but notice that he made love with the same concentration he gave everything he did in life. As if he had something important to prove . . . all the time. He got back as much satisfaction as he gave in lovemaking, she was sure, but his primary focus was her pleasure.

Accompanying his long strokes were softly whispered endearments and murmurs of encouragement.

"Aaah, Reba, it feels so good to be with you . . . inside you."

"Like that, honey. Yeeeesss, like that."

"Touch me."

"Open."

"I love you, baby. I do . . . I do . . . I do . . . "

She, on the other hand, was beyond speech.

It seemed like an hour, but was probably only minutes before Sam came with a guttural cry of release. At the same time, her orgasm accompanied his with strong convulsions of pleasure. He collapsed atop her, his heavy weight a caress in itself, to Reba's mind.

Reba had no idea what the future would hold for them, but for now, all she could say was, *Welcome home, Sam.* She hoped one day she would be able to say the words aloud.

It was the middle of the night, and still they had not slept. Sam was insatiable.

She was insatiable.

Isn't insatiability grand? she thought with a giggle.

"What are you giggling about?" Sam said, nipping her ear. "I thought I cured you of giggling the last time."

"The last time?" she sputtered. "That was three times ago, buddy."

"Are you complaining?"

"Heck, no."

"Good." He tugged her even closer into his embrace.

Actually, the "last time" was their fifth bout of lovemaking . . . sixth if you counted that little modeling demonstration she'd done with Maudeen's tacky negligee. Yes, she had let Sam talk her into donning the dumb thing. And, yes, it had generated heat . . . when Sam had generated heat . . . which had caused her to generate heat. And, boy oh boy, had they played "Jingle Bells," which Sam declared from now on was going to be his favorite song.

Of course, Sam had reciprocated by showing her how pilots and astronauts did this little trick with their abdomens called "hooking." It involved tensing the abdominal muscles to prepare for G-forces, or fierce gravitational pulls, in high speed jets or rockets. If they didn't do it, they would pass out. Of course, every time Sam tensed or untensed his abdomen, another of his body muscles—*her favorite*—tensed and untensed, too. He claimed later that, yep, he'd almost passed out from the force of *her* gravitational pull.

Now, they were cuddled under the quilt in the high bed, spoon style, watching the fire which still roared. Sam had fed it a log every hour or so to keep it going. It was the only source of heat in the cabin, which was now covered to the eaves with snow. Most of the candles had long burned down, but it was light enough to see with the fire and the whiteness of the snow outside the bedroom window, along with the two living room windows.

There wasn't a part of Reba's body that didn't ache, and she relished every twinge for all it represented. "I love you, Sam," she said suddenly . . . not that she hadn't said it a time or two . . . or twelve during the night.

"I love you, too, baby."

After they lay for awhile, half-dozing, Sam asked, "I wonder if we'll be able to leave today . . . with all this snow? I'd hate to miss George's wedding . . . especially after coming so far."

"Not just the wedding. We have a shelter stop scheduled for tomorrow, actually today, in Portland, Maine. But I'm not going to worry about it now," she said, turning in Sam's arms and snuggling up against his chest. "I'll bet, even now, Betty is on the phone with all her contacts. She'll have a cavalcade of snow plows here if that's what it takes to get us to our next stop on time."

"Well, at least we put together enough last minute gifts, thanks to that Big-Mart, and the expertise of Callie and Dana, plus everyone chipping in to help."

She nodded, loving the feel of his chest hairs rubbing against her cheek. She loved being in bed with Sam. She loved making love with him. She loved . . .

"You're purring."

"I am not."

"Yes, you were. I heard it. A definite purr." Sam sat up abruptly, knocking her over onto her side. "Holy hell! I can't believe I forgot."

"Forgot what?" She sat up, too, and pulled the quilt up to her shoulders. Despite the fire, there was a chill in the air.

Sam was leaning over the side of the bed, which gave her a most excellent view of his backside. She thought about whistling, but decided she'd boosted his ego enough during the past night.

"Ta-da!" Sam said, handing her a paper bag, which he'd apparently stashed in a bedside table. "I got this present for me from you."

She raised her eyebrows at him. "You got yourself a present? And it's from me?"

"Yep." He folded his hands behind his neck, leaned back on the pillow, and didn't even bother to cover himself. Which prompted her to consider whistling again. And not at his backside, either. "Well, are you going to keep on ogling me, or are you going to open my present?"

She opened the bag, pulled out the object within, and laughed out loud. "Chocolate body paint!"

"It was a last minute 'purchase,' but enlightened, if you ask me."

"Last minute, huh? Like, dare I say the name Maudeen?" His reddening face was answer enough. "Tsk-tsk-tsk! We're going to be the talk of the bus tomorrow."

By the time, dawn finally rolled over the mountain and filled the inside of the cabin with glaring whiteness, Sam and Reba were still unable to sleep. They were "suffering" from a chocolate high.

And they could have cared less whether they were the talk of the bus or all of New Hampshire, or the whole blasted country.

CHAPTER ELEVEN

KEVIN

Wednesday night, less than forty-eight hours before George's wedding

"You can uncuff me now."

"You're my prisoner, and I'll uncuff you when I feel good and ready."

Callie sighed. "JD, you know darn well I couldn't cut and run even if I wanted to. We're snowed in here, for crying out loud. Where would I go?"

Kevin was sticking to his guns, so to speak. He wasn't letting her out of his sight for a moment. Not before he had his way with her. They had unfinished business.

"And how dare you drag me out of the lodge like a caveman?" Callie added.

"You weren't coming willingly."

"You noticed that, did you?"

"Bopping me over the head with a Raggedy Ann doll was a pretty handy clue."

"You're lucky it wasn't a baseball bat. We have a few in stock, you know."

Her use of *we* was telling; kind of sweet and irritating at the same time. Callie was already considering herself part of the team. Which made sense, considering she'd organized the purchase and then construction of a ton of toys tonight. He'd actually truly admired her take-charge attitude. She'd even had Colonel Morgan practically saluting as he ran around following her orders.

The really aggravating part, though, was that she'd hit the bus, then the lodge, as if nothing had happened between them in the Big-Mart. In fact, she'd pretty much ignored him altogether, other than to make fun of his yarn efforts. He wasn't putting up with that. They'd

185

almost made love in a store dressing room, and she was damn well going to acknowledge that fact.

But Kevin was nothing if not patient. Unlike Slick, who was hitting on Reba like a desperate Blue Angel on a mission, Kevin was thinking Callie needed a more subtle approach.

"We're finishing what we started today," he informed her. "I'm making love to you tonight, over and over, 'til you cry uncle. And you know you want that too, so don't give me grief."

Callie didn't react at all, except to study the cuffs on her hands in major detail. When she finally glanced up, her eyes were so filled with fire, Kevin almost took a step back to keep from getting singed.

She stalked him regardless. "First of all, mister *Juvenile Delinquent*, what happened today was zipper burp, compounded by my fuzzy brain, thinking you were kind of attractive."

That was good, he thought. Although he had a real strong desire to ask if he was Harrison-Ford attractive. A *younger* Harrison Ford, of course.

She took another step forward. "Second of all, I was feeling overwhelmed, and I needed to be held. You just happened to be there. A teddy bear would have worked just as well."

That wasn't so good.

"Third of all, I was brought up to save making love for men I cared for, for men I knew, and who knew me and loved me as well."

That wasn't good either, although he was willing to tackle it. "I think I know a lot about you."

"You don't know a thing about me, Wilder."

"I know you're very talented."

"So is a chimp in a circus."

"I know you really seem to like kids."

"So does Santa."

"I know you have about the most wild, sexy hair I've ever seen on a woman. And you *can't* say that about Santa."

That stopped her forward progress. But then she shook her head. "You also know I'm breaking the law, I've stolen from you twice, and I occasionally have a temper."

"Occasionally?" he answered without thinking.

That was the wrong response. Her occasional temper decided to rear its pretty head. "You're a jerk."

"And you're a perp."

"You self-righteous idiot! How dare you judge me? You don't

have a clue what's happened in my life. You don't even care why I've made the choices I have. You're just looking at me like there's a money sign on my head. 'Callie Brandt—pay dirt.'"

"Oh, honey, you are *very* wrong about that."

"Ha! Every time you look at me, I see the wheels turning in your head."

"If you think that's due to looking at a monetary payoff, I have to check my wheels."

"You're not getting free-for-all, stranger sex, either."

Kevin glanced around. He'd done some pre-preparation after dropping in on Slick, but not nearly enough, and not nearly as cool. He really sucked at this stuff.

"Look," he said, "how about if we start a fire and grab a glass of wine and just talk? I'm not forcing myself on you, no matter how tempting that sounds. Let's just relax."

Callie looked around, too. "Not exactly the Ritz, is it?" She glanced back at him and smiled. "But it sure has atmosphere."

"Wine?" he asked, his heart suddenly pumped up.

"That sounds good, but JD, can I ask a favor?"

"Anything," he said, figuring that smile of hers earned her a free ride to anywhere she wanted to go.

"Would you be so kind as to take off these handcuffs?"

The fire crackled, offering warmth. The candles JD had somehow obtained and placed all around them gave off scents that sort of warred with each other. Still, Callie felt happy, and strangely at home, for the first time in many years.

They sipped wine that tasted wonderful and sat on a shag throw rug that most likely had been popular in the sixties.

"JD?"

"Yes?"

"Is your family in Snowdon?"

"Biological? No."

"Why aren't you with them? It's Christmas."

She felt the tension that came over him, even though they weren't touching, and she knew she'd struck a nerve. But curiosity and the desire to understand this man kept her from backing away from the subject. "Kevin? JD?"

He didn't answer for close to a minute. "My family is Sam and

Stan and Reba and especially George. That's my family. Period."

Callie knew that 'period' meant she should shut up right now. Good thing she never believed in periods. "Your parents?"

"Exist only in my genes."

"I'm sorry."

He rolled from his back to his side to face her. "You know, I'm not. I'm not sorry about anything any longer. I have the best friends anyone would be proud to call family, I have a career that matters, I have Harrison Ford—in his younger days—good looks . . . "

He glanced at her, but Callie wasn't about to stroke his ego. Still, she had this funny feeling inside her. "I think you happen to have an incredible family."

"I think so, too."

"But it hurt that the folks in your town 'misunderstood' you."

"They misunderstood all of us, Callie. We were all virtual orphans, and we were all angry. We were young brats. They were right to worry. They just didn't understand the power of George."

"What do you mean?"

"George was our savior. All three of us. He's a veterinarian, and he worked our butts off in his clinic. When we'd get in trouble in school or in town, he always showed up to stand up for us. Then he'd chew us out but good."

Kevin smiled, and Callie's heart melted just a little more. "It was George who encouraged each of us to follow the paths that seemed most right for us. Stan was an aggressive, angry kid. He was ready to let his fists do the talking at any given moment. George told him to harness the anger and use it constructively. Thus, football. Slick pretty much liked discipline and order. And he was nuts about flying. George steered him toward the military. He said, 'Let the government pay for your flying lessons, son.'"

"And you?" Callie asked "Did George realize you have James Bond fantasies?"

"I do *not* have James Bond fantasies."

Callie had to stifle a giggle, seeing as he looked so cute when he was indignant. "Then what drove you to become a private spy?"

"Money."

"Money?" Callie couldn't believe how disappointed she felt. She'd been sure he'd had a nobler purpose than strictly financial incentive. After all, she'd seen this man testify in untold number of trials, and he'd always appeared on the stand as someone who was hell bent on working for truth and justice.

JD laughed at her. "Aww, honey, don't be upset. I'm not as selfish as that. The truth is, George encouraged me to get into law enforcement. He always said, 'Boy, I know you have a fierce sense of justice, but it might be better in the long run if you took that passion and used it within the confines of the law.'" He shrugged. "There's no arguing with George, so I became a cop."

"You were a cop?"

"Yep, for five years."

"Why'd you quit?"

"Like I said, money. A cop's salary is pretty pathetic, and there's no way I'd have been able to save enough for law school."

"Law school? You're going to law school?"

He nodded. "Next fall."

"What kind of lawyer do you want to be?"

"You know, funny enough, three days ago I'd have answered absolutely that I wanted to be a county prosecutor. Put the bad guys away and all that. But I might rethink that some. All along this trip we've met women and kids who could really benefit from sound legal advice. Take that woman in New Hampshire. She and her two kids are forced to come to a shelter for basic needs, simply because her scum of a husband ran off, and she had no idea there are resources out there to help her track him down and make him help pay support for the kids. I'd really like to help out people like that."

Callie's disappointment vanished fast." Oh, JD, that sounds like a wonderful idea!"

"Well, it's not something that's going to happen tomorrow, but it feels right as a long range plan. And trust me, George was a stickler for long-range planning."

"I think he'll be very proud," Callie said quietly. She knew, for some reason she couldn't define, she felt proud of him. Very, very proud. And somehow, after all of this was over, she hoped there'd be some way to check up on Kevin to see if he ever accomplished his long range plan. She fervently hoped so.

There was a long silence. Kevin got up and added another log to a fireplace that probably violated about fifty codes at this point. He sat back down and picked up his wine.

"Your turn, sweetheart. Happy family, yes?"

"Yes and no. At least, I'm not sure you can call it that."

"Tell me."

"My parents were the best. But then my mother got sick right after Jenny was born, and I sort of had to take over."

Kevin refilled her glass, then settled back down in front of the fire. "So you became the mommy of sorts?"

"I did, I guess. Jenny was my father's baby, and I was the one who had to have supper on the table."

"Ow."

"Oh, I'm not complaining! I'm really not. I adore Jen, so it was no problem. And my father's a wonderful man."

"Did your mom . . . pass away?"

"Yes, when I was eight and Jen was three."

"I'm sorry."

"Me, too. She was a great lady."

"Did she teach you how to design clothes?"

Callie laughed softly. "Actually, no. That would have been Emma Peachey, the Amish woman whose farm bordered our property."

Kevin's gorgeous jaw dropped an inch. "You learned how to sew sequins from an Amish woman?"

Callie grinned. "She'd deny it if anyone ever called her on it." Kevin's gaze swept her face. "You have a beautiful smile."

Heat traveled straight down Callie's body, and she didn't think it had anything to do with the wine. "Thank you," she said, feeling suddenly shy and awkward.

"Anyway, that's basically my life in *Reader's Digest* form."

"How about your sister? What does she do?"

"Besides get herself into trouble whenever possible?"

"She's a little hellion, is she?"

"Oh, no! She's the sweetest kid in the world. She just has . . . poor judgment when it comes to some of her acquaintances."

"How so?"

"Is this off the record?"

"This is totally personal, I swear."

"You know the trial I skipped out on?"

"The Morris case, right."

"Dylan Morris is Jen's boyfriend."

"Wow. Poor judgment is right. That guy's slime. No offense."

"None taken. I agree with you. Jen, on the other hand, thinks he's the greatest thing since fast drying nail polish. That's how I got involved in this mess. She wants me to lie on the stand to give him an alibi." Callie turned to him, knowing she looked pathetic, but she needed him. "I can't lie, JD. But I can't hurt my sister, either. And I can't hurt my dad. He treasures my sister."

"Basically, your sister's asking you to commit perjury."

Callie had to swallow twice. "Yes. But she's confused. She doesn't think it's that big a deal, and she swears he's innocent, but just can't prove it."

"So she's asked you to lie on the stand for him?"

"Well, to remember history a bit differently."

"To lie."

"Yes."

"And you're running because you don't want to lie on the stand, am I right?"

"Right."

"And you only stole my wallet not once, but twice because?"

"The first time? I really needed lipstick."

"Come up with a better excuse, just to make me happy."

"I needed to buy food to feed the homeless?"

Kevin grinned. "Works for me. Now, the second time?"

She laughed. "That one's easy, you were being a jerk. You pretty much deserved it."

"Right."

"You're not arguing."

"That's because I'm too busy figuring out how to talk you into making love. And I'm coming up empty."

"Well, some sweet-talking might work."

"You've got me confused with Slick. He's the master of that sort of stuff."

"He doesn't seem to be all that smooth when it comes to Reba."

Kevin cocked his head to the side and looked at her intently. "You know, you pay real good attention."

"Doesn't take a rocket scientist to know sparks when they're blazing."

"Are there sparks blazing here?" he asked, pointing back and forth between them.

"You tell me."

"Well, darlin', I just about burned up in that dressing room."

Callie hesitated. Did she really want to get into a fling with this man? Well, yes, she really did. The point, though, was whether it was a good idea. On the other hand, was denying what they both were feeling any more brilliant? How many nights would she spend kicking herself for not making love with this man?

Too many. She grabbed Kevin's wine goblet and pushed him onto his back. Straddling his hips, she grinned down at him evilly. "Burned up, huh?"

He looked up at her, and there was definitely a bonfire blazing in his eyes. "Have I mentioned you are the most beautiful woman I've ever met?"

"No, but feel free to mention it."

"Have I mentioned you are the sexiest Amish woman I've ever met?"

"You've met a lot of them, have you?"

"No, but you'd make me convert, for sure."

Callie began kneading his chest, loving the muscles that tensed and relaxed under her fingertips. She itched to tear his shirt from him and feel him skin on skin.

His chest expanded as he heaved a breath. "I'm getting lots of sparks here. They can't all be mine."

"Oh, no."

"Are you going to let me make love to you, or are you just torturing me for fun?"

"I'm just torturing you for fun."

Before Callie knew it, she was on her back. Kevin gazed down on her, his brown eyes hot and focused. "Torture me, Amish designer babe."

Callie batted her lashes. "How, sir? I know nothing about the sins of the flesh."

"Let me show you."

Callie's heart just about leaped from her chest as his mouth lowered to hers. She hadn't been able to think about anything *but* the way he'd touched her and kissed her in that dressing room. She'd never had any man make her see how she looked when she was mindlessly aroused. It had been so erotic and almost scary. His fingers on her flesh, his mouth on her neck.

"Touch me again like that," she said out loud.

"I'm getting there. First I want to play with your hair. Do you know you have hair that's sexier than anything I've ever seen? I mean, I was turned on by your hair even before I met you."

"Then play, already." She was getting impatient for the better parts.

"This is better than anything *Playboy's* ever put out."

She was going crazy. He was running his hands through her hair, and she loved it. She didn't think women were supposed to get turned on by a man going wild through their hair. But what did she know?

"You . . . read *Playboy* a lot, do you?"

"Great ads."

"Right."

"I'm getting you naked now," he informed her. She wanted to ask him if he was always into play-by-play, but she was too busy enjoying him making her naked to bother.

He nibbled at her shoulders. "Your arms are so tiny."

He slid his mouth down her body. "And your breasts. Two of them. They are so beautiful."

She was having trouble breathing. "JD?"

"Call me Kevin," he said, then licked a nipple, almost making her scream. "I don't mind JD in every day conversation, but when I'm making love to you, it's Kevin."

She had to breathe or pass out. "Kevin, are you making love to me or taking inventory?"

"Both. One belly button, and it's gotta be the cutest I've ever seen."

"This is . . . wonderful," she said.

His hands roamed all over her, his mouth followed his hands. Callie felt like a starving man's double chocolate fudge sundae. "Honey?" he breathed against her neck.

"Yes?"

"Did you—God, I love touching you—steal those condoms?"

"No. Touch me here," she said, directing his hand.

"God, baby," he said as he stroked her and penetrated her with his fingers.

"Oh, Kevin. Please don't stop. Never. Never."

"Not planning on it," he said, his voice harsh between breaths.

"I only have one of those, by the way."

"One is all we need. God, baby."

"Kevin? Please!"

"Do we need condoms?" he asked roughly. "I need to know right now, baby."

He thrust two fingers deep into her, and Callie cried out and came apart right there on the floor of a dilapidated cabin. The raging storm outside had nothing on what was happening inside of her. "Oh, God, Kevin," she whispered.

He made her come until she almost melted into the shag. Then he looked at her, his eyes so piercing, she almost smiled. The man needed relief. And soon. She loved that her body had made him that needy.

"Baby, do we need a condom?" he asked, his voice pure grit.

Callie smile up at him. "Not for what I have in mind."

She traced the contours of his jaw before shoving him off of her and onto his back.

Right there, to a man she barely knew, but felt like she'd know all her life, Callie Brandt, the dutiful, obedient, *good* daughter, rendered a man helpless and at her utter mercy.

And she loved each and every powerful moment of it.

"Get up, and for goodness sakes, put clothes on her," Maudeen squawked into the phone.

"Who says she's naked?" Kevin asked.

"Give me a break, buddy boy. Now listen, the cops are on their way. The Parkers, bless them, tried to stop the badges, but they couldn't hold off for long. Get your acts together pronto."

Kevin shook his head to try to bring some semblance of brain back to life. He was utterly exhausted in the best possible way, and was having trouble assimilating the situation.

"What are they doing here?" he asked.

"They got a tip from somebody. Who knows? The point is, they know she's here, or somewhere near, and they're on their way. Wake up, boy!"

He sat up and assessed the situation. Callie was naked. Under any other circumstances, that would be the best situation he could possibly imagine. But no one, *no one*, was taking Callie away from him at this point. And most definitely not naked. That body was his. And he wanted it, and her, for at least a hundred more years.

Maudeen practically screeched. "Are you awake, boy?"

"Yes, I'm getting there."

"Let me tell you, if you let that gal get booked, I'm going to come after you and you won't like what's coming."

As much as Kevin wanted to enjoy gazing at Callie in all her naked glory, fear crawled in. Maudeen's warning sent a chill through him that drove all the lust straight from his body. He dropped the phone without even thanking Maudeen for the warning.

"Callie, honey, you need to put on some clothes."

The woman slept deader than dead. If he didn't see her fabulous breasts moving for himself, he'd be sure she'd bought the farm. Kevin ran around, grabbing everything he could.

"Callie, baby? I need some help here. We need to get you dressed."

She "mmm'd" then flopped over on her back.

"Darlin'" he said, trying to shove a T-shirt over her head, "Some cooperation would be greatly appreciated, if you don't want to flash your sweet tush to strangers."

She mumbled some more.

"What?"

"Green is my favorite color."

"That's good to know, baby. I'll keep that in mind. Now pick up your hips."

She continued to mumble nonsense, but she helped a little by rolling around while he stuck clothes on her, wherever they could fit. Kevin had the feeling she wasn't actually awake, but in some zone. At least she wasn't having nightmares, like she'd had the first couple of nights.

By the time someone knocked on the door, Callie had a beaver hat on her head, men's sweats covering her bottom, and a T-shirt that unfortunately and appropriately stated, *I'm not dead, I just look that way* on it.

But she was covered.

"Merry Christmas!" he greeted the two uniformed officers. "What can I do for you?"

"Sir, we believe that a woman named Cassandra Brandt, who's wanted in New York City on an outstanding warrant, is in residence here."

"Yep, she's here," Kevin said. "And a real pain in the butt she is, if you ask me."

Callie clawed her way out of a fog to discover she was in gloriously sated pain. Every inch of her body hurt. She stretched and smiled and decided Kevin Wilder was a wonderfully adult JD.

Then it occurred to her. She was wearing clothes. Weird ones at that. And she had a hat on her head. What in the world—?

"Yep, she's here," she heard Kevin say. "And a real pain in the butt she is, if you ask me."

She'd spent a night with him letting him have access to her body, she'd confided the most intimate parts of her life, and he'd turned her in. Somehow, someway, she'd pay him back. The moment her heart worked again.

She kept her eyes closed as someone entered and leaned over her. She recognized the snake's wonderful scent instantly, and she wanted to rake his face so much. But she kept still.

"Play along," he whispered in her ear.

"What?"

"If we're getting out of this, play along, baby." He shook her a little. "I plied her with a bit of liquor to keep her close, if you get my drift," he told the strangers.

"That doesn't look like her. The picture's . . . different."

"Oh, it's her all right," Kevin said. "You know how those glamour shots lie."

She was going to kill him.

"If you can wake her up, we'll take her off your hands. New York County wants her bad."

"Don't I know it. You wouldn't believe what I had to do to track her down. Then this snow storm happened, and . . . well, you know."

"If you could just wake her up."

"That'll be the day. This woman could sleep through a hurricane, and God knows she snores louder than one."

Dead. He was dead. And it would be a slow, lingering, painful demise.

It took everything in Callie's soul to keep from sitting up and screaming at the man who was about to double-cross her.

And kill every bit of hope she'd built during the night that what they'd done and been together wasn't just born of lust. That the sharing and intimacy stemmed from something deeper. How stupid could she be?

"I'm afraid I can't let you do that," she heard Kevin say.

"Excuse me?"

"She's *my* catch, and I'm turning her in myself. I worked hard for the money, and I'm not giving it up."

"I'm afraid we'll have to insist. The warrant—"

"Is a bunch of bunk, actually," Kevin said. "But I'll do anything for a buck. She's not guilty of a damn thing, and the second they have her they're going to have to let her go. And probably deal with a civil lawsuit to boot. But at this moment she's worth a good chunk of change if I hand her over myself. So she's mine, boys."

"Civil lawsuit?" one of the men croaked.

"Millions," Kevin averred.

"Well, I don't know . . . " the other man said.

At that moment the door banged open. "Timothy Dugan, get your hands off of Callie."

Callie recognized Betty Morgan's demanding voice. "Betty, honey, I haven't touched her. But this warrant—"

"Means less than squat," Maudeen chimed in. "She's a goodhearted, law abiding citizen, and she's not going anywhere." There was a pause. "Why is she wearing Morey's hat? Morey, isn't that your hat?"

"It is, but she's welcome to it."

"Still," Maudeen huffed. "Kevin Wilder, what have you been doing to this poor little girl?"

"Her head was cold," Kevin explained.

"So why are her clothes scattered all over the floor?"

"The floor was cold."

No one contradicted him.

It took monumental effort for Callie to keep from busting out laughing. Or crying. Or both. In such a short time she'd grown to love and respect these hard-working, huge-hearted people. She was going to miss them *so* much. Especially if she went to jail.

"The point here is," Kevin said, "you folks have no reason to worry. I'm taking care of this. So you can just wade on back out of here, now."

"But—" one of the officers began.

"Timothy!" Betty barked. "Out. Now."

"Everyone out," Kevin said. "Callie needs her beauty sleep." He was definitely dying a slow death for that one.

She heard a bunch of hemming and hawing and shuffling, and then a lot of scuttling of boots across the pine wood floor.

After a short silence, Maudeen said, "So, everything okay here?"

"Yes, thanks," Kevin answered her. "But when you get back to the lodge, you might want to remind Morey to zip up his pants before he goes out again. No false advertising there. Those things really *do* glow in the dark."

Kevin slammed the door shut and came over to her. Callie felt the chill of the outside air hanging on his clothes and body. He bent down and kissed her, and his lips were cool, too. But in a really hot way. "Wake up, Sleeping Beauty," he said, caressing her cheek. "All clear."

She cracked open one eye. "All clear?"

"They're all gone, baby."

She kicked him in the shin.

"Ow!"

"You're still taking me in."

"That's true."

Her heart and hopes and mind splintered. "You want the money."

"That's true, too. I'm getting the money from the scumbags. They deserve to pay."

Callie sat up. "You're doing a really lousy job of keeping me from hating you right now."

"You love me."

"At this moment? I don't think so."

"You will."

"You know, you don't look a thing like Harrison Ford."

"That's a real low blow. Good thing for you, I know you're just acting out in anger."

She kicked him again.

CHAPTER TWELVE

STAN

Late Wednesday night, a bit more than one day 'til Christmas Eve.

Dum, dum, dum lovin' feelin'…um dum dum lovin' feelin'…
Stan cursed and tossed another log on the fire.

He was going to kill Slick. The damned song had been playing in his head ever since he'd spotted Dana with those twins, over and over and over again until he wanted to hit something. Or scream. He'd never been a screamer, but this … this *torment* was definitely provocation to scream. And hitting something.

Or making love to someone. Hot, sweaty, heart pounding, can't-get-your-breath-because-you're-dying kind of love.

From the other room came the harsh *creak screech creak* sound of someone shifting position in the old wooden bed.

Stan clamped his hands over his ears.

Screech, groan, creak, creak, creeeeak.

At least he wouldn't be making the same sorts of noises. Since the mattress on his bed had been as bad as Dana's, he'd had one of the Parkers' teenage helpers drag it onto the floor in front of the fireplace. It still wasn't comfortable, but lumps were better than sags, and at least the floor didn't squeak every time he shifted position.

The trouble was, lying here like this, with the light from the fireplace the only illumination in the room, the only thing there was to do was listen to the soft crackling of the fire and the protesting creak-groan-creak of Dana's bed as she tossed and turned.

He was more than willing to offer a solution to her problem. Unfortunately, she'd moved a really heavy dresser in front of the door that joined the two rooms. It would take a three hundred pound lineman to force the door open now. He'd tried, and he couldn't budge it by as much as an inch. When he'd tried to talk to Dana about it, convince her the dresser wasn't a good idea, he'd been met by a chilly silence.

Squeak squeak squeak.

Cursing, he stared at the ceiling and considered flinging himself head first into the nearest snow bank.

He sure as hell wouldn't freeze to death. He was so hot right now, it would take an iceberg to cool him down.

Or Dana, which came to pretty much the same thing.

Screeek!

Stan dug his fingers into the blanket and tried to think of England. Or something. Anything except Dana.

It didn't work. Thoughts of Dana consumed him.

Dana, laughing. Dana with a bright-eyed child on her lap. Dana tossing back her hair or chatting with Penny or sewing doll clothes or—Hell, Dana doing anything at all.

Dana, naked.

That lovin' feelin'—

Creak, creak, screech!

Stan groaned and dragged the pillow over his head.

The bastard. The bum. *The . . . the jerk!*

Dana punched her pillow twice, hard, then wadded it into a ball, slammed it back on the bed, and turned onto her side.

Screeeek!

Damn it all, anyway!

Here she was, going crazy, tossing and turning and driving herself nuts with thinking about him, and the big lummox was already fast asleep. She hadn't caught so much as a whisper out of that room for the last hour, let alone a creak from his bed.

The bum *had* to be sound asleep. She'd seen that bed. She'd be hearing it if he were tossing and turning even half as much as she was.

Maybe the darned thing had simply collapsed under his weight and he was buried in the wreckage.

For a moment Dana lay there, face burrowed into the pillow, trying to focus on the mental image of Stan—cheery, grinning, let's-have-sex-for-the-fun-of-it Stan—folded into a pretzel by the collapsing bed.

All she could picture was Stan, naked except for a sheet and a smile.

No, Stan naked except for the smile.

Stan. Naked.

Dana groaned and flopped over on her back, cursing the accompanying chorus. If the man had any decency, he'd be suffering like she was. He was the one who'd started it! The teasing. The smiles. The chocolate frosting he'd insisted on wiping off the corner of her mouth at dinner.

The kisses . . .

He didn't *deserve* to have a decent night's sleep!

With an angry huff and an obnoxiously loud squeal of wood against wood, she flopped on her right side, then, after a moment, back on her left. When that didn't help, she started counting all the hellish ways she could make him sorry.

After five minutes of disappointing silence when he wondered if Dana had actually managed to fall asleep and, if she had, what that said about his usually irresistible sex appeal, Stan was relieved to hear another wooden shriek from the room next door. The shriek was immediately followed by a hard thunk as her feet hit the floor. The thunk, in its turn, was followed by silence, then the sound of feet—properly shod this time—crossing the floor to the door. Her door to the hallway opened, then shut. A moment later her footsteps faded into silence.

Stan awkwardly got to his feet—he hadn't considered the challenge that getting up would be when he'd had that teenager dump the mattress on the floor—then scrambled as best he could into his clothes, slipped his feet into his shoes without bothering about socks, and followed Dana.

The hallway was cold and dark; nothing shone beneath the doors he passed. He halted at the sixth door down, startled. Now he knew why the Parkers, under Slick's encouraging direction, had made such a point of keeping an empty room or two between each occupied room—the Rosses had gotten a bed that was every bit as squeaky as Dana's.

Stan grinned at the rhythmic squeak-squeak-squeak coming from the couple's room. If this was what a happy marriage could do for you, even after all these years, he'd have to reconsider his opposition to getting shackled.

Squeak-squeak-squeak.

The sound pursued him down the hall, growing fainter with every step he got closer to Dana.

With every step, his need to find her grew more urgent.

One night with her, that's all he asked. One long, hot, passionate night in front of the fire, and to hell with the lumps in the mattress.

One night ought to do it. Just a few hours of her—*all* of her—should be enough take the edge off this hunger that had tormented him from the first moment she'd walked around the corner of her house and into his life.

Not that he wouldn't want more, of course. He couldn't imagine settling for just one night with her if he didn't have to.

And not that he was thinking serious, here, or long-term or anything foolish like that. That wasn't going to happen. Not to Stan Kijewski. Not if he could help it.

But first he had to find Dana.

She wasn't in the main hall, but she'd turned on the Christmas tree lights and laid a couple more logs in the fireplace beside the tree. Tiny orange tongues of flame were beginning to stir in the embers and dance across the logs. The lights were reflected in the night-dark windows like jewels on black glass.

The glass-paned doors to the dining hall stood open. A streak of light under the door into the kitchen drew him on.

Dana was just taking a steaming mug out of the microwave when he entered. At the sight of him, she froze.

"Cocoa?" he said. "And you didn't make any for me?"

"Here's a cup." She grabbed a mug from the shelf and set it on the counter in front of him. "Milk's in the fridge," she added coolly. "Instant cocoa's in the can."

She was trying to freeze him out, but he knew how to handle that. "This mug has a bunny rabbit on it."

"Easter's right around the corner. Live with it."

"This the milk?"

"You're asking me? And wipe up the spills. I'm not your mother." *Thank God!*

"How long do I heat it? How do I turn this thing on?"

"What? You've never used a microwave?"

He gave her his best hurt-puppydog look.

She rolled her eyes, then heaved a sigh. "Two minutes. Punch this, and this, and Start. You can manage that, can't you?"

Stan stifled a grin at the growing irritation in her voice. She was getting hotter by the second. There wasn't a trace of frost in sight.

He picked up the can of instant cocoa and scowled at the label. "How much cocoa do I add? A cup? Two cups?"

"Oh, for pity's sake!" She snatched the cup out of his hand and started mixing it herself.

Pleased, Stan leaned back against the counter and watched her work. He could have fixed it himself, of course, but then she would have raced back to her room and locked him out. When you were planning a blitz, you didn't give the opposing team a chance to grab the ball and run.

Mug in hand, he followed her back to the fire. With a wary glance at him, she settled at the end of the old leather sofa nearest the fire, then tucked her feet up under her.

With a groan, he settled on the opposite end. Fortunately, it wasn't a very big sofa—two broad cushions that tended to sag toward the middle. Very convenient. And you could slide on leather a lot easier than over cloth.

"Great cocoa."

She took a sip from her cup and pointedly ignored him.

"Love the tree."

The tree was spectacular. Just what a Christmas tree should be—a little lopsided and covered from top to bottom with the motley collection of ornaments unearthed from Mike's boxes, stray items like toy trumpets and plastic teddy bears from the Big-Mart box, and nineteen big, red bows. Wishing ribbons, Morey had called them when he brought out the roll of ribbon, the scissors, and the marking pens. At his insistence, everyone from the Parker twins to the colonel had written their Christmas wish on the ribbons, then tied the bows so the wishes were hidden in the knots.

Stan knew right where Dana's ribbon was. He'd watched her hang it on that scrawny little branch right there near the bottom, not too far from the slightly lop-sided ribbons that Tyler and Taylor had hung with such care. He hoped it counted with Santa and the elves that he hadn't pulled hers off and read the wish, like he'd wanted.

Unfortunately, she hadn't tried to read his, either. Since his wish was to find her in his bed come Christmas morning, maybe it was just as well.

"I always wanted a tree like this," she said softly. Her knees were drawn up to her chin, her hands clasped around her ankles. Like the boy earlier when she was telling stories, he thought. The memory made him shift uncomfortably on the old sofa.

"I liked your tree," he offered. "I liked your whole house, actually."

Her head came up at that. He could see the reflections of the Christmas lights in the corner of her eye.

"Really? You liked the house?"

"Oh, yeah. Great house." He meant it, and he could tell she knew he did because the tension in her shoulders eased a little and she let go of her ankles. "Thanks."

"If Beerson's was anything like White Mountain, the holiday decorations were pretty generic."

"Yeah, they were. It wasn't a bad place, though," she added quickly. "They did their best for us."

"But there were too many kids and never enough money."

She nodded. "Guess it was like that at White Mountain, huh?"

"Yeah. If it hadn't been for Slick and JD, I doubt I'd have made it through high school."

"And George?"

"George was . . ." He groped for the right words that would explain exactly what George had meant to them, how much he'd done, but there weren't enough words in the dictionary for that. "George was great. If it hadn't been for him, the three of us would have ended up in neighboring cells in the state pen. As it was, he had to fish us out of detention more than once. We must have driven him nuts, yet he was always there for us, every single time."

She smiled at that, a wide, warm, wonderful smile that spiked right through him. "He told me that you three were his toughest job . . . and his proudest accomplishment."

"George said that?"

She nodded.

Stan shifted, uncomfortable with the undeserved praise, then winced at a stab of pain in his hip and leg. All this climbing on and off buses—and getting off mattresses on the floor—wasn't doing his hip any good. Fortunately, Dana was on his right so there wouldn't be any trouble sliding his good right arm around her . . . if he got the chance.

Under cover of propping his legs on the battered coffee table, he slid closer. Half a cushion to go and he'd have her. Casually, as if he didn't really notice what he was doing, he stretched his right arm along the back of the sofa. He had to fight against the urge to run his fingers through her hair.

"So George thought we turned out okay after all?"

"He has scrapbooks of all his 'kids.' Did you know that? Every single one. But the books for you three are enormous. He's got programs from Blue Angel demonstrations, newspaper clippings about JD's exploits, sports articles about you. George swears he doesn't have to lift weights to keep in shape, he just hauls your books around."

Guilt slammed him. "We should have come back more often, come visit instead of just calling."

"He understood. And at least he could watch your games on television. He gave me my first poster of you."

"You're *first?*"

"*A* poster," she hastily amended. She wasn't a very good liar.

Stan slid closer still, close enough so he could catch the scent of flowers in her hair. Creme rinse, he told himself, even though he knew it was really magic. Her magic.

"You said *first,*" he insisted. He tipped her chin up, forcing her to look at him. "How many other posters do you have?"

"Uh . . . mmm . . ." She chewed on her lower lip, which was a waste, because he should be the one chewing on it. Kissing it. Sucking it. Licking it.

Stan dragged his thoughts back from that dangerous precipice. "How many?"

"Eleven?"

He grinned. "You're asking me?"

"I . . . uh . . ." She was having a hard time breathing.

Good thing he knew how to provide mouth-to-mouth resuscitation. But not yet. Not quite yet.

He shifted slightly, trying to relieve the pressure in his groin. It didn't work.

"I don't recall seeing any posters of me in your house."

"What do you think? That I framed them?"

Stan leaned closer. He was starting to have a hard time breathing. Her eyes were huge, her mouth wet and open for him.

"How many did you frame, Dana?"

She was looking at his mouth, mesmerized. Her breath was quick and warm on his chin. "Three. I only framed three."

"And where'd you hang 'em, Dana?"

"I . . ."

"In your bedroom?" he murmured, his lips mere inches from hers. The ache in his groin was exquisite. "Did you hang them in your bedroom?"

She closed her eyes, struggling to still her breathing. "Yes."

His fingers squeezed convulsively around the silken strands of hair he'd captured.

God! He was going to explode if he couldn't kiss her! But she was still fighting against her need for him. He wanted her to admit that she wanted him, wanted her to recognize that this fire that was between them was right and good and sweet instead of something to be feared.

"Dana?" He said it low. Almost a whisper, definitely a caress.

Gently, he ran the tip of one finger down the side of her face, tracing the delicate curves, the perfect features. The motion hurt a little—he had to lift his hand higher than his damaged shoulder liked—but he was damned if he was going to let go of the golden silk he'd trapped in his right hand.

He had her. He knew he had her. The only thing left was for her to realize that she had him—any way she wanted him.

Instead of kissing him, though, she shifted away from him, and glanced at the tree. If she noticed the grip he had on her hair, she didn't show it.

"What did you write on your wishing ribbon?" she asked.

"What?"

"Your wishing ribbon," she repeated, deliberately not looking at him. "What did you write on it?"

"If I told, I might not get my wish. Isn't that the way it works?" He'd get it. He'd never been more sure of anything in his life.

"Taylor and Tyler, they wished they could stay here always."

Stan flinched. He wasn't really in the mood to think about the dreams and hopes of a pair of six-year-olds. Not right now.

On the other hand, he couldn't help but understand exactly how they felt. Years ago, he'd longed for a home, too, a place he belonged, a family who loved him. The closest he'd come to having that dream was Slick and JD and George. Friends that good and true and strong didn't come along every day of the week, either, so he guessed he'd been lucky.

Hell, yes! he'd been lucky.

But right now, watching her stare at that Christmas tree, he wondered if maybe, after all these years, there wasn't a chance for all the rest of it, too.

It was a crazy idea, but somehow, with Dana . . .

"What did you wish for?" he asked, very softly.

Without a word, she tugged her hair free of his fingers and got to her feet—gracefully, like everything else she did. He didn't have to ask which ribbon it was she plucked from the tree. It was hers.

For an instant, she just stood there, head bent, her back to him, her hair liked liquid gold in the firelight. Then she squared her shoulders and turned to face him, the ribbon tightly clutched in her hands.

"I wished for you."

I wished for you.

It wasn't a total lie. She *had* wished for him. But in writing his name, she'd asked for more, too. Love. Marriage. A home. A family. All the things neither one of them had ever had.

The wish was so big and bold, so . . . so *greedy* that it took her breath away.

Making a wish that big was asking for trouble. It was dangerous because the minute you risked your heart, life was pretty well sure to take it and stomp it into the ground. She'd learned that the day her mother dropped her off at the Beerson Home, then disappeared without a word of farewell.

Stan would know what that was like.

At least he'd had his friends as well as George. She'd had George and her fantasies. But George had warned her about letting the fantasies be substitutes for the real thing.

"Don't let wishful thinking run away with your good sense," he'd told her when she was young and uncertain. "And don't ever be afraid."

Now she was grown and she was still uncertain and afraid, and she was definitely letting her wishful thinking get the upper hand, at least when it came to Stan Kijewski.

Right now, she didn't much care. Right now was *now*, and Stan was here in front of her, and he wanted her as much as she wanted him. Of that fact, at least, she was absolutely certain.

It was nice to be absolutely certain about something.

The protesting rustle of the ribbon she was crushing brought her back to her senses. What she had left of them, anyway.

With a calm she was far from feeling, she tossed the crumpled bow aside and moved to stand in front of Stan. He was leaning back on the old leather sofa, trying to look casual and sure of himself and not doing nearly as well at it as she would have expected. His hunger for her hit her like a wave.

She leaned forward to prop her hands against the sofa on either side of his head. The old leather was soft against her palms. She caught the faint scratch of his hair against it as he tilted his head back to meet her gaze.

For a moment—for what seemed darn near eternity—they remained like that, their faces a foot apart, the air between their bodies charged with the electric need arcing between them. The only sounds she could hear were the crackling of the fire and their low, too-fast breathing and the pounding of her own heart.

Dredging courage out of the hunger that threatened to consume her, she closed the gap between them. Her mouth crushed down on his, forcing his head deeper into the cushioned back of the sofa.

Stan didn't seem to mind. He gave a low, growling moan of pleasure, then clamped his hands around her waist and dragged her forward and down until she was on her knees on the sofa, straddling his lap.

His erection pressed against her center, hard and demanding even in the strait jacket of his jeans, yet he let his hands slide up her body, up under her sweater, up the bare skin over her ribs. Not down to the zipper on her jeans. Up.

When his hands closed over her unbound breasts, she gasped and pressed against him. Their mouths were open, their lips still locked in a kiss that threatened to consume her if the heat rising from below didn't do it first. Tongues touched, tangled, plunged deeper. His hands burned her skin. His palms cupped her breasts, flattening them even as her nipples tightened painfully.

She gasped and broke the kiss, fighting for breath.

"I've been driving myself crazy trying to figure out whether you'd be wearing silk or sensible cotton under that baggy sweater," Stan said, his voice ragged. "I never once thought you'd be wearing nothing at all."

Her eyes closed against the exquisite pleasure of his touch—he'd shifted his hold on her breasts until her nipples were pinched between his thumbs and the first two fingers of each hand—and the even more exquisite ache where their bodies pressed so close together.

"I want you, Dana. *All* of you. Now. Please."

She was a sucker for please.

"Your room?" she whispered, arching into his touch, forcing

herself against him. "Or mine?"

"Mine," he said between gritted teeth. His grin looked a little mad and very, very hungry. "Your bed would make enough noise to wake the dead, let alone all the busybodies in the lodge."

"I didn't think you noticed."

"I noticed. Believe me, I noticed!"

She wasn't sure she could have found the strength to get off him if he hadn't slid his hands out from under her sweater, then, with a groan, pushed her away. For an instant she worried that she'd hurt him, but one glance at those dangerous green eyes told her it wasn't his old injuries that were bothering him right now.

Feeling just a little smug, she held out her hand and hauled him to his feet.

"Damn," he groaned. "Remind me to avoid soft leather couches for a little while longer. Unless," he added with a wicked grin, pulling her close against him, "we don't bother sitting up."

They made sure the fire screen was properly set in front of the dying fire, but didn't bother turning off the lights on the tree. The combined glow was just enough to show them their way back.

It also gave them a brief glimpse of a tiny little figure in a long nightgown disappearing around a corner and up the stairs to the second floor.

"Wasn't that Dr. Maggie?" Stan demanded, stopping dead in the middle of the hallway.

"I think so." Dana tugged him back into motion. "The Colonel's room is upstairs, you know."

"Well, damn!" said Stan, chuckling. He pulled her close against him. His arm was strong and warm around her shoulders, his body hard against her side. "Looks like we're the slowpokes, here. Guess we'll have to do something about that, now, won't we?"

He swung her around for a quick, hot kiss, then dragged her down the hall, straight to his door.

At the sight of his mattress on the floor in front of the fire, Dana stopped dead. Though it had obviously been neatly made up at one time, the sheets were now tumbled and tossed. The heavy old quilts were half on, half off the bed. Two of the four pillows lay on the floor. The two that were left had been pounded into shapeless lumps.

"*That's* why I didn't hear a sound from your room! I thought you'd fallen asleep!"

He laughed and shot the deadbolt on the hall door. "Not on your life. The sound of you tossing and turning in that damned creaking bed just about drove me mad."

"Did it?" she murmured, and felt a rush of confidence flood through her.

"Don't look so smug," he said, ripping his sweatshirt off over his head. "You weren't having any better time of it."

"I was in hell," she admitted, "and madder than hops that you'd fallen asleep so easily."

"Good." He opened a leather dop kit on the stand by the abandoned bed and pulled out a shiny strip of little foil packets. His body gleamed golden in the firelight. His grin was pure wolf. "It's only fair that you suffered some, too."

"I suffered. *Believe* me, I suffered!" She eyed the foil strip with misgivings. "Are you always this well prepared?"

The wolf grin widened. "I wasn't prepared at all, but the manager at Big-Mart was nice enough to turn one of the registers on when I asked."

She could feel her eyes go wide and round with horror. "Did anyone see you buy those?"

"Only Maudeen," he assured her, flinging the strip down beside the bed.

"Maudeen?" It came out more as a squeak than a question.

"And Dr. Meg."

"Dr. Meg, too?"

He nodded, then casually tossed another couple of logs on the fire and set the screen back in place. "And Morey and Slick and—"

"They all saw you buy those . . . *things?*"

"And not one of 'em said a word," he assured her, grabbing her hands and pulling her to him. "They know I'm crazy about you."

"They do? You are?"

"Absolutely nuts," he murmured against her mouth, and kissed her.

She wasn't quite sure how they made it down onto the mattress— Stan's awkwardness from his injured leg and hip was compounded by the fact that they were wrapped around each other like leeches— but by the time she dragged the wayward pillows back onto the bed and he arranged the quilts so they didn't get tangled in the folds, they were both stark naked and breathing hard.

"God, you are so beautiful," he murmured, holding her away from him. His eyes glittered with a hunger that set her blood burning. His hands slid up her arms under her hair. The mingled touch of rough, warm, male skin and familiar silk roused her nipples to a peak and started a throbbing in her belly that made her muscles squeeze.

"And you." She touched his injured shoulder, ran her fingers over the puckered scars that criss-crossed his skin. The firelight gilded his uninjured right side and cast his left into shadows.

She didn't need to see the damage to know it was there. Neither did he.

His grip on her tightened. "You realize I can't make love to you the way I'd like, that you'll have to do a lot of the work?"

She laughed and bent to kiss him, forcing him down onto the mattress. "Who says I would have let you do all the work, anyway?"

Whatever he might have answered was swallowed in his groan of pleasure as she trailed her hand down his chest, over and around his nipple, then across his belly and down to his groin. At her touch, his engorged penis twitched.

"I figure . . . we . . . can work . . . out . . . a compromise," he gasped. He shuddered as her hold on him tightened.

Excitement filled her. She had dreamed of this so many times, alone in her bed in her house in the trees. She'd fantasized about making love to him and having him make love to her, about how he would touch her, there, and she would kiss him, here, and how their bodies would fit together. But never once had she dared dream of such power. It had never occurred to her that he could want her so much, or be so helpless beneath his body's craving for her.

No, not just his body's need, she realized, and felt her heart stop. This wasn't just sex—not for him, and not for her. Despite her inexperience she could see it in his face, feel it in his touch. He hadn't yet admitted it, not even to himself, but there really was something between them. Something strange and wild and wonderful. Something fat with promise for the future.

She wished, suddenly, that she hadn't left her wishing ribbon on the floor by the tree, then dismissed the thought. She'd retrieve the bow tomorrow. For now . . .

She reached for the strip of foil on the floor beside the bed.

They laughed, fumbling to tear off a packet, getting in each others' way. The laughter was sweet and often choked off by kisses and groans and their involuntary cries of pleasure.

And then she was above him, straddling him as he guided her down. Their joining was swift and sure and utterly right. She gasped at the shock of it, arched away, then down and into his hands. Her hands were braced on the either side of his shoulders, his hands wrapped around her waist, helping her balance, pulling her back.

She rode him, then, rode him until her body seized in a fierce, galvanic climax that wrenched a strangled scream from her throat and a strangled laugh from his. His own climax hit him a few seconds later. The laughter turned to a groan as he arched into her, thrusting hard and straight and true, the beautiful, damaged body suddenly rigid with the strength of his release.

As it turned out, they didn't use all the packets in that strip, but it wasn't for lack of trying.

CHAPTER THIRTEEN

SAM

Thursday morning, one day 'til Christmas Eve.

"No! Absolutely not!"

"That's what you said when I asked you to—"

"Don't you dare bring *that* up again, you louse. And stop smiling at me. You're not coaxing me into one more thing, and that's final."

"Please, Reba, just try it. For me."

Famous last words! "Hah! You're crazy if you think I'm going to sled down a mountain in a wheel-less wheelbarrow."

Sam had kicked off the single front wheel and the two back braces of his deep wheelbarrow and was trying to talk her into his own version of a lost-your-mind Olympic luge event . . . the one that resembled bobsledding, but was ten times more dangerous. The only difference was that she would be the point man in this extreme sport fiasco.

"Aaah, c'mon, baby. It'll be fun. Besides, there's no way to shovel our way down to the lodge with that crust of ice that's formed over a good two feet of snow. Not that I have a shovel."

"I repeat, I am not sledding down a mountain in a wheel-less wheelbarrow. Sam, I don't even like roller coasters. I'm afraid of heights. Scary movies are not my cup of tea. I am not a thrill seeker and never have been. Mother Teresa is my idea of a hero, not Evil Knievel."

"I know what you're thinking now. Just stop it." Sam raised a forefinger warningly at her. "You are not going to start the we-are-just-too-different-to-make-it-work crap."

"Well, we *are* different, Sam."

"Compromise . . . we can learn to compromise," he said, a note of desperation in his voice. "You could probably learn to love things I do, like . . . oh, let's say . . . skydiving."

She made a snorting sound that equated to, "In your dreams!"

He ignored her snort. "And in return, I could . . . I could . . . ," he stammered for the right answer.

"Yes?"

His face brightened. "I could learn to love Oprah."

They both laughed at the absurdity of both extremes.

He decided to try a different tact. "Don't you trust me?"

Oh, that was a low blow. And Sam knew it.

Just then, his cell phone rang. Not for the first time, either. Betty had called several times to alert them to road conditions and the prognosis for them being able to leave for Maine anytime today; it was still up in the air. A worried George kept tabs on them, too. And JD had called to inform them of an unexpected visit from the cops late last night. Stan was oddly silent . . . well, not so odd, she supposed, considering the surreptitious looks he and Dana had been exchanging over dinner last night.

"Hey, buddy!" Sam said into the phone. "How's it going? Really? Well, did you do what I told you to? And it worked? Great! Uh-huh. Uh-huh." Sam turned his face away from her as he spoke, and his side of the conversation was rather terse, as if he didn't want her to know who was on the other end.

At first, her female shackles went up. A woman . . . could he be talking to a woman? No, he'd used the term *buddy*. She didn't think he would call a girlfriend *buddy*. Oh, geez, where did the idea of a girlfriend come from? After the night she'd just spent with Sam, how could she be so insecure?

"Who was that?" she blurted out the minute Sam clicked off the phone.

Sam shuffled about and made great work of tucking the phone into a leather pouch which he attached to his belt. Finally, he admitted. "Richie."

"What? What did you say?"

He cursed under his breath, and his face flushed. He was embarrassed for some reason. "If you must know, that was Richie . . . the kid from the Littleton shelter. I gave him my cell number . . . in case he ever had a problem. And he . . . uh . . . had a problem."

Tears stung her eyes and she put the fingertips of one hand to her mouth to stifle a sob of emotion. *The big-hearted louse!* "Oh, Sam," was all she could say.

"Don't go getting all soppy over this. It's not like I'm adopting the kid or anything. I just didn't want him to think there were no lifelines out there when things got rough."

She walked up to him, looped her arms around his neck and gave him a quick kiss. "Sam, I'm not surprised at all that you would do such a thing. But I'm moved." She put a hand over her heart and patted it for emphasis. "Deeply moved."

"Yeah?" he said, looping his own arms around her waist and tugging her closer, belly to belly. "How moved?"

She laughed, not un-*moved* by the inviting twinkle in his eye. "We're not going back to bed . . . especially with all those chocolate stains on the sheets. And I don't care what you say, I'm not jingle belling again. As for the handcuffs—"

"Tsk-tsk, sweetheart. That's not what I meant. I was hoping you were *moved* in another direction." He was kissing her ear as he spoke . . . in fact, he was doing lots of stuff to her ear . . . sinfully tormenting type stuff that he knew darn well turned her melty and unable to resist any outrageous thing he suggested.

"Like?" Fool that she was for punishment, she was arching her neck to give him better access to her ear.

He chuckled softly. "Wheelbarrow sledding."

"Well, would you look at that!" Colonel Morgan was standing at the window of the lodge, staring up at the steep, snow covered path that led to the cabins. "Unbelievable!"

All the seniors who'd been sitting about the fires dropped their sewing and craft materials and rushed forward to see what Bob was referring to.

"Is it an avalanche?"

"Betcha it's a bunch of snowplows. Betty knows this guy from Bangor."

"Maybe it's geese. I saw a flock of geese fly over this morning."

"I hope it's not more snow. We'll never make it to George's wedding if it snows again."

"If the Colonel's tryin' to trick us into going outside for more calisthenics, I'm gonna scream."

Once they all arrived with a skidding halt, there was a communal gasp.

Stan took Dana's hand and dragged her over to the window to see what all the commotion was about. It didn't take much to excite this group. It was probably just a "super keen" icicle, or something equally non-exciting. "Super keen!" was a favorite expression of the Colonel's. God knows what Marine Corps he'd served in. Stan had known lots of Marines over the years and not one of them would be caught dead saying, "Super keen!"

But it wasn't an icicle, super keen or otherwise.

As one, fifteen sets of jaws dropped open with amazement.

"Holy Smoke!" Stan said. Even he wouldn't have expected this.

Slick and Reba were barreling down the wide mountain path in what appeared to be a wheel-less wheelbarrow, of all things. The closer they got, they could hear Slick whooping with glee, and Reba screaming with terror.

The twins, Taylor and Tyler, were jumping up and down, squealing with glee. For sure, they would be cajoling Slick into giving them rides on his improvised sled. In fact, the seniors were grabbing their jackets and hats and gloves. Stan wouldn't be surprised if some of them wanted a test run, too.

Dana giggled at the spectacle before them as they stepped out on to the wide porch. Slick was sitting flat on his ass in the snow, where Reba had pushed him, once they'd disengaged themselves from the overturned "sled." A royally pissed Reba was standing over him, hands on hips, giving him a tongue lashing that would blister the stripes off a referee's uniform.

"You told me it would be fun."

"It *was* fun."

"It was not fun. It was insanity. It was the kind of wild thing imbeciles do, before they smash what little brains they have to smithereens."

"Are you saying I'm an imbecile?" Slick was clearly amused and not taking Reba seriously enough. That became evident when he tried to stand and she shoved him back down.

"I'm not done with you yet, buster."

"You're not?" Slick lifted his eyebrows with exaggerated innocence.

"Uh-oh," Stan said.

"What?" Dana asked him.

"I recognize the look on Slick's face. Reba's about to get her comeuppance."

"Comeuppance? Is that a Maine word?"

He cuffed her playfully on the chin for her teasing. "Shhh! Watch Slick in action."

And sure as sin, Slick stretched out one leg, hooked Reba's right ankle, and in one fluid move had her on the ground, flat on her back. Then the two of them were rolling over and over down the rest of the hill. It was hard to tell which one was on top, and by then they were both laughing and kissing and having a jolly ol' time. Stan wished he could have been there in that same situation . . . with Dana, of course. He was in sore need of a jolly ol' time . . . minus the roughhousing.

Dana squeezed his forearm, as if in understanding.

On the other hand, who needed wet snow? He had Dana, and a roaring fire in the fireplace, and a beautiful tree, and what was turning into the best Christmas of his life.

As the seniors started to straggle back in, Dr. Meg was heard to comment to Dr. Maggie, "I predict another wedding besides George's."

Dr. Maggie nodded. "Probably before spring."

Stan grinned at that prospect. Sam Merrick, the first of The Three Musketeers to bite the dust. He couldn't wait to razz him about it. Maybe he'd sing the Queen song, "Another one bites the dust. Another one bites the dust . . . "

But then Dr. Meg levelled her direct gaze on him, even as she addressed her sister. "Yes, indeed. In fact, sister, I wouldn't be surprised if there were *two* weddings."

Stan felt his face turn hot. Beside him, Dana was shaking with suppressed laughter at his discomfort. He would take care of her later.

Maudeen must have overheard the whole thing because she provided the zinger. "Why stop at two? I'm predicting a triple-header. Anyone seen that JD since last night?"

With perfect timing, Slick walked up, Reba in tow under his arm. He was beaming like a bloody Christmas star. And she was staring at him as if he'd just invented something wonderful, like chocolate . . . or sex.

Everyone exchanged knowing glances, and burst out laughing.

Sam was outside, behaving like a wild kid who'd never outgrown the need for childhood thrills. Reba was inside, behaving like a responsible adult, having just cleaned up from the midday brunch. She wasn't making any judgment calls about Sam—in fact, it warmed her heart to see him so openly exuberant—but she wasn't even a tiny bit envious of the scream-ridden events taking place before her eyes. She and Sam were so different.

Smiling, she stood at the window of the lodge, watching. A cup of hot cocoa was cradled in her hands. You'd think she would have been sick of chocolate after the previous night, but apparently it had only whetted her appetite. Sam had handed her the beverage before heading outdoors, accompanied by a wicked wink and a whispered promise . . . also wicked.

He'd just completed five sled rides down a short stretch of the mountain path with Taylor and Tyler squealing happily in his protective arms. Sam didn't realize it, but he would make a wonderful father someday. She wondered idly if those children would be made with her, then immediately banked the twinge of distress that question ignited. *Not now*, she told herself. There were too many other things she had to worry over, like the road conditions and George's wedding.

Still, she idled time away, too, as she watched Sam, now engaged in a snowball fight. Also involved in the free-for-all were JD and Stan and Morey and Mike and the colonel. New additions were Callie, wearing the silliest, most adorable fur-lined hunter's cap with ear flaps, Dana and Penney, wearing oversized plaid hunting coats that must belong to Mike, with stretch ski caps, Maudeen in a fuchsia spandex running outfit that defied description, and the sisters, Doctors Meg and Maggie, elegant as always in big wool sweaters and tailored slacks. Everyone was laughing and issuing challenges and sputtering with indignation when they slipped and fell or were smacked dead-on with lightly packed snowballs. Even Stan, with his injuries, was getting his fair share of licks in, from behind a snow fort.

With a sigh, Reba turned back to the activity in the great hall with its two enormous stone fireplaces blazing away at either end. John and Ethel Ross sat on an overstuffed sofa by the Christmas tree, close to each other, as they invariably did after fifty years of marriage. They were checking over the gift request list Maudeen had printed out that morning from the remaining homeless shelter they were supposed to visit. It was no small job to compare the list with the Brigade's current abundant inventory, thanks to Big-Mart and the frantic, last-minute work of Callie and Dana, and all the seniors, really.

Reba set her cup on the massive trestle table in the center of the room where Emma was completing the gift-wrapping for the newly refurbished Barbie dolls. Betty sat on the other side of the table, a cell phone pressed to one ear while she traced a finger over a map laid out before her.

Reba glanced at her watch and winced. It was already two p.m., and their last shelter stop of this trip had been scheduled for five p.m. In all the history of The Santa Brigade, they'd never missed a booking, but things were looking pretty hopeless for this year, even if they were able to reschedule for a few hours later.

Their original plans had been to finish their last shelter stop early tonight and be home in Snowdon by midnight or the wee hours of the morning, thus leaving all of Christmas Eve day to relax and prepare both for George's evening wedding and the holidays in general. Ah, well, the best laid plans and all that!

"How's Betty doing?" Reba whispered to Emma.

"Not so good. Every plow from here to the Maine line appears to be engaged by state and county crews. A state of emergency has been declared for all of New Hampshire. Betty's working on her last resort now."

Reba cocked her head quizzically as she followed Emma's silent cue and pressed a fingertip in the center of a bow which Emma was tying.

"It's an old boyfriend of hers who owns a small trucking company. A boyfriend that Betty 'done wrong' at one time apparently," Emma informed her with a roll of the eyes.

"Now, Lester, don't be like that," Betty cooed.

Holy Cow! Betty cooing? It would seem she could learn a thing or two from this over-the-hill femme fatale.

"I did not dump you, Lester. No, no, no, you've got it all wrong, sweet cakes. It was all a misunderstanding. Remember. I caught you . . . I mean, I thought I saw you in that vibrating bed at the VFW convention motel with that hairdresser from the Curly Q."

There was a long silence while Betty listened to the male voice on the other end of the line. The whole time she was making faces at her and Emma, as if to say, "What a crock!"

"Oh, yeah, sure, I understand. You were just lending her a Phillips to adjust the vibrations on the bed. And then you had to test out the . . . uh, vibrations. Perfectly understandable." The expression on Betty's face now translated to, "This is one helluva schmuck!" She was practically gritting her teeth to stop from saying what she really wanted, Reba could tell.

"New Year's Eve? The American Legion party? Well, I don't

know, Lester. That is really short notice. Oh, all right. What can I say? You always were irresistible." Betty looked as if she might just puke on those last words.

Lester must have been talking up a storm now because Betty was listening intently.

"You will? You are? Three plows? God bless you, my man!"

Betty clicked off her phone, pumped her fist in the air with the victory sign, and smiled at her and Emma. "Tomorrow morning. First thing. Lester will be here with his crew at six a.m. We'll reschedule our shelter engagement for ten or eleven, but we're gonna make our last stop. Hot damn!"

"We better go tell everyone," Reba advised, feeling exhilarated about this turn of events, but not all that surprised that Betty had pulled off a miracle . . . once again. Frankly, she kind of liked the idea of another night at the lodge cabin with Sam. And she had no doubt that everyone else would welcome another night here, too.

"Yep, lots of changes to make, but this works out just fine. We'll still have plenty of time to get home to Snowdon, the way I figure." Betty was smiling with well-earned satisfaction as she gathered up her maps and trusty cell phone.

Emma stood, a large woman almost twice Betty's size. She walked around the table, leaned down, and gave Betty a big hug. "Thank you, Betty, for making such a sacrifice. It sounded as if you're going to have to date a man you despise."

"Are you kidding me?" Betty laughed, her eyes twinkling with mischief. "Haven't you heard, there's this strange virus visiting Snowdon this holiday season. Betcha I'm gonna catch it by New Year's Eve."

They all laughed then. Everything always seemed to work out in the end.

At least, Reba hoped they would, especially where she and Sam were concerned.

Sam was sitting on the sofa near the Christmas tree, practically hyperventilating.

The snow plows should be here practically at daybreak tomorrow. Everyone had pitched in a short time ago to shovel around that godawful red Santa bus, while Betty had polished up the godawful Rudolph hood ornament, and the Doctors Meg and Maggie had decorated the inside with a godawful amount of fresh holly and mistletoe. All the gifts and the personal belongings of the Brigade members were stashed on the bus.

In essence, they were in a holding pattern. But they should be arriving at the Maine border within the next fifteen hours, God willing and the snow plows arriving. Not that Sam was counting. *Hah!* That's what had him practically hyperventilating. *Snowdon!* A part of him wanted to run in the opposite direction and avoid confronting all his old ghosts. But he had an anchor that forced him to stay put. *Reba.* If the only way he could hold onto Reba was return to I-wish-I-were-anyplace-else-in-the-world Maine, then he was going to do it . . . even if it killed him.

To his surprise, John and Ethel Ross dropped down on the couch on either side of him, bracketing him in like bookends. It would have been rude to get up and walk away, which was exactly what he felt like doing. He had a sneaky suspicion that he was in for it, senior style.

"I've been married to Ethel here for fifty years," John told him suddenly, as if he'd asked. He smiled around Sam at his wife, who smiled sweetly back at him as she adjusted her hearing aid. Sometimes he wondered if Ethel didn't turn her hearing aid off at times, just to tune out the chaos of the Santa Brigade. They could be a rowdy bunch.

"Hasn't been easy at times, either."

Shall I play the violins now or later?

"I remember that time you got the job offer in Snowdon," Ethel said. "I had a good teaching position in Maryland. My family lived nearby. And it was cold in Maine, I'd heard, very cold."

I know exactly how cold it is in Maine. Heart chilling cold.

John and Ethel laughed softly in remembrance.

Sam did not laugh softly in remembrance.

"But love means compromise. And I decided that John was more important to me than anything else in the world. What difference did our surroundings make, if John and I could be together?" The whole time Ethel spoke in her gentle, though firm, voice, she looked at Sam, not her husband.

Sam was beginning to get the message. He'd have to be a dunce not to.

Just to make sure, John asked him pointedly, "How important is Reba to you? Does geography really matter in the scheme of things?"

"Of course Reba's important to me." He wasn't about to get involved in the geography discussion. They would never leave then.

But they didn't even wait for his answer. The two of them had already risen, smiled at each other as if to say, "Mission Accomplished," and went off to join their friends in drinking another cup of farewell egg nog. If these seniors drank much more egg nog, Betty would be making pit stops every five miles from here to Snowdon.

Snowdon? Aaarrgh! There are reminders everywhere.

Before he had a chance to digest John and Ethel's well-meaning words, speak-of-the-devil Betty sat down beside him.

Uh-oh! Since Betty Bad-Ass rarely sat down and always seemed to be bustling about, he knew he was in for it, again. *If Betty mentions one single thing about protection, though, I am out of here.*

"She would probably follow you wherever you wanted to go," Betty started, right off.

"Who?"

"Who-schmoo!" Betty said and socked him a good one in the upper arm with a fist. And it hurt, too. "Reba, that's who, you idiot."

"Listen. I would never ask Reba to leave Snowdon. It's her home. Winter Haven is there . . . it's been in her family for ages. Besides, she loves Maine."

Betty clucked with disgust at his apparent thick-headedness. "Reba loves *you*. The rest is immaterial."

"No, it's not, Betty. I learned a lesson on this trip. Sometimes when you love someone, the best thing you can do is let them go."

Betty stared at him in horror. "You're going to let Reba go . . . *again?*"

"I didn't say that. I was just thinking out loud."

"Dumber than dirt, that's what men are," Betty exclaimed as she stomped off. "Shouldn't be allowed to think, the whole lot of them."

"I hope that doesn't mean you're going to make a life altering mistake." It was Dr. Maggie now who dropped down on his one side, looking pretty in a lavender turtleneck sweater and gray wool slacks.

"Now, sister, don't jump to conclusions," her sister, Dr. Meg, said from the other side. She wore a similar outfit with the colors reversed, gray on top, lavender on the bottom. Regular geriatric Bobbsey Twins, that's what they were.

Sam made a resolution right then and there. He was for damn sure going to leap off this sofa next time someone got up. He was not going to be cornered by one more Dear Abby type interfering senior.

"What were you muttering, dear?" Dr. Maggie inquired.

"I think he's just confused and thinking aloud, aren't you, Samuel?" Dr. Meg patted his arm reassuringly, as if it was perfectly all right to talk to himself. Evidently Dr. Meg didn't have the same opinion of thinking men as Betty did.

"I met a man once in the Himalayas," Dr. Maggie began.

Sam groaned to himself. *Here it comes.*

"Are you referring to Doctor Welsh?"

Dr. Maggie nodded at her sister. "He had a sweetheart waiting for him in Tuscaloosa. Phyllis Bancroft, a university professor. But he had this yen to travel. One more month, he kept saying. Then, one more year. And before he knew it, twenty years had gone by. He'd seen the world, every inch of it. And by the time he finally returned to Alabama, Phyllis was gone."

"Died of a broken heart, some said." Dr. Meg actually seemed to have a tear in her eye.

Sam felt kind of sick to his stomach . . . and he hadn't even drunk any egg nog.

"Some people think that dreams last forever," Dr. Maggie said. *Oh, God, I thought the story was already over.*

"They don't," Dr. Meg said with a sigh.

It's a never-ending tale. Arabian Nights *with a Geritol twist.*

"Don't be offended by our advice, dear," Dr. Maggie concluded.

"We're only trying to help," Dr. Meg added.

Thank God, the story's over! "No offense taken," he said gruffly, and was about to push off from the sofa when Dr. Meg reminded him, "Don't forget. You promised to let us interview you for our next book. *Sex Habits of Warriors: From Cavemen to the Modern Military.*"

He plopped back down. *I'm really am getting sick to my stomach.*

"The ancient Hittites allegedly had fixed sexual rites they performed before battles," Dr. Maggie added.

What the hell do I know about Hittites?

"I'm sure there are rites that modern soldiers follow as well," Dr. Meg said, a hopeful tone in her voice, as if she expected to interview him now.

The only rite I can think of is "Get Laid." Or the ever hopeful wish of men to hear, "Hey, soldier, wanna get lucky?"

When he didn't volunteer any information, the twins got up, giving him quick air kisses before they left.

Maudeen stopped in front of him, before he had a chance to escape. Wagging a bony finger in his face, she said, "Second chances don't come often in life, big boy. Don't mess it up."

"I don't intend to," Sam exclaimed, "if everyone would just leave me alone a minute to gather my thoughts."

"A thinking man? Now that's an oxymoron." It was Emma Smith who spoke now as she breezed by on her way to the egg nog . . . and, man, Mrs. Smith could create one big breeze. She and Betty ought to form a club, *Women Who Think Men Can't Think*, or some such thing. Mrs. Smith was smiling at him, as she spoke, though, which made him think she was only teasing.

"I have a super keen suggestion for you, son. A never-fail method for snagging a woman." The colonel had come up on him from behind the sofa and about scared the crap out of him. Leaning over the back of the sofa, the colonel cupped his hand near Sam's ear to hide his undertoned message. "Remind me to tell you about it once we board the bus. We military men need to share our secrets."

Oh, yeah, I'll do that, all right. Super keen.

"Have faith," someone else said, but when Sam glanced around he realized that, suddenly, he was alone. It must have been a voice in his head. *How odd!*

He looked up then and there was Reba standing at the Christmas tree with her back to him. She was examining the red Christmas bows which everyone had put on the tree last night . . . Christmas wish bows, actually. He and Reba had written their wishes on the ribbons with black markers, then hung them on the tree. He knew just where they hung, though, and so did Reba apparently. She had just pulled *his* off the tree. He stood and walked toward her, snagging *her* bow off in the process.

She looked down at his wish bow and let out a little sob. He looked down at her wish bow and felt like sobbing.

The only word on his Christmas wish bow had been, "Reba." What he discovered now was that the only word on Reba's wish bow had been, "Sam."

Well, that settles it. He held out his hand to her. "Come on, baby. Let's go somewhere private. There's something I need to do before we get on that bus tomorrow."

"Can't it wait 'til later . . . at the cabin?"

"No way. If I don't do it now, I'll probably chicken out."

She nodded, but not before he saw the fear in her eyes.

Oh, ye, of little faith!

"Reba."

"Sam."

They both spoke at the same time.

Sam had pulled her into a pantry just off the kitchen. It was one of those old-fashioned rooms with floor to ceiling oak cabinets for storing supplies and a special sink for washing crystal and polishing silver. The scent of clover and cinnamon and licoricey anise hung in the air. Sam must have a thing about storage rooms. She was beginning to, as well.

"You go first," she said. Her heart was beating so fast it was scary. Reba could see that Sam had something important to tell her, and since he'd already told her dozens of time that he loved her, she just knew there was going to be a "but" attached to the statement this time. Returning to Snowdon . . . to home . . . filled her with pleasure, but Sam obviously dreaded the prospect with a passion.

She could see what was coming. Oh, Reba had prepared herself for this inevitability. When she'd made love with Sam last night, it had been with her eyes wide open. But that didn't make it easy.

"I bought you a gift."

Huh? That's not what I expected. Oh, wait. I get it. A good-bye gift. As if I need some memento of him. The big jerk!

He was digging in his pants' pocket, and, oddly, his face had turned red with embarrassment.

"This is really, really tacky, Reba. Don't laugh. I pulled the manager of the Big-Mart aside, and he sold me the best one he had, but it was really small, and probably not very good quality. Hell, how could it be? It only cost a couple hundred bucks. And, oh, God, I am really bungling this."

Reba tilted her head in confusion. "Sam, whatever are you talking about? I thought you brought me in her to read me the `I love you, baby, *but . . .* ' speech."

"You thought *that?*" There was hurt and disbelief in his voice.

"Sam, I told you before. No commitments. You are free to do whatever you want. There are no strings tied to our having made love last night, or any other night, past or future. No matter what happens, I love you. I probably always will."

"Damn straight. You better. I'm going to hold you to that promise, honey."

Sam was still fumbling in the tight front pocket of his pants. "Must have gained five pounds from that freakin' chocolate," he mumbled.

Finally, he pulled out a little black velvet box.

And Reba's heart stopped.

Sam got down on one knee and gazed up at her. The expression on his face was totally serious and so vulnerable she could have wept. "I hope I'm doing this right because it's the only time I intend to do it in my entire life."

Reba was already weeping, big fat tears that welled in her eyes and spilled over onto her cheeks.

"Reba Anderson, will you marry me?"

Reba sobbed aloud.

"Is that a yes?"

She opened the velvet box with the Big-Mart logo on it, and sobbed again. Inside was a tiny diamond solitaire in a plain gold setting.

"I told you it was tacky."

It wasn't tacky at all, in Reba's opinion. In fact, it was the most beautiful ring Reba had ever seen. Perfect.

"We can always get a better one later," Sam said, and his voice was a little teary, too.

She shook her head vigorously from side to side. "This is the one I want." She flung herself into Sam's arms then, kissing him and hugging him and stopping to look at her ring, then kissing and hugging him some more, all the time saying over and over, "I love you, I love you, I love you."

Of course, he had to reciprocate by kissing and hugging her and telling her over and over, "I love you, I love you, I love you."

Finally, when they both settled down, Sam set her up on the cabinet and scooted himself up beside her.

"I'm so happy, Sam, but I don't understand. How are we ever going to make it work?"

"I have a few more months to go in the Blues, and I can opt out of the Navy come spring. It's something I've been considering for some time. To tell the truth, the excitement is gone. Instead, my life's been feeling a bit frayed on the edges lately. Everything I thought was important has been unraveling . . . 'til I met you again. Don't worry. I'll find something to do in Maine. Flying, PR, administration . . . I'm not sure what. It doesn't matter, as long as we're together."

"I've been thinking, as well, Sam. We don't have to stay in Maine. I've been selfish. You can stay in the military, if you want. Wherever your work takes you, I'll go. I can always hire a director for Winter Haven."

He smiled softly at her and kissed her on the forehead. "It's sweet of you to offer, honey, but, no, we'll stay in Snowdon. It's time for me to . . ."

" . . . come home," she finished for him.

And Reba realized in that moment . . . that's just what they needed to do . . . especially Sam. They needed to go home to Snowdon and a lifetime together.

"I promise you one thing, Sam," she said in a breathy voice, "if you come home with me, I will give you all the excitement you could ever find anywhere else in the world."

He flashed a dazzling, pure Sam smile then, and hugged her closer. "Honey, that's a promise I intend to collect on for the rest of our lives."

It was a scene right out of a Hallmark TV commercial, in Sam's opinion.

Enormous Yule logs burning in fireplaces at both ends of the great hall of the log-paneled hunting lodge. A Christmas tree twinkling with strings of lights and antique ornaments, not to mention hand-tied red bows. Holiday music playing softly in the background on a high fidelity system—Andy Williams, still roasting chestnuts on an open fire and Bing Crosby, still anticipating a Blue Christmas. The seniors, having run out of egg nog that afternoon—*Thank God!*— now sipping at fifty-year-old brandy, which had been found at the back of the wine cellar.

The Doctors Meg and Maggie had challenged the colonel and Emma Smith to a game of chess, which was still going on after two hours. John and Ethel Ross sat on a settee, holding hands, and dozing off occasionally. Maudeen and Morey had disappeared to God only knew where. Betty was in the kitchen talking on her cell phone to one of her beaux. A few minutes ago, Mike and Penney had dragged their two droopy-eyed boys off to bed after they'd beaten JD and Callie at three games of checkers.

JD and Callie were still lying on their sides on the floor before the fire, talking softly, the checkerboard shoved to the side. Occasionally, JD would reach out and touch Callie's hair, as if entranced. He was entranced, all right. That was obvious to everyone.

Dana and Stan were sitting on a sofa in front of the other fire, Stan's long legs stretched out onto the coffee table before them. He was talking earnestly with Dana, but then he threw his head back and laughed at something she'd said, followed up with a quick kiss. You could say Stan was entranced, too.

There was such a strong family spirit in the room, and it wasn't just because it was Christmas. These people had come together for a common goal . . . a noble enterprise . . . and in the process, they had become bound to each other as strongly as any blood ties. Sam basked in the atmosphere that surrounded them.

"This is exactly how I always pictured that Christmas should be," Sam confessed to Reba, who was cuddled up on the sofa next to him. She was holding out her hand, admiring the ring he'd given her that afternoon. She'd been doing that practically nonstop, when she hadn't been weeping with happiness, that is. Earlier, she'd taken his wish bow from him, and said she planned to press both his and hers in the family Bible.

He would have been embarrassed by all this sentimentality . . . if he wasn't so touched.

"Oh, Sam! We're going to have so many Christmases like this . . . only better."

Sam didn't see how it could get any better than this.

"Think about it," Reba said dreamily. "We'll have our own home . . . maybe even by next Christmas. Oh, my goodness! How could I have forgotten? Remember how we always used to admire the Olsen place . . . that big old Victorian on Summit Street . . . the one with the wrap-around porch? I think it's for sale again."

"Reba! What would we do with such a big place? Jeez, that place must have six bedrooms."

She punched Sam playfully in the upper arm. "Silly boy! You and I could fill every one of them . . . with all the children we're going to have."

Sam's heart clenched with such strong emotion he could barely breathe.

"Sam? What's wrong? Don't you want children?"

He put a palm to his mouth and blinked several times before he was able to speak. "Reba, I would love to have children with you."

"I'm so glad you're coming home, Sam," Reba whispered, snuggling even closer.

Sam's misty gaze swept the room. He saw his two old friends. He saw new friends. Then his gaze came to rest on Reba . . . and he saw in her eyes all the promise their future held for them. The answer was right there, and had been all the time.

"I'm already home, baby."

CHAPTER FOURTEEN

KEVIN

Friday morning, Christmas Eve

They were inching along at a snail's pace, but considering the conditions outside, it was a miracle—and a testament to Betty Badass's mind-boggling connections—that they were moving at all.

While they watched yet another man with a plow lead the way ahead of them, Kevin turned to Stan and Slick. "Is it possible Betty's actually had . . . ummm . . . relations with all these guys?"

Slick winced. "If so, I don't want to know. I don't even want to form a mental picture, here."

"Well, they're doing a whole lot of plowing, if you get my drift," Stan chimed in, then laughed at his own wit. "Drift, get it?"

Slick rolled his eyes. "The man has obviously been tackled on his head a few too many times." He glanced over his shoulder toward the front of the bus, where Callie and Dana and Reba were wrapping up the remaining toys to be delivered to their final stop. Apparently assured that the women were busy and out of earshot, he turned back. "Speaking of plowing, you two look awfully relaxed today."

"Speaking of plowing," Kevin shot back, "You apparently plowed right into a marriage proposal."

"Yeah, Slick," Stan said, grinning. "And so romantically, too. What bubble gum machine did that ring come from?"

"Hey! Reba likes it."

"So did Dana," Stan said, looking perplexed.

"So did Callie," Kevin added, feeling as puzzled as Stan looked. "And when I made a joke about it, she got all huffy and told me I was about as romantic as a rock, and just as intelligent."

Slick puffed up with pride. "The old Merrick charm wins again."

"Right. So when's Reba inserting the nose ring?" Stan asked.

Sam frowned. "Reba's not like that, and you know it. Besides, you two have been following around a couple of females like you're in heat. So you have no room to talk."

Kevin couldn't argue that. The last two nights had been the best of his life. He couldn't seem to get enough of Callie.

It scared the hell out of him to contemplate any future without her in it. Although they hadn't discussed anything beyond their strategy for returning her to New York after George's wedding, he couldn't even fathom them just going their separate ways.

Kevin had made a phone call to his client last night, informing him that he *had* tracked down Cassandra Lee Brandt, but after discussing the case with her, he strongly advised the defense attorney not to call her to the stand. The man wouldn't like what she'd have to say.

He'd done that only after gaining Callie's reluctant permission, and only after he'd given her a chance to contact her sister and let her know that Callie couldn't commit perjury.

It had been a tearful phone call, but once she'd hung up, he could tell that the weight of the world had seemed lifted from her delicate little shoulders, and she'd sniffled and smiled as she informed him that her sister wasn't angry at all. In fact, her sister was learning a whole lot about her thug boyfriend through other trial testimony that she'd never known before. Didn't look like that relationship was going to survive for long, and it was on to the next dysfunctional boyfriend.

Immediately after he'd called the attorney, Kevin had turned to her and said, "Looks like you're off the hook, sweetheart. We'll have to clear up the warrant situation, but that'll be easy. I've got connections."

"So I can return to New York?"

"Anytime you want, darlin'," he'd said, smiling at the excitement in her eyes. But then his smile had faded. "Tomorrow, even, if you want."

Her grin had disappeared instantly, too. "Tomorrow? You mean, leave the bus?"

"If that's what you want."

She'd chewed on her thumbnail. "Is that what you want?"

"It's not my decision to make, sweetheart."

He'd held his breath as she mulled it over. He hadn't known what he would do if she chose to leave him. The possibility of cuffing her and forcing her to stay with him until he himself returned to the city had definitely taken root in his mind.

"Well," she'd finally said, "I'd feel like I was leaving the Santas in the lurch."

Kevin had nodded solemnly. "I don't know how they managed before you came along."

"And besides, the Santa bus is about the only transportation on the roads these days."

"Also true. You'd probably just get stranded somewhere."

"And . . . well . . . " She's practically shuffled her feet.

"What?"

"I know George doesn't know me and I'm not invited to his wedding—"

"Sure you are. I'm inviting you."

"Really? You don't already have a date?"

He'd almost laughed at that, but he just shook his head. "Nope. Wanna be my date to a wedding?"

She'd smiled slowly, then threw herself at him. "I'd love to." And then after that they'd spent the night celebrating in the best way possible.

Which was why, this morning, Kevin was having a hard time picturing the nights ahead when he wouldn't have Callie to celebrate with.

Just then she glanced up and smiled at him, and an explosion blasted through his chest. He'd known this woman all of a few days, and already he couldn't imagine even a single night away from her, much less the rest of his life. Which was scary. Although they'd enjoyed the best sex he'd ever known, he had the feeling that this was a temporary thing for Callie. That once she returned to New York and her lucrative and busy clothing business, she'd forget him faster than lightning.

He had to find a way to stay in her life, but considering how they'd started out, he had the feeling she'd just as soon dump him and put that rotten time in her life behind her.

"Boy, talk about having it bad," Stan said. "JD looks like someone just kicked him in the teeth."

"Kiss ass, pigskin boy," he said, then stalked up the aisle toward Callie.

Her eyebrows rose as she watched him approach. "What's wrong?"

"Come with me," he said, dragging her by the arm to an empty seat furthest from prying eyes.

"JD, what is your problem? I've got work to do."

"We need to talk first. This won't take long. Sit."

She got a mulish expression on her face that he was beginning to know well. But he was feeling just a bit mulish himself at the moment.

She sat. "Fine. What?"

"You're not dumping me when we get back to New York," he said.

Her mouth popped open. "Excuse me?"

"You heard me."

"I heard you, I just don't understand what in Hades you're talking about."

"New York."

"Big city, right."

"We both live there."

"Thanks for letting me know."

"Well, when we get back there, we're still going to see each other. You can't dump me."

She stared at him like he'd just gone over the edge, which was pretty close to the truth.

"Here's a concept for you. 'Dumping' a person sort of presupposes that there's a previous relationship in place."

"Your point being?"

"My point being that what we've got going here could hardly be considered a relationship."

"Is that right? What would you call it, then?"

"Ummm, a holiday fling, maybe?"

"This is not a fling and it *is* a relationship and you aren't dumping me. Got it?"

"He's telling her she can't dump him," Emma Smith said in a whisper that could probably be heard in Canada.

"I knew it," Maudeen said triumphantly. "Morey, you owe me five bucks."

"Not until she agrees not to dump him," Morey argued. "She hasn't answered him yet," Mrs. Smith said.

Kevin scowled. "A little privacy here, folks?"

All of the seniors pretended to return to their various tasks, but Kevin didn't miss Mrs. Smith fiddling with her hearing aid, probably turning it on full blast so she could eavesdrop even if they spoke in sign language.

"Can we talk about this later?" Callie said.

"There's really not much to talk about."

Her eyes blazed. "Is that right? You've decided and therefore it just is?"

He could tell he was jogging right into very dangerous territory. But he couldn't seem to help it. This was too important. "Well, no, I realize this will have to be decided by mutual consent. I'm just saying that you need to consent right now, so we're clear."

"Uh-oh," Mrs. Smith muttered.

"I'll think about it," Callie said, standing up. "I'll get back to you."

Kevin wanted to drag her back and insist she do her consenting without too much thought, because he was afraid if she thought about it—or him—too much, she'd find plenty of reasons to dump him.

But when he glanced up and caught Doctors Maggie and Meg shaking their heads in silent warning, he decided to take their unspoken advice and just let Callie go. For now.

Four hours and the Portland stop later, Callie wanted to be angry. She really did. Problem was, she was bubbling inside with excitement. Ever since JD'd told her she was free to go, she'd been scared to death that she'd never see him again. And the thought of that had been thoroughly depressing.

But if she understood him correctly, in his utterly macho, irritating way, he was declaring that he didn't want them to end when the trip to Snowdon did. And that thrilled her. She just wasn't ready to admit it. Yet.

Maudeen had bullied JD about the state of his hair, so he was now sitting docilely while Maudeen had at him with scissors. Callie hoped Maudeen didn't cut it too short, because she had really grown fond of his shaggy head, but she wasn't dumb enough to mess with Maudeen when the woman was on a mission.

Funny enough, while lots of the seniors gathered around to watch Maudeen do her thing, they began talking about Kevin in his hellion days. And she wouldn't miss that for the world, so she surreptitiously moved up closer to the action.

"Remember the time in high school when Kevin put some concoction in Missy Prescott's shampoo, and it turned her hair blue?"

"No one ever proved that was me."

A chorus of snorts greeted that announcement.

Reba sat down beside Callie, smiling. "He did that for me."

"Really? Why?"

"Missy Prescott was the homecoming queen. She wondered aloud in homeroom how it was possible that I'd received all of three votes. She decided, again out loud, that I must have paid three people to vote for me."

Callie's heart melted just a little more. She could imagine exactly where those three votes had come from. The more she got to know the man, the more she figured that was exactly what JD would do to defend his friend. "Creative justice," she murmured.

"Exactly," Reba said. "He was really good at that. Although more often than not, it landed him in hot water."

"I'll never forget," Mrs. Smith chimed in, "the time he locked Bobby Wallace in George's barn overnight."

JD groaned.

"He'd caught Bobby Wallace teasing George's horses," Reba elaborated, "and he wanted the boy to learn what it felt like to be treated like a defenseless animal."

"Enough, already," Kevin said. "If you all keep this up, you're going to scare Callie and then she's going to dump me for sure and I'll never know the love of a good woman and it'll all be your fault."

She smiled behind her hand. Far from scaring her, these stories were making her fall just a little more and more for the man. How could she not love a guy who would risk the wrath of an entire town to dispense justice?

"You're done," Maudeen said to him. "Now get moving so I can check my email."

Callie's view of Kevin had been blocked by Morey, so she didn't know what Maudeen meant by *done*, and considering Maudeen's own preferences in hair-dos, Callie was just a little worried.

She shouldn't have been. His hair was still that gorgeous and silky teak brown, and Maudeen had only cut it enough that it now just brushed his collar. Callie's breath stuck in her throat at the sight of him. He was gorgeous and he was sexy as sin and he was sweet and he didn't want her dumping him.

How could she not love a guy like that?

He came and sat across the aisle from her. "Have you made up your mind yet?"

"I'm still thinking about it," she lied. Not that she wanted to torture him or anything, but she couldn't have him thinking she was *too* eager. Not to mention, she didn't really want to make any declarations in front of a crowd, no matter how adorable this particular crowd was.

"You know what I'm thinking about?" he said, his voice pitched low for her ears only. And maybe Mrs. Smith's Miracle Ear.

"What?" she couldn't help but ask. Especially when his eyes got all smoky like that.

"Last night. And the night before. And this morning."

Callie felt a blush rise up her throat to her cheeks. For as long as she lived, she'd never forget their time together at that lodge. It had been magical. She didn't have tons of experience, but she didn't think there was a man alive as sexy and giving and . . . creative. There was no way in hell she was dumping the guy.

"Listen up, people," Maudeen called out. All activity ceased, as everyone turned to Maudeen.

As soon as she got everyone's attention, she said, "I just got an email from Jill Broughton at the Snowdon Good Hope Shelter. Apparently they've had a huge influx of folks, due to the weather and such. She's got about thirty new kids who weren't there when we visited on the way out of town. She wants to know if we possibly have enough toys to stop in again."

"We have plenty," Callie said.

"Thanks to you," Morey graciously added.

"Oh, no. Thanks to all of us," she said, shaking her head. "We did it together."

"We did, didn't we?" Meg and Maggie said simultaneously, amidst a sea of nodding heads. "We make a great team."

They sure did, and in that moment Callie knew that she'd be joining the Santa Brigade every year for the rest of her life. If they'd have her. The work was important and meant so much to so many people.

"Betty, when do we hit Snowdon?"

"Twenty minutes," Betty said, "if we don't have to call in any more plows."

Maudeen checked her watch. "Another hour to hand out the gifts and put on the short version of the show, and that gives us less than a half hour to get to George's wedding. That's cutting it awfully close."

"That leaves no time to change out of our Santa suits and into our wedding duds," Morey said.

"That's true," Maudeen said, frowning. "And you wouldn't believe the gorgeous pink sequin and feather number I bought for it." She glanced over at Callie. "Sorry, it's not one of yours, unfortunately."

"Thank the Lord and pass the rhinestones, huh, babe?" Kevin mumbled.

Callie stifled laughter and managed to just smile and shrug. "So let's take a vote," Maudeen continued. "Do we visit the shelter, or get dolled up for George's wedding?"

Everyone talked at once, and Maudeen held up a hand. "Vote of hands. Dolled up?"

Not a single hand went up.

"Hit the shelter?"

All hands zoomed up, except strangely, Kevin's. Callie shot him a quizzical look, and then he, oh-so-reluctantly, it seemed, lifted his hand to make it unanimous. That seemed so out of character, Callie was truly puzzled. Kevin was one of the most enthusiastic performers on the shelter circuit, and always seemed to get excited as they approached another stop.

But she didn't have time to question him, because Maudeen announced, "The shelter it is! Santa suits everyone!" And chaos, as always, erupted.

As everyone filed off the bus in front of the Good Hope Shelter—actually a converted brownstone—Callie glanced back at Kevin, who was dawdling with his Santa belt, and occasionally glancing out the window, only to quickly look away.

She backed up from the steps of the bus and walked to him. "What's wrong?"

"Nothing," he grumbled.

"Like hell. What is it? Are you mad because we aren't going to have time to change for the wedding?"

"Hell no!"

"Then what?"

He cocked his head toward the shelter and swallowed. "I've been here before."

"Yeah, so? This is your hometown."

He sat down heavily. "No, I mean I've been here before. Not as a volunteer."

It took her a moment to understand. When she did, her heart cracked a little. "Oh." She sat down, too. "I see. When you were younger?"

"Yeah. When I was ten. My old man brought me here for a meal.

We ate, then he went to the bathroom and never came back."

"I'm so sorry."

"I'll never forget what it felt like to realize he'd dumped me, like garbage."

Dumped him. Callie's heart shattered even more. *When we get back there, we're still going to see each other. You can't dump me.*

No wonder he was afraid she'd abandon him. She'd fix that in a minute, but first she felt an overwhelming need to fix the hurt from so long ago.

"You know what I think?" she said softly, her hand on his padded shoulder.

His Adam's apple slid up and down his throat a couple of times before he croaked out, "What?"

"If you are an example of what good can come from a place like this, then every single stop we've made in the last few days is worth it, a million times over."

He finally looked at her. "That's nice of you to say."

"I'm not trying to be nice, you turkey. Think about it, JD. You, Stan, Sam, even Dana, were products of a system that is so often flawed, kids like you fall through the cracks. But you didn't. None of you did. You succeeded and became successful, moderately well-adjusted adults."

That produced a ghost of a smile. "That's debatable."

"You know what I mean."

"Yes, I do."

"If nothing else, you should be bounding into that shelter, letting every kid in there know you've been here, done that, and look at you now. Give them hope. They desperately need the hope of knowing this isn't necessarily the end, but a good place to start."

He stared at her for an endless minute. "Have I told you I love you?" he asked, his voice a little gravelly.

Callie's knees practically buckled on her. "No, but I sort of got a little inkling of it with the 'no dumping' rule you tried to establish."

"I love you."

She stroked his hair, her heart so full it was almost painful in the most glorious way. "I love you, too."

"Really?"

"I'm pretty darn sure," she said dryly.

He stood up. Does that mean—"

"Yes. I'm not dumping you."

"Never," he said, and it wasn't a question.

"Never," she promised, and knew, without a doubt, that she meant it. This man was hers. Forever.

"I'd kiss you mindless right now," he said, caressing her cheek, "but I'm afraid I won't be able to stop."

"I'll take a rain check for later tonight. For now, let's go hand out some toys."

"And hope," he said softly.

"And hope."

CHAPTER FIFTEEN

STAN

Christmas Eve

The kids in the Snowdon shelter were great—bright, eager, excited—yet as Stan watched them pester JD for more magic tricks and hit up Slick for more tales about the Blue Angels, he was conscious of a pain deep in his gut. The kids, the people in the shelters, were getting to him. They were getting to them all.

Slick Merrick might be walking around in a happy, lustful daze, but from a couple comments he'd made, Stan could tell he hadn't forgotten the boy from the shelter on Wednesday—what was his name? Richie?—or the boy's mother. Callie had been muttering imprecations on the clothes most of the kids wore, clothes which were often scraggly, ill-fitting hand-me-downs. JD had almost come to blows with the colonel over a discussion of the shelter residents' rights to decent legal representation and advice. If it hadn't been for Reba stepping in—firmly on JD's side, of course—they might have had their first real quarrel of the trip.

And Dana . . .

Stan smiled, just thinking of her. Kids flocked to her like bees to honey.

Hell, *he* went for her like a bee to honey, a trout to a fly, a . . . a lusty male to a fantasy come true. The past two nights had been heaven, the hours they spent together during the day pure bliss.

He'd deliberately put all thought of tomorrow away, refusing even to consider what would happen once George's wedding was over and they all went back to their lives. Well, all but Reba and Slick, of course. They still hadn't decided exactly what came next, except it was clear that whatever it was, it would be the two of them facing it together. And then there was JD and Callie. They hadn't officially announced it yet, but any fool could see they'd end up tying the knot, too. But Dana had her work while he—

What *did* he have? A house that wasn't a home, investments that made him enough money so he wouldn't have to work another day in his life if he didn't want to, and not much of anything else. Certainly nothing that mattered. And sure as hell nothing that made a difference to anybody.

A week ago, he'd been thinking about going into investment management or something. He hadn't been real excited about it, but he'd figured if he couldn't have football, there wasn't much else he was good at, so why not? But now, just the thought of it chilled his blood.

A week ago, he'd been wishing he'd taken that blonde—or had she been a brunette? Bonnie or Betty or something—down to Cancun. Now, just the thought of a mindless liaison with a woman whose face he couldn't remember was enough to make him shudder.

He didn't even want to go back to San Diego.

Sure, he had friends there, but not one of them was as crazy as Maudeen or as smooth as Morey or as ready to mind someone else's business as the twins, Maggie and Meg. Good drinking and carousing buddies. Good men, every one. But he'd been trying to imagine them on the Brigade's bus, scrubbing old Barbie dolls and having to watch their language because of Emma Smith, and he just couldn't picture it.

Yet for some crazy reason he could see himself there. Not just now, but next year, and the year after that, and the year after that.

Hell, he could even imagine himself on the bus when he was ninety, and that scared the very devil out of him!

But only so long as Dana was there beside him. He didn't even try to picture himself without her.

And that scared him even more because Dana wasn't a great fling to be forgotten. Dana was a forever kind of woman, while he had always been a short-term kind of guy. She was cocoa in front of the fire and Christmas trees with old ornaments and big red ribbon bows and—

And he couldn't think of anything he wanted more.

Thinking of her, Stan shifted on the stool where he sat. The motion made the two crumpled bows in his pocket rustle. His wishing ribbon, and hers. He'd retrieved them both yesterday morning while everyone was rushing out to see if Slick and Reba had survived their wild ride down the mountain.

He still hadn't found the courage to untie her bow and find out what she'd written, but he was pretty sure he knew, anyway, and he was pretty sure she was going to get her wish. All of it, and more.

But there'd been other bows on that tree, other wishes. Some of the wishers, like Slick and Reba and Callie and JD, were probably going to get what they'd wished for, too. Some—he grinned at the thought—like Morey and Maudeen and Dr. Maggie, probably already had. But what about the Parkers? What about Tyler and Taylor's wishes written in black marker with all the faith and hope that six-year-old hearts could hold?

And what about the kids in the shelter here, who didn't have any wishing ribbons at all? What about little Richie and his mother, who was fighting her inner demons with everything that was in her? What about Mrs. Eisenstock, whose family had ended here in a town she didn't know in a shelter full of strangers on the very holiday when one most wanted a home and a place to belong to?

When she'd unwrapped the wall hanging that Dana had cleaned and repaired with such care, the poor woman had burst into tears, then run to hang it on the wall of the crowded cubicle their family shared, desperate to add a little color to a life that was painted in grim shades of gray right now.

What about all the rest of them?

He'd never forgotten what it was like to be on the outside looking in, but for a long, long while he'd conveniently ignored the memories. Besides, he'd always had Slick and JD and George to help him over the hard parts.

He scanned the room, looking for his friends, and spotted Emma Smith, presiding over the punch bowl. Not far away, Betty was on the phone, dredging up the last bit of help to get them from the shelter to the church while Maudeen, who'd dyed her hair holly green in honor of the day, was clattering away on her computer. Probably figuring out where to deliver the last of the Brigade's toys and presents before Christmas morning dawned.

As if sensing his gaze, Emma looked up and caught his eye. For a moment he had a flash of panic, just like what he'd felt years ago when he'd blown a test because he hadn't studied. But this time she didn't frown, she smiled, then winked, as if the two of them shared a secret. Stan was still staring, open-mouthed, when a couple of kids clamoring for more punch dragged her attention back to her job.

Come to think of it, maybe he'd had Emma Smith on his side, too. It hadn't seemed like it at the time, but her constant demands that the three of them shape up, work harder, and do more had really just been another way of saying that she knew they were capable of a lot more than even they had imagined.

There'd been others like her through the years, now he thought of it. The head administrator and the counselors at the home, teachers and coaches and, yes, even some of the cops who'd regularly hauled their butts up for getting into trouble. The three of them had had more supporters than they'd ever realized.

And always, always there'd been George, who'd stood by them through thick and thin, and kept scrapbooks of their achievements, and been proud . . . and told them so.

It came to him right then in a blinding flash, just as it used to when he'd been at a crucial point in a difficult game and he'd known, somehow, exactly what he had to do next. He knew what he wanted to do with the rest of his life and he was pretty sure he knew exactly how to get started doing it.

Stan grinned and glanced across the room to where Dana sat with half a dozen little kids grouped around her, enthralled. She was the heart of it, the key that would make it all worth while, the dream he'd written on his wishing ribbon that was more than he'd dared imagine.

With his gaze glued to his golden Madonna, Stan dug out his cell phone and punched in a number he'd already learned by heart.

"Hurry, hurry, hurry!" Betty stood beside the open door of the bus, urging her flock of red-suited Santas across the snowy parking lot and up the steps. "Come *on*! We gotta get to the church. No time to waste. George isn't going to wait for us forever. Gotta go, gotta *go*!"

She was almost dancing with impatience as, one by one, the Brigade members made their way onto the bus. "What're you planning to do, Morey? Take root here in the parking lot? Move it!"

Morey grinned and blew her a kiss, then bounded up the steps, spry as any fifty-year-old. Two ladies in the shelter had almost come to blows over which one got to dance with him. He'd resolved the problem by dancing with both of them, turn and turn about, until they'd worn circles in the shelter's floor. His face was still as red as his suit from the exercise, but he'd brushed off Reba's concern with an airy wave.

"Couldn't disappoint the ladies!" he'd informed her, then winked at Maudeen, which had made that doughty lady turn crimson, too.

From her seat by a window at the front of the bus, Dana watched as Stan slowly made his way across the snowy ground. He had his cane, but he wasn't paying attention to the ground—his cell phone had been glued to his ear for the past half hour, at least.

She'd tried to eavesdrop, had even resorted to an overt attempt at seduction to find out what could possibly hold his attention like that, but he'd deliberately turned away and lowered his voice . . . and kept on talking.

"Come *on*, Kijewski!" Betty called. "You move any slower, you'll freeze to the ground and we won't get you unstuck 'til spring." Stan punched off the phone and stuck it in his pocket, then stumped across the lot.

Watching him, Dana found her heart speeding up and her breath catching. Her body ached just at the sight of him, reminding her of all the secret, passionate pleasures they'd shared in the past two days . . . and nights.

Before they'd left Moose Lodge, she'd gone back to retrieve her wishing ribbon. To her disappointment, it had disappeared, no doubt swept up in the confusion or kicked under a chair, forgotten.

Not that it mattered, she'd assured herself. She'd gotten part of her wish, at least. She was just being greedy and unreasonable to wish that she'd been granted more.

Still, she couldn't help hoping. That was what love did to you, she supposed, made you think anything was possible.

She watched as Stan negotiated the stairs on the bus with Betty hot on his heels. Just the sight of him was enough to start that hungry ache deep insider of her. The ache that only he would ever be able to ease.

Yet with the ache came a bubbling joy that made her feel like she could fly from the sheer wonder of it all.

Maybe, just maybe, when it was Stan Kijewski you were in love with, every good thing you'd ever dreamed of really *was* possible after all.

"We gotta talk." Snow dusted Stan's head and shoulders and the folds of his Santa suit, but he didn't seem to notice. His whole face was alight with an eager, joyous light. He leaned down and grabbed her hand, pulling her out of her seat. "Come on."

"But—"

"Later." Heedless of the wild plunge and bounce as Betty roared through a wall of snow and onto the main road, he dragged her down the aisle toward the back of the bus.

Halfway there, he halted suddenly, swept her into his arms, and kissed her. Violently. Hungrily.

Dana kissed him back and came up gasping for air. "Oh, my!"

He grinned, but refused to let her go. "I love you, Dana Freeman. Will you marry me?"

"*What?*"

"Of course she will!" Maudeen snapped from the row ahead. "What kind of stupid question is that?"

"Hah! Pay up, Morey!" Dr. Meg crowed. "I *told* you he'd pop the question before we ever hit the church!"

"I heard that!" Ethel chirped. "Isn't that romantic?"

Stan leaned closer, oblivious to anyone but her. "*Will* you? Marry me, Dana. Say yes. Yes!"

"Uh . . . " Her head was spinning, her heart was pounding, but her lungs had stopped working entirely.

"Good heavens, girl, say yes!" cried Emma Smith. "It's a simple enough word! Yes!"

"*Nooo!*" howled Morey. "Not until after George and Molly get hitched. Tell him no! I got twenty bucks riding on it!"

Stan leaned closer still, so close his breath was warm on her mouth and his eyes seemed to fill her vision, ardent, alive, brimming with promise.

"Yes," he coaxed.

"Yes," she said. It was barely a whisper, but it was enough. His mouth crushed down on hers, robbing her of the last bit of breath in her lungs.

A cheer went up, almost loud enough to bury Morey's anguished groan.

Stan let her go so abruptly she staggered and had to grab for the nearest seat back to keep from falling. "Now that's settled . . . "

"Stan!"

He dragged her all the way back to where Reba and Slick and Callie and JD had claimed two rows of seats.

"Stanley! Stanley!" JD chanted, pounding on the seat in front of him and grinning like a fool. The others, laughing, instantly took it up. "Stanley! Stanley! Stanley!"

Stan just grinned and wrapped his arm around her shoulders and dragged her hard against him. They didn't quite fit side-by-side in the narrow aisle, but Dana didn't care. She was soaring, anyway.

"Shut up, you guys," he said without heat. "I got an idea."

"You've already had that idea," Slick teased. Since his arm was around Reba's shoulder, holding her close against his heart, nobody paid him any attention.

"This one's almost as good, but it needs all of you to make it work." Stan looked around the circle of his friends, then straight into Dana's heart. She didn't know where he was going, but she had a feeling it was going to be quite a ride. She'd always liked interesting rides.

"What would you say to turning Moose Lodge into a center to help kids like we were? Kids *and* their families?" Dana could feel the excitement surging through him and into her. The other four sat up, faces alight with sudden interest.

"I've already talked to the Parkers," he continued, "and they're all for it. They'll run the place. I've got some money that can get the ball rolling, cover some of the repairs the place will need."

"And buy new beds!" everyone chorused.

Stan grinned. "And definitely buy new beds. I figure I can manage investments and the team sports programs." He glanced down at her. "I thought you could develop an outdoor skills program, maybe one of those life challenges things like folks pay thousands to take for a week. That is, if you'd be willing," he added anxiously. "And if you can get time off from your work."

"I'd be willing!" Her head spun at the possibilities rushing through it. George had introduced her to the wilderness, and saved her soul in the process. The thought of sharing the wild world she loved with others who might find the same solace and salvation she had made her breath catch in sheer excitement.

"I can handle the legal side!" JD offered. "And the juvenile delinquents that want to take after Stan."

"Hah!" said Stan, and swung a punch that JD easily ducked.

"Mr. Merrick here can do the fundraising," Reba volunteered, grinning up at her husband-to-be.

"And Reba can boss us all," Slick said, grinning down at her with proprietary pride.

"A whole lodge full of people won't be half the problem you'll be, all on your own!" she shot back.

"You got that right, sweetheart," Slick drawled. "And I intend to keep you on your toes."

Dana would swear that Reba added "and on my back," in a

delighted whisper, but she might have been mistaken because an instant later Slick silenced her with a kiss.

Callie eagerly jumped to her feet. "I'll handle team uniforms. We can give classes for the women, too. Dress for success, building a working wardrobe on a budget, that sort of thing." Her eyes lit. "We might even start our own design studio!"

"What about the men?" JD demanded, dragging her back down beside him.

"The men?" Callie grinned and punched his shoulder. "We'll keep them as naked love slaves."

"I'll go for that," JD murmured. He would have kissed her, but Callie tickled him in the ribs and distracted him.

"Don't think you're leaving *us* out!" Emma Smith called from the front of the bus. "Those children will need help catching up with their schooling!"

"They'll need haircuts!" Maudeen said.

"And someone to drive 'em!" Betty added.

"Count us in!" Dr. Meg and Dr. Maggie chorused.

"And me!"

"And me!"

"And me!"

"Dang tootin!" Morey said, and snapped his suspenders loud enough for everyone to hear.

"And I know just the kid to start it off," Slick added. The usual teasing glint in his eyes was missing. His jaw was set rock hard with sudden determination. "We'll start it off with Richie."

He glanced around their circle as if daring anyone to disagree.

"And Richie's mother," Reba urged, lacing her fingers with his and squeezing hard.

Slick's gaze snapped back to her. Reba met it unflinchingly. For a moment they simply stared into each other's eyes, their silent communication so intense and powerful that the rest of the world might not have existed. Slick was the first to yield. Slowly the hardness faded from his handsome face, replaced by a dawning wonder.

"And Richie's mother," he said softly, his gaze still locked on Reba. And then he smiled, and lifted her hand and kissed it. "*Definitely* his mother."

Reba laughed and blinked back tears, then dragged him to her for a kiss that had real fire in it.

"I know a great treatment program to help her kick the drugs," JD offered.

"I know of a great scholarship program for single mothers," Dana added.

"We'll deck her out in some great clothes." Callie gave JD a teasing wink. "A woman always feels more confident when she knows that she's well dressed."

Slick reluctantly abandoned Reba's mouth. "So what are we gonna call this thing?"

Stan blinked. "I don't know. I didn't even think about that part of it."

"Moose Lodge Maniacs," JD suggested.

Slick waved a dismissive hand. "That's for the managerial staff, dummy. Stan's talking about a name for the program here."

"Oh, yeah?"

"Yeah."

"Good Chance Ranch?" Reba suggested.

"In *New Hampshire?*" JD, Slick, and Callie chorused in disbelief.

"It's got a nice ring to it!"

"I know!" Dana cried. The five turned to her expectantly. "We'll call it George's Place."

The vote was unanimously in favor. Further discussion was postponed, however, for at that moment Betty pulled the bus to a flourishing halt in front of the church.

"All out for a wedding!" she called, shoving the door open so the Brigade could pour out.

Snowdon Church had been built of stone and native timber almost two hundred years before, but it still served its people well. Some families had twelve generations listed in the church records, all baptized, married, and, in their turn, buried here.

Stan leaned across Dana to peer out the window. Fresh snow blanketed the church and the trees around it, softening the golden light that poured out of the high arched windows. Despite the cold and the snow, George and his bride stood at the top of the stone steps, welcoming their guests. It wasn't the way most weddings were run, but it was exactly the sort of thing Stan would have expected from a man who had taken three troubled young boys to his heart all those years ago.

Something at George's side moved. Stan leaned closer, squinting against the light. "Is that really George's old St. Bernard, Mammoth?"

Dana nodded. She was making a last, desperate attempt to comb her hair and rub out the punch stain a little boy at the shelter had added to her Santa suit.

"George insisted on including all his dogs, and Molly was too smart to argue. Mammoth is there, and Screwball and Oedipus Tex and Jingleberry and Mutt Man and Fudge." She grinned. "Doodlebug, however, is not. He was cut from the guest list when he peed on the minister at practice last week. George says being stuck at home with three cats, a parrot, and a half dozen ferrets will teach him a lesson, but Molly's of the opinion the old mutt just wanted to have the sofa all to himself for a change."

"I don't think I've met Screwball or Mutt Man."

"You will."

"You two coming?" JD hovered at the top of the steps.

"You bet." But when Dana slid into the aisle, Stan pulled her back.

She came into his arms easily, willingly. In the dim light her face looked like an angel's, delicate and incredibly beautiful.

"I love you, Dana." The words came out in a hoarse whisper. His throat was suddenly too tight for normal speech.

"And I love you, Stanley Kijewski," Dana whispered back, an instant before she kissed him.

"Kijewski!"

"Coming!"

They were the very last arrivals. The six of them—Stan and Dana, Slick and Reba, JD and Callie—walked toward the golden light spilling out of the church's open door, toward the man and woman who waited, hands linked, at the top of the steps.

As Stan mounted the steps with Dana at his side, peace settled over him like a blanket. This was what he'd wanted, what he'd *always* wanted—friends, family, a wonderful woman who loved him, a place where he belonged.

He glanced at his friends and saw that same peace, that same contentment in their faces. Slick grinned and gave a cheery thumbs-up, then stole a quick kiss from a willing Reba. JD laughed and drew his Callie closer. Stan glanced down at Dana, tucked so close and tight against him, and saw a miracle in her eyes.

"Welcome home, boys," George called. "We've been waiting for you a long time, so you all had better hurry up and come in out of the cold. We've got a wedding to get on with!"

EPILOGUE

You are cordially invited to join in our celebration

of the weddings of

SAMUEL MERRICK TO REBECCA ANDERSON,
KEVIN WILDER TO CASSANDRA BRANDT,
AND
STANLEY KIJEWSKI TO DANA FREEMAN.

June 1st, 2011, 1:00 P.M.

George's Place

Moose Lodge, New Hampshire

Reception immediately following, at which we shall

be celebrating the grand opening of George's Place

and welcoming our first summer guests.

Transportation, food and lodging provided.

Please join us on this joyous occasion.

LaVergne, TN USA
31 October 2010
202941LV00004B/3/P